Sun
Killers

Book One of the
Felis Alliance Series

Peter Amsel

A portion of the proceeds from the sale of this Book is being donated to Amnesty International (Canada).

For more information, visit http://BordofskyProductions.ca

PUBLISHING HISTORY
Bordofsky Productions Electronic Edition / August 2016

Cover design by Bordofsky Productions

Excerpt of *Time Changers* published with permission of the author.
Time Changers is Copyright © 2016 by Peter Amsel
Published in arrangement with Bordofsky Productions

This is a work of fiction. Names, places, and events are either the product of the author's imagination or they are used fictitiously. Any resemblance to a perceived reality, to any individuals, or anything that you may have imagined, is highly unlikely; recognition of any actual locations, either in this Sector or another Sector of the Universe, is strictly coincidental. References to historical events are used exclusively within a fictional framework; no inference is meant to be made as to any accurate representation or depiction therein.

This book is dedicated to my mother. She always insisted that if I wanted to accomplish something, I could: it was only a matter of not giving up and applying myself to the task.

It is also dedicated to everyone who believed in me throughout this long journey.
Thank you: you mean more to me than you could possibly imagine.

CONTENTS

ACKNOWLEDGMENTS

Every creative endeavor requires three things: space, time, and inspiration.

I am especially indebted to my family for providing the space I required and the time in which to write, as well as a tremendous amount of encouragement. Without them, this book would not have been possible. It is also necessary to mention *Dr. Seuss*, a sweet tuxedo cat who provided a great deal of the inspiration for the character of Sovereign Sayoose while in the form of the cat. Unfortunately, he died of cancer and his spirit was ushered into the Wellspring during the editing of the early drafts of this book; he is deeply missed. His successor, *CC*, is a wonderful companion, as well as an occasional hindrance to my work.

Of no less importance has been the encouragement provided by my dear friend, Billy: his enthusiasm for this project has kept me going through several different drafts and edits: thank you for your comments, criticisms, and unique perspective. More than anyone, I must thank my Editor, Patrice Bordofsky, for her patience and guiding hand. Without her coaxing and coaching this book would not have taken on the life that it has; she has allowed it to bloom, and allowed me the freedom to write, the dream of every writer.

Finally, although we have never met, I am deeply indebted to the wisdom of Doctor Neil deGrasse Tyson for providing scientific advice, albeit obliquely, through interviews seen on television. As a result of what he said regarding things that bothered him in Science-Fiction for not being realistic enough the *Temporal Compensator* in this novel was introduced; without it certain elements relating to travel near stars and other gravity sources would seem far less plausible and more problematic in regards to the distortion of the continuum for the travelers. Thanks to Dr. Tyson the science in this book is, I hope, more plausible than it might have been had I not paid attention to his sage words. Even so, this is a work of fiction.

It is my hope that even though this book is Science-Fiction, it does not have to sound as though it is pure Fantasy.

Peter Amsel, Ottawa, Canada

PROLOGUE

"In the beginning God created the heavens and the earth, and the earth was without form, and void; and darkness was on the face of the deep, and the Spirit of God was hovering over the face of the waters. Then God said, 'Let there be light,' and there was light."
The First Book of Moses called *Genesis*

(*|*)

"How did life evolve on Alliance member planets and Protectorates? Let me start at the beginning: Science Vessels of the Seeding Project first assess the probability of the development of intelligent, or sentient life, as has occurred countless times throughout the universe. Once it has been ascertained that a planet possesses the requisite factors for hominid evolution our scientists employ the Life-Development Formula, which precisely calculates the amounts of Beryllium 8 and other elements required to facilitate the development of intelligent life that will ultimately emerge as the planet's dominant species. After the elements have been inserted into the biosphere the final result, the hoped for result, will be the expression of a genomic pattern virtually indistinguishable from those found on other planets populated by humanoids."
Excerpted from a Q&A Session with Sovereign Sayoose after her Keynote address to the 137th Symposium on *Planet-Seeding*

(*|*)

For many people consigned to dwell on a planet incapable of traveling amongst the stars it is sometimes easier to deny the possibility that intelligent life exists beyond the boundaries of their planet rather than accepting that they are only one member of a crowded universal community. It may be difficult for closed-minded individuals to gaze beyond their planetary horizons, finding themselves unable to comprehend the breadth of the truth, even when it is staring directly at them, or is accompanied by abundant evidence. With minds filled with superstitions and fairy tales as buffers against the truths contradicting their canonized beliefs, these same individuals sometimes find it necessary to construct plausible fictions to explain what they undoubtedly find too difficult to accept simply because it violated what had been established as their paradigm of an accepted reality.

An undeniable fact is that life did exist on other planets, and it *had* evolved, but not in the way most experts had postulated: sentient life had been part of a sophisticated operation in which an appropriate planet had been carefully cultivated to produce the intelligent species commonly referred to as humans.

Planets found suitable of sustaining life were classified along the *Green Zone* scale, assessed according to their technological development in the furtherance of intergalactic travel. After their initial classification planets were carefully cultivated over several millennia to maximize the possibility that the entities living on them might one day join the pan-universal Felis Alliance, the largest organization of its type, which not only cultivated life on other planets, it also mined precious elements from dying and extinct stellar bodies, particularly Red Giants. As the most successful of the organizations that mined the stars the Felis Alliance presently comprised over thirteen thousand member planets, representing over thirty-three trillion Citizens, which made it the largest association of sentient life-forms in the known universe.

Cultivating a planet took place through a fine balance of science and art. It was an ancient practice perfected over many millennia in which elements within each portion of the genome were capable of being manipulated in various ways during the evolutionary process. Scientists were now capable of controlling the chemical balances of every element required for the development of life, particularly the precious Beryllium 8, an unstable element which had to be added to the biosphere of the planet in just the right quantities at the opportune time in order to stimulate the development of life. Art came into play when both scientists and xenobiologists found themselves in the position of aiding in the cultivation of the biosphere during that stage when mammalian bipeds began emerging as the dominant life-forms on any Green Zone planet. It was at that point when the myriad ethical issues had to be addressed; they were never easy, but could never be ignored. One of the fundamental rules of the Planet Seeding Project was that if another sentient life-form had established a foothold on a planet the Alliance would not intervene. No other form of life could be usurped in favor of humanoid dominance, not even if it was viewed as inferior by humanoid standards; sentience was considered the standard.

As a result of this rule, known simply as *The Standard*, the Alliance had left several planets uncultivated, though many were declared Protectorates in the event that others might show interest in their resources, which would be disastrous to the life-forms living there peacefully. In the case of one planet found in Sector 0002, the neighboring Sector to the home world of the Felis Alliance and its orbiting capital city, Felis Prime, *The Standard* had resulted in something quite positive for the Alliance. When Volana III had been discovered it seemed ideal for seeding, to spur on the development of the hominid life-forms teeming in the jungles of the planet, but on closer observation the xenobiologists found that the mammals in the trees were not the dominant species: there was another, even more intelligent life-form, sharing that world.

Creatures calling themselves *Torgon* were not only sentient, they communicated using a form of telepathy that surprised the xenobiologists who had arrived to survey the planet. Their first encounter with the Torgons had also been remarkable considering the unique method of propulsion used by the creatures. Possessing neither arms or legs, Torgons resembled a rather large furry ball with a lump on top, which turned out to be their head. Some confused it as a tail if the creature had their eyes closed, it was, however, where their eyes and mouth were located, though witnessing a Torgon consuming food or water was rare. When first encountered it seemed as though the creatures could fly; they compressed their bodies into a tight ball, which was possible since they did not seem to have much of an internal skeletal structure to interfere with the process. Once a target had been selected they would release their collected energy against whatever they had been resting, propelling themselves through the air at tremendous speeds, often at terrifyingly high altitudes, at least for a Torgon. From humanoid perspectives it appeared to be an absolutely insane method of travel, but the creatures seemed to enjoy the process, and their options were quite limited; they could opt to roll around for a few paces rather than jumping for short distances, but jumping definitely seemed to be their preferred method of locomotion.

When the Alliance first encountered the Torgons it was discovered that the creatures enjoyed the companionship of the visiting humans and also appeared to be quite desperate to leave their planet. This raised a dilemma for the survey team that had never before been encountered: The Alliance scientists had been sent to assess the local fauna, not relocate indigenous life-forms. Ultimately, most of the peaceful Torgons decided to leave Volana III. Several of the peaceful creatures expressed an interest in becoming companions of the humans who had visited their planet, while the rest sought to become companions to residents on Felis Prime and Felis Magoris, when the survey vessels returned, though it had been made clear to them that this was explicitly against the policy of the Alliance. Even with that explanation, the Torgons were unwilling to relent in their request to leave their home world: things had become insufferable for them and the human visitors represented their salvation. Escaping from Volana III was something they had been dreaming of for generations but had never had the means to achieve; the arrival of the humans from the Alliance was, to them, a sign of good fortune which they could not allow to pass by if they were to escape their tormentors.

"We must need go," the creatures cried, almost desperately, filling the minds of their new friends with the Torgon equivalent of pleading and desperation.

"Torgon must cannot remain here," many of the creatures said in concert. Their voices sounded sweet to the minds of the visiting humans, but their pleading was relentless.

"Some might choose remain stay, perhaps, yet many Torgon already make choice to leave this life … you now offer Torgon chance see life beyond this small rock, to live free of nasty tree-climbers. You we like. You not use violence against Torgon; besides, nasty tree-climbers steal joy of Torgon." They were referring to the monkey-like creatures that had evolved alongside them on the planet, *"All time make much noise, throw things at Torgon. Kill many. Tree-climbers not nice. Torgon not do this to nasty tree-climbers, but they kill many Torgon. All Torgon want live in peace. Now is time to expand horizons."*

Several of the small creatures launched themselves into the arms of the humans, snuggling up against them, and to them the matter seemed settled. It was all true: the tree-climbers were both noisy, and violent. They had also thrown things at the humans, injuring a few of the scientists surveying the territory around where the Torgons had been encountered. It was difficult to see the creatures as they moved through the dark canopy of the trees. Their actions and screeching cries convinced the humans that the Torgons were telling the truth; they could be heard from the edge of the tree line, all the way to the clearing where their shuttles had landed. To those who heard the sound it conveyed both fear and dread.

By flying through the air in coordinated patterns it looked as though there were more of them than there were; in the end, however, there were fewer of the creatures than the scientists had estimated. Torgons also reproduced extremely slowly, with a female having one kit every ten years after reaching maturity, which occurred at around the age of thirty. Due to the many deaths resulting from the constant assaults from the tree-climbers only about five hundred of the gentle creatures remained on the single continent of Volana III, and all but a few of the oldest of them decided to leave with the survey teams that had arrived.

Ordinarily, the discovery of sentient life was far less dramatic and disruptive than with the Torgons, but it always posed ethical dilemmas for Alliance scientists. Once a level of sentience was evaluated it had to decide which directions along the evolutionary trail the life-forms might take in order to maximize their chances of survival and development. In many ways it was an interpretive dance as scientists performed complex ballets around the possibilities of genetic expression. Numerous genes involved in the explosion of life developed over countless millennia, with each iteration of the genome bringing minuscule and practically imperceptible changes until they expressed the necessary adaptations found in the hominid version of the life-form. Once those changes expressed themselves, only then would scientists know whether their dance had been successful, then they would know whether the new life-forms would thrive in their environment, or if they would simply return to the jungles from which they had emerged, or die. Usually the seeding process would result in positive effects on other life-forms, if it was determined that they would similarly benefit from the intervention, but that remained an argument that the ethicists were likely still having, one which would not likely end for several thousand years to come.

For those living on Earth the idea that their existence constituted everything there was in the universe rather than embracing the possibility that they might be part of something far greater was simply more than the average person was willing to accept. That, however, was the truth represented by the enormity of the Felis Alliance: the universe was truly gargantuan, and it was teeming with life on thousands of planets. Humans living on Earth would have to learn, at some point, that they were not alone.

CHAPTER I ~ ALLIANCE

"Mining of Red Giant Stars posed countless difficulties, not the least of which includes the issue of sustaining the integrity of their shields of the mining vessels while maintaining stationary orbits within the star's corona, the temperature of which could range between 2,900° – 5,700° Lats, or even higher. Other factors include monitoring gyro-stabilized probe projectors used during the sampling process to ensure quality control of the elements being mined while coordinating the targeting sensors for the Beryllium 8 collectors, the most sought after element. Perhaps the most critical aspect of the process involved the operation of Temporal Compensators which prevented vessels anywhere in the vicinity of a stellar body from moving slower within its relative time stream due to the intense gravitational forces exerted by the violent and unpredictable changes of the gravimetric forces of the star, resulting from its advanced age and rate of stellar degradation.

"These and other variables were assigned to the A-ConCom, the Automated Control Command module, a sophisticated computerized component capable of running virtually every operation onboard the ship, allowing the crew to focus on other parts of the mining operation. Most functions on the latest generation mining vessels employed by the Felis Alliance have been automated to such an extent that the operations may be carried out with only a Pilot, an Engineer, a Communications Officer, a Stellar Analyst, and a Supervising Mining Technician."

[...]

Excerpted from: *From Star to Soil [Pamphlet for Children in the Felis Alliance School System]* (Authorized by ASIS, the Alliance Security & Intelligence Services)

(* | *)

With over thirty-three trillion Citizens living on the nearly fourteen thousand member planets scattered across numerous Sectors of the universe it would have been impossible for any single bureaucratic organization to effectively oversee the judicial needs of those living under the flag of the Felis Alliance. Ensuring that the rule of law was not an issue had been dealt with by the first Sovereign of the Alliance who had envisioned a system which provided for a generous amount of self-rule and regional autonomy for the governance of member planets, removing a tremendous amount of the administrative burden from the Alliance home world. This also had the benefit of allowing member planets to maintain their cultural identities and traditions, while ensuring that they did not conflict with the established tenets of the Alliance.

General Guidelines, as set out by the Sovereign and their advising Cadre, guaranteed anyone traveling throughout the Alliance that they would encounter certain commonalities when dealing with specific laws, even if the interpretation of particular codes and precepts might be slightly different from planet to planet, depending on how a particular judiciary chose to interpret a particular set of laws or regulations.

After several hundred thousand years of careful planning and artful maneuvering within the fields of diplomacy and military dominance, the Felis Alliance had risen to prominence as the single most powerful organization in the known universe. Many mutually-beneficial treaties had been negotiated with diverse planetary governments, representing so many life-forms that the Alliance was ultimately acknowledged as a governmental body unto itself, one which superseded all others in both scope and authority. By the time the Alliance represented over ten trillion Citizens it was the largest organization of its type in the known universe, recognized as the first pan-galactic para-governmental organization of its type, with the authority to supplant other planetary governments.

Now, with over thirty-three trillion Citizens living within the Felis Alliance, it was beyond gargantuan, perhaps even unwieldy by some estimations. It was also without peer within the vast cosmos, though that did not mean that it was without opposition, or that it lacked competition. Located on the opposite side of the Great Shadow

Nebula, in Sector 1009, was Ursus Minor, the home world of the Ursus Consortium. Unlike the Felis Alliance, the Ursus Consortium was relatively small, encompassing under two thousand Green Zone planets, with approximately six and a half trillion citizens. While the Ursus Consortium was only a fraction the size of the Felis Alliance, they compensated by possessing an extreme determination and tenacity, being led by maniacal leaders who refused to accept that they were anything less than the greatest of organizations, destined to rule the universe. Nothing could divert the leaders of the Consortium from their desire to possess what they did not control, thus transforming them into an explicit threat to the peace of every planet within the Felis Alliance, and extraordinarily dangerous in everything they planned.

Members of the Alliance had little to fear and few complaints regarding their security as they were provided more than adequate protection from anyone, or anything, that might threaten their planet and the system in which they existed. This protection extended to cover any forms of intimidation that might arise from attempts to induce planets to leave the Alliance in order to join the Ursus Consortium, which thought of itself as a viable alternative to the Alliance. Anyone who had dealings with the Consortium, however, recognized that the only thing viable about them was their propensity for violence: they ruled with a combination of brutality and cruelty, their only true interest being their profits. Any planet was welcomed into the Consortium, but the Alliance would do everything within their considerable power to show them the error of their thinking before the ink was dry on the treaty, a treaty which had no hope of being honored.

As much as the leadership of the Alliance may have enjoyed a total monopoly on the stellar mining operations that enriched their economy, both the Sovereign and the Cadre recognized better than anyone that this was simply not possible. The Stellar Mining Bureau, known to all within the Alliance as the SMB, maintained a tight control over the mining rights of every Sector of the known universe, only allowing certain types of stellar bodies, in uninhabited systems, to be mined for their precious elements. Any system which contained a Green Zone planet and had any signs of life was considered to be strictly off limits when it came to the Stellar Mining Bureau. Even the Ursus Consortium was sworn to follow the regulations of the SMB, knowing that if the Mining Inspectors, or the Board of Governors, revoked their Mining Certificates, their operations would be shut down faster than if a division of ASCAR commandos had seized their operations, and nobody wanted to mess with the ASCAR.

Unfortunately, the tight controls set out by the Stellar Mining Bureau did little to thwart the ambitions of the Consortium's leaders who were determined to expand their holdings. If this could not be done through their mining operations, they had to find other ways to accomplish their goals. In recent years the Consortium had become so desperate for new member planets to exploit they began attempting to poach members of the Alliance, or planets declared as Protectorates. Doing so violated the *Protectorate Treaty of Gersh*, which provided the Sovereign the prerogative to declare any planet that had been seeded by the Alliance a Protectorate if it exhibited the potential of eventually becoming an Alliance member. Even though most Protectorates were several hundred thousand years away from being offered membership, the Sovereign found many of them worthy of being protected, resulting in the deployment of ships and troops from the Unified Armed Services. Alliance forces were deployed in orbit and, in some cases, on the Protectorates themselves; their presence was usually more than sufficient to thwart the Consortium and prevent armed conflicts.

This had led the Sovereign to adopt a casual attitude when it came to the threat posed by his counterpart. He had believed that the Consortium would not wage an overt war against the Alliance, or risk breaking the treaties that had been established, even though they already had violated the *Protectorate Treaty of Gersh* by moving against several Protectorates. Since the Alliance had been able to defend those planets, Sovereign Martok did not act as though there was any great threat, making some within the Alliance and the Unified Armed Services, to whisper about whether or not he possessed the fortitude to send Alliance forces into battle for a worthy cause. Sovereign Martok had not been fully persuaded that the Consortium would make any violent move against Protectorates of the Alliance, that were fully defended by the UAS; all of that would change on Sarkiss II.

Ninety-five thousand years ago Alliance Security & Intelligence Services determined that the Consortium was moving against Sarkiss II, in Sector 1009, a Protectorate of great interest to the Alliance; it was located in the Orek cluster, and had the potential for future riches once the planet qualified for membership. As a result, both the Cadre and Fleet Commander made recommendations to the Sovereign that the planet be vigorously defended against interference from the Consortium. Sarkiss II also happened to be strategically important to the Alliance as it was located in the same Sector as Ursus Minor, the home world of the Consortium. Despite the recommendations that Sovereign Martok received he decided to only send a small contingent of UAS vessels under the command of General Hertzmal to defend the planet, believing in the superiority of Alliance technology and relying on the belief that the Consortium would back down at the sight of their ships. He grossly miscalculated.

At that time the Consortium had been led by Factotum Efaris Mar, a distant relative of their current leader. Efaris Mar deployed far more of his fleet to Sarkiss II than any strategist would have imagined reasonable, and they were waiting for the Alliance ships in high orbit over the magnetic poles of the planet, using its strong magnetic fields to shield them from the sensors of the Alliance ships. As they made their transition into sub-light speed they discovered the Consortium vessels lying in wait when they were most vulnerable to attack. Like a group of hunters waiting for their prey to emerge from the forest so they could kill them quickly and efficiently, the Consortium vessels were prepared.

It was a battle that only lasted a matter of seconds, if it could even be called a battle; most of the Alliance vessels, including General Hertzmal's flagship, were destroyed while still transiting from sub-light speed into planetary orbits where they would have taken up defensive positions against the opposing Consortium forces. Since Mar's vessels had been hiding within the magnetic field of Sarkiss II the sensors of the Alliance ships were blinded as they approached from Argis IV, located in the Argato Nebula in neighboring Sector 1008, which had served as their departure point. As far as General Hertzmal had been concerned no Consortium vessels were anywhere near the planet, or anywhere within 200,000 Krenar of Sarkiss II. As the ambush took place none of the ships were even able to make an emergency transmission back to Felis Prime to report their situation; all hands had been lost without a single shot having been fired by the Alliance. News of their destruction was only received thanks to Emergency Sensor Logs which were deployed once the ships were destroyed, transmitting the final images that had been recorded before the destruction of the ships at the hands of the marauding forces that had been lying in wait for them at the time of their arrival in orbit over the planet.

Since that fateful day the Felis Alliance and the Ursus Consortium had been watching each other with guarded animosity; they were not in a state of war, but it seemed perilously close. While the Consortium was acutely aware that they were much smaller than the Alliance and could never hope to outmatch them in a protracted military campaign, they seemed to want to constantly test the boundaries that had been established, pushing the treaties they had painstakingly negotiated and signed to the point where, if they did not actually break, they seemed to be mangled to the point where they were about to crumble. Diplomacy had, in many cases, become a weapon wielded as a sword rather than words spoken by diplomats.

Serving in the military was one way for Citizens of the Alliance to guarantee a career for themselves within the much larger bureaucracy, once their military service ended. While the extended lifespans afforded by the advanced technologies provided by the Alliance now meant that careers were measured in centuries, or longer, people still often chose to move from one career to another, taking the time to explore the opportunities afforded within a particular field. At the same time, many elected to remain within the military for as long as possible. Assuming someone survived their service, which was far more likely than not, the military was something that many young and talented Alliance Citizens volunteered to enter enthusiastically, with many having the desire to serve in the most elite group, the Alliance Special Combat Armed Response Corps, more commonly known as the ASCAR, or simply as the Corps.

(*|*)

Thanks to the advent of the Advanced Genomic Manipulation Program it was no longer necessary for people to worry about age when considering what they wanted to do with their lives. When someone wanted to join the military they simply went to the nearest Recruitment Center and attempted to pass the induction tests. If they passed, they were sent to one of the training facilities, depending on their aptitudes and interests. Since one of the codified rights guaranteed to Citizens of the Alliance was the right to an education, something that people took advantage of with great enthusiasm, most who joined the military had already completed their advanced education. People would often take several advanced degrees, in a variety of subjects, before deciding to join the Unified Armed Services. Joining the military afforded an individual the opportunity to explore even more through the specialized training unique to the specific programs within the UAS to which someone had been inducted.

Before the advent of the Advanced Genomic Manipulative

Program the average humanoid lifespan on Alliance planets ranged between ninety and one-hundred-and-eighty-years, with the occasional individual living to be as old as two-hundred-years-old, especially if they treated their bodies better than average. After the AGMP was introduced the average lifespan increased from hundreds to thousands of years. As scientists and geneticists further enhanced the Program it became possible, and not at all unusual, to see perfectly fit individuals living well past the age of one-hundred thousand years of age, though there were still some fluctuations, depending upon their planet of origin. Most critical to the AGMP had been identifying the aging process as a disease. Once it had been discovered that most diseases affecting humans stemmed from age, preventing untimely death was a matter of unlocking the sequences responsible for that process. As soon as that had been accomplished life was extended by reprogramming the genome and wiring cells to cease producing anything not beneficial to the system. Cells that developed into things like cancers, or failing organs were merely re-programmed at the source; it was an elegant, simple process that allowed life to proceed in a completely harmonious manner.

Even the peaceful Torgons had benefited from the AGMP after leaving their planet and becoming members of the Alliance. While they normally lived about one hundred and fifty years on their planet their lifespan was extended to upwards of fifty-thousand years thanks to the AGMP therapies. Longer lifespans allowed people to indulge in things they would never have had the opportunity to do otherwise; they were able to spend hundreds, if not thousands of years exploring things they would have otherwise only dabbled in, if they had bothered to try them at all. Artists could now spend a thousand years, or longer, working as apprentices, learning from great masters who had honed their skills and talents for unimaginable lengths of time. Music, the arts, literature, and all of the 'humanities' were prized beyond anything else on Alliance planets, and those who created things for others to enjoy were held in the highest esteem. When someone spent years, or even decades, composing a piece of music for others to enjoy it was considered one of the highest accomplishments for society and lauded by all; the Alliance had truly entered an age in which culture was cherished by all, considered far greater than anything that could be done by humanity. Museums, concert halls, and libraries had become the temples of the Alliance, housing the works that were now enjoyed by all Citizens.

While many welcomed the opportunity to appreciate the

challenges of several different careers, others used their time to enjoy life in ways that would simply not have been possible if they were not able to live as long as they were enabled thanks to the AGMP. It had reached the point that genomic manipulation was as common as ordinary space flight, or the mining of the Red Giant suns, which had provided the tremendous wealth that ultimately allowed Citizens of the Alliance to live without knowing the meaning of poverty, which was one of the main reasons the Ursus Consortium detested them so deeply. While the Felis Alliance believed that the wealth they accrued from their mining operations was something to be shared amongst its Citizens, effectively eliminating poverty and want from society, the Ursus Consortium was diametrically opposed to that concept: theirs was a highly developed class system, and their Ruling Class maintained an iron grip upon the wealth created by the Working Class. Those with wealth were in fierce control while those who worked to create that wealth lived in a constant state of need and fear, possessing no power to stand against those who ruled over them, particularly the Factotum and those and those in his service, who had little tolerance for anyone who stepped out of line for even the slightest reason. Any deviant action was dealt with publicly, using the harshest punishments. Few infractions were ever repeated.

(* | *)

Simply wearing the uniform of the Unified Armed Services was the fulfillment of a dream for many; for others, their dream could only find its satisfaction if that uniform included the patch of the ASCAR, indicating they had completed the rigorous requirements to become members of the most elite special forces Corps in the universe. For those who managed to earn the ASCAR patch, it was the ultimate achievement as far as they were concerned. Completing the training alone required skills found amongst less than one tenth of one percent of those who applied. For every thousand who took the tests to enter the training program only about six could pass muster, demonstrating they possessed the skills to be trained to become members of the elite forces of the Alliance. Anyone showing interest in entering the Alliance Special Combat Armed Response Corps, after having already completed their basic UAS training, received further evaluations to ensure they would survive the rigorous training ASCAR commandos endured. If someone who made it as far as wearing the uniform of the UAS had felt it had been difficult to get that far they would be shocked once they reached Tarak III, the planet where cadets for the Corps were trained. It was euphemistically known as the *Planet of Many Terrors* by those who underwent the arduous training that took place beneath the binary suns of the Ventu System.

Tarak III possessed rugged terrains, desert regions, and rain forests, making it an ideal place for the training of commandos. As a Green Zone planet it had been left untouched by the Alliance Seeders so it could be used as a place to watch the destruction of *Slugs*, the term applied to cadets who were trying to get into the Corps. Every Slug spent between six and eight months on the planet, depending on their specialty. They returned every few years of service for a one-month refresher of their skills and to learn any new techniques as they were developed. That month was often referred to as the *Holiday*, though it was anything but one for those returning. Without any doubt the training program for the ASCAR was the most comprehensive within the universe; those who completed it were prepared for anything. Once they had received the training the Corps had to offer each commando became a force unto themselves, possessing enough skills to survive through situations that would ordinarily kill twenty or thirty regular soldiers: each was trained to think, and they believed, without a shadow of a doubt, in their hearts, that they were unlike any other soldier, and it was the truth; the training had not only changed them, they had the history of the ASCAR to support that belief.

It was only after the tragic defeat at Sarkiss II, losing the planet to the Ursus Consortium ninety-five thousand years ago, that the Felis Alliance had introduced the ASCAR to the Unified Armed Services, although everyone agreed that their presence would not have made any difference on that mission. Officially, they had been introduced a few years later as a grand experiment, but their initial success as both support troops and elite commandos made their permanent presence within the UAS a necessity that could not be minimized considering the ongoing tensions between the Alliance and the Consortium. Given the directions the Consortium was taking with the development of their own military, including their own elite group of commandos, the idea of having a permanent force of highly-trained commandos available seemed more than prudent considering the risks posed by the enemy, which was how many within the Alliance viewed the Ursus Consortium. Now, with their training program under the direct supervision of the current Commandant of the ASCAR, a highly decorated commando from the planet Ventia by the name of Llashar, those who were earning their patches were the best ever. Commandant Llashar had begun her tenure twenty-five thousand years ago, and she had no plans of retiring anytime soon, not when things were heating up between the Alliance and the Consortium.

After an uneasy truce that had lasted several millennia, thanks in part to the diplomatic skills of Sovereign Sayoose, the most recent leader of the Felis Alliance, it almost seemed as though the idea of peace between the Alliance and the Consortium might be possible, and it would have been, had it not been for Factotum Ebla Mar, the Supreme Leader of the Ursus Consortium. As leader of the Ursus Consortium he possessed a maniacal desire to usher in the demise of the Alliance and the emergence of the Consortium as the dominant organization in the universe. It did not bother him that the task was impossible, requiring a military undertaking the likes of which had never been seen. Factotum Mar was nothing if not ambitious, and had no intentions of allowing the Sovereign to live under the illusion that there could be peace between their two organizations. If Mar had his way, he would launch an immediate attack against the home world of the Alliance itself; the only thing stopping him was his acutely awareness of the size and disposition of their defenses. He understood that his forces would be wiped out, much as the Alliance's forces had been when they arrived to defend Sarkiss II.

Factotum Mar had an advantage over his predecessors that Sovereign Sayoose was unaware of: thanks to his contact with the Premier of the Stellar Mining Bureau he had gained access to the AGMP, the life-extending technology developed by the Alliance. Unlike his predecessors, who usually only lived to the age of one hundred, Ebla Mar now expected to live for thousands of years thanks to the technology that the Premier of the Stellar Mining Bureau had brought back with him after one of his frequent trips to Felis Magoris, the home world of the Alliance. As Premier of the SMB the Paragon was in a unique position to travel freely between the territories of the massive organizations, without fear of his vessel being searched or confiscated, which was something he routinely used to his advantage. Factotum Mar had paid him handsomely for the medical technology and, in a rare gesture of familial beneficence, shared the treatments with his twin cousins Laranna and Teerana, the two remaining members of his family living in the city of Hydra; they had spent time together as children and he still claimed he cared about them, though the truth of the matter was that he needed one of the women for his plans to infiltrate the Alliance.

Since Sayoose had assumed the position of Sovereign things had improved tremendously for the Alliance. Sovereign Sayoose had shown that she was not afraid to use the Unified Armed Services to both strenuously, and effectively, defend both the members of the Alliance and Protectorates that were blissfully unaware of the existence of the pan-universal organization. Without realizing their position within the universe many planets had numerous heavily armed vessels in high planetary orbits, or patrolling their solar systems, preventing the Consortium from making aggressive moves against them while they continued to evolve. With the countless reforms that Sovereign Sayoose had instituted there was a major problem which potentially left the security of the entire Alliance at risk: she was missing from the capital, and could not be found.

She had disappeared without a trace from Felis Prime, and had not been seen or heard from for days. While her Cadre could rule in her absence, their jurisdiction prevented them from making any critical decisions requiring the Executive Authority provided by the Sovereign. By the grace of Caiphus, nothing would take place requiring Executive Authority, but it would be impossible to conceal her absence for an indefinite period. Due to the inordinate size of the Alliance's bureaucracy it was not unusual for important decisions requiring the attention of the Sovereign to wend their way from one department or another for several months or even years before they reached the Sovereign, making it fairly easy to keep the secret that the Sovereign was missing. But that secret could not be maintained for long.

Her Cadre was so faithful they had not even admitted that she was absent from the Alliance; they merely explained her lack of visibility to her excessive workload and a desire to spend what little free time she had alone. It was an excuse that was accepted without question; it was not unusual for the Sovereign to be sequestered for weeks or months due to the demands of her work. Nobody asked why she was not making public appearances, and nobody offered any explanations. It was the way of things within the Alliance.

At least, that was the way things usually operated.

CHAPTER II ~ MISSING

"Engineers developed the Automated Control Command module, the A-ConCom, as the finest development in Artificial Intelligence after Synthetic Intelligent Living Systems; both devices used Nano-processors capable of executing up to ten Exaflops: one million-trillion calculations per second. An A-ConCom provides enough computational power to keep any mining vessel from burning up in the corona of a star while simultaneously extracting the precious elements from the stellar body; it also provides the computational power other vessels in the Alliance fleet require to navigate through the universe at beyond the speed of light, moving through space that was unseen rather than traversing through that which was visible. It was only through the development of the A-ConCom that travel through pan-dimensional space stopped being a theory and became a reality."

[...]

Excerpted from: *From Star to Soil [A pamphlet for Children in the Felis Alliance School System]* (Authorized by the Alliance Security & Intelligence Services), by Laxapro, Premier of the Stellar Mining Bureau

(* | *)

An uncomfortable silence had fallen over the chambers of the Sovereign's Cadre, the room used whenever they met to discuss matters pertaining to the Alliance, or when they encountered visiting dignitaries from any of the numerous Alliance planets, as well as the countless bureaucratic officials that seemed to require something but, for various reasons, would not rate a private meeting with the Sovereign. For the most part, the Cadre served as an effective buffer against the demands against her limited time. Today, however, the

Cadre was meeting with the one group that could not be intimidated by their power, the one group that was closer to the Sovereign by virtue of their constant interactions with the leader of the Alliance. They were meeting with the three individuals who provided the Sovereign with close security, the Guardians.

When the Sovereign was in her office, had any meetings with visiting dignitaries, or during her various day-to-day activities, her Guardians were close at hand. Aside from providing close security, they provided a level of companionship the Sovereign found difficult to obtain due to the rarefied nature of her life and the grueling demands of her unique position. Enjoying leisure time, if such a thing existed in her life, was not an easy thing for the Sovereign to do, if she managed to find the time for it in the first place. On those rare occasions when she did manage to find some time for herself, the Guardians would be there, and she knew that she could trust them with her life. More than that, the Prime Guardian also served as the Sovereign's First Advisor and advised her in various matters pertaining to the Alliance and the Unified Armed Services. Some of the advice provided by the Commander Dragar went against what was provided by Regar, the First Counselor of the Cadre, which had earned the First Advisor more than a few harsh words from the First Counselor, though there was nothing that the First Counselor could do about the First Advisor: Commander Dragar had been personally chosen by the Sovereign and nobody but the Sovereign could remove him from his position. Based on how pleased she had been with the services of Guardians, particularly those of her Prime Guardian, First Counselor Regar was acutely aware that he stood little chance of ridding himself of the man standing before him in the chambers of the Cadre.

As the most powerful leader in the known universe the Sovereign did not rely exclusively on her three Guardians for security; they served as an inner phalanx, which appeared to cling to her wherever she went, as well as accompanying her anytime she left Felis Prime. Her security was augmented by a platoon of thirty specially trained ASCAR commandos known as the *Sovereign's Guard*, hand-picked from the division of the Corps assigned to protect Felis Prime, the capital of the Felis Alliance. They came from the best trained, most feared commandos around, and were under the capable command of Lieutenant Kar, but the Sovereign had still managed to slip past them unnoticed. It had, apparently, been her plan from the beginning. Ordering the Guardians to go on leave was one thing, but managing to distract thirty commandos, that was something that Commander Dragar, who had spent much of his life in the Corps, could simply not comprehend.

Wherever the Sovereign went, so went the Guardians: that was the rule. Except for this one time. For the past four days she had been missing, and despite their vast resources, not even the Alliance Security & Intelligence Services, known as ASIS, had been able to locate her. On the one occasion that the Sovereign had ordered, quite literally demanded, that her Guardians take some time off for themselves, something they had been extremely reluctant to do given their dedication to their duties, she had managed to disappear without a trace. Now that they had returned from their five days of vacation on Tarla IV, a planet favored by those needing a few days of rest and relaxation, they were both ready and anxious to return to their duties. Instead of returning to their duties they had been greeted by the shocking message from Lieutenant Kar, the platoon leader of the Sovereign's Guard.

Before agreeing to leave Felis Prime for their short vacation Lieutenant Kar had hand-picked five members from her platoon to provide close protection for the Sovereign while the Guardians were absent; it was the only way Commander Dragar and his companions would agree to take their leave, knowing that the highly trained commandos would have the Sovereign completely protected. They also knew that the Sovereign was not scheduled to travel anywhere off of Felis Prime in their absence, making the security a much lower-risk than if she were to leave the safety of the capital. At the same time, it had seemed that the Sovereign had managed to slip past the contingent of five commandos from the Sovereign's Guard and had managed to disappear without a trace.

Commander Dragar immediately demanded to see the First Counselor of the Cadre, summoning the rest of Cadre as well, which was the last thing they had expected to be doing upon their return to Felis Prime. Somebody would answer for this treachery, if there was any treachery involved, and Dragar was not about to stand around waiting to see who was being blamed: he was looking right at the top of the food chain.

Commander Dragar and the other two Guardians were standing in the chambers of the Cadre, looking around at those assembled while he attempted to contain his rising anger, "What do you *mean* Sovereign Sayoose is missing, First Counselor Regar?" the Prime Guardian and First

Advisor to the Sovereign boomed. Lieutenant Kar was not present; she had already fully briefed the Guardians immediately upon their return to Felis Prime regarding everything that she knew, which was, admittedly, not a great deal. Dragar could not blame her as she had done exactly as the Guardians had been ordered, apparently as the Sovereign had planned in order for her to leave Felis Prime for reasons unbeknownst to him, which was that much more frustrating to the dedicated Guardian. He could not find it within himself to be angry at the Lieutenant for following the orders of the Sovereign, since it was exactly what he and the other Guardians had done as part of the grand deception to help the Sovereign leave Felis Prime. Anger was something he could not help feeling, however, and at this point it was entirely directed toward the First Counselor of the Cadre.

Dragar was unsure why he distrusted the man so much, but he did, and he trusted his instincts more than anything; as a professional soldier they had saved his life on more occasions than he could count. First Counselor Regar had never appeared to him as anything less than a man who was opportunistic and intensely driven in his desire to gain a greater position for himself. Being the First Counselor of the Cadre should have made the man intensely proud of his achievement, but Regar always gave the impression that he wanted more from his career, and that was not how the bureaucracy of the Alliance worked. He was a tall man, though still half-a-head shorter than the towering Commander Dragar; First Counselor Regar was extremely thin and had a nervous disposition was only exasperated under stressful conditions.

Dragar's voice filled the room as though he were once again addressing a thousand troops as a battalion commander in the Corps. He glared at the First Counselor in as menacing a fashion as he could muster, then asked, his voice low and fierce, "Tell me, exactly, what you are talking about," he shook his head, "no, on second thought, why don't you just start from the beginning," it was, of course, all a ruse: Lieutenant Kar had already told him everything she knew, and Dragar had spoken with ASIS officers about what they had been able to discover, which had, admittedly, not been a great deal. Commander Dragar was simply checking to ensure the First Counselor was not holding anything back from him; anyone who had overheard the request would well be forgiven to think that the person making it had been threatening the First Counselor of the Cadre. In truth, it was all a test; if the First Counselor of the Cadre failed, the consequences were far worse than the threats he might be able to imagine coming from the man facing him.

Lying was the last thing that anyone would want to do to the Prime Guardian, particularly when it had anything to do with the safety and well-being of the Sovereign. Commander Dragar was not only the First Advisor of the Sovereign, he was her friend. Even more than that, he was fanatically dedicated to his role, though it was a relatively new position, having only been created fifty years ago. His primary responsibility was for her safety, and now, she was missing; all he was trying to do was sort out where she was, before anything could happen to her. It was all so insufferable: on the one occasion that the Sovereign had gone somewhere without her escort, the one time she had convinced her Guardians that they should take some time for themselves because her schedule did not require their presence on Felis Prime, she had managed to disappear without a trace.

As First Counselor of the Cadre it fell upon Regar to lead the Cadre, a group of five which served as the special counselors and advisors to the Sovereign of the Alliance. Their role was particularly important in the absence of the Sovereign as they were tasked with the responsibility of serving, in a limited capacity, in her stead, making all but the most critical decisions. At this moment, however, Dragar was uncertain whether or not the man standing before him truly knew more than what he was revealing. If he found out he was being lied to, Regar would live to regret having been born.

"Let me put it to you this way, First Counselor Regar," Dragar said, almost in a whisper, making the First Counselor shiver. Few people, Regar knew, could utter his title and make it sound as much like an epithet as Commander Dragar. "I know, for a fact, that we can find others to become members of the Cadre, but there is only *one* Sovereign. If you do not tell me everything you know, by Caiphus, I shall invoke the wrath of the *Fallen* upon you," his eyes seemed to bore into the man's soul, "and trust me," he continued, his tone making the other man tremble, "I've sent more than enough soldiers to their graves to know that there are more than sufficient amongst the *Fallen* who would be more than willing to come take their wrath out on a tasty morsel like yourself." Dragar was pleased to see a trickle of sweat coursing down the face of the Cadre member as he struggled to swallow.

Regar grew pale as he avoided the eyes of the former ASCAR Commander. It was perfectly clear to him that Dragar could not only do what he was threatening, he would; on top of that, he would enjoy it, which frightened the man terribly. He opened his mouth, trying to answer, but his mouth was so dry he could not produce a sound. His mouth was gaping, his lips moving in a silent pantomime as he struggled to speak. After taking a sip of water from his hydrator his eyes met the penetrating black eyes of Dragar, a characteristic of people who hailed from the planet Ventia, "It, it's ..." he stammered, taking a breath, "it," he took another breath, and another sip from his hydrator before trying to speak again. "It would seem," he finally managed to say, with some effort, "that the Sovereign has taken a ..." he stammered, "a ... a vacation ... of sorts," he finally said, his voice trembling, his eyes darting everywhere except making contact with the piercing black eyes that seemed to see through wherever they looked. "But," he added hastily, "I know she doesn't want to be found." He took another sip from the hydrator, a device that hung from two straps over the shoulders, providing fresh, cool water whenever it was desired.

"Really?" Dragar asked skeptically, "How would you possibly know this?" Regar was a tall man, but the Prime Guardian was still able to make him look as though he was an insignificantly slight individual, frail, and easily crushed by the giant towering over him. In truth, Dragar was only taller by half-a-head, but his shoulders were extremely broad and his chest was thicker than most, giving the impression that he looked indestructible. It was an illusion that served the Guardian well by dissuading most people from wanting to engage in any sort of violent action when he was nearby, which suited him fine, especially when he was guarding the Sovereign. But now, things were different: he had never known the Sovereign to intentionally seek being so far out of contact with everyone, especially her Guardians and the Cadre, even if the First Counselor of the Cadre was a sniveling ... he allowed the thought to go unfinished as he considered the situation, looking at the First Counselor, who was nodding, confirming what he had just stated.

First Counselor Regar spoke again, his voice stronger, "She arranged for her own transportation," he began, "she transformed into another form, traveling as a passenger on an Alliance patrol vessel transiting through Sector 0108," he glanced at the menacing Dragar and took another deep breath, "but when the patrol vessel returned to Felis Magoris, the Sovereign was ..." he glanced away for a moment, before resuming, "not on board, and there were no records of her having left the vessel."

As much as it angered him, the explanation matched what Lieutenant Kar had told him, and it made sense. He knew that the Sovereign was from the planet Tarlos II, which was one of the oldest members of the Alliance. Only those born on the southern continent of Waylacor had the power to change their physical appearance. Such individuals were known as shapeshifters, or genomorphs. If the Sovereign had decided to modify her appearance, it would have been impossible for anyone to detect her presence as a passenger on the patrol vessel. She could have looked like anyone. *By Caiphus,* Dragar thought in frustration, *she could have even gone looking like him and nobody would have raised an eyebrow.*

Even so, Dragar was not quite ready to let the First Counselor off so easily, "You're telling me," he stopped, shaking his head, when he felt the gentle touch of one of the other Guardians touch his left arm. He looked over and saw the pixie-like face of Captain Pertu looking up at him, nodding slowly. Her hand remained on his arm just long enough for him to feel the pressure of her soothing touch through his uniform, causing the hairs on his arm to twitch in response.

Her raspy voice penetrated the depths of his frustration, "Commander," she began, her voice as much of a whisper as she could make it without exhaling nothing but air, "I don't believe anger is going to help us at this juncture, do you?" she looked into his eyes, allowing him to see that he was putting his emotions before what was truly important; he could see that she was as deeply concerned as he was, but he also knew there was another way of approaching it rather than by attacking the messenger. Captain Pertu was not only one of the best pilots in the fleet, having been decorated with some of the most prestigious awards given to pilots for flying in the Unified Armed Services, she was also one of the most level-headed people Dragar knew, either within the Corps or otherwise. Dragar nodded, grudgingly, his memory flashing back to the first time they had met.

(*|*)

One of the decorations Captain Pertu had received during her career in the Unified Armed Services explained the raspiness of her voice; it was also the reason she been asked to join the Guardians. As a pilot in the UAS fleet she had been one of the many pilots deployed to guard the planet Marnse IX, a Protectorate in Sector 0920, when her ship was ambushed by a patrol from the Galactic Armed Forces of the Ursus Consortium which had been lying in wait for them, concealed behind one of the three moons of the planet. Captain Pertu not only outmaneuvered and destroyed the marauding patrol, she helped to save the planet by eliminating the threat from the marauders. As a result of the battle she suffered severe injuries to her throat and larynx from plasma discharges from the helm, leaving her permanently scarred and her ship heavily damaged, resulting in Pertu having to make an emergency landing on an uninhabited part of the planet. Several members of the crew were also injured during the battle, but they all survived thanks to her exceptional piloting. Even with the damage done to the ship and the severe injuries she had received, Pertu managed to safely land her Cruiser, well away from any developed areas, where the injured survivors waited to be rescued by another Alliance vessel, later that day.

After several months at an Alliance Healing Center on Felis Magoris, where her wounds healed and she went through rigorous physical rehabilitation, Captain Pertu was presented with the prestigious Bleeding Heart, with Clusters. Her citation read: *For injuries received while demonstrating distinguished valor in battle*. She was also presented with her second Golden Wings citation, for exceptional flying and tactical skills in battle. This led to her being offered the opportunity to choose her next assignment, once she was physically fit to resume duty. It was a dream situation for any pilot. Flying had always been her aspiration, since she had first seen an aircraft fly overhead as a young girl of seven, on her home world of Ventia. Since that day her sole desire had been to fly for the Alliance, a dream which she had fulfilled. After achieving advanced degrees in aeronautics, mathematics, military diplomacy, and a few other things she had felt would serve her well in a military career, when Pertu finally applied to join the Unified Armed Services she passed the aptitude tests to become a pilot with flying colors, excelling quickly and dramatically. Her first assignment had been as a pilot of an Interceptor onboard one of the fleet's massive Carriers, which she flew with such distinction she was presented her first Golden Wings citation, as well as her first of several promotions.

That was, however, not to be the end of Pertu's dream, it was only the beginning: she had always wanted to be the commanding officer of one of the great ships of the Alliance; now she was being offered that opportunity. She would be able to command one of the greatest ships ever constructed. She had often imagined what it would be like to be at the helm of one of the UAS Battlecruisers, the greatest vessels that the Alliance had ever designed, especially after the latest upgrades had been made to the fleet, or perhaps even one of the mammoth Carriers, which she had served on as a pilot. A single carrier could convey hundreds of different Interceptors into a battle while also bringing to bear weaponry that was almost as impressive as that found on the Battlecruisers, but the Battlecruiser was something unmatched in the fleet, in any fleet.

Her decision would have been far easier had things been as simple as choosing between whether or not she should merely take the helm of one type of ship over another, but fate had intervened, making her choice much easier. In the end, it was not what she had expected, but it turned out to be far better than she could have ever imagined. Her decision was easy because she had been approached by the Prime Guardian of the Sovereign, Commander Dragar, who had been made aware of what she had gone through on Marnse IX; he had been told of the exploits of the young Captain Pertu, and he had been impressed. If there was one thing that anyone who knew Commander Dragar would tell you it was that he was not easily impressed.

When Commander Dragar arrived at her room at the Rehab Center on Felis Magoris Captain Pertu was exercising with her Rehab Technician. One look at the hulking figure of Commander Dragar and she instinctively knew that this was not a man you fooled with; he possessed the air of a man who not only demanded, but deserved the respect he received from those around him. Captain Pertu quickly discovered that he had earned every bit of it as well, but her first impressions of the man were simple: he was massive. She recognized him as a fellow Ventian thanks to his eyes, which were as black as her own. His piercing black eyes seemed to see everything all at once. Dragar was also built like an Alliance Land-Crawlers, an armored vehicle used to transport troops on planetary missions that were well-armed and virtually indestructible. That was exactly how Commander Dragar looked: indestructible. Captain Pertu did not share the physical characteristics of her fellow Ventian; people from Ventia had as much variety in their body-type as many other planets, it was only their eyes that were distinctly black, a defensive system that had evolved to protect their visual organs from the increased radiation given off by the binary suns in the Ventian system. Without their darkened eyes any visitors to Ventia find themselves going blind in a short period of time, unless they use protective lenses.

When Dragar entered the room he looked at Captain Pertu and nodded at the Rehab Technician. She nodded in return and excused herself to provide them some privacy, shutting the door quietly behind her. That was when he gave her the first smile he had shown, changing the hardness of his face into something she had not expected. His rugged handsomeness was transformed by that simple act; rather than a severe soldier he now looked like someone she would want to sit and have a conversation with, someone she would like to get to know. Pertu immediately noticed the rank insignia on his collar, and the *Ghost Corps* badge on his shoulder. ASCAR; but there was also something else, he wore the unique patch indicating the most elite unit membership within the Alliance: Black Wings over his service ribbons indicated he was a member of the Guardians of the Sovereign.

"How are you feeling, Captain Pertu?" he asked, his voice surprisingly gentle, catching her off guard.

She found she could only nod mutely in response at first until, after a moment she found her voice and stammered, "Uhm, better … doing well," she managed, her voice a strangled whisper, "thanks for asking," she smiled, which made the big man's heart skip a beat. It pained him to see anyone injured, let alone someone who seemed as delicate as Captain Pertu, which was deceiving since she was quite tall and extremely athletic. She could definitely hold her own in any hand-to-hand situation, as could anyone who had gone through the training to become a member of the Unified Armed Services.

Dragar nodded, seemingly satisfied with her response as he examined the weights she had been using. He casually lifted the heaviest of them with his left hand, performing a few easy curls before gently replacing it on the rack, "I'm really pleased to hear that," he said, not exhibiting any strain at having lifted such a heavy weight. He gave her another smile, putting her more at ease, "I suppose you're wondering why I'm here?" he asked, pleased to see her nod at the question. "Let me explain," he said, pulling over the stool the Rehab Technician had vacated. He looked directly at the young woman's face, observing the bandage that still covered the wound on her throat, "First of all, I promise, you won't have to do much talking, alright?"

Pertu nodded, smiling at the Commander. She gave him a thumbs-up gesture to indicate that was fine with her; the less talking, the better. Her throat was still extremely tender thanks to the plasma burns. It would take another several weeks before she would be fully recovered. Even then, the doctors had warned her there were no guarantees she would ever have the sweet sounding voice with which she had loved to sing.

"Good," Dragar replied, his deep voice resonating richly in the sparsely decorated room. He smiled again as he leaned forward, "I understand you've been given the opportunity to choose your next posting, which is an honor for any pilot," he saw her nod in agreement, "well, you've certainly earned it," he continued, "but, before you make any decisions, I'm here to give you something else to choose from, an offer that I can assure you isn't on your list right now," he paused for a moment, watching her face. She looked confused, and he smiled again. He was obviously enjoying this, "You can only choose this assignment if you've been invited, which is what I'm here to do. After hearing about what you did over Marnse IX, how you managed to save your crew," he continued, "I've decided you deserve the opportunity to command the single most advanced ship in the fleet, one which cannot be flown unless you are in a particular branch of the UAS," he paused for the briefest moment as he saw the confusion on her face grow deeper. Pilots in the fleet generally regarded the newest Battlecruisers to be the best vessels developed by the Alliance; what could possibly be better than the Trans-Light Battlecruisers?

That was when she made the connection: Commander Dragar was a member of the Guardians of the Sovereign. It was no secret amongst pilots in the Unified Armed Services that the Guardians flew in a hybrid design of the Trans-Light Battlecruisers, specifically designed for the Sovereign. It was known as Helios-2, or He-2, when the Sovereign was not on board. When the Sovereign was onboard, it was known as Helios-1. As a ship it had the appearance of a luxury space yacht: something that might be found transiting between planets routinely these days, but Helios-2 was far more than any space yacht that someone could order from some black market Shipyard. Helios-2 was the equivalent of the most advanced Battlecruiser, with enhancements, many of which would be incorporated into the next generation of Alliance Battlecruisers. The main difference between Helios-2 and a Battlecruiser was its size, the Sovereign's ship was designed to be small and relatively inconspicuous while Battlecruisers were designed to intimidate, delivering the maximum amount of weaponry that could be brought to bear in battle. Helios-2 was flown by a single pilot, while the other two Guardians served in supportive roles. It could easily carry fifteen in a state of luxury, or up to forty, though that would make for close quarters.

Commander Dragar nodded as he saw the look of realization in Captain Pertu's eyes. He could saw that she understood, but he still had to officially make the offer, "Yes, Captain," he said, his voice low, "I'm here to offer you an opportunity to join the Guardians of the Sovereign, as both a Guardian and, of course, the Commanding Pilot of Helios-2," he looked into her eyes, searching for an answer. It was apparent he wanted her to make a decision. "I can give you some time, if you need ..." he began, but she interrupted him.

"No," she blurted out, causing her more pain than she expected, "I mean ... no, sir, I don't require more time ..." she grinned as she brought her hand up to her throat and gently rubbed the bandage. "Yes," she smiled broadly, "it would be an honor to accept your offer, it would be my pleasure to serve as a Guardian to the Sovereign, and to serve as the pilot of such an incredible vessel as Helios-2," her face lit up the room. "I don't know what else to say," her voice turning more into a strangled hiss with each word.

Dragar raised his finger to silence her, "I don't need to hear anything else, Captain," he said. "Your acceptance was all I needed, all that I wanted," he reached over and patted her on the arm. "All you have to focus on now is your recovery, which I gather," he looked around the Rehab Room, "is going quite well," he was pleased to see her nod in agreement. "Good," he said, rising from the stool, which rolled to the other side of the room, "when you're ready, and not a day before, report to the Training Facility on Felis Prime. You'll have to go through a few weeks of auxiliary training, but that shouldn't be an issue for someone with your training." She nodded, knowing the training would be difficult, but welcome after her time in the Rehabilitation Center. Dragar gave her a crisp salute, but since she was not in uniform she did not return it, only nodding appreciatively at the gesture.

"Welcome to the Guardians, Captain Pertu," he smiled again, "I'm looking forward to getting to know you better, once you're able to talk without straining yourself," he held up his hand to prevent her from responding, knowing she was still in pain from their exchange. Instead, she just nodded enthusiastically. He turned to leave the room but stopped himself. He turned to face her again, reaching into a pocket in his uniform.

"I expect you'll want to have these applied to your uniform when you're ready to report for duty," he said, handing her a pair of White Wings. They were identical to his, only different in color. Dragar's were pure black, indicating his position as the Prime Guardian, while hers indicated that she would be in Command of the Sovereign's ship, which was fine with her; white had always been a good color for Pertu. She smiled at the tall Guardian as he turned again to leave the room, looking back once more as he closed the door behind him.

That had been eleven years ago, eleven short years, and Captain Pertu had not regretted making her decision to join the Guardians once. It had not only been the easiest decision of her career, it had undoubtedly been the best. Working with the other two Guardians had taught her more in the past eleven years than in her previous eighty-seven serving in the UAS, and she was looking forward to spending a long time serving the Sovereign, whom she had grown extremely close to over her time as a Guardian. Sovereign Sayoose may have been the single most powerful figure in the known universe, but she was also a genuinely wonderful person to be around. Few Alliance Citizens had an opportunity to meet her, let alone speak with her on a regular basis. Having the chance to get to know the Sovereign while doing her job made things all the more interesting. Captain Pertu considered herself to be the luckiest pilot in the Alliance, if not the entire universe.

(*|*)

As a member of the Guardians Dragar knew he could always count on Captain Pertu to provide an angle on things that others might not be able to see when it came to situations that seemed impenetrably dark. He always appreciated having her agile sense of humor around, especially as a foil to his friend and comrade, Tactical Sergeant Brem, with whom he had served in the Corps. Brem was the most capable soldier that Dragar had ever encountered, but he also had a knack for rubbing people the wrong way if he thought he could do so without serious ramifications. In truth, Brem enjoyed pushing people's buttons, regardless of who they were. Unfortunately, as a Guardian that usually meant playing games with dignitaries or other high-ranking officials, none of whom seemed to appreciate the sense of humor of the short, plug-like man who was as tough as they came. Fortunately for Brem, Dragar was usually able to keep him in check, and the Sovereign also happened to like him, which helped tremendously.

After taking a deep breath to calm himself, Dragar nodded toward Pertu, acknowledging that her message had been received. He turned back to the First Counselor of the Cadre, struggling to keep his anger in check, "Well then, *First Counselor* Regar," he asked, his voice dripping with sarcasm, "how do you suppose the Sovereign is supposed to get back home?" he glared at the Cadre member with a ferocity that made the man cringe, cowering visibly as the Prime Guardian took a small step toward him. "Don't you think it's just a bit ridiculous to have allowed the Sovereign of the Alliance to leave the capital without any escort?" Dragar realized he was being hard on the man considering how the Sovereign had managed to slip past those guarding her, but the truth of the matter was, he was enjoying seeing the man fearful of what he might do to him, and it did not help matters that he could hear the snickering of Tactical Sergeant Brem from behind him. After casting him a warning glare he returned his focus onto the First Counselor, who seemed grateful for the brief distraction.

First Counselor Regar was now visibly shaking, nodding his head in agreement, then shaking it again, "There is," he began tentatively, "a … well, she has a communicator with her," he managed to spit out, hoping this might mollify the angered Prime Guardian, "the Sovereign can call for assistance whenever she desires, or anytime she feels threatened; she's perfectly safe," he took a quick breath and another sip from his hydrator, trying to satiate his seemingly unquenchable thirst. After another small sip from the long flexible straw he continued, "My understanding is that it's a lovely world, somewhere around a Green Zone Six, or … perhaps even a Seven."

Dragar felt his stomach drop and he was genuinely infuriated, "Did you say Green Zone *Six* or *Seven*?" the words sounded like explosions, echoing off the walls of the chamber with a pronounced reverberation. "Are you *serious*? That's horrific! That practically puts them in the Iron Age, how can you think the Sovereign might be safe on a world in such a backwards state?" before Regar had an opportunity to answer the Prime Guardian held up his thickly muscled arms, "No. Don't even bother saying anything else," he turned to look at the other two Guardians who looked equally mortified at what they had just heard. Turning back to Regar he said, "I'm going to find her." Before leaving he looked directly into the eyes of the First Counselor and said, "if that's okay with you and your precious Cadre?"

His question caught First Counselor Regar by surprise as he stood there, mute and paralyzed by the confrontation. After a brief moment he nodded his head, "Of … of course …" he stammered, "yes, of course," he finally replied, his voice gathering strength, "by all means, Prime Guardian, please, do whatever you must in order to find the Sovereign," he looked to the other two Guardians for a moment. "We'll do whatever we can to support your efforts," he added hastily, glancing at the other four members of the Cadre who had remained conspicuously silent during the encounter. None of them had any interest in being on the receiving end of the rage of the Prime Guardian and were quite content to observe First Counselor Regar be the target of his rancor. "You must know you'll have our full support in your endeavors," he smiled at the thickset Guardian and was rewarded with a withering glare in return. He wisely decided to remain silent.

When the Guardians had reached the door of the chambers Commander Dragar turned toward him again, "I don't require your support, First Counselor Regar," Dragar spat, "I require your silence. If you, or the Cadre," he gestured toward the others, who shrank behind the First Counselor, "do anything to hamper our efforts …" he left the threat hanging; the tone of his voice severe enough to convey the message with a clarity that did not require any further explanation. Without another word the three Guardians left the chambers of the Cadre, entering the long hallway that connected the many administrative offices on the Executive level of Felis Prime. For a moment the three stood in the busy hallway, watching the bustle of the many people as they went about their business in the orbiting capital of the Alliance. Some were walking while others were riding on AG Floaters, one or two-person vehicles that employed an anti-gravity field to travel a few feet above the ground at various speeds.

Dragar turned to his two comrades, shaking his head slowly, "I can't believe that fool," he said, his voice a hiss of a whisper, "but, we cannot allow anyone to know what's going on, is that clear?" Brem and Pertu nodded in agreement, their eyes filled with a combination of anger and sadness. At the same time, the two Guardians recognized that nothing good would come if information about the Sovereign being missing, or even absent, was released without them knowing where she was located. "Good," Dragar continued, "now, here's what I want you to do," he said, keeping his voice barely above a whisper, "I want both of you to carry on as though things were normal: report for duty and maintain your schedules, regardless of the present situation. In the meantime, I'm going to pay a visit to Marta and see what I can find out," at the mention of Marta both Brem and Pertu's faces lit up. They knew exactly where he was going and what he would be doing while they carried out the charade of guarding someone who was not around.

"Yes sir," the two Guardians replied in unison, holding up their left hands next to their faces, palms out, in crisp salutes. Dragar returned the salute and smiled grimly as they went off in opposite directions, each with heavy hearts.

CHAPTER III ~ SEARCHING

"Mining Red Dwarf Stars led to the greatest source of economic enrichment since the splitting of the atom and the harnessing of the fusion process, which led to the single worst disaster in the history of humanity: the complete destruction of Delar IX. It is difficult to imagine the devastation that could be caused by the power of fusion until seeing the remains of the planet, the ruins of which may be observed in orbit around the sun in the Delar system. Subsequently, the Felis Alliance established strict protocols regulating the use of Atomics, banning the development and use of all fusion weapons."

[...]

"Of primary importance to the Alliance is the economic well-being of member planets and their Citizenry; the priority was of such importance that personal wealth was no longer considered an issue when it comes to an individual's station within society. Every Citizen of the Alliance lives in accordance to a simple precept: access to a quality education, healthcare, housing, and nutritious, unprocessed foods are all considered Inviolable Fundamental Rights, regardless of where the person lives within the Alliance. Each of these rights, among others, are entrenched within the Pan-Universal Alliance Charter of Rights and Freedoms. More than enough resources exist within the Alliance to provide for the needs of each Citizen without anyone having to experience privation.

"It was discovered that once the prospect of poverty and all forms of discrimination were eliminated, once the prospect of suffering due to having been born someplace where you had no control over your destiny was eliminated, people began to reach their full potential far sooner, and the petty strife that had beleaguered so many worlds was similarly eliminated.

An era of enduring peace spread across those planets that has lasted for many millennia."

[...]

Excerpted from: *A Brief History of the Felis Alliance*, by Sovereign Sayoose

(*|*)

Felis Magoris, the home world of the Felis Alliance, was one of the most densely populated and heavily developed planets within the pan-universal Alliance. Over nine billion people lived on the planet, with more than another billion living on the over eight thousand orbiting cities that had been constructed in orbit, high above the surface of the planet. Each of the orbiting cities was a phenomenon unto itself, each version bigger and better than the previous iteration. Several of the early versions had faced near disastrous ends when they were first introduced, but after many years of development, a few tragic and unfortunate accidents, the building techniques of these technological marvels had advanced to such an extent it was now common to see orbiting cities around almost every planet in the Alliance. Scientists and engineers had mastered the building techniques, allowing those Citizens of the Alliance who chose to live off-world to cultivate the space above their planets as easily as they did the land below. One of the most elaborate of these technological sensations had been commissioned to serve as the orbiting capital of the Alliance and home of the Sovereign, as well as serving as a home for the thousands of administrative and bureaucratic offices required to run the Alliance.

For anyone visiting the orbiting capital, Felis Prime was a splendor to behold. Any visitor arriving at one of the many spaceports located along the rim of the city was rewarded with a view that could only be described as spectacular as they approached the immense double-sided city in high orbit over Felis Magoris. It was only after the orbiting cities began to adopt the double-sided design that they were able to become fully self-sufficient, allowing them to cut all ties to their home worlds and cut the invisible tethers that kept them reliant on the planets below, so long as they were prepared to deal with any contingencies that might arise while in orbit. Having two sides meant the orbiting city could dedicate enough space to growing the requisite food for its inhabitants without needing to send a constant stream of supply ships back to their home world every few months. Since the design of the city allowed it to cultivate the food it required there was another benefit: the plants helped produce some of the much needed oxygen required to sustain life, which was also supplemented by trees interspersed throughout the city and the massive Power Generation Unit, which used elemental conversion techniques to synthesize essential substances, such as water, which was an incredibly heavy cargo to transport from the surface of the planet.

As a visitor approached Felis Prime they would see the Ag-Domes on the side facing Felis Magoris and the Hab-Domes on the side facing space. Between the two parts of the orbiting city was a section that appeared as a thick core which housed the most essential parts of the city; it was here that a great deal of work went on, far more than could be imagined by anyone living within the city. Aside from housing the spaceports, which were large enough to accommodate a contingent of Battlecruisers, Carriers, and Transports, the core of Felis Prime served as the location for the repair facilities for all the ships traveling to and from the city; the core also contained the Power Generation Unit and the Central Computer Core, without which Felis Prime would be powerless and dead, a dark satellite orbiting Felis Magoris like a piece of abandoned space garbage. With the Power Generation Unit, it was possible for the orbiting city to use its powerful thrusters, installed at various points along its rim, to make fine adjustments to its orbit, including raising or lowering its altitude. If necessary, Felis Prime could even leave orbit if desired, though there was little chance of this taking place as traveling anywhere through deep-space onboard the city would take centuries without the assistance of a Star Drive or Trans-Light Drive.

More important than being able to adjust the immense city's position in orbit, or even move it through space was that the Power Generation Unit provided the energy required to sustain life on the orbiting city, allowing it to remain in orbit and maintain the environmental balance required to keep the city and its residents comfortable. With the Power Generation Unit, the city was a paradise for the quarter-million inhabitants. It enabled them to simulate the light and energy of the sun from the Felis system, providing the perfect climate for human life in the Hab-Domes while providing ideal growing conditions in the Ag-Domes, where foods and other plant-life was cultivated. Each compartment within the Ag-Domes could be adjusted to suit any crop or desired habitat, allowing the caretakers of the city to provide growing conditions that could only be replicated in space, making the city's gardens ideally suited for any crop that had been planted. Since the Ag-Domes faced the planet natural light from the sun was channeled through the city, allowing the crops in the Ag-Domes to receive the ideal amount of natural light while people living in the Hab-Domes enjoyed the natural sunlight, filtered through specially tinted panes of multi-layered glass designed to protect them from harmful solar radiation, making it feel as though they were living on the planet's surface.

Each pane of glass had been an engineering marvel unto itself, taking years to master before the design had been perfected to the point that something as large as the Felis Prime domes could be constructed. Other domes had been built on orbiting cities but they had to use much smaller windows. Felis Prime had been one of the first cities to be able to take advantage of the new lattice design that had been developed from interlocking panes of laminated glass. It was an elegant design in the shape of a hexagon, based on the honeycomb used by bees. Scientists had discovered the design during one of their survey missions to Terra and had brought samples of the structures back to Felis Magoris for further study. It immediately became apparent to the engineers that the arrangement of the cells within the honeycomb was an ideal structure for proving the strength they required for the proposed dome structures in the orbiting cities. When a scale model was produced it was determined that it was capable of withstanding far more stress than it would ever have to endure under the most extreme conditions in space, and the design was approved for Felis Prime.

An advantage of the design was that it allowed for the replacement of an individual pane of glass, or an entire cell, should the need arise, without having to evacuate the entire dome. All that would be required was for an isolation module to be placed over the affected area. Thanks to the space created by where each cell abutted against the neighboring cell there was room for the isolation modules to be installed as safety feature. Each module consisted of a synthetic material that was automatically activated whenever the sensors in the dome determined that a repair was necessary. If a pane became damaged from the outside of the dome the isolation module would deploy from within the dome, creating a temporary impenetrable barrier which would allow for the complete removal of the damaged cell, if required, or just the single pane of laminate, if that was all that needed to be changed.

With the advent of the Synthetic Intelligent Living Systems the dangerous task of scaling the heights of the inner walls of the dome could be accomplished without fear of someone falling and injuring themselves. SILS were also able to affect the repairs in less time than their human counterparts due to their greater strength and agility, and they were not distracted by working far above the city's floor in necessary. It was also possible for SILS to travel along the outside of the dome without any cumbersome gear since their synthetic bodies did not require protection from the harshness of space. Once the repair had been completed the devices would simply return through one of the maintenance ports along the rim of the city and they would return to their normal duties. As a testament to the quality of the strength and design of the materials used in the construction of the domes only three panes had required replacement in the four hundred and seventy years since Felis Prime had been completed in orbit, and their design life was estimated at over one thousand years, but the plan was to change all of them well before that time.

One of the most important features of the Power Generation Unit to Commander Dragar was that it provided energy for the Communications Array, which served as the eyes and ears of the city. There seemed to be an endless number of antenna protruding around the circumference of Felis Prime that any approaching visitor would notice, including the largest array coming out of the central portion of the city, located on the side of the Hab-Domes; a smaller structure located on the Ag-Domes side permitted clear communication with Felis Magoris. It was the Array that allowed the Alliance to maintain communications with the fleet of the Unified Armed Services, as well as the encoded communications between the member planets of the Alliance.

Without the Array the Alliance would be blind and deaf. Low priority messages and unencoded communications could be sent through a system of transmission nodes scattered at various points throughout the universe, but if someone was looking for something or someone, the Array was the place to start. Besides, Commander Dragar thought to himself, the system of Communication Nodes, or Comm Nodes, as they were commonly referred to, which made up the architecture of the Central Communications Hub that accommodated all non-military transmissions, was not what Dragar needed; he required the Array, which was reserved for top-level, high-security, military communications. Felis Prime was equipped with the most advanced radiographic telescopes within the Alliance; what few people realized was that it was possible to use the Array to locate specific people, if certain conditions existed.

The Communications Array on Felis Prime was only one of several throughout the vast Alliance, and it was essential in order to process the enormous number of messages and vast amounts of data that were regularly transmitted between the massive fleet of the UAS and the members of the Alliance. Messages were sent through an Array because of security measures established to prevent unauthorized interception of the communications, otherwise, using the pan-universal Comm Nodes were an expedient method of transmission. Any messages dealing with high security issues, such as the movement of the fleet, required the use of the Communications Array since it was completely secure. All of the communications and data transmitted over the Array were encoded using an unbreakable system unique to each message, with a new key sent with each message generated by the system to each sender. The system had been designed with such complexity that no living being could possibly decode any message without the use of the advanced computers used to create them: each message carried a unique 24-digit identifier at their beginning, indicating the unique key by which the message would be decoded, followed by another unique identifier at the end of the message, providing the code which would be used to encode the messages originating from the recipient in response, if necessary.

Each Array had the ability to generate new identifiers to initiate a communication string, as it was known, without having had an initial message, thanks to the sophisticated Automated Control Command modules which could decipher an original message using a predetermined algorithm based on the stellar coordinates of the message's sender. This would permit a one-time communication under emergency circumstances, which could then be responded to using the predetermined identifiers. It was an encryption system devised in such a way that the Alliance felt confident that their communications were completely secure, particularly from the prying eyes of the Consortium, who routinely attempted to intercept Alliance Comms signals. They were less concerned with Consortium intercepting their messages, so long as they knew they would not be capable of decoding and reading the materials that had been intercepted.

(*|*)

Even as he walked toward the Communications Array the mind of Commander Dragar was reeling after his encounter with the First Counselor of the Cadre: he may have been restrained from striking the sniveling fool by Captain Pertu, but he had a strong feeling that he might have an opportunity to do so sometime in the future. He shook his head as he thought about Pertu; he had definitely made the right decision when he had offered her the position to join the Guardians eleven years ago. He had not had any doubts about her abilities as a pilot or whether she would be able to fulfill the physical demands of being a Guardian; his only concern had been about her ability to recover from her injuries. These thoughts had been quickly allayed when she reported for duty only six weeks later, after having spent three weeks in the Felis Prime training facility. She proudly wore the White Wings of the Guardians on her uniform and was fit for service; the only remaining signs of her injury were the angry scar on her neck, which was only visible when she looked up, and the raspiness of her voice. He would never admit it, but deep down inside he even found that to be an endearing feature of the extremely attractive pilot who managed to outperform at every opportunity.

Dragar shook his head, brushing aside thoughts of Captain Pertu as he considered the missing Sovereign. He knew there was one thing on their side when it came to seeking her in the vastness of the universe: several years ago she had agreed, at his urging, to have a subcutaneous transmitter implanted behind her left ear that would act as a passive homing device should something happen to her. It was a simple device developed by the Alliance Security & Intelligence Services, the group the Guardians were attached to for administrative purposes, though both Dragar and Brem would always consider themselves members of the Corps. ASIS had developed a number of devices used for keeping track of soldiers in the field, but the Sub-C Tracker was the most advanced that had ever been created by the scientists and engineers in the ASIS labs. It had been designed to only send out a signal, or a beacon, once it had received an activation signal from an Alliance Array. This was a safeguard so that it would not be detected by the enemy while the soldier was in the field. An activation signal could be received from anywhere across the universe from an Alliance Array. Once activated, the Sub-C Tracker would emit a unique beacon that travelled through subspace; it would be detectable only by equipment tuned to that frequency.

Such devices had been designed to protect soldiers in the event of their capture by the Consortium, but had never been tested in practical terms, or across anything beyond one universal Sector. Soldiers had not received the devices yet thanks to an ethical debate about the use of them in humans, but the Sovereign was not bothered by the ethics of the tracker and had believed it to be a wise precaution. Dragar knew that the beacon could be detected from vast distances, but it might also be possible to miss the signal, depending on where the Sovereign was located. First, however, the activation signal had to be transmitted; after that, it would only be a matter of time before the Guardian found his charge. All these thoughts were going through his mind as he entered the Communications Array and went directly to the office of the Administrator.

As he entered her office Administrator Marta was sitting behind her desk. She looked up, seeing the broad shoulders of Commander Dragar approaching, and frowned; she knew the Prime Guardian extremely well and did not think dealing with him was going to be particularly enjoyable based on how disconsolate he looked. Even so, Administrator Marta thought to herself, taking a quick sip of the warm herbal tea from the cup sitting nearby her console, she knew that if the Prime Guardian had taken the time to come down to the offices of the Communications Array, something important had to be transpiring.

"Good day, Commander," she said, forcing herself to sound cheery, "what can I do for you today?" her green eyes reflected the light from her console.

Dragar looked at the Administrator and gave her as much of a smile as he could muster under the circumstances, "Hello Administrator Marta," he replied softly, using her title to subtly convey that this was definitely not a social call. He had visited the Array on a number of occasions, just to chat with the affable Administrator, but this would not be one of those times, and she knew it by his affect. "I must speak to you," he hesitated, looking around, "about an extremely sensitive security issue, something for which I'll need a seat at a console," he said simply, nodding to the private Security Office next to her workstation. Without another word she rose from her seat and led the massive Guardian into the nearby Office and closed the door, activating the Privacy Shields to ensure their conversation would not be overheard by anyone, even someone with a listening device.

Once Dragar had inspected the Privacy Shields and seemed satisfied he turned to the Administrator, who was a small woman and barely came to the middle of his chest, "Marta," he said, his voice gentle, placing his large left hand on her shoulder, "what I have to say cannot leave this room," she nodded, intrigued by the mystery, encouraging him to continue with her dazzling green eyes. After taking a breath and removing his hand the Guardian revealed everything he knew about the missing Sovereign, everything that the First Counselor of the Cadre and Lieutenant Kar had told him only a short time before. Part of him was pleased to see that the news shocked the Administrator. It was news he did not want spreading throughout the Alliance, particularly when the Ursus Consortium still posed such a threat to their security.

"Now," he continued, his voice quiet despite the Privacy Shields, "the main reason I came here is because I have some serious work to do," he took another look at the panel controlling the Privacy Shields, confirming that the device was still in its Secure mode. "Several years ago I convinced the Sovereign to have a Sub-C Tracker implanted; before it can be used, however, I have to send out the activation signal and then, hopefully, find the response beacon," he paused, "alone." Marta had gasped at the mention of the Sub-C Tracker. Passive Tracking Devices had been used for hundreds of years to track companion animals but the debate had been raging regarding their use in humans. Apparently, she thought to herself, the Sovereign had not been concerned with those arguments. Even the Torgons had been reluctant to have the devices implanted, until their popularity as companion animals became so great that a few of the gentle creatures were ransomed by inscrutable individuals. They had turned out to be miscreants, compelled to act in antisocial manners, and were dealt with accordingly by the Justice System. Nonetheless, it had the result of making tagging the creatures routine, which made all future thefts impractical since the creatures could be traced in a matter of hours once they were taken.

As though Dragar discerned her thoughts he shook his head, "I understand," he said sympathetically, "as you know, there've been some threats against the Sovereign and both the Guardians, and the Cadre," he shook his head and made a face at the utterance of the word, "felt it prudent to use everything available, including the Passive Tracking Device, to guarantee her safety. To tell you the truth, I really don't care," he exclaimed, his voice rising, "all I really care about *right* now," he stabbed the air with his right index finger, "is finding the Sovereign, and returning her home safely," he looked directly into Administrator Marta's eyes. "Nothing else matters."

She nodded, "Of course," she said softly, barely above a whisper, "I understand."

Without another word she gestured for the Prime Guardian to follow her to the back of the Communications Array's Headquarters. They walked into the darkened main level of the Array, where the consoles of the Array that the Communications Specialists sat at were located. Communications consoles were located on three levels, with over five hundred individual stations, but the Administrator knew that there was one station on the main level ideally suited to the needs of the Commander, which she led him to directly. It was one of several stations sequestered from the others and had the advantage that it was one of the few stations located in a small office. These stations were usually reserved for visiting dignitaries who needed privacy for their transmissions. Since there were a few such stations, and given the importance of his search, Administrator Marta felt comfortable dedicating one to the Prime Guardian, knowing the others would still be available, should they be required. "Is there anything else I can get for you?" she asked, as Dragar settled himself into the small office and began working the dials on the radio and transmitter, adjusting the settings to the frequencies he had committed to memory. She gently patted his broad shoulders, trying to comfort him.

He shook his head slowly, "No, my dear friend, but thank you," he clasped her small hand in his, giving it a gentle squeeze before releasing it, turning back to the console. His voice was low, already focused on the task at hand, "All I need is time." Marta nodded, patting him on the shoulders again as she turned to return to her desk to oversee the operations of communications for Felis Prime, and the Alliance. She had the feeling that she would be seeing a great deal of the Prime Guardian considering the enormous task ahead of him as he searched for the Sovereign.

In the end, Administrator Marta had been correct: Dragar returned every day for almost three years before he located the unique signal that identified where the Sovereign was located. As soon as he found it he understood why it had taken so long to be located: the planet the Sovereign was on was in orbit in a system around a fairly young sun, in Sector 0107. There was a micro-singularity in the adjoining Sector which had blocked the signal from the tracking device until the rotational shift of the two systems had moved enough to compensate for the Arrays to relay the signal back to Felis Prime. It made no difference now, Dragar thought to himself: now that he knew where she was he would find her and bring her home.

(* | *)

Once Dragar had identified the location of the Sovereign he summoned and briefed the Guardians; delivering some good news to his friends after such a long search felt wonderful to the beleaguered Prime Guardian. Dragar had been keeping them apprised of his efforts, but now that her beacon had been located he needed his team more than ever: he could not get to the Sovereign without the assistance of Captain Pertu and Helios-2, the Sovereign's ship. Aside from the means to get there, Dragar wanted his friend and comrade, the third of the Guardians, Tactical Sergeant Brem. They seemed an unlikely pair, but the two friends worked extremely well together. Had Brem remained an active member of the Alliance Special Combat Armed Response Corps he could have ascended through the ranks, earning a position at the Officer's Training School, where he would have easily become a Major, or even a Colonel, given his exceptional skills, but his temper had short-circuited his career, not to mention his proclivity for inappropriate humor. It all came to an abrupt end after Brem had an unfortunate confrontation with a fresh-faced Lieutenant who decided to order the Sergeant's squad into a situation that the more experienced Sergeant believed was unsafe for both himself and his squad. If there was one thing that Brem would not tolerate, it was an order that put lives at unnecessary risk.

When Brem voiced his opinion the Lieutenant decided to demean him in front of the squad rather than take his advice; that was the second mistake the LT had made: issuing the order had been the first. Not only did Brem not take that well, he demonstrated his disdain for the young LT by breaking his jaw with his fist, a punch which barely took any effort, but did require the LT to have his jaw wired shut for several weeks. Of course, none of the squad members were able to remember having seen anything, so it came down to the word of one man against another, but Brem still ended up in the stockade for three months, after which he had to face a Disciplinary Hearing, which could have resulted in his discharge from the Corps. Before the three months had ended Brem found himself looking into the face of his old friend, Commander Dragar, who had come to visit him in the stockade. Dragar offered him the opportunity to enter the Guardians once everything was cleared up with the DH. At that point, it was an offer that Brem could not turn down given his limited career options.

At the Disciplinary Hearing the Lieutenant testified about the incident, where he demanded that Tactical Sergeant Brem be discharged from the Corps, but the issue of the orders that had led to the conflict were raised, which led to a surprising turn of events. After hearing his friend's side of the story, Commander Dragar was convinced that he had acted in the best interest of his squad and did not feel he should be punished for refusing to follow an idiotic order. At the Commander's urging ASIS conducted an intensive assessment of the situation and concluded that the mission would have been a total loss: Tactical Sargent Brem was declared a hero for his actions, though his methods were seriously frowned upon; he had ultimately saved the lives of the twelve commandos under his command. Instead of being discharged, Sergeant Brem was awarded the Golden Cluster citation, with Distinction, for exceptional leadership skills, and given an unconditional pardon. At the same time the Lieutenant was demoted to the rank of Corporal, discharged from the Corps, and returned to the Unified Armed Services. Worst of all, his Ghost Corps patch was removed from his uniform.

There was no question in Dragar's mind that Tactical Sargent Brem was the best soldier he had ever met; he was also his best friend, and that was probably more important than anything when it came to the Corps. Being able to survive the ASCAR training was one thing, being able to maintain a friendship with someone like Tactical Sergeant Brem was something altogether different. He seemed to go out of his way to push Dragar's buttons, but it was something the big man enjoyed and tolerated far more than he would have from anyone else. He certainly would not have tolerated his actions if Brem was not as competent as he was; Dragar knew that he could trust the man with his life, and had done so on more occasions than he could count. They worked well together, and that was the most important thing. When it came down to protecting the Sovereign Dragar knew that Brem would be there, putting his life on the line without hesitation if necessary. That was all he could ask from any Guardian.

While both Dragar and Brem were extremely competent pilots, perhaps excellent by most standards, Captain Pertu was who Dragar wanted at the helm of Helios-2 on the off-chance that they encountered anything out of the ordinary. Besides, Dragar thought to himself, Pertu had been as concerned as anyone since the disappearance of the Sovereign; she deserved the opportunity to help return her to Felis Prime. Whatever the case may be, it only took a short time once the Guardians had been notified that Dragar had found the Sovereign for the ship to be readied for departure. Captain Pertu had made a point of ensuring that Helios-2 was maintained in perfect condition while Dragar had been conducting the search, taking it out for regular check-flights in the event that the ship would be needed sooner rather than later.

With all three Guardians onboard they were ready to depart within an hour of having identified the Sovereign's location. After ensuring that everyone was settled into their seats Pertu looked at her comrades, "You two Slugs strapped in?" she asked in her raspy voice, flashing them both a smile as she adjusted the halo device that allowed her to interface with the ship. ASCAR Cadets were called *Slugs*, something which neither Dragar nor Brem had been for several millennia. "I don't want to have to come back there and pick up any pieces after we make the jump through trans-light." She smiled again as Brem let out a disdainful grunt. Pertu knew the stocky Guardian hated transiting through pan-dimensional space, but had been forced to tolerate it thanks to his career. He greatly preferred remaining planet side, or on Felis Prime for that matter, for extended periods of time. Unfortunately for the Tactical Sergeant, as a Guardian of the Sovereign he was often forced to accompany her on trips to various locations across the universe. He would only grudgingly admit that traveling on Helios-2 was much more comfortable than on the transports used to move thousands of commandos at a time. They were a different class of ship altogether, and Brem would be quite content if he never had to set foot on one of those mammoth vessels again.

"Well then," Pertu's raspy voice called out, "hold on boys, next stop…" she stopped, mid-sentence, "Uh, wait a second," she turned, looking at Commander Dragar, "you haven't told me where we're going," a note of annoyance in her voice as she looked back at the Navigational Console of the A-ConCom, the Automatic Control Computer. "Would you mind giving me some coordinates, Commander?"

Brem let out another low grunt from his seat, one of his less than subtle ways of razzing his friend when he made one of his infrequent mistakes. Dragar shot him a glare, a warning to remain silent, then looked at his wrist device on which he had entered all of the navigational information, "Sorry," he muttered, almost too quiet for her to hear, but loud enough for Brem, which only made him grunt harder, earning another stern glare from Dragar. "Coordinates are," he read out, his voice loud and clear this time, "A:7916 R:3952 X:5655 Sector 0107," he could hear her entering the coordinates into the Nav Con as he read them out, and then, per regulation, she repeated them back to him, ensuring they had been entered correctly. In all of the trips they had made together Captain Pertu had never entered a coordinate incorrectly, and he did not expect her to start now, not on such an important mission.

"Excellent," she replied, once the Nav Con indicated the data had been accepted. "We're ready for departure. Again," she added, looking back over her shoulder at her two colleagues, both of whom had completed strapping themselves into their seats. Without another word she activated the orbital thrusters and began to deftly maneuver Helios-2 from the Felis Prime Spaceport bay where they were docked, moving into the stream of the other ships flying around the satellite-city and the many thousands of other orbiting cities above the crowded space over Felis Magoris. It only took a few minutes before Pertu had left the high orbit of Felis Magoris and had maneuvered them into deep space, toward the transition point where they would activate their Trans-Light Drive.

As the ship approached the transition point, where ships were allowed to engage their Trans-Light Drive, Pertu turned her seat once again toward Dragar and asked, "You sure we're ready to go?"

"Absolutely," he replied, slightly annoyed at the interrogation. He was not used to being doubted.

Pertu felt his annoyance, but was not overly concerned. She held up a hand in a disarming gesture, "I'm only asking because the Nav Con shows that the coordinates you gave is a recent Protectorate; I'm just wondering what could have led the Sovereign to have gone there?" As she spoke her fingers were flying over the Navigational and Engineering Consoles, going through the final system checks that were required before the Trans-Light Drive was activated. Once the Automated Control Command module had been coordinated with the Navigational Array on Felis Prime Captain Pertu entered her final authorization key, making it possible for their journey to begin.

Dragar was shaking his head, "It's okay, Pertu," he replied, his voice softer, tinged with contrition, "I'm not upset with you," he turned to Brem, "You," his voice hardened, "… that's another story," the stocky man grunted, letting out a harsh laugh. "But I honestly have no idea why she's done anything, Pertu. I couldn't possibly tell you why she might have gone to a recent Protectorate," his eyes had an almost crazed look as he tried to understand the situation. After three years of searching for the Sovereign the Prime Guardian had, at times, become nearly sick with worry, "All I can say is I just want to get there, and return her to Felis Prime, before somebody else has an opportunity to find her." A silence descended over the cabin as the two other Guardians looked at Dragar, nodding in agreement.

Pertu finally asked, "Do you honestly believe Factotum Mar would make a move against her?" there was a note of genuine fear in her voice. "Surely," she began to say something more but Dragar interrupted, his tone suddenly angry.

"What," his deep baritone cut her off, "you don't think Mar would jump at the chance to kill the Sovereign?" He snapped his fingers, "In an *instant*, as quickly as he'd kill an entire planet if it served his warped purposes, he'd destroy an entire system if he thought it would eliminate her in the process." To emphasize his disdain for the leader of the Ursus Consortium he pounded his massive fist into the palm of his hand, causing the ship's cabin to reverberate with the sound of his thick flesh. "No, my friends," he glanced over at Tactical Sergeant Brem, "if we can't find the Sovereign, we risk losing her, forever."

Pertu's eyes widened at his outburst, then narrowed as she regained her focus on the task at hand. "Well then," she said, trying to sound more upbeat than she felt, "let's get there before anyone else, alright?" she turned back to her controls, refocusing her attention on them for a moment. "Engaging Primary Activation of Trans-Light Drive," she announced, and after the briefest pause, "Secondary Activation in 3-2-1," as she reached the number "1" the ship, everything in it and around it ceased to exist in normal space, and simultaneously became everything and everywhere within the universe, all at once. It was the nature of the Trans-Light Drive to seemingly allow the ship to travel far beyond the speed of light, moving across vast distances in such a way that the ship travelled as though all of the energy in the universe was somehow interconnected, guided by the principle that all matter was composed of a matrix of commonalities through which the ship, and space itself, were able to transit through one another, without having to move any great distances since their commonalities were constant from one end of the universe to the other.

(* | *)

When the theory of Trans-Light Drive had first been proposed it was viewed with great suspicion and even some trepidation, mostly because the theory of a single vessel being everywhere in the universe at one time seemed to be too fantastic for the average person accept and far more than could be comprehended. After the first successful test flights, however, opinions were quick to change. Journeys that had once taken months, and even years, through the use of the previous generation of Star Drives, the latest generation of which were now used in conjunction with the Trans-Light Drive, were now accomplished in a matter of minutes, including the time required to maneuver at sub-light speeds using the Star Drives to achieve an orbit around the planet or stellar body to which it was transiting. On top of that, there did not seem to be any extra risk involved, assuming the navigational settings did not steer the vessel into an uncharted singularity, which was always a risk during spaceflight. Fortunately for the testing phase of the Trans-Light program, uncharted singularities were now extraordinarily rare and none had been encountered.

As Dragar tightened the 7-point straps that held him into his seat he thought about how traveling in a vessel only equipped with a Star Drive had not necessarily been such a hardship. As his body and mind registered the all-too familiar sensations that felt as though his insides were being turned inside out for the brief instant that Helios-2 travelled through pan-dimensional space, the term scientists used to refer to Trans-Light travel, he felt himself straining against the discomfort of the straps, almost grunting at the restraints. He understood that during the transition multiple dimensions literally folded upon themselves, making space come together as though a piece of paper had been folded over an infinite number of times in order to bring every point of space and time converging at that single point from which the ship was departing. Once that had been accomplished, an operation that was performed as a result of the Primary Activation of the Trans-Light Drive, the Secondary Activation took place. In every practical sense, once the Secondary Activation took place the ship existed in throughout the universe, in each of the 1,024 Sectors of the universe. It was a phenomenon that only lasted for a fraction of a nanosecond, until the central part of the A-ConCom, paired with the

Navigational Array, focused the substance of the ship, along with everyone and everything onboard, to the desired destination. Even though these infinite pathways only existed for the briefest amount of time, the actual duration of the flight, that time before the ship arrived at its destination, lasted several long seconds before the Trans-Light Drive and Nav Con successfully brought the ship to its selected coordinates. With the other pathways closed the ship was inexorably drawn to its ultimate destination, as though it was meant to be there; it was as though all of the other pathways had never existed and, for all intents and purposes, they had not existed; their only reason for being was to provide the necessary pathway through pan-dimensional space for the ship to travel through fantastic distances in the blink of an eye. This took place as a direct result of the guiding principles that governed the operation of trans-light travel which specified that the active state of the universe in which matter originated provided a more profound pull on reality than the existence of theoretical multidimensional multiverses, which could well be exerting their influence on both the universe and the continuum, even though it was presently beyond the ability of scientists to detect their presence or influence of these phenomena. Scientists had demonstrated, on numerous occasions, that simply because something could not presently be observed that did not necessarily mean that it was pointing to a particular conclusion, or that absence of evidence disproved something. Certainty was a word that science viewed with both discretion and caution; it was never advisable to jump to conclusions based on a single finding or experiment, especially if the lives of others were at stake. That was how people lost their lives.

Things changed dramatically when Trans-Light Drives were introduced to the fleet of the Unified Armed Services, which also transported the troops of the Alliance Special Combat Armed Response Corps. It was quickly discovered that the new Trans-Light Drives could not simply be retrofitted onto the older class ships, which had been designated as SD class vessels. Merely replacing the Star Drives had at first seemed logical, but the results were far less than satisfactory when tested. First to be tested was a Light Cruiser, normally used for planetary patrols and escorts, which was sent out under automated control. The increased stresses made as a result of the tests during the transition through trans-light travel proved to be too much for the already aged hull of the ship, which had a long service history of being stressed through the gravitational forces applied by the exertions caused by the standard Star Drive. As a result of the highly focused non-symmetrical gravitational forces applied during the transition through trans-light travel LC-Aurora-213 was, quite literally, shredded before it could complete its transition out of pan-dimensional flight.

Not surprisingly, that test was declared an unmitigated failure, but the engineers and developers of the Trans-Light Program were not prepared to abandon the project. Despite the failure there had been many promising results, including the overwhelming successes of the initial tests, which had taken place on a purpose-built vessel which had functioned perfectly, which ultimately led the Felis Alliance to decide to replace their entire fleet. For several years many of the older class ships, particularly the Battle Transports and Carriers, were still used in limited capacities for intra-system travel, which took place comfortably with the use of Star Drives. But eventually, the entire fleet was replaced, utilizing the new technology, allowing Alliance ships to travel anywhere in the universe, as soon as they desired. Each new ship was also equipped with a completely redesigned, hybridized Star Drive that was both smaller and more powerful, allowing the new ships to have the best of both worlds in regards to stellar travel. Still, Star Drives were generally only utilized while patrolling within star systems or for sub-light travel, otherwise it was far more practical to engage the Trans-Light Drive.

As Dragar grappled with the sensation of his body being torn into a trillion disparate pieces, something he understood was entirely a construct of his mind and would not, in fact, happen, he recalled the relatively long cruises he had taken as Commander of the *Fighting Fifth*, the battalion of the ASCAR he had commanded for nearly five thousand years. He thought about how it had been the greatest honor of his life to lead them, even as it felt as though the molecules of his body were being scattered across the universe, then regathered and reassembled, as though nothing untoward had happened. As an active member of the Corps, Dragar had thought nothing about stepping onto one of the massive Battle Transports that were tasked with taking troops from one Sector of the universe to another in order to protect members of the Alliance or their Protectorates. Journeys sometimes took months at a time, but that was part of their job and nobody complained. Sometimes, by Caiphus, more often than not it was a dreary journey, but at least they had never felt as though their own molecules were being ripped apart from the inside. By the time they arrived at their destination they were well-rested and ready for action. If the journey was going to take too long, they simply put the troops into Cryo-sleep for months at a time, if not longer, but those days were long gone. None of the troops minded that the same technology that prevented them from aging while on those long spaceflights was also used to punish prisoners convicted of crimes. It was part of their job and they had chosen to serve the Alliance.

Only one thing had managed to make Dragar prouder than when he was in command of the *Fighting Fifth*: the moment he had been approached by the Sovereign herself and asked if he would be a member of her Guardians. He had been unable to turn down such a request as he had always held her in such high esteem, but when he had arrived on Felis Prime to fulfill his duties the Sovereign surprised him and presented him with the Black Wings that indicated that she was appointing him to be her Prime Guardian. Since he had never officially retired from the ASCAR he was still permitted to wear his *Ghost Corps* patch on his uniform, an honor permitted those who left the Corps in good standing. Dragar always thought that the Black Wings went well with the ASCAR patch and gave his uniform a suitably imposing presence. Few people could say they had earned the right to wear the insignia of the Corps, even fewer could claim the Wings of the Guardians.

Dragar recalled the first time his troops travelled to a planet on a Battle Transport equipped with Trans-Light Drive: it was onboard the BT-Hercules-783. They had been ordered to the planet Curtos, a GZ-7 Protectorate in the distant Fortars System which the Ursus Consortium had been displaying too much interest in, making it imperative to send forces to protect the defenseless planet. Two Battlecruisers were dispatched, as well as a Carrier which had been on patrol and was already on station in the Fortars System. With that amount of firepower on hand the Sovereign still wanted the ASCAR present, though they would remain concealed from the indigenous population by patrolling well away from any populated areas.

Battle Transports are capable of carrying two regiments of 14,000 highly trained soldiers in the Felis Alliance's Unified Armed Services, but it was the ASCAR that many children throughout the Alliance dreamt of joining, not because they wanted to kill, but for the honor of protecting and serving the Alliance, to do their duty as Citizens. That was something instilled into all children as they went to school on any Alliance planet. Only the toughest, strongest, most intensely prepared, however, could manage to endure the rigorous training required of an ASCAR Initiate. Before you were even accepted into the

Corps you had to get through the training, and before you could get through the training, you had to endure the Initiation.

(*|*)

Initiation into the ASCAR did not involve the brutalization of a candidate, but, to be sure, it was a violent affair. Anyone who hoped to wear the *Ghost Corps* patch of the most elite commando Corps had to be ready to do anything in order. Before any Initiate was accepted into the training program they had to demonstrate that they were capable of surviving and solving problems. In order to be accepted into the Program, there were three stages to the Initiation: the first stage involved comprehensive tests and examinations that looked into the psychological profiles of each candidate. It was necessary to determine why someone wanted to become a member of the Corps as much as it was necessary to determine if they were capable of becoming a member. Failing the psychological test did not lead to a candidate being removed from their position from the UAS, though it could trigger an investigation, depending on the seriousness of the issue that was detected. The last thing any commander wanted was to find themselves with a commando who wanted to go around killing people when their mission was to rescue people. It had, unfortunately, happened, and the result had led to far more stringent screenings of candidates. After that policy had been initiated the ASCAR became known as the most efficiently run group within the UAS, resulting in the fewest number of misconduct and incident reports for all the UAS. Considering the size of the Unified Armed Services, it was an impressive accolade, but it said also said a great deal for the training the Corps provided to those that it did accept as Initiates. Those who were accepted understood that their failure would be a reflection on the entire Corps, as was their success.

After passing the psychological screenings the second stage involved a test in which a subject was provided with three items: a knife, a short length of rope, and the ubiquitous T-17 Plasma Rifle. In actuality, the test was simplicity itself: each candidate was placed in a sealed room, with a single barricaded door, and only fifteen minutes to discover a way out using the provided items. After the allotted time candidates were told there would be no opportunities for retesting: this was their only chance to take this test. Again and again ASCAR supervisors would watch as a potential Initiate would sit on the floor in the middle of the room, staring at the rope, the knife, and the Plasma Rifle, desperately trying to figure out how the objects might work together. There had to be a clue somewhere, but they could not see it anywhere. Every corner of the room, from the floor to the ceiling, was searched, but nothing helpful was ever found. One after another the Initiates would enter the sealed chamber, sit down for several minutes, search the room despondently for some time, and leave, their heads hanging in failure. It was little consolation to most that they still had wonderful careers within another branch of the UAS; the Corps had been their dream, and that was all that mattered: they had failed to enter the next phase, they had failed to advance to the third stage.

Eventually, somebody would enter the room, look at the three items and recognize you did not require all three items: the only thing that was needed was the T-17 Plasma Rifle. As soon as an Initiate raised the rifle to their shoulder and aimed it at the barricaded door the light above it would flash and the door would swing open. "Congratulations," one of the observers would announce over the loudspeaker, "you have passed this test."

It was just as well that they did not allow the potential Initiates to fire the Plasma Rifle inside the training facility; the T-17 was designed for long range engagements and would have easily penetrated the door, as well as the wall of the outer office, and probably the next building before the plasma energy had dissipated, although none of the candidates knew that the Plasma Rifle they had been provided lacked the all-important Power Cell that generated the plasma slugs it fired. Still, the test was a puzzle, and they had discovered the solution. That was why it was the favored weapon of ASCAR commandos. Beyond that, however, the preferred weapon of the Corps was their mind. Every commando was expected to be able to think, to reason their way out of a problem. While it was understood that violence was sometimes necessary, and unavoidable, if it could be avoided, that was preferable.

Anyone who managed to pass the first two stages was given an appointment to return to the testing facility, where they would be taken to Tarak III, the training planet of the ASCAR, for final their physical tests. There were no questions as to the physical fitness of the candidates since they had all completed their initial training and some had already been serving in the UAS for a number of years. This was different. After undergoing the first two stages the candidates would now undergo an endurance test to see if they could survive the scenario. They were provided with an ASCAR uniform, which provided them with potable water, kept them warm, or cool, depending on the environment, and allowed them to stay in a battlefield for weeks at a time without needing to be changed. A Battle Pack was provided, which contained everything they required for the mission, including their only weapons: a single knife, with which they could build a shelter to remain concealed from the enemy. Their mission was to provide reconnaissance on an enemy position and remain concealed. If they were captured, they would be considered eliminated from the program.

After being briefed while in orbit the candidates would be sent down to the planet and expected to evade their simulated enemy while, at the same time, making regular reports back to their ship which would be monitoring their every move through the use of sensors embedded into the surrounding flora which were virtually impossible to detect by the naked eye. It may have seemed like an unfair test to the uninitiated, but every UAS soldier had undergone intensive evasive training as part of their standard training procedure. This test merely pushed that training to the next level and tested to see which of the candidates was capable of thinking beyond what they had already learned and were able to apply other skills to the task. Those who succeeded were allowed to remain on the planet and begin their training immediately. Those who failed were returned to their UAS units; nothing more was spoken about the test.

After three days in the wilds of Tarak III, sometimes nearly crazed from sleep deprivation and exhaustion, the test was concluded. If the candidate had managed to make their reports every three hours as required and had not been observed by their enemy, they passed. It was easy to tell if they had been observed: the enemy used photonic detectors that scanned the area surrounding their encampment. Any movement was immediately identified, recorded, and transmitted up to the orbiting ship with the officer overseeing the test onboard. So long as nothing had been recorded and all transmissions had been made, the test was considered passed. As the final test it was considered the most difficult considering the endurance and the psychological elements of being alone, unable to speak to anyone for three days. Making the report was not the same as interacting with a human since all that had to be done was entering the coordinates of the enemy into the wrist communicator. You did not speak or hear the voice of your companion in orbit. For all intents and purposes, you were alone, facing an enemy on an alien planet. It made little difference that it was a simulation, you still had to get through it to face the next day, and achieve your ultimate goal.

Those who managed to find the strength within themselves to silence those inner fears that rose up out of the depths of that despair, especially in the darkness of the second evening, usually managed to succeed. Their training came back to them and they quickly discovered that the river by which they were encamped had a silty bottom which could effectively darken their uniform. This helped to camouflage them in the piebald vegetation of Tarak III and managed to serve another purpose that they could not have realized at the time. Those who used the silt from the river had managed to discover the weakness of the photonic detector: it was incapable of penetrating the silt due to a crystalline presence which caused the photons from the sensors to be reflected around the wearer as though they were not even there, acting as though they were effectively invisible. In the end, only those who managed to use the camouflage, who thought beyond their initial training, managed to pass the test and go on to begin their training on the road to becoming members of the Corps.

Once they managed to pass these preliminary tests the Initiates still had a long road ahead of them before they earned their *Ghost Corps* patch, but they had successfully passed the first hurdles to fulfilling their goals of joining the ASCAR and becoming one of the elite commandos of the Alliance. They had gone further than most who had applied to the program. An ASCAR Commando was expected to be available for service to the Alliance for longer periods than other members of the Unified Armed Services, partly due to the amount of time dedicated to their training. Most of those who went through the rigorous training felt the commitment was worth the honor of representing the Alliance, not to mention becoming members of such an elite group within society. Of the massive population of over thirty-three trillion in the Alliance, less than 2% chose to serve within the Unified Armed Services. Even though that figure represented about six hundred and sixty billion people, comprising troops, pilots, and the various support personnel required to maintain the massive fleet, service within the UAS was entirely voluntary. There were also the Reserve Forces, comprising the retired members of the UAS which were capable of being called up for duty on short notice. This meant that the forces of the UAS could be augmented by almost twice its size if necessary. Out of the six hundred and sixty billion of the regular forces was a much smaller contingent of only seven million who had been found to be qualified to wear the *Ghost Corps* patch of the ASCAR. On the surface it may have seemed like a large number, and perhaps it was, but Commander Dragar always reminded himself that the battalion of one thousand commandos that he had been in command of was a mere drop in the bucket compared to the number of Citizens who lived within the Alliance, not to mention the Protectorates that the Unified Armed Services were sworn to protect.

(*|*)

Each commando on board the BT-Hercules-783 was wearing their Battle Packs, armed with their trusty T-17 Plasma Rifle, the PPD-77 Pulse Plasma Device, the hand-held version of the Plasma Rifle, as well as twenty-five of the small, marble-sized grenades, known in the Corps as *Shadow Makers* because of what they did to those unfortunate enough to be in their blast zone when the devices were deployed. When a Shadow Maker was thrown anything within a fifteen-foot radius was, quite literally, reduced to shadow: it made little difference if an item was organic or mechanical, it ceased to exist. It was quick, painless, and irrevocable. If you only found yourself partially within the blast zone you would discover whatever part of your body was exposed to the blast had been cleanly amputated. It was a weapon the commandos used as a last resort, but were glad to it have on hand when things were tough.

Dragar was acutely aware that if the Alliance was forced to deploy forces to every single planet they were obliged to protect it would be a logistical nightmare. Some planets would be left with nothing more than a Light Cruiser accompanied by a single battalion or two of regular UAS troops, as there would undoubtedly be hot-spots where more forces would be required. Fortunately for the Alliance the Ursus Consortium was considerably smaller and far less prepared militarily than the Alliance, though that had not stopped them from waging an aggressive campaign in their attempts to annex several Protectorates in the past, which was why the BT-Hercules-783 had been ordered through pan-dimensional space to meet the other forces waiting for it at Curtos.

Dragar watched in dismay as his entire battalion was turned inside out, while his own body was twisted beyond recognition, if only for the span of a few uncomfortable seconds. As this was the first time the new Trans-Light Drive had been used on the Battle Transport they had all been briefed on the phenomenon, even though they had all gone through simulated transitions to acclimate themselves to the sensations they would feel during the actual flight. When the scientists had briefed them about the transition through pan-dimensional space they seemed particularly concerned with something they referred to as the GTMI, or *Gross Temporal Mass Inversion*, which supposedly meant that while the Trans-Light Drive was causing the entire ship, and everything onboard, to travel simultaneously to every point within the universe, a similar operation was taking place locally, within their bodies. It did not change the fact that they felt as though they were being ripped apart from the inside out, then reassembled in a fraction of a nanosecond. What it actually felt as though they were experiencing, though they were assured this was quite impossible, was that their conscious mind was observing the phenomenon; the scientists assured them that the reality of the situation was that nothing was really happening to their bodies. For some reason the scientists giving the briefing seemed to laugh at this point in the presentation; apparently, according to the brain-trust, what the commandos were seeing was an expression of their imagination seeking an explanation for the unfamiliar sensations that the body was experiencing at that instant particular. It was perfectly harmless the scientists had claimed.

They had been assured, numerous times, *"Nothing could possibly go wrong."*

(*|*)

Nothing could possibly go wrong, unless, of course, you were the LC-Aurora-213, but that had been during the testing phase. Fortunately, nobody had been onboard the Aurora.

The same could not be said for the BT-Hercules-738. As Hercules came out of pan-dimensional space Commander Dragar looked up in horror from his own personal discomfort to see that several of his commandos, several of his friends, had failed to survive the transition. Those sitting closest to the bulkheads of the immense transport vessel had somehow become embedded in them, their bodies becoming bonded to the superstructure of the ship. Thirty-seven of his friends and comrades died without ever having seen the planet they had come to protect. It had been the first accident causing fatalities involving the Trans-Light Drive. After their mission, which had been successful, the Hercules returned to its point of origin using its Star Drive, a trip that took four months. A full investigation revealed that even the slightest movement of the passengers while the ship transited through pan-dimensional space was enough to scramble the molecules of one person with another, or with portions of the ship, which could lead to tragic results. This lead to the development of the newest version of the A-ConCom, the most powerful Automated Control Command module ever devised, along with the 7-point harnesses that kept passengers fully immobilized during the transition phase of the flight. Fortunately, thanks to the lessons learned at Curtos, the results had not been repeated, but pan-dimensional travel still left a bad taste in Dragar's mouth every time he had to travel using Trans-Light Drive.

He knew it was far faster than taking a ship equipped only with a Star Drive, especially when traveling as far as they were going: Terra was located in Sector 0107, in the distant Pinwheel Galaxy, which had been named by the daughter of the Chief Astronomer when she saw a picture of it and proclaimed that it reminded her of her toy pinwheel. It was a trip that would have taken approximately 92 months using the Star Drive. Not using the fastest means possible for getting to the Sovereign was something that Dragar could not imagine, not even with his feelings regarding pan-dimensional travel. With the Sovereign already having been missing for three years, another 92 months was inconceivable. A few moments of discomfort were well worth fulfilling his duty of returning the Sovereign to Felis Prime, which was where she belonged. Besides, he reminded himself, the Hercules was ancient history. There had not been an accident involving Trans-Light Drives since they had been introduced to the entire fleet.

(*|*)

Transmission Starts:

Encryption Begins: Z-232-4T5-565-322-LCD-X

To: Factotum Ebla Mar, Supreme Leader, Ursus Consortium; Ursus Minor
Subject: Transmission Intercept from Felis Alliance, Felis Prime Communications Array

The following was intercepted by the GAF-Tralta-9; Patrolling region bordering Sec. 0106.

Updates as available.

In Your Service,
Captain Tiernat

INTERCEPTED MESSAGE FOLLOWS:

Codex Identifier: ¤ RTS2B1Q03SX4R8T5R4E5R49X ¤
Rating: EOF [Eyes Only Fleet Commander]
To: Marshal Salzat, BC-Orono-001
From: First Counselor Regar, in the Name of Sovereign
Sayoose

Message Follows:

Updated list of certain Green Zone Protectorates,
with their classifications and coordinates. Please
note: several were not included on previous lists:

Planet   GZ Designation;   A: R: X: Coordinates
Andar II GZ-5 Cd: A:2918 R:6391 X:1197 Sec. 1007
Cygnar IV GZ-6 Cd: A:0191 R:9019 X:0109 Sec. 0198
Cunars GZ-4 Cd: A:9899 R:1209 X:8417 Sec. 0021
Exnar VII GZ-7 Cd: A:2712 R:1211 X:7396 Sec. 0110
Fartuhn GZ-5 Cd: A:0010 R:1121 X:9819 Sec. 0198
Gol GZ-7 Cd: A:0383 R:2989 X:9979 Sec. 1001
Jannu GZ-4 Cd: A:1197 R:8913 X:3727 Sec. 0424
Kar II GZ-7 Cd: A:2119 R:7313 X:9917 Sec. 0002
Lamu XI GZ-3 Cd: A:1929 R:2997 X:0131 Sec. 0001
Marnse IX GZ-4 Cd: A:0021 R:4937 X:9199 Sec. 1019
Okrat III GZ-7 Cd: A:1998 R:0209 X:3129 Sec. 0297
Patrust Retrus GZ-4 Cd: A:7921 R:1979 X:2712 Sec.
1007
Qius GZ-5 Cd: A:1945 R:1105 X:2015 Sec. 0409
Resta Arv GZ-6 Cd: A:1952 R:0711 X:0015 Sec. 1001
Slarta Sals GZ-7 Cd: A:1616 R:0808 X:2621 Sec. 1013
Terra GZ-7 Cd: A:7916 R:3952 X:5655 Sec. 0107
Umbac Kal GZ-5 Cd: A:0012 R:0213 X:0009 Sec. 0958
Waxca GZ-6 Cd: A:9987 R:9901 X:9919 Sec. 0958

After discussions with the Sovereign it has been
decided that our existing policy of aggressively
guarding all Protectorates should be examined on a
case by case basis. After considering the status of
the above planets, taking into consideration that
each are several centuries, if not longer, from being
offered entry into the Alliance, it has been agreed

that it would be wasteful to continue to expend
Alliance resources to guard each of them against a
threat that does not seem to exist at this time.

Therefore, it is the recommendation of the Cadre, in
the Name of Sovereign Sayoose, that the Marshal of
the Fleet reallocate the resources of the Fleet from
the above named Protectorates and their stellar
systems, unless such a time manifests when a direct
threat develops, which seems unlikely at this time.

None of these planets seem to be of any particular
significance or strategic value, or have any other
potential value to the Alliance at this time. We find
it both unlikely and highly doubtful that the Ursus
Consortium will show any interest in any of these
planets at this time, or in the near future.

Should such a threat develop, the Fleet will be
capable of deploying sufficient forces to circumvent
any move by the Consortium. Until such time, we
believe a withdrawal is both prudent and expedient.

In the Name of Sovereign Sayoose,
First Counselor Regar,
First Counselor of the Cadre of the Felis Alliance

Encryption Ends

ENCODED: ¤ X3154C7SA987423ES2U87ER4 ¤

Transmission Ends.

(*|*)

Onboard the flagship of the Alliance, the Battlecruiser Orono-003, Marshal Salzat studied the latest message he had received from the First Counselor of the Cadre. It was not unusual for him to receive messages pertaining to the security of the Alliance from the Cadre, but it was definitely out of the ordinary to receive operational orders directly from the First Counselor. Only the Sovereign was empowered to command the Fleet, and the First Counselor was keenly aware of that fact. He studied the wording of the message, noting that it had been carefully formatted to state, *In the name of Sovereign Sayoose*. That was still not the same as having originated *from* the Sovereign herself. He had been elevated to the rank of Marshal of the Fleet by the Sovereign and answered directly to her; he was not about to start defying the orders he received. There was a proper order to things in the Unified Armed Services of the Felis Alliance, and this message went against that order.

Looking up from where he was seated at the bridge he called over to his Second in Command, "General Taran, take a look at this for me. I'd like your opinion."

Taran crossed the bridge in a few easy strides and took the datapad from the outstretched hand of the Marshal, frowning as he read its contents. He shook his bald head, "What in Caiphus?" he muttered as he read the contents of the message. "No sir, this isn't right. Not at all. Regar ... First Counselor Regar ... he knows damn well that he doesn't have the authority to do this. He can't order you to reallocate the Fleet, not even in a message that states, In the name of Sovereign Sayoose. Only the Sovereign herself is able to do that."

Marshal Salzat smiled. "Well, there is one other," he reminded his Second in Command, who nodded in response, referring to the one person empowered to convey the orders of the Sovereign.

"Yes sir, but *he* didn't send this," Taran quipped.

Salzat nodded, he knew that he could always count on the General for bluntness. Taran had been his 2IC for as many years as he had been Marshal and he trusted him with his life. He was the most capable officer that he knew, with a sharp intellect and sharper tongue. "Thank you, General," he said, taking back the pad. "What would you recommend?"

Taran smiled, "I would start by increasing the fleet's presence around the Protectorates."

"Good. Make it happen."

General Taran returned to the Communications Officer and began to prepare the messages that would be sent to the various Sector fleet commanders while Marshal Salzat gazed at the view screens scattered around the bridge, looking out over the ships that comprised the Battle Group of the Orono. He was still not satisfied; something odd was going on and he was worried. Receiving a message from the Sovereign was something that did not happen with regularity, which made this message *in her name* even stranger. If the Sovereign had something to say to her Fleet Commander she had always managed to take the time to send the message. She had never entrusted such a communication to the First Counselor of the Cadre.

Before Lieutenant Carif could send out the first message the Marshal's powerful voice called out, "Hold on that," and Salzat appeared next to the Communications Station. "Tell me something, Lieutenant," he asked, his voice lower, "when was the last time we received a direct communication from Sovereign Sayoose?" It was not unusual for the Flagship to be out of contact with the Sovereign for extended periods of time since the Alliance was not in an active state of war. So long as they had clear orders to follow, which was something they had at the present time, they conducted themselves accordingly.

Lieutenant Carif looked through the Communications Log for a moment before replying, "That would be three years, two weeks, and three days ago, sir," she replied.

"I see, and what were the contents of that message, if you don't mind refreshing my memory," he smiled. He could remember the message perfectly, as he glanced over at General Taran, who was looking at him questioningly. He had a feeling that the General could also remember the message since they had discussed it at length after it had arrived. They had been waiting for this message for quite some time.

"Yes sir, it said," she paused for a moment as she reread the message herself, seemingly confused by what it said, then proceeded, "This is an EOF Priority One Message from Sovereign Sayoose; Eyes Only Fleet Commander Priority One Message from Sovereign Sayoose: Expect to receive conflicting orders. Cannot reveal more at this time. Contact Commander Dragar if and when such message arrives. Salzat, I am sorry. Message ends from Sovereign Sayoose, EOF."

"Yes, that sounds about right, doesn't it? Where does that leave us, General?" he asked softly, looking at General Taran.

"I suppose we contact Commander Dragar. Where do you think he is?" Taran replied.

"Perhaps we should be asking the question, where is *she*? Where in Caiphus is Sovereign Sayoose, and why is the First Counselor of the Cadre sending messages that conflict with our standing orders?" Salzat's voice was rising, indicating that he was getting annoyed, a step away from anger; it took a great deal to kindle the man's anger, and it never ended well for those who managed to accomplish that feat.

"Lieutenant," he said, reigning in his irritation, "find Dragar. Be discreet. Whatever you do, don't contact anyone in the Cadre. Try Helios-2 if you can't locate him on Felis Prime. Something strange is going on and I want to find out what it is," his frustration was evident. "In the meantime," he sighed, taking a deep breath, "I'll be in my Ready Room. General Taran, you have the bridge," he announced tersely as he walked off the bridge, entering the room used as his private study and refuge. His Ready Room was where he preferred to be when he was not on the bridge, only reluctantly retiring to his private quarters to sleep when absolutely necessary. On many occasions, however, the Marshal had managed to take a series of short naps in his Ready Room and feel refreshed enough that spending too much time away from his beloved bridge was not required. Hopefully, he thought to himself, he would be able to do the same thing today, before solving this riddle regarding the Sovereign. If something nefarious involving the Sovereign was transpiring the last place that Marshal Salzat wanted to be was sleeping.

He had only been in his Ready Room for about fifteen minutes when the alert chime sounded, indicating that Lieutenant Carif had found Commander Dragar. "I'll be right there," he responded, speaking into a small microphone next to the view screen on his desk.

"Sir," Lieutenant Carif said, once the Marshal had reentered the bridge, "Commander Dragar is not on Felis Prime, he's in orbit over one of the Protectorates that was mentioned in the message from the First Counselor," her cheeks had grown flushed with excitement.

"Well, Lieutenant, where in Caiphus *is* he, and what about the Sovereign?" Salzat asked, growing slightly impatient.

"That's just it, sir, they're in orbit over Terra, in Sector 0107, Commander Dragar and the other Guardians that is, and they went there to find the Sovereign. She's been missing from Felis Prime. She apparently disappeared just after she sent that message to you, three years ago."

Marshal Salzat looked stunned. None of it made any sense to him, and yet, perhaps it did: what was the Sovereign expecting that she might have the foresight to send such a message three years before such an act might occur? It certainly seemed to imply that she had a profound sensitivity to the situation, but why leave the safety of Felis Prime for such a strange planet, he wondered to himself. His standing orders were to patrol the region several Sectors away from that particular Sector, and at the moment he had no reason to countermand them, at least, not yet. If the life of the Sovereign were at risk, he could justify changing his orders, but not for a supposition.

"Signal the Commander. This is an EOG Priority One Message from Marshal of the Fleet Salzat; Eyes only Guardian One from Marshal of the Fleet Salzat: BC-Orono-001 and her Battle Group will remain on station, as per our operational orders from Sovereign Sayoose, performing patrols in Sector 0021, but shall be available, at your disposal, should the need for our presence arise. Message ends from Marshal Salzat. EOG." After thinking for a moment he looked at the General, then at the Lieutenant, "Send the Commander the message we received from the First Counselor. My authority."

"Yes sir," came the quick response from Lieutenant Carif as she sent the transmissions, thinking to herself that things were definitely getting interesting onboard the flagship of the Alliance.

CHAPTER IV ~ THE CAT

"The universe is a dangerous place; I like it that way."

Factotum Ebla Mar, Supreme Leader of the
Ursus Consortium: *Notes to Posterity*

(*|*)

Music from Beethoven's *Pastoral Symphony* flowed out of the speakers of the small car, playing on the FM radio as it drove down the country road. It was music that matched the day: sunny and beautiful, the type that would have been perfect for lying outside, basking in the sun, but Tanya Little hardly noticed the weather as she drove toward town. Normally, the young woman would have allowed herself to notice things like the weather and the scenery as she drove her little red Mini over the Old Iron Bridge that led into town from the rural outskirts where she lived with her grandfather, but she was too preoccupied today. As a result, she was barely listening to the music of her favorite composer. Instead of taking in the scenery, or enjoying the music, Tanya was worried about her precious cat. She was taking the creature to see the Vet for her annual check-up, hoping there would be nothing wrong with her. There was really no reason to worry, she knew, but it was in her nature to worry about such things, especially since she had lost one cat to a nasty case of Feline Leukemia. Although she had grown up with pets, this particular cat meant more to her than any other she had shared her life with, and Tanya wanted to be certain that she remained in perfect health. Regular visits to the Veterinarian were key to maintaining that health.

Tanya had moved back to the bucolic paradise where she had grown up only five years ago, shortly after her grandfather suffered his second heart attack. His first heart attack had occurred two years before the death of her grandmother, his beloved wife of fifty-seven years. The second attack came only a year after her death. Her grandparents, Bob and June Little, had helped to raise her after her parents had been killed in a car accident when she was only three-years-old. They had been returning home with her maternal grandparents, after picking them up to visit with their granddaughter when an unexpected spring snowstorm caused their car to swerve into oncoming traffic on the interstate; they drove directly into a tractor-trailer that could not avoid their car as it crossed into his lane. Tanya had no memory of the event save for that she never left the home of Grandma and Grandpa Little after that day. From then on, this small town had been her home, and she loved it here.

Tanya had not wanted to leave the beautiful town, but once she completed her high school studies there had been no place for her to continue her studies. All she had ever wanted to do since she had been a little girl was to pursue a career as a writer; she had been honing her skills since she could remember, writing short stories, poems, essays, and anything she could imagine in order to prepare to eventually write the Great American Novel that every writer dreamt of, but so few managed to ever complete. While she was still a student she had entered every writing contest she could find in the many writing magazines that she could get her hands on at the local bookstore or in the library, and she won more of them than she lost. That was how she eventually earned her scholarship to university. When she applied for entry into the program she sent along a package of her best work, a glowing recommendation from her English teacher, and several of the pieces that had won prizes in the competitions she had entered, including the works that had been published, and then she waited. Her grandparents had nearly burst with pride the day the acceptance letter arrived from New York. It was not enough that Tanya had been accepted to one of the best schools in the nation, she had also been awarded a full scholastic scholarship.

"You're going to go places," her grandma had said on the day Tanya had left for school with her cherub grin lighting up her face. When Tanya graduated, at the top of her class, her grandmother pulled her aside and whispered in her ear, "I knew you could do it, darling, I knew it; you're going to be a star." Tanya had cherished those words as they had been the last words her grandmother had spoken to her in person. They had spoken to each other on the phone a number of times, but that had not been the same, not like standing next to her, smelling her, felling her grandmother's hand resting on her arm as she leaned in close to talk to her. No, speaking to her grandmother had always been an intimate affair, and she missed those moments. Four years after she finished university, her grandfather telephoned; her grandmother had gone into the bedroom to take a nap and had simply stopped breathing. It was over. She had not been sick, she just died.

After returning for the funeral, and receiving assurances from Gramps that he was fine, Tanya reluctantly returned to the hustle and bustle of New York. She had already found success as a writer, but she knew that her grandfather needed her; he was not getting any younger, and was increasingly having trouble getting around the house and doing things for himself. Once he had the second heart attack everything had been decided: Tanya quickly settled things with her landlady, who had been extremely accommodating, and moved back in with Gramps, as she had always called him. It had been an easy decision knowing that Gramps was not able to do as much for himself as he had once been able to, especially since his doctors wanted him to stay off of his feet, which was easier said than done. She also knew, even if he had not always admitted it at first, that he really did like having *his little girl* back home again. While her leaving for New York had been difficult for her grandmother, Tanya knew that it had been hardest on her stoic grandfather.

Convincing the old man to do something that he was not particularly interested in doing, even if that advice came directly from his doctors, was not going to happen without a battle, or a protracted argument. Getting Gramps, or Bob as he asked everyone he met to call him, to do something he believed was a stupid idea, or a waste of his time, was as easy to accomplish as getting someone to pull teeth without an anesthetic: it could happen, but not without a great deal of pain, and screaming. As Gramps liked to say, "I survived fightin' the Goddamn Nazis in Europe, then I survived fightin' the Goddamn communists in Korea, *and* in Vietnam; there ain't no way I can't survive no Goddamn heart attack," and he was serious. When he retired from the army, after thirty years of service, he was a full-bird Colonel, and still felt a stirring in his heart when he heard the sound of a bugle. Any heart that had the temerity to quit on him, he warned, had another thing coming. The same warning went for anyone who asked him to do stupid things: when he was in the military if he gave an order he expected it to be followed, but if someone gave him a stupid, or dangerous order, it would be challenged. He had always said that nobody was going to die under his command as a result of stupidity.

Even so, Gramps was the only family that Tanya had left and she was not about to surrender him to something as absurd as heart disease, not when the man had survived three wars and received so many decorations for his service to the nation. In Tanya's mind ordinary people died of heart disease, and her grandfather had to be the least ordinary person she had ever encountered in her life. Colonel Bob Little was, without question, the most brilliant man that Tanya had ever had the privilege of knowing. Even after having been surrounded by academics at the university, she had yet to meet anyone with a greater understanding of life than Gramps, and that did not include what he knew about the military. His knowledge of tactics and military history was phenomenal. He would spend hours entertaining his granddaughter with stories of historical battles from ancient wars all the way through to his time in Vietnam, but it did not end there. He was still a keen student of current affairs and kept up on the developments around the world. If something was happening with the military somewhere in the world, Bob Little knew about it, and had an opinion about what the United States should be doing to remedy the situation. Tanya marveled at his clarity of mind and exceptional mental acuity. His occasional lapses were all the more disturbing to her, but she dismissed them as being the results of either age or fatigue.

After moving back to the small home she had grown up in as a little girl she established her daily routine of cooking and doing all the shopping and cleaning that was necessary, before settling down to work on her second novel. She was pleased to discover that she was able to do far more writing than she had expected to do when she had first returned. Truth be told, she was surprised at how well her writing was going, but she gave most of the credit for that success to the black and white cat sitting next to her in the car. Tanya had met her writing partner, as she liked to call the cat, three years ago, and it had been a case of love at first sight: the name of the cat was Sayoose, though Tanya probably would have chosen a different name herself; the odd thing was, unlike most cats, this one actually responded to her name. She was the sweetest, smartest cat that Tanya had ever encountered.

She still recalled how she had met her amazing friend, as though it were only yesterday. One evening, while she and Gramps had been sitting on the front porch of the small house, reminiscing about her grandmother and the times he had been away while on duty, she heard the sound of plaintive mewing off in the distance. It had sounded as though the creature was in distress, causing Tanya to immediately seek it out; after only a few minutes of searching she had found the cat, at the base of a one of the shrubs, near the fence surrounding their property. Somehow the cat had become entangled in a long rope that had seemed to be wrapped around her legs and body, and looped through her collar. As soon as the cat saw Tanya approaching she calmed down, allowing her to loosen and untangle the rope, as though she had known somebody would come to her assistance. Once Tanya had freed her from the rope she had assumed the cat would run off, but instead of running away she jumped into her arms, allowing her to be carried back to the house.

"Well," Tanya whispered to the purring creature, "I guess this means you want me to take you home," Tanya whispered to the cat, eliciting an even louder purr from the creature, which did not seem any off worse for the incident with the rope. As she carried her back to the house the cat gently rubbed herself against its human companion, purring loudly and insistently.

"What shall we call you?" Tanya asked as she arrived back at the house, showing the cat to her grandfather, who seemed surprised to see such a healthy looking cat. That was when they noticed the small golden medallion hanging from the thin metallic collar, inscribed with the name *Sayoose* on the tag. It was not any type of registration tag that Tanya had ever seen: it had no numbers to call, it was just a fancy looking name tag.

"Well," Tanya said, combing her short auburn hair with her left hand as she sat down again next to her grandfather, the cat still cradled contentedly in her right arm, "I guess we'll call you Sayoose." At the mention of the name the cat let out a satisfied sounding mew, as though in response, which made both Tanya and her grandfather laugh. "Tomorrow morning I'll call into town and see if there's a record of you anywhere, and if not," she looked at Gramps, "then I guess you'll just have to stay here … right?" she smiled, her green eyes sparkling in the light from the porch as the old man nodded his head, winking in return. Tanya knew that he had always been an animal lover, even though he had not had a cat or dog for several years. His faithful dog, Chip, had died of old age several years before, shortly before his beloved wife June had passed, and he had never had the heart to replace the beloved cocker spaniel. Just seeing Sayoose, however, seemed to stir something in the old man. He had already risen from the bench, with a slight groan, and retrieved a small bowl of milk from the kitchen; he then retrieved a soft pillow from the spare bedroom and set it down next to Tanya's bed, so Sayoose would have a comfortable place to sleep, though she ended up sleeping quite contentedly on the corner of the bed, which was fine with Tanya.

Before turning on the coffee pot the next morning, Tanya called into the town's Animal Shelter to inquire if anyone had reported a lost cat with markings like those on Sayoose, or with the same collar and name tag, but nothing had been reported. She left them her name and phone number, but nobody called back. In truth, she was not upset about that at all, and had been quietly hoping that nobody would call regarding the lost cat. It seemed that she had found herself a new friend and, after a week had gone by, Tanya allowed herself to believe that Sayoose would be there for the rest of the cat's life. Growing up in the country had meant that they had always had animals around, so having Sayoose in the house was something that made things seem so much warmer, especially since Gramps could not get around as easily anymore. Tanya knew that when she went out the cat would curl up next to him and he would stroke her soft fur, enjoying the purring of the gentle creature. Often was the time she would return home after running her errands and find the two of them asleep on his favorite chair, his newspaper sprawled across his lap. The oddest thing was that sometimes it looked as if the cat had actually been reading the paper, looking away when she entered the house.

On more than one occasion Tanya had muttered to herself that she was in desperate need of a vacation.

(*|*)

Tanya marveled at how perfect Sayoose looked: her fur was a deep black, darker than anything she had ever encountered with other cats. Her front paws were white, as though she was wearing a pair of elegant gloves that barely reached her wrists. On her belly the fur was also white, which gave the impression that she was wearing a tuxedo vest, as though she were dressed for a formal affair, ready to step out at any moment. In truth, she never showed any interest in leaving the house, save to sit on the front porch in the evenings, enjoying the cool night air with her and Gramps. A splash of white extended from between her ears to just above the tip of her nose, forming a T-shape, but it was her eyes that truly caught the attention of anyone looking at her for more than a few seconds: her eyes were beyond mesmerizing, they were downright bewitching. When Sayoose looked at Tanya it was as though she were being hypnotized: it was as if the cat was, and Tanya knew it was crazy to even think this, but it felt as though the cat was reading her mind. Throughout her life Tanya had shared her home with several cats, but none of them had ever looked at her with this sort of preternatural intelligence: none had possessed eyes that were anything like those of this cat. These eyes not only glowed, as did the eyes of many cats; they were orange, and seemed to penetrate into your soul, looking beyond the surface. They gave the impression of a tremendous intelligence and wisdom that was far beyond anything a normal cat possessed. As impossible as it seemed, it was as though the creature understood everything that was going on around her. When Tanya looked at Sayoose she felt as though the creature was not only looking directly into her soul, but that she knew what Tanya was thinking; not only that, it felt as though this cat knew *why* she was thinking something as well.

Having staring contests may have been enjoyable with other cats but that was definitely not something Tanya did with Sayoose; looking directly into her eyes was like looking into the eyes of a wizard: when she looked into her eyes it felt as though she was being cross examined. As much as she had grown to love this cat it was a deeply disturbing experience that never failed to leave her unsettled. When she had first found Sayoose and brought her into the house she immediately noticed the odd sensation that she experienced when she met the creature's gaze, but dismissed it as simply not having had a cat for several years, until one morning, a few days after her arrival, when Tanya was preparing scrambled eggs for herself and Gramps for breakfast. She noticed that Sayoose was not eating the food she had set out for her. Tanya looked over at her and asked, half-jokingly, "What's the matter, my sweet, don't you like your cat food?"

To her surprise, Sayoose immediately responded with a loud, "Mrraw," walking away from the bowl of Turkey Stew she had served her. Sayoose then rubbed up against Tanya's leg, purring loudly, "Meeew, meerow," as though asking for what Tanya was preparing for herself and Gramps.

Looking down at the sleek creature Tanya could only laugh, "Well, I'll be," she had never heard of a cat eating scrambled eggs, but it seemed to be what she wanted; *why not*, she thought to herself. She added another egg to the bowl and tossed out the Turkey Stew. She had only bought a few cans, and the stuff smelled terribly anyway, what did it matter? That had been the last time she tried to give Sayoose any cat food, and when she took her to see the Veterinarian for her first checkup, the Vet had declared that she was the healthiest cat she had ever seen, so there did not seem to be any reason to change what she was feeding her. Sayoose seemed especially fond of the salmon steaks that Gramps liked to grill out back when the weather was warm. There did not seem to be much of anything that the cat did not like to eat, except for cat food, and eggplant. Much to the surprise of her human companions, she even enjoyed pasta.

Gramps was the one who had figured out, in his own mind at least, what was wrong with Sayoose, if you could call it a real problem: he had put his finger on it the first time he had noticed it, a few weeks after she had entered their lives. He had been sitting in his favorite chair in the living room, reading the newspaper, when he happened to notice that the cat was lying near a discarded section of the paper, on the floor. He glanced over and saw her looking up at him, and their eyes met for a brief moment. He had the strangest feeling that she had been reading the discarded section, but quickly dismissed the idea; but he continued looking into the cat's eyes, holding her gaze. No man alive could scare or intimidate Colonel Bob Little; he had spent the best years of his life in the army, fighting his way across Europe as an enlisted man during the Second World War. He served in South Korea as a junior officer, and fought the last war of his career commanding a battalion as a Lieutenant Colonel during the Vietnam War; the idea of having a staring contest with a cat was not something that the old man was going to turn away from, until it began. Once he locked eyes with the small tuxedo cat he had the uneasy feeling that he was in the presence of something far more than an ordinary cat. "That ain't no ordinary cat," he whispered to himself, as he looked away, thinking about the last time he had ever lost a staring contest.

When their gazes locked he had expected that the cat would turn away after a few seconds, like most cats did when they got into staring contests with humans, but that did not happen with Sayoose. Bob remembered the time when he, as a Lieutenant Colonel, had stared down a Brigadier General after the idiot had decided that his battalion should take on what was, in essence, nothing more than a glorified suicide mission in order to capture a piece of territory in Vietnam that had been passed back and forth between the Viet-Cong and the U.S. Army so many times that nobody could even remember why they even wanted the damn thing anymore. Bob could tell by after studying the Intel and the maps of the area for himself that the Intel for the operation was lousy, as lousy as the chow they had been serving the men for the past few months, and there was no way he was going to allow his men to risk their lives just so some damn officer could earn himself another star for uniform. Certainly not by shedding the blood of his men. After some persuasive arguments from Lieutenant Colonel Little the General finally backed down, and the VC were eventually bombed out of the area by a flight of B-52s and a handful of F-4s, each of which delivered a shit-load of hard iron and Agent Orange that transformed the forest into a scene from some horror film that nobody would ever want to see. But, the important thing was that his men had lived to see another day.

That staring contest with that Brigadier General helped earn him his promotion to full-bird Colonel. Bob would have been able to become a Brigadier General himself, but based on the way Vietnam was headed, which was not a direction that he particularly liked, all he wanted to do was hang up his helmet and return home to his wife. After all the time he had spent in the army he could see that the guys calling the shots in Washington were making a massive mess out of things in Vietnam; they were not allowing his men to fight to win the damn war, but they did want them to fight hard enough to die, and that was leaving a bad taste in his mouth. No, Bob had always thought that if you entered into a conflict it had to be for a good reason, a moral, justifiable reason. War had to have some righteous excuse behind it, and he did not see that in Vietnam. Defense of a nation was one thing, but he really did not understand what the hell was going on over here, on the other side of the world. Fighting the Nazis had been easy to understand, their evil had been palpable, their threat to Europe and the world existential. Stopping the North Koreans had been less clear in his mind, but the *Red Menace* had seemed like a justifiable enemy that seemed worth fighting, at the time. But now, here in Vietnam, it all seemed so senseless. So many young Americans were being killed and maimed, and for what? What the hell did bombing these little villages filled with a bunch of women and children have to do with fighting the enemy? Oh, they were told, they were the VC ... that was the excuse for everything: the damn Viet-Cong.

But it was also an excuse that was being used to turn good soldiers into cold-blooded killers. At least, that was how Bob was seeing it, and he was not pleased with what he was seeing. Not in the least. Then, on March 16, 1968, the village of My Lai was massacred. It was a day that still haunted his memory even though he had been anywhere near My Lai and My Khe, the locations of the slaughter. According to the United States Army only three-hundred and forty-seven were killed, but the Vietnamese government listed the total number of dead at five hundred and four. Five hundred and four unarmed civilians that had been murdered, slaughtered, by soldiers from Company C of the 1st Battalion, 20th Infantry Regiment, 11th Brigade of the 23rd Infantry Division. It really did not matter, Bob knew, because even if it had only been *fifty* it was a war crime of unspeakable proportions. There were supposed to be in Vietnam to save these people, not murder them. It had been such a traumatic event for Lieutenant Colonel Little because his Battalion, the 3rd, had been slated to take that mission, but he had traded the assignment with the commander of the 1st Battalion. His battalion had only returned from a grueling patrol the day before and Bob had wanted to them a day of well-earned rest. Had he known that things would have turned out the way they had, he would never have traded the assignments, but that was what sometimes happened during a war. You could not read the future or the minds of others. Three years later, after thirty years in the army he figured that having fought in three separate wars he had spent more than enough time away from his wife, and nobody was about to argue with him.

When Tanya returned from the market, a few hours later, he was waiting for her at the door, taking some of the grocery bags from her hands despite her protestations and said, "That cat's got an old soul, ya know," nodding his head toward Sayoose. Tanya looked over at Sayoose, who was contentedly basking in a sunbeam streaming through the living room window. "She looks at me," he continued softly, as though he did not want the cat to overhear him, carrying the groceries into the kitchen, shaking his head slowly. "Don't know how," he sounded in awe, "but ... she knows things," he grunted as he lifted a heavy bag onto the counter, "she knows things that no cat should know." Tanya was about to say something but he held up his hand to stop her, "Child, don't even try to say nothin', I ain't blowin' smoke out my ass," he grunted again as he moved out of the kitchen, wheezing with the exertion. "After thirty years in the army I can tell ya one thing I know," he said, lowering his voice to barely above a whisper, "that ain't no ordinary cat ya got," and he turned back and returned to his chair, being careful to avoid disturbing Sayoose, who was now watching him from half-closed eyes as he passed by her position on the floor.

For her part, however, Sayoose seemed to have the sweetest disposition of any cat that Tanya had ever encountered. She never had any issues with her and, after spending nearly three years together, she had become as much a part of the family as anyone. She was such an integral part of her life, Tanya could not imagine it without her. Every morning, after she had prepared their breakfast and run whatever errands had to be done, she would settle down at the old roll-top desk she had inherited from her grandmother. She had her trusty laptop with her, and with it would do whatever writing she was able to for that day. Some days were better than others, of course, but things had definitely improved thanks to the presence of Sayoose. There was a small portable stereo on the desk that Tanya listened to while working and, much to her surprise, she discovered that Sayoose also seemed to enjoy the music. When there was nothing of interest on the radio Tanya would simply use her laptop to provide the musical backdrop for her work. She had allowed herself to indulge in an expensive model after her first book had been published, rationalizing that it would help her with future projects, and it had proved to be helpful. At the same time, she could not help but be impressed with the amazing sound quality the computer had, as well as how sleek it looked with its aluminum case.

"Dude, you've got a Dell," she would whisper as she turned on the laptop, giggling to herself. Several years before she had watched a compilation of old television ads and saw one for the computer company that used that line. At the time she had thought it was tremendously inane, but now that she had one of their computers she found it difficult not to repeat it to herself whenever the computer was coming to life. Aside from using the laptop for all of her writing needs it had her much of her musical library stored on its hard drive, available to be listened to at the touch of an icon on the screen. Having a touch-screen was something that made it extremely easy to use as well, speeding up her workflow quite a bit compared to her previous computer. It was hard to imagine how Dell would be improving on this model, but she was sure they would come up with something, she always thought to herself.

Her favorite composers had always been Beethoven, Bach, and Schumann, and she was especially fond of chamber music, which seemed to keep her ideas flowing with greater fluidity than when worked in silence, which she would often do when she was editing. Whenever the music was playing Sayoose would curl up in front of the small speakers on the desk and listen intently to the music; her tail twitching to the beat of whatever they were listening to at the time. It was the strangest thing she had ever encountered. The oddest thing Tanya had discovered was that Sayoose had figured out how to turn on the small stereo all by herself. She was able to press the 'on' button with her nose, activating the play feature, which would automatically play the last recording that had been left in the machine. She would also press the button to turn the stereo onto the classical radio station that Tanya had entered into the FM preset, so that she often came home to the sound of the radio playing.

It had reached the point where Tanya said that Sayoose had been the one to rescue her. Her purring was so relaxing it inspired her, blending in with the music, allowing her to work faster than she ever could have done without the creature around. She was able to do so much more, in less time, that she managed to complete her second novel faster than she had thought possible. Whatever the trick was, her publisher had been thrilled, and her third book was finished several months ahead of schedule and she was now working on a much-anticipated fourth. At this point, her most difficult task was trying to figure out what she would do with the generous advance her publisher had sent for the book she was currently writing.

As they drove down the small Main Street Tanya turned to make sure Sayoose was still alright; she was sitting on the passenger seat, looking out the window as though she was acutely aware of what was happening. "You know where we're going, don't you, sweetie?" Tanya asked as she reached over and gave the cat's sleek fur a gentle stroke.

"Merrow," she replied, as though she were replying, "Of course I do," which caused Tanya to laugh in response.

"That's my girl, always replying," she giggled. It was truly uncanny, she thought to herself; whenever she spoke to Sayoose it seemed as though she would reply, but not just with a single *meow*, but with actual syntax, with ... with cat grammar. "Oh, Tanya," she muttered to herself, "you really do need a vacation."

"Mroww mew," came a quick reply from Sayoose, as Tanya's Mini turned into the parking area of the Village Veterinary Clinic, where she had been bringing Sayoose for her annual checkup for the past three years. She had brought the cat to the Clinic a few weeks after she had found her, asking Doctor Vera Micholson, the only Veterinarian in the town to make sure there was nothing wrong with her new-found friend. To her relief the Doctor Micholson had examined Sayoose and declared her to be in perfect condition.

"This may be the healthiest stray I've ever encountered," Doctor Micholson had said, much to Tanya's delight. After giving Sayoose all of the necessary vaccinations she took her home and had been bringing her back once a year for her annual check-up.

"Okay, young lady, it's time to go see the nice Doctor, alright?" Tanya looked at the cat, knowing there would be no troubles, but she still said it, "no troubles, right?" She stepped out of the car and went around to the passenger side to collect Sayoose, who was now facing the door, patiently waiting for her to open it; Tanya knew that the cat would allow herself to be picked up and carried into the clinic without complaint. "That's my sweetie," Tanya whispered as they walked into the empty waiting room. She did not notice that Sayoose was looking over her shoulder toward a shimmering light behind them, several feet over their heads.

One of the Vet Technicians was at the front desk when Tanya and Sayoose entered the Clinic, "It's so good to see you again, Sayoose, and your companion, of course," she smiled broadly at the two, "how have you been?" she asked, as she pulled out their file and brought them to the Examination Room.

"Fine, well no, better than fine, we've been great," Tanya replied.

"That's great to hear; Sayoose looks terrific," she winked, "as usual," she gave the cat an affectionate scritch under her chin and was rewarded with a loud purr and a rub by Sayoose as she nudged her head against the Tech's hand. When they were situated in the Exam Room the Vet Tech chatted with Tanya for a few minutes, asking her about her writing. She had read her latest book and had loved it and was looking forward to her next book. "Well, I'd love to chat more, but I *must* get back to work," she winked, "Doctor Micholson will be with you shortly," she said, turning to leave the room.

"Thanks," Tanya replied She liked the Vet Tech, she was a perky young woman who always seemed to be in a great mood and was extremely gentle with the animals. It was always great to meet people who had read her books, Tanya thought to herself, it made the writing all the more worthwhile.

Sayoose was sitting placidly on the stainless steel examination table which had a bath mat on it to make it more comfortable for those visiting the clinic. After waiting about two minutes the sliding door opposite the one they had entered opened and a small woman with shockingly red hair and bright green eyes walked in; she was carrying a small tray containing the immunizations Sayoose would be receiving.

"Hello," Doctor Micholson said, her voice soft and gentle, "It's good to see you again," she said to Tanya. "So, how has my favorite patient been?" she asked, lifting the small cat from the mat on the table so she could better see her belly. As soon as the Veterinarian had entered the room Sayoose began looking around, as though she were a bit nervous, which seemed quite uncharacteristic for her and immediately made Tanya wonder what was wrong. Sayoose did not seem to mind being handled by the doctor, but she was still looking around the room nervously. It was as though she was distracted or worried about something. Both the Vet and Tanya dismissed the movements as the anxiety a normal cat might display while visiting the Vet, but they had no idea what was going on virtually over their heads.

CHAPTER V ~ CONTACT

"When Torgons were introduced as companion creatures a great dilemma arose as to whether the creatures were being subjugated considering their intelligence. Many Ethicists believed their rights were being violated by keeping the creatures in such a manner, but, it was argued, the alternative had been to allow them to remain on their home world and die. Torgons had chosen to leave their planet and wanted to live with humans. In the end, it was the creatures themselves that settled the matter by stating unequivocally that they enjoyed being companions: if they did not, they would definitely say something about the situation. The matter had been settled."

[...]

Excerpted from: Ethical Issues in Resettlement: Symposium on the Torgon Question

(*|*)

"What in Caiphus are you two Slugs looking at?" Dragar growled, his eyes snapped open when he sensed he was being stared at; he was trying to sound intimidating as he attempted to rise from his seat and failed, forgetting the 7-point harness that still held him in place quite securely. With the combination of the harnesses that had been recommended by the Alliance Board of Inquiry, convened after the tragedy on board the BT-Hercules-783, along with the extra stabilization provided by the A-ConCom, the problems associated with the first test flights of the Trans-Light Drive had been eliminated, though the flight still made you feel as though you were being turned inside out while transiting through pan-dimensional space, which was exactly how Dragar currently felt. He was sure his stomach was still several Sectors behind them, far closer to Felis Prime than the planet over which they were currently orbiting.

He regarded his fellow Guardians as he released the harness, allowing himself to float out of the seat into the zero-gravity environment, "Are we …" he began to ask.

"Shielded? Yes, sir," Pertu replied, anticipating the question. If there was one thing he knew he could count on from the Captain it was professionalism, which was one reason he had recruited her in the first place. She was the best. "All systems are fully functional; the transition came off without any issues. Our shields have been modulated to a rotating frequency; none of the planetary observational equipment can detect us. Anything pointing our way will register nothing more than a reflection of their own sun's light from their atmosphere, or starlight in the evening; it will appear as a perfectly natural phenomenon," she said, her scratchy voice quiet, so as not to strain her vocal chords. "We're presently in a geosynchronous orbit above the target area; current distance from planet surface is 60,000 Krenar, quite a bit higher than any of their own satellites," she smiled and gave him a wink, "I didn't think it would do to have us crash into any of their satellites if we're trying to remain undetected." Brem grunted, before Dragar could respond.

"Satellites?" Dragar asked, "This planet shouldn't have any …"

"Take a look for yourself, Commander, they have hundreds, and then there's *that* thing. It isn't anything close to one of our orbiting cities, but it demonstrates that they've been taking an active step out into space, even if it isn't into traveling beyond light speed." She was directing his gaze toward the largest object in orbit which was moving below them over the planet. It had eight large reflective panels extending out from either end of it, with another modular section in the center.

Tactical Sergeant Brem had already been monitoring the communications and announced, sounding a bit perplexed, "It's called the International Space Station."

Dragar looked at it for a few seconds, and shook his head in dismay. At the same time Pertu moved back to her seat at the helm and strapped herself back in, in case something had to be done that the A-ConCom could not handle, which was highly unlikely. She knew there was little chance that the A-ConCom would not be able to handle any emergency situation, but she was an extremely hands-on pilot and liked nothing more than being at the helm of the ship. In truth, Dragar preferred to see her there as well. He knew that the technology was both sophisticated and trustworthy; he also knew that Captain Pertu could fly circles around any other pilot in the universe, himself included, and he liked to think that he was a pretty damn good pilot, though he figured Brem would probably like to claim otherwise.

Dragar continued to look out of the portholes at the pale-blue planet, thousands of Krenar below, marveling at the beauty of the wispy clouds brushing across its face; for a moment he could understood why the Sovereign would want to come to such a place. Unlike Felis Magoris, which was heavily covered with cities and built-up areas, this planet looked like a genuine paradise; it was covered with water, with vast undeveloped spaces that were covered by green, lush forested areas and grasslands. He turned to the monitors next to his seat and made a few scans and grunted softly to himself. Life, Dragar could see, even from this far up in space, the planet was teeming with life. Ecosystems on this planet were diverse, though he could also see that there were many problems: it had an atmosphere with an extremely high carbon content, as well as rising acidification levels in the oceans. Classic signs of a civilization burning through their most precious resources: their own planet. There was no way this planet was what they had been told by the Cadre.

He turned to Brem, who seemed to have a similar reaction to the transition through pan-dimensional space that he had, "Alright, Tactical Sergeant, we know these humans have managed to leave their little planet, so tell me something," he asked, his voice quiet, "what Grade would you estimate the planet to be, based on your observations, on atmospheric pollutants, radio signals, and other factors?" Brem was already looking through the array of scopes and dials next to his station, each of which had something to tell him about the planet. While Helios-2 was not a research vessel it was equipped with sophisticated probes that enabled it to test for the levels of certain pollutants in the atmosphere that would indicate when a planet entered a different phase in its development.

Brem let out another of his grunts, "Well, according to what we were told, this planet was labelled GZ-7, but that was an obvious miscalculation …"

"Or an outright lie," Dragar interjected, sounding angry, to Brem's surprise.

He nodded his head and continued, "That may be, but let me tell you, they have everything needed to qualify as a solid GZ-9, and they're well on the road to becoming a full-blown 10 within the next century, perhaps sooner. All they need is to develop sub-light technology, there are enough satellites out there for a Torgon to skip across. I don't know what the Sovereign has been doing, but this could be a lot more serious than we imagined," he gestured for Dragar to lean closer, "and, uh … Commander," he sounded even more serious than usual, "have you taken a look at their sun?"

Dragar twisted around to look out the opposite side of the ship to see the bright white disk of light shining through the rear porthole, making him squint even with his black eyes, which were well suited to the bright light. Squinting, he turned back to Brem, "Alright," he said, as he retook his seat. "It's a fairly young sun, quite bright, I'll give you that, …" he was about to continue, but Brem cut him off.

"No, no, it isn't that," Brem said, pulling one of the monitors over on its swinging arm, "look here, at the out gas expulsion rates, look at these Hydrogen conversion levels … and the sheer mass of the thing. Can you imagine anyone that might be interested in that much raw Hydrogen? Not to mention the other elements within that beauty?" He looked intently at Dragar, but the Guardian could not take him seriously. It had been several millennia since anyone had attempted to mine the sun of an inhabited system; it was an inviolable rule of the Stellar Mining Bureau: *where there was life, there could be no mining*. There were no caveats and no exceptions. If a planet in the system had life on it, that sun could not be mined. Relocation of the life-forms was not permitted, and if they were sentient, asking the life-forms to move of their own volition was strictly prohibited; intimidation of any sort was expressly forbidden.

When the issue was life on a planet in a Red Dwarf system, of course, the company performing the mining operation simply had to be patient: life on any planet in that system would surely not survive for too long once the star continued to progress in its death throes, though not everyone had the patience of the Felis Alliance, which was why they not only mined the stars, they acted as the legal enforcers for the Stellar Mining Bureau, upholding the regulations that some seemed too impatient to accept and far too willing to flout. As a result of their commitment to protecting others from those who seemed willing to violate their rights so casually the Stellar Mining Bureau consistently awarded the Alliance with the most favored mining concessions, whenever they became available.

Unfortunately, that also meant that the Ursus Consortium had become increasingly desperate and highly jealous of Alliance and their position. As a result, the Consortium had been making increasingly unethical moves in their attempts to collect the precious elements which they required to keep the machinery of their organization, and economy, in operation. Dragar was acutely aware of the fact that Factotum Ebla Mar did not care about the lives of others, but that did not make it easier for him to imagine the maniacal Consortium leader of intentionally killing billions of people to achieve his goals, sending involuntary chills down his spine as he once again looked at the burning disc of light through the rear porthole of Helios-2. Even with rules designed to protect those who were defenseless, there were circumstances where those rules were sometimes bent to the point where they either broke, or were twisted so far their breaking was an inevitability. Regardless, the thought of the sun of this system being mined for its resources was an absolutely horrific proposition, the results of which would lead to its destabilization and, ultimately, the end of all life on the planet.

"Well, there's no way anyone's going to be mining this sun as long as the Sovereign has declared this a Protectorate of the Alliance," the irritated voice of Dragar filled the bridge of the ship; he looked to Brem, who was nodding, then added, "especially if she's somewhere down there." He turned to Pertu who had activated the artificial gravity on the ship and the large view screen over the helm, which was showing a small building with a red vehicle sitting on a strip of rough-looking material that extended to the road. Next to the car was a large tree, which Dragar could see might provide a good vantage point for observation should the need arise.

"She's in that structure," Pertu said; the three Guardians watched as a young woman emerged from the building carrying a small, black and white creature in her arms. She then placed the creature in one side of the vehicle and then entered on the other side, and a few seconds later began to drive out onto the road, then she drove away down the road, but there had been no sign of the Sovereign. Pertu looked back at Dragar, shrugging, "I don't know what to say, Commander, according to the beacon, she's in that vehicle." They watched in silence as the little red car made its way toward a bridge and continued on into the town.

Dragar nodded his head, leaning forward to retrieve something from under his seat while the other two stared at the display, "Send me down wherever they stop," Dragar said calmly. He quickly took the small pack and strapped it onto his back; it immediately blended into his uniform as though it were invisible. He reluctantly walked to the one thing on the ship he hated even more than the Trans-Light Drive: the

LDMT. Long Distance Matter Transporters were, as the scientists and engineers liked to say, "Safer than walking across the street on Felis Magoris," but that did not make Dragar feel any better after feeling as though his molecules had already been scrambled once today. One saving grace about the LDMT was that he could activate his Personal Shield Device and arrive somewhere virtually invisible, and continue to remain completely hidden until he knew it was safe to reveal his presence. Terra may have all the markings of a GZ-9 planet but they were still, technically speaking, in a barbarously dangerous level of development and it was not something the Prime Guardian wanted to get involved with, not when the safety and life of the Sovereign was at risk.

Dragar was about to move to the aft section of the ship, where the LDMT was located when Brem called out to him, "Commander, you're going to want to take a look at this, it's a message from Marshal Salzat."

Dragar looked at the view screen over the bridge and saw that the little red vehicle was still moving, and turned his attention to Brem's monitor. Marshal Salzat was asking about the location of the Sovereign. "I guess three years is a long time to keep this kind of secret," Brem whispered.

"They are friends," Dragar agreed, "I would think if anyone should know, he would be one of the people. Besides, if it comes down to a fight, we may need the Orono on our side. I can't imagine Regar sending us any help from the fleet, can you?"

Brem just looked at him, horrified, "You don't think ..."

"Commander, you can't be serious ..." the croaking voice of Pertu interrupted.

"Deathly. Think about it. Regar told us that the Sovereign was on a Green Zone *Seven* planet. Why? Why would he mislead us so much? Alliance records could not be so out-of-date regarding one of its Protectorates, you know that as well as anyone, right?" Both Guardians nodded in agreement.

"Send the Marshal the response. Tell him where we are, and what we're doing," Dragar responded.

A few minutes later, while the littler red vehicle was still moving down the road, approaching what seemed to be a small town several Krenar away, a response from the Marshal arrived.

"It's for you," Brem announced grimly, showing Dragar the monitor. Dragar leaned forward to read the message, *"This is an EOG*

Priority One Message from Marshal of the Fleet Salzat; Eyes only Guardian One from Marshal of the Fleet Salzat: BC-Orono-001 and her Battle Group will remain on station, as per our operational orders from Sovereign Sayoose, performing patrols in Sector 0021, but shall be available, at your disposal, should the need for our presence arise. Message ends from Marshal Salzat. EOG." Both Dragar and Brem read the message, the Tactical Sergeant grunting loudly as he reached the end. He looked over at his friend who was also shaking his head.

"By Caiphus, that man is incredible," he muttered. "What's the next part? It's still encoded."

Brem clicked a few keys, activating the decryption for the attachment and the message from the First Counselor was displayed.

"By all that is sacred!" Brem exclaimed, gripping the armrests on his seat so hard they shook. "I'm going to rip that Tarvok's head off ..."

"Relax, my friend," Dragar said, placing a hand on the Tactical Sergeant's broad shoulder, "he's just making things easier ... we'll get him, don't worry."

Brem looked up at his friend and nodded, "Oh yes, we will ..."

"Commander," Pertu interrupted, "she seems to have arrived at her destination, you'd better get down there."

Dragar nodded toward Pertu and pulled his friend along to the LDMT, to activate the device. Although the Long Distance Matter Transporter could be operated with a timer, he preferred to have someone working the controls. "Don't take any unnecessary chances, my friend," Brem said as he entered the coordinates the sensors indicated were close to where the Sovereign was located.

"You know me," Dragar grinned.

"Yes, I do, that's why I'm saying ..."

"Just activate the ..."

"Initiating transport." Before Dragar could complete his sentence the Tactical Sergeant had initiated the transportation cycle, sending the Commander down to the surface of the planet.

Once activated it took less than four seconds to cycle through the entire LDMT process, transporting the object on its targeting pad to its designated location. Dragar usually closed his eyes and held his breath, fully expecting to have his molecules resolved into oblivion; this time he had barely had time to close his eyes, but when he opened them he was in the branch of a large tree, next to the building the young woman had parked her vehicle beside. Dragar watched as she carried the small creature into the building and was surprised to see the orange eyes of the creature gazing directly toward him despite the fact that his Personal Shield Device had rendered him virtually invisible. He immediately knew that he had seen those eyes before. Maintaining his shielded state Dragar lowered himself from the tree and went around to the back of the building, slipping in through an open window while being careful not to make any noise.

He could hear the voice of two young women as the detector indicated that the Sovereign was in the room just beyond the next door. By activating his anti-grav belt Dragar was able to rise to the level of the ceiling. He entered the room at the same time as the woman with the red hair, completely invisible, save for a slight shimmer of light which was generated by his Personal Shield Device. Once in the room he observed the young woman and Veterinarian as they talked about the creature on the examination table. He was not surprised as the creature once again looked directly at him again and seemed to nod at him, even though he was shielded.

(*|*)

"She's been great," the young woman replied, "there haven't been any ..." her voice froze, mid-sentence, as though her breath had caught in her throat. Dragar had twisted the inner ring on his Temporal Shield, allowing him to temporarily stop the flow of the time stream in a localized area, for a brief period; the resulting ripples caused by the stoppage would eventually cause the time stream to correct itself if the stoppage was not rectified. He knew he only had a few moments, but this was the only way he could act without revealing his presence to such primitive life-forms.

"Hello, Prime Guardian," the creature spoke, her voice soft, "I've been expecting you."

Dragar was not sure whether to be overjoyed or annoyed at having discovered the Sovereign, "What in Caiphus are you doing here, my Sovereign?" the deep voice of the Prime Guardian asked. He was trying to keep his voice low, since the Temporal Shield did not extend far enough beyond the door of this room to effect the person in the outer office.

Sayoose looked toward the ceiling again and stretched, then sat down on her haunches, looking slightly annoyed, "Well, Dragar, how did you find me?" she sounded almost impressed, and was genuinely pleased to see her old friend. She knew it had been a mistake to leave Felis Prime without having told him and her other Guardians of her plans.

Dragar's form came into view as he deactivated his shield, allowing the light of the room to reveal his presence. As he settled to the floor he began to answer the cat, "It wasn't difficult, my Sovereign, well," he corrected himself, "it *was* difficult, it simply required time. As you recall, you were injected with one a locator implants quite some time ago. I activated it, but it took a bit longer to find you due to your proximity to the young sun in this system, and a micro-singularity in one of the adjoining systems which temporarily blocked its signal. We never imagined you would seek refuge on a Protectorate planet," he tried to glare at her, but found her gaze, even in this strange form, unsettling. "Imagine our surprise when we found that our leader had, quite literally, run away from home," he was not laughing, but was truly pleased to have found his charge. "But, my Sovereign, a *Protectorate*? Do you realize the dangers you have placed yourself in?"

"Dragar, you are far too serious for your own good," she replied, without hesitation, then she laughed. "I have been perfectly safe here, under the care of this human," she nodded toward the young woman who was standing frozen with her mouth open in mid-sentence. "However, I do understand that the Alliance might feel the need to have its leader back, but at this point, quite frankly," she yawned, "I really do not see why I should leave," she saw the look of surprise on the face of her Prime Guardian and laughed again. "Oh, come now, Dragar, you know better than anyone how long it has been since I have had any serious time away from the insanity involved in running the Alliance. Do you think I really want to do nothing but sleep all day? Of course not, but the amount of noise that the Alliance creates in my mind, not to mention the mess that the Consortium and Factotum Mar have been causing, well ..." she stretched and yawned dramatically, "it is enough to make me *want* to sleep," she began to purr, as though to emphasize how much she enjoyed her current state. "Besides," she added after a moment, "this planet may not be an Alliance member, but it is a Protectorate, what is the problem? It is guaranteed protection under our operational mandates." She looked at Dragar with what must have been a look of annoyance, though it was difficult to read given her present form.

Dragar was also slightly annoyed, "My Sovereign, I'm sorry, it simply won't do to have the most powerful woman in the universe living her life as …" he looked around the examination room, "what in Caiphus are you supposed to be, anyway?"

Sovereign Sayoose laughed and sat up straight, "I am a cat, silly, they are one of the most popular companion creatures here on Earth," she saw the confusion on his face. "Oh, that is what they call this little planet. Cats are much like the Torgons in the Alliance," she laughed again, a strange sound coming from a cat, but it was music to his ears after not having heard her voice for three years.

He shook his head, "What would possess you to take on such a form as," Dragar was gesturing toward the Sovereign's body, "this? Why not just come here as yourself; we are, after all, of the same Genomic family. It would have required virtually no adjustments for you to fit into the human population." He looked at the Sovereign, shaking his head in dismay. "As for the Protectorates, it's true that this is a Protectorate, according to the mandates, but you should know that strange things have been going on of late."

Sovereign Sayoose leaned forward, "Indeed, such as?"

"Well, for one thing Factotum Mar has been making a great deal of noise since your disappearance," he shook his head, anticipating her question. "No, my Sovereign. Nobody save for the Guardians and the Cadre, and a few others, including Lieutenant Kar and Administrator Marta, know of your absence. Everyone else, including Lieutenant Kar's platoon, believe you've been out of sight due to the commitments of your office for the past three years," he was quick to add, "it doesn't look like things are going to be getting better with Factotum Mar; it's almost as if he knows that you've been away, as though someone has been funneling him information about your status," Dragar shook his head in frustration.

"Just as I was preparing to come down here Marshal Salzat sent us a message stating that he'd received a message from First Counselor Regar directing the Marshal of the Fleet, in your name, to stop protecting certain Protectorates … including this one," Dragar was shaking his head again, trying not to show his overt disdain for the First Counselor, but Sovereign Sayoose was well aware that the two men did not like each other.

Sayoose was genuinely concerned, but tried not to display her feelings, "I understand, Dragar, but you must realize," her voice lowered, as though she expected others to be listening, "there is more to this than you recognize; I cannot leave until I am ready and, quite frankly, that time has not yet arrived." Dragar was going to reply, but she held up her left paw, stopping him, "I want you to do two things: make contact with Operations and inform the Cadre that they are to aggressively, is that understood? I said aggressively, defend each and every Protectorate, and every Alliance member, regardless the cost. Is that clear enough?" The tone of her voice even while in the form of this cat creature left no doubt as to her meaning. Dragar smiled as he nodded; he was not really happy, but it was clear that the Sovereign was, and that was what was important. If he could not return with her, at least he would have crystal-clear instructions from her for the Cadre.

She continued, "Send a message to Fleet Commander Marshal Salzat, under your authority as First Advisor, *in my name,*" she was looking directly into his eyes. "Any messages he receives from the Cadre is to be ignored. Protectorates are to be defended at the same level as they are currently defended, unless there is a threat which indicates more forces are required to repel the invaders, in which case the Marshal is to use his discretion to increase the forces necessary to crush any opposition. He is to consider this an operational command and continue under communication blackout," her tail was wagging. "Have I made myself clear?" She asked again, though she did not sound impatient.

Dragar nodded, impressed at the speed at which the Sovereign was able to appreciate a situation. He knew that Marshal Salzat would be relieved to receive that message and would understand the order to operate under blackout conditions. He might question the reasons, but he was a good soldier, and an order from his Sovereign was enough to let him know that everything was as it should be: Sovereign Sayoose was safe, and thanks to the Marshal and his forces, the Alliance would be as well.

Sayoose continued, lifting a white-tipped paw to rub against the side of her head, "I really had not expected you to find me so quickly, you know, but you have, so I shall have to live with that," she looked directly at him, giving what must have been the cat equivalent of a smile, "I suppose I should not have expected anything less from my Prime Guardian and First Advisor," she paused for a moment, hanging her head. "I do owe you an apology, Dragar, it was never my intention to cause you to worry over my safety, but I assure you," she added quickly, before he could reply, "I have been perfectly safe here; this human," she nodded toward the thin female, "has been treating me … well, like royalty. So, it is my intention to remain here, in this form, at least for now. I shall return to the Alliance when I am ready; besides, there are still some things that must be resolved," she let the thought hang, looking into his eyes again. Dragar knew better than to argue; after all, she was the Sovereign of the Alliance. If she wanted to take a vacation, in the guise of a cat, he was powerless to stop her; now that he had found her, however, he would do everything within his power to ensure that she was safe on this planet.

"As you wish, my Sovereign," he said, performing a low bow, "if I may..." he began to ask, but she cut him off.

"Yes," she sighed, knowing it would be impossible to get him to leave now that he had found her. "You may remain, but *discreetly*. You may not interfere with the family with which I am staying; they deserve better," Dragar had to respect the Sovereign's sense of loyalty.

After bowing once again he stepped back a bit. "I shall remain in touch with Operations through Helios-2; they'll remain in orbit over while you and I remain here. Should anything critical arise, we will be able to execute an expedient extraction. That way, you will be able to be kept apprised of any important developments," he stepped back another step. It was almost time for Dragar to release the Temporal Shield, otherwise those within the localized time stream would begin to noticeably stutter around them as the time stream attempted to catch up with the area that had been isolated by the device. Once the Temporal Shield had been released the only residual effect would be that chronometers in the area where time had been paused would be found to have lost about two or three minutes, but few people ever noticed the loss of time unless they happened to compare their devices simultaneously.

"I shall see you, soon, my Sovereign," Dragar said, a genuine smile on his face. He had hoped to be returning to Felis Prime with her, but would have to be satisfied with remaining on Terra, on Earth, once again acting as her Guardian. At least he knew where she was, and that she was safe. Once he reported the situation to Operations and to the Marshal, which would be done through Helios-2, he would be free to establish a post from which he would observe her and provide the Sovereign protection from any threat that might manifest itself. Finally, after three years of searching, Dragar was once again fulfilling his role as Prime Guardian, a position he relished, but had felt he did not deserve while the Sovereign was missing, after disappearing without a trace. Once he reactivated his Personal Shield Device and disappeared again he deactivated the Temporal Shield that had frozen the examination room for the past few minutes.

As his form shimmered and vanished into the corner of the examination room the young woman and Vet resumed their conversation as though nothing had happened. Neither noticed that Sayoose was facing the opposite direction she had been a second before, but that was the way the human brain worked: it was sometimes more difficult to detect large, obvious changes than something small and subtle.

"… problems," the young woman finished saying, as Sayoose resumed her position, although she now faced the window instead of the wall. In the meantime, the Vet continued her examination: Sayoose was weighed and checked to ensure there were no tender areas, which almost made her laugh out loud, but she managed to restrain herself. Being a cat was a real challenge at times considering the human she lived with enjoyed talking to her so much. She began talking to her the moment she woke up in the morning. Even while she was writing her books she continued carrying on one-sided conversations with what she thought of as an ordinary cat, assuming the creature could neither understand, or respond. For Sovereign Sayoose not to respond took a tremendous amount of will, but she knew that if she did reply, nothing good would come of it: on this planet talking companion animals were unknown. Torgons were one of the rare exceptions in the universe, but they communicated through a form of telepathy, and people had become used to hearing their thoughts over time; it was unlikely that a talking cat would be considered anything less than highly unusual on this underdeveloped planet, and the Sovereign did not want to attract any undue attention to herself, so she remained silent.

One of the saving graces, thus far, had been the human woman's love of music. It was something that Sovereign Sayoose had always enjoyed and was particularly pleased to discover that Tanya was fond of listening to chamber music while she worked. She found that she had a particular fondness for the Earth composers named Beethoven and Schumann, though many of them appealed to her at this point, and she enjoyed listening to the radio when Tanya was not there, if she could manage it, listening to the various broadcasts of different concerts that were played throughout the day on something called *Public Broadcasting*, which seemed to play a great deal of lovely music. There was only one problem with that, of course: Gramps, as Tanya called him. He seemed quite surprised to observe a cat turning on the small stereo. She had solved that problem by staring at him for a few seconds: he simply forgot about the situation and went back to his newspaper, believing that he had turned it on himself.

Thanks to her lack of communication, aside from being able to use a cat 'vocabulary' she had devised, her wordless vacation had turned into a semi-monastic retreat; she was beginning to understand how the Monks on Cygna 7 must begin to feel after spending such protracted periods in silence. Cygna 7 was a dreary planet in Sector 0899; it was mostly barren, save for a series of monasteries that had been established several millennia ago by the Order of Caiphus and was a place where monks from across the Sector, and now the universe, went to seek enlightenment through prolonged periods of meditation. After three years without speaking to another human the Sovereign was beginning to understand how some of the monks must have felt after spending anywhere from 50 to 500 years in silence, depending on the commitment they made to the monastery.

Those who managed to last 50 years were permitted to utter seven words, which usually led to the phrase, "Please, I would like to go home."

Other Monks were quoted as saying, "I cannot eat another bowl of soup," before lapsing into another commitment of silence.

One clever Monk summarized his feelings with the phrase, "I despise soup; let me go home." For Sovereign Sayoose the choice to take on the form of a creature that was non-communicative on this distant planet had been less of a spiritual choice and far more practical in nature: she had taken on the form of a cat primarily for her health.

While the Sovereign had not been silent for nearly as long as the Monks on Cygna 7, three years for her was still quite a stretch. She was not looking for sympathy: the entire thing had been her idea, right down to transforming into the likeness of one of the platoon members that guarded her, in order to gain access to Felis Prime's Spaceport. She then transformed into the likeness of a xenobiologist in order to gain passage onboard the Alliance patrol vessel that brought her to this planet. She had chosen this planet for a number of reasons, not the least of which being that she felt it would make an irresistible lure for those who might want to seek her out, if her suspicions about certain things proved to be correct.

It was in a Green Zone, but the technological development of the population were still many years away from what was deemed necessary for it to be offered entry into the Felis Alliance, not to mention the state of the system's sun, which could prove to be quite enticing to certain unscrupulous individuals. Sovereign Sayoose had personally declared the planet, named Terra, a Protectorate of the Alliance. Even so, Earth, as it was known by its inhabitants, would not be ready to join the Alliance for at least another sixty years based on its present rate of development. Which, of course, assumed that they did not destroy themselves in that process. Unfortunately, based on what she had been reading in the old man's newspapers, when he was not looking, that possibility seemed quite likely at the moment. In the intervening time, however, the Sovereign had taken a personal interest in the development, and safety, of the planet.

Regardless of the planet's development, the Sovereign had chosen this beautiful world, and the form of the cat, for other reasons. Not so much to see the planet, which she could have done far more effectively from the comfort of a patrol ship, which would have afforded her the ability to see far more of the planet than she was able to experience now, as a companion animal. No, the Sovereign came from a long line of genomorphs, also known as shapeshifters, and found there were many benefits, as well as great comforts, in taking on the form of other creatures; doing so rejuvenated her in ways that the medical technologies of the Alliance could not, extending her life far beyond what could only have been imagined possible, even by the standards of those whose life spans were measured in the thousands of years, as was the norm amongst those who lived on most of the planets within the Felis Alliance.

While it was true that Sovereign Sayoose could have achieved this on Felis Prime, she would not have been able to maintain the transformation for an extended period while also carrying out her duties as the Sovereign. She had sought out the privacy of an unknown planet to allow herself an uninterrupted period in a transformed state while testing her theories regarding the deceptions within the Cadre. Spending uninterrupted years in this alien form provided her body the time it needed to renew itself, which would radically extend her life.

With the eradication of disease through the Advanced Genomic Manipulation Program medical scientists had discovered that the most pernicious disease that affected the body was age itself. Science came to discover that ageing was the result of the body's inability to regenerate the correct types of cells at the appropriate time. While the AGMP had tremendously enhanced the lives of genomorphs from the southern continent of Waylacor, what extended their lives the most was spending time in the form of another creature. As a result of these physical shifts, or changes of form, would come corresponding modifications to genomorph metabolisms which would have a dramatic effect on their cells and their ability to regenerate. It did not hurt that the Sovereign enjoyed the sensation of spending time in the form of a different creature for protracted periods of time. Now, as she was over 121,000 years of age, Sovereign Sayoose did not look a day over thirty.

As a genomorph the Sovereign knew that living as another creature was good for her health, but it was also a sensual, and extremely enjoyable experience; as her cells were rejuvenated she could feel her mind grow stronger with each passing day, knowing that every day spent in the form of this creature would add another several thousand years to her life in humanoid form. She could have taken on the form of a Torgon back on Felis Prime, but the truth of the matter was that she had never been particularly fond of the way the creatures flew through the air. While she loved the creatures, and enjoyed their company as companions from time to time, their form of locomotion frightened her. Cats, on the other hand, were far more docile. She had discovered their existence while reviewing a routine report from Terra from one of the survey vessels that had visited the planet. Data Stream Terra-73X412 showed several examples of the flora and fauna, including companion animals kept by people in their homes; that was when she had decided to make her trip to see the planet for herself.

(*|*)

After Doctor Micholson injected Sayoose with the routine vaccinations, which her immune system immediately neutralized, the examination was officially over. "Once again, you leave me with little to do," the Vet laughed. "All I can say is … I'll see you again in one year," she smiled as Tanya scooped Sayoose from the table and gently carried her back to the reception area. Sayoose quietly sat on the counter, licking her paw, while Tanya paid the bill for the examination. She then allowed herself to be carried out to the car, where she curled up on the front seat and promptly went to sleep.

"Did you hear that, sweetie?" Tanya said to the sleeping cat as she began to drive home, "Doctor Micholson said you're in perfect health!" Sayoose looked out the window and watched as Dragar kept up with their progress thanks to his anti-grav belt and a firm grip on the side of the vehicle. She could not help imagine how annoyed her Prime

Guardian must be at following her in such a manner but figured that introducing him to Tanya would have likely been too much of a shock to the young woman.

"We're going home and have some treats to celebrate, okay?" Tanya continued, oblivious to the passenger that had latched onto her car. She was so happy at the news from the Vet it was hard not to share in the enthusiasm, so Sayoose looked over and mewed sweetly, adding to Tanya's smile. "That's right, my sweet, we're going home now." Sometimes, Sayoose thought to herself, it would be nice to respond to the human, but she had a feeling that if she did want to talk to someone, the old man was probably a better choice.

Tanya's grandfather, had been having some issues with his memory, though Tanya was afraid to admit it was anything beyond the forgetfulness that came with advancing age. He was, after all, in his nineties; who would not forget something at that age, she would ask defensively. Even with the occasional lapse in memory, Tanya would remind people, Gramps could spend hours regaling someone with stories and facts regarding military history and tactics. He knew more than some historians had forgotten. She liked to say that he forgot things that were simply unimportant to him, leaving room for things he wanted to keep at the forefront of his memory. At least, that was what she liked to say; in truth, she was afraid that he was beginning to experience something more serious. Sayoose really liked the old man, and he seemed to like her as well. He would talk to her in a sweet voice, calling her his *Princess* as he stroked her fur while sitting on the front porch of the house on the swinging bench. Sayoose would sit with him there, especially on the rare occasions that Tanya needed some time to work alone, or when she was out.

There had been times, the Sovereign thought, when it would have been possible to speak to him and he would have been fine with it, but what if he told someone? Well, that was the beauty of the idea: who would believe him? *Tell us again about the talking cat, Colonel?* But, she really did not want to get him into trouble, he was a nice old fellow. Still, Sayoose thought to herself, maybe the next time they were alone.

A short while later they were pulling onto the country lane leading to the small house that Tanya shared with her Grandfather. As she opened the door she felt a slight draft behind her and quickly pulled the big oak door shut behind her, making sure it was firmly closed before letting Sayoose out of her arms, though she never worried about the cat escaping: this cat never showed any interest in going out, not even when the door was left open by accident. Even when she had the opportunity to go out, she would ignore it, unless it was to sit on the porch when she and her grandfather out there, or sometimes alone with her grandfather; she was definitely an inside cat, which was just fine with Tanya. Once Sayoose was back in the house she walked to the center of the room where the sun was shining onto a small area rug. After turning around so the sun was on shining her back she curled up and went to sleep in the middle of the sunspot, relishing the warmth as it drifted through the window, the conversation with Dragar still playing through her mind as she drifted off to sleep.

CHAPTER VI ~ VIGIL

"Without question, the ratification of the Pan-Universal Alliance Charter of Rights and Freedoms was the most significant act undertaken by the leaders of the Felis Alliance. Without it, the Alliance was merely an organization dedicated to the creation of vast amounts of wealth, a business without regard for those involved in its production. Once the Charter came into being the Alliance was transformed into an organization that transcended the planetary governments it represented; it took on the role of an overseeing authority which had been granted, by both the member planets and the Stellar Mining Bureau, Executive Powers to oversee Extreme Moral Authority in areas relating to how Citizens conducted themselves while simultaneously codifying their rights and freedoms under the law. It also defined the critical place of workers within the Alliance, guaranteeing them unassailable rights as the Creators of the wealth enjoyed by Citizens living within the Alliance.

"By ending the exploitation of workers, slavery and poverty was abolished on thousands of planets. Since its ratification every planet entering the Felis Alliance agreed to adhere to its precepts, bringing the number of signees within the Alliance to over 13,000 planets. Guaranteed Rights and Freedoms include: All Citizens within the Alliance are to be treated equally under the law in all manners, without exception; Citizens are free to Express Ideas, unless such expression may be deemed harmful to others or promote hatred; all forms of discrimination are expressly forbidden. [...] No Citizen shall possess weapons used within the Unified Armed Services without a Special Dispensation from an Alliance Tribunal, unless they are active members of the UAS, members of the ASIS, or active members of a reserve branch of the UAS.

> *"All Citizens have the right to an education and to attain any number of advanced degrees of their choice, pending qualifications. [...] Citizens shall have free access to quality food, clean potable water, housing, the right to vote for local representation in free elections on their home worlds, as well as having full access to medical care and medicine; none of these shall be denied to any Citizen of the Alliance."*
>
> *[...]*
>
> Excerpted from: *Pan-Universal Alliance Charter of Rights and Freedoms: a History* by Sovereign Martok

(*|*)

By using the anti-gravity belt on his uniform and tethering himself to the small vehicle Dragar had been able to follow the little red car back to the structure from which they had departed without much difficulty. He almost had a mishap before the small vehicle had crossed the Old Iron Bridge when another approaching vehicle came perilously close to dislodging the Guardian from his position. It was a terrible way to travel, he swore to himself, but he had not been willing to use the Long Distance Matter Transporter to travel back to the ship and then have them send him back to the Sovereign's location. This way he was able to keep her in sight for the entire journey. After they had arrived he watched as the young woman carried the Sovereign in through the front door of the small structure and carefully entered behind her, completely concealed by his Personal Shield Device.

Once inside he quickly discovered that she shared the dwelling with another human, a much older male who seemed to be both ancient and relatively harmless. After scanning the building for potential threats Dragar was not pleased to discover that there were two projectile weapons on the premises. One seemed to be a primitive rifle of sorts that employed metallic projectiles that were loaded individually through a breech system. It was not unlike the training weapons used by Initiates of the Alliance Special Combat Armed Response Corps, which fired nonlethal encapsulated plasma rounds. He estimated that the weapon had a range of about one Krenar at best, but Dragar was more concerned about the second weapon: it also fired metallic projectiles; unlike the rifle this was a hand-held device that held a total of nine projectiles. Based on its design it looked as though it would be able to fire all of its projectiles in rapid succession, making its potential for lethality quite serious. Although it had a range of less than 0.5 Krenar, it was still a something that Dragar did not want anywhere near the Sovereign. Unwilling to take any chances, Dragar used his Shield device to fuse the moving parts on both weapons, rendering them unusable. Then, as quietly as he had entered, Dragar left, though Sovereign Sayoose looked up from her spot on the area rug at the shimmering light as it silently moved overhead through the living room.

Once he was back outside Dragar found a suitable observation point in a large oak tree next to the house, which allowed him to remain concealed while close enough to have the Sovereign under constant surveillance. He was not particularly pleased with the prospect of spending an indeterminate amount of time away from home or his fellow Guardians, but at least the Sovereign had been found, and seemed relatively safe. Well, perhaps that was debatable, he thought to himself wryly. He was not quite sure Operations would understand hearing that the Sovereign had taken on the form of a cat, the human version of a Torgon. Dragar stifled a laugh as he thought of how much Factotum Ebla Mar, the Supreme Leader of the Consortium, would appreciate the current state of Sovereign Sayoose: it was often speculated that Mar was cruel enough to even kill the harmless Torgons; he would no doubt find a cat an object worthy of his scorn. Anything that others found adorable Ebla Mar despised, declaring it worthy of destruction.

Factotum Mar had a well-known, and earned, reputation for cruelty and violence across several Sectors of the universe. Unlike the Felis Alliance, which had worked arduously over several millennia to establish itself on the foundations of mutual trust and a reliance upon one another, the Ursus Consortium operated on the principles of conquest, intimidation, and military dominance. Once a planet was invited to join the Alliance they knew they were becoming an important part of a greater whole; they were made aware that they were making an important contribution to the organization which was now vastly superior with them as members than it would be without their presence. Alliance members also knew that each of their Citizens were protected by the Pan-Universal Alliance Charter of Rights and Freedoms. It was a document that was derided and mocked by many living outside of the Alliance, but secretly envied by countless people who were not protected by the rights conferred by the Charter.

Unlike the Alliance, once surveyors from the Ursus Consortium had identified a planet they felt was ready for membership within their organization they would initiate talks with a delegation of its leaders. In contrast with the Alliance, talks with the Consortium were only a ruse for the imminent military takeover that was already underway. What the leaders of the planet in question would not know was that the Ursus Consortium already had a large contingent of their Galactic Armed Forces in place, ready to support their negotiating position to convince the leaders that they wanted to join the Consortium. It was routine for the GAF to fly under a misleading flag, calling themselves the *Galactic Freedom Forces*, which was a cruel joke more than anything else; they were the military bullies of the Factotum, used to force unsuspecting planets into joining the Consortium. Those did not accept the invitation would face the consequences for their resistance. It was the Factotum's way of saying, *Join, or we'll destroy you; then take what we want afterwards*. A compliment of the Galactic Freedom Forces would typically arrive with at least two Battlecruisers, two Star Cruisers, and one Carrier, taking up orbits with their weapons trained on the main cities of the planet, ready to rain down the end of days for that world should their leaders decide they were uninterested in accepting the terms being offered by the Consortium negotiators.

By the time the Consortium and the planet's leaders had entered into the serious stage of negotiation the planetary contingent were usually informed by their aides of the presence of the alien forces in orbit since the Consortium made no efforts at concealing themselves. It was a tactic of the Consortium to allow whatever sensors were available on the planet, or in orbit, to detect the threats that had arrived over their heads; they wanted the people they were negotiating with to be afraid of them as they believed it provided an advantage in the negotiations. Consortium negotiators were not afraid of having their underhanded tactics discovered as they relied upon the intimidation provided by their display of force. What they truly feared was returning to their home world without having a planet becoming a signatory of what they referred to as the Consortium's Treaty of Planetary Association. Disappointing Factotum Ebla Mar was, above all else, something a Consortium negotiator could not live with, especially since the price for failure was often summary execution. Consortium negotiators only failed once in their career.

Most of the time the presence of so much firepower considerably aided in the satisfactory conclusion of the signing of the

Treaty of Planetary Association between the Consortium and the planet in question, though calling it a treaty was truly a matter of convenience; once it had been signed, the planet, and all those living on it, were essentially enslaved. Planets rich in natural resources were the first to be targeted by the Consortium, unless it had been declared a Protectorate of the Alliance by the Sovereign, although even that had not stopped Factotum Effris Mar, Ebla Mar's grandfather and predecessor, in the past. Effris Mar, and his many predecessors, had managed to absorb a few Protectorates into the Consortium by taking advantage of the fact that they had not been heavily protected when Consortium forces arrived, forcing Alliance forces to withdrawal. Consortium Factotums had counted on the belief that Sovereign Martok did not relish the prospect of an open war between their two organizations. It had seemed that the Consortium knew that the Alliance vessels guarding Protectorates in the past had standing orders that they were to retreat in the face of superior forces, unless they knew that reinforcements were immediately available. It was something that the Factotums had taken advantage of quite often, much to the dismay of many Alliance commanders.

Then things changed: while it had not been the policy of Sovereign Martok to send reinforcements for the protection of many Protectorates because of his reluctance to engage the Consortium in a conflict, when Sayoose ascended to the position of Sovereign, 27,000 years ago, the policy of abandoning Protectorates to the Consortium was revised. Sovereign Sayoose decided that it was in the best interests of both the Protectorates and the Alliance to do as much as feasible in order to prevent the Consortium from exploiting the Protectorates. Since then it had not been possible for the Ursus Consortium to absorb any planet that had been declared a Protectorate of the Alliance.

Factotum Ebla Mar still suspected, as did others, that Sovereign Sayoose did not possess the fortitude to put the lives of others on the line, if only because she had never committed to a full-scale battle, but he was also aware of the fact that the forces of the Unified Armed Services of the Alliance were far superior to anything that the Consortium possessed. Even if the Consortium were to utilize their entire fleet in an assault against the home world of the Alliance the UAS would have little trouble deflecting the assault, leaving plenty of vessels in reserve to defend the rest of the Alliance. At the same time, the idea of committing to an all-out assault was something to which Ebla Mar, or his predecessors, had few compunctions. In the mind of Ebla Mar sending ten thousand men to their deaths, or even one hundred thousand, was merely something that had to be done in order to attain the goals of the Consortium.

If some had to die in order to fulfill those goals, that was the price required. A Factotum simply looked at it as the cost of doing business; the needs of the Consortium came before all else, certainly above the rights of the individual. Ebla Mar did not consider himself soft like the Sovereign of the Felis Alliance, a mere woman. He had been born a warrior, and would always be a warrior. His father had been a warrior, as had his grandfather, Factotum Effris Mar. Ebla Mar knew that no woman had ever served as Factotum of the Consortium; none ever would: women were incapable of fulfilling the responsibilities of the office.

Having been raised on Ursus Minor, the home world of the Ursus Consortium, in the capital city of Hydra, Ebla Mar knew what it meant to live through hardship, though much of it had been self-imposed in order to improve himself and gain battle and leadership experience. Hydra had areas where only the hardiest could survive due to the horrific crime rates and terrifying living conditions. Mar's family lived in the First Quarter of the city, where he could have grown up totally insulated from those hardships, instead, he had sought them out; from a young age he enjoyed spending his time running with the gangs in the Fourth Quarter. It was the poorest, most violent portion of the city, filled with a number of gangs and other criminals that roved freely. Ebla Mar had joined the gangs which called themselves *Gujos*, a word which meant *Killers* or *Wicked Ones* in the dialect spoken in the city of Hydra, and the members of the gang spent their days living up to their name. It did not take long for Ebla Mar to rise to the top, like the natural leader his grandfather had recognized him to be when he had recommended the young Ebla to the *Seventeen* to become the next leader of the Consortium, succeeding him as Factotum.

Ebla had first become a member of one of the local gangs, which killed anyone that entered their territory, using blackmail, and graft to develop their private kingdom in the capital of the poverty-stricken Fourth Quarter. Then Mar used his connections with his grandfather to further manipulate the group, ultimately becoming the leader of all the *Gujos*, who were, for the first time, united under one charismatic, maniacal leader.

Ebla Mar's ascent as leader had all been thanks to the introduction of a powerful and highly addictive substance that his grandfather, Factotum Effris Mar, had provided in order for his grandson to gain control over the vicious gangs. Consortium scientists had developed Neurotetrahexadrine several hundred years ago as a psychoactive drug that was also highly addictive. It was primarily developed as to provide Consortium troops with an advantage over their opponents during their missions. It had been a simple concept: when administered in controlled doses, the drug, known as NTHD, allowed users to perform with optimal efficiency, performing far better than they might under normal circumstances.

It was also discovered that NTHD had the extra benefit of enhancing aggression, making a soldier far more effective in battle. Unfortunately, there were also some serious dangers associated with the use of the drug. After it was introduced into several active battalions of the Galactic Armed Forces it had been discovered that while under the stress of combat there were several instances of spontaneous catastrophic intracranial bleeds, causing many members of the battalions to suddenly die when blood vessels in their brains ruptured due to the massive increased pressures caused by the drug in their systems and a corresponding weakening of the surrounding tissues.

As interested in the program as Consortium Commanders had been, they were forced to abandon it nearly as quickly as it had begun, but not before several hundred lives and numerous ships had been lost.

Consortium scientists did not want to give up on the idea, however, and kept pursuing the dream of enhancing their troops with drugs. After altering the formula of the NTHD a new molecule was created which was named Trexhexadrine. TRAX, as it was called, proved to be nearly as effective, but not in the way the scientists had hoped. One clear disadvantage of TRAX, in the opinion of the military, was that it did not affect the aggression center of the brain, which made it useless for the troops. Scientists postulated that the reason for this was as a result of the changes that had been made to make it safe for consumption. It turned out that the component of the drug that affected the aggression center of the brain was the same component that was killing users. But, it was quickly discovered that there were other, even more important uses, for this new drug.

Throughout his tenure as Factotum, Effris Mar, Ebla Mar's grandfather, had been hearing rumors of discontent and dissent spreading throughout the Consortium. Many people were displeased with the way things were being done, and they were demanding change. Something had to be done or the despotic leader of the Consortium would be facing its greatest challenge, and that would not be coming from the massive Felis Alliance. If the people of the Consortium rose up and demanded reforms, Factotum Effris Mar would have to respond by either answering their demands, or conducting a massive purge, the likes of which had never been seen. It was an insufferable situation, but Trexhexadrine provided the solution.

One of side effects of TRAX was that it created a feeling of euphoria that lasted for almost an entire day. One dose was enough to keep someone in a state of bliss, completely at peace, without any deleterious effects. When using the drug in controlled, recreational doses, it was found that this completely blinded people to the dreadful conditions they were living under within the Consortium, allowing them to accept the things that they had otherwise been enraging by were it not for the mind-altering drugs.

At the order of Factotum Effris Mar the drug was made available on every planet in the Consortium, and it was given away free of charge. It was disguised as a dietary supplement, something that even children should be given as part of their regular diets, and most people took the drug without question. Shortly after the program began the rumors of dissent disappeared. There were, however, some people who were, for whatever reason, reluctant to take the supplement, but the scientists determined that only a micro-dose was required to keep the population content in regards to the situations under which they lived, preventing them from expressing any desires to rise up against the despotic leadership. It was concluded that the appropriate dose could be delivered through the water systems, making it possible to reach virtually every person living within the Consortium, even those already taking full dosage in their daily allotment. Even if someone missed their daily supplement they would still receive the micro-dose through the water system. Dissent was defeated.

For this reason, the rule of the Factotums endured without opposition, and the current despotic regime of Factotum Ebla Mar was able to continue without the threat of being overthrown.

While NTHD had been abandoned for use in the military, the Factotum willingly provided it to his grandson to help him gain control over the fanatical *Gujos*. Neither were particularly concerned about the health or welfare of the brutal gang members, nor would they have shed a tear over one, or more, of the bullies dying from their use of the drug. Control was the only thing that mattered to him, along with maintaining his dynasty within the Consortium. Effris knew that his son, Effrin Mar, was a weak-minded imbecile who was unqualified emotionally to take over as Factotum. Effris had been grooming the young Ebla to be his successor since he had first proudly observed the cruel nature of the boy when he was still quite young.

Effris had also been impressed by his grandson's intelligence, but also knew that intelligence was not the most important part of the equation for a Factotum. His own son had been a smart young man, but had developed to become the worst kind of weakling: he was disappointingly kind to others and showed a disturbing amount of sympathy to people, even if they had nothing to offer him in return. It was an insufferable characteristic in someone who might potentially be the future leader of the Consortium.

It was a despicable situation and had grieved the Factotum for some time, but not enough that it had prevented him from having the man put to death once he knew his grandson would serve as a fine successor to his position. He also knew that the *Seventeen* would eagerly accept his recommendation that Ebla be permitted to take over as Supreme Leader once they saw in him what he was seeing. With enough time to groom the boy, it would be a simple choice.

By the time Ebla Mar had gained control over the eleven fragmented factions of *Gujos* in the Fourth Quarter he had command of nearly two thousand *Gujos*, each of whom was fanatically dedicated to the dynamic young leader. They were also completely addicted to NTHD, which Ebla was, of course, now providing thanks to the largess of his grandfather. They understood who their new leader was, and where he was from, but they also recognized that he had something that they craved: strength and leadership. He could also provide them with something that they lacked, which was legitimacy. Ebla also guaranteed a steady, uninterrupted supply of the drug which each of them had become hopelessly addicted to and could not live without, even if it had cost some of them their lives. That was something Ebla had counted on when he started providing the *Gujos* with NTHD: he knew they were so self-absorbed they would neither notice nor care about one of their comrades dying, even if it happened right next to them. None of them would question the circumstances of the death, and they certainly would not blame their demise on the drug that made them feel so wonderful.

When Effris Mar died and Ebla was selected to become the Factotum by the *Seventeen*, the secretive group that controlled everything from the shadows of the Consortium, select members of the *Gujos* became his personal guard and enforcers, while others became members of his private army. What Factotum Ebla Mar desired, his enforces provided, regardless of the cost to others. A new reign of terror had begun with the rule of Ebla Mar, and its focal point was the home world of the Ursus Consortium, Ursus Minor.

What Ebla Mar did not fully comprehend was that unlike himself, the Sovereign of the Felis Alliance was not an absolute ruler. It was possible for things to happen within the Alliance without requiring direct orders from the Sovereign. While large military operations required direct orders from the Sovereign, when it came to guaranteeing the security of individual planetary members within the Alliance, that was something within the jurisdiction of the Governors or Chancellors of the individual planets, who were empowered to request whatever aid they might require from the Military Commanders posted to their Sectors.

At the same time, Commander Dragar knew that if there were any overt danger posed by the Consortium the Sovereign would never hesitate in ordering the deploying of the appropriate military forces and interventions. He knew that she was not fond of violence, unlike her counterpart in the Consortium, but she was also not as afraid of conflict as Factotum Mar believed, nor would she shy away from it, not if the lives of Alliance members were threatened. When it came to the Unified Armed Services of the Alliance Sovereign Sayoose was supremely confident in the skills of the forces available to her, and she believed in their abilities to defend the Alliance. Had that not been the case she surely would not have survived as long as she had in her position. Dragar shook his head as he thought about the brutality of the Consortium and how they maintained control over the planets under their sphere of influence. His entire life had been spent under the freedom of the Alliance, but he knew many, including several friends and colleagues, who had come over from former Consortium planets that had been liberated by the Alliance. Liberation of a planet did not usually involve too much violence, but that was only due to the Sovereign wisely sending at least ten ships for each one the Consortium would have guarding the planet in question, along with several divisions of the ASCAR, which was more than sufficient to dissuade Consortium forces from pursuing a battle.

Of course, any adversary with half a brain showed fear when they knew the ASCAR were coming, but most of the time there was no warning. These commandos had been trained to attack using stealth techniques, coming at the enemy in such a way that their opponents never even knew they were under attack, until it was too late and the battle had already been lost. An entire battalion of one thousand men could encircle an enemy camp and defeat it, often without even firing a shot, which was how the ASCAR had become known as the Ghost Corps, and it was a name they wore proudly. Once a cadet completed the rigorous training program they were welcomed into the Corps with the awarding of the ASCAR insignia, a yellow lightning bolt striking a Red Giant Star, with the words *Ghost Corps* stitched beneath the star in small script while *Alliance Special Combat Armed Response Corps* was emblazoned across the top of the insignia. For most members of the Corps, receiving their patch during the Presentation Ceremony was the proudest moment of their lives.

Once they had made it into the Corps the commandos were assigned to protect the various Alliance planets, and they were always prepared for the worst. They did not care about what others thought about the leadership of the Alliance, it was their job to protect the planets within the Alliance, as well as the Alliance itself. A special short division of 5,000 members, known as the Home Guard and was assigned to protect Felis Prime. It was under the command of Major General Scarth, an accomplished Ionian who had much in common with Tactical Sergeant Brem, both of whom hailed from the same home world. Regardless of how some may have viewed the leadership of the Alliance, nobody in the Consortium, particularly Factotum Ebla Mar, seemed to be in much of a rush to see their forces pitted against ASCAR commandos. For those who had managed to earn the insignia of the Corps, the thought of a war with the Consortium was merely another possibility for which they had trained. If asked about their prospects against the Galactic Armed Forces they would provide the standard Corps reply, "We're prepared, and we're ready: bring 'em on." In truth, they were ready, and more than prepared. Dragar only hoped it would not be necessary for his old friends to go to war too soon, although he was cognizant of the fact that events were constantly changing, bringing the chances of a full-blown conflict closer than they had been in thousands of years.

(*|*)

As he watched the building in which he knew the Sovereign to be safely ensconced Dragar decided it was time to contact Helios-2 and make his report. Once Operations had been contacted he might be able to relax a bit knowing there would be some protection for this planet thanks to the orders of the Sovereign. It was time to let the Cadre know they were not alone in ruling the vast Alliance, though he was certain that particular bit of information would come as some disappointment to the First Counselor, who had seemed, in the opinion of Commander Dragar, to have been taking a bit too much pleasure in the absence of the Sovereign. Regar's role as the First Counselor of the Cadre had never been to act as a substitute for the Sovereign but rather as one of her advisors in matters of leadership relating to the running of the Alliance. Dragar shook his head as he reminded himself, not for the first time, that Sovereign Sayoose had once been in the same position that First Counselor Regar presently held. He did not know the circumstances behind how the Sovereign had been selected to become the First Counselor of the Cadre, but he did know that she had been asked to enter the position after a remarkably successful career within the Unified Armed Services, which was something she never spoke of in their times together. He shook his head at the thought; it was unusual for the Sovereign to keep things from him, but he had always believed that if there was something he needed to know, in time, he would be told. It would have been easy enough for Dragar to discover what the former First Counselor of the Cadre for Sovereign Martok had done before assuming her new post, but he had too much respect for the Sovereign to invade her privacy by going behind her back in that manner.

No, he thought to himself. What was important was the fact that she had served as the First Counselor of the Cadre to Sovereign Martok, and had ascended to the position of Sovereign when he had retired, just over 27,000 years ago. She had been the obvious choice as the replacement for Sovereign Martok, considering she was highly regarded by the Sovereign, as well as the rest of the Cadre, and every dignitary with whom she had encountered or worked with from across the Alliance. Everyone had agreed that First Counselor Sayoose was eminently qualified to assume the role of Sovereign, and the Stellar Mining Bureau agreed. When the Board of Governors made their decision it was without equivocation and unanimous: First Counselor Sayoose had been the only name put forward for the position. Dragar could not imagine First Counselor Regar receiving the same treatment from the Stellar Mining Bureau should something happen to Sovereign Sayoose.

He shook his head again, thrusting the thought from his mind: nothing was going to happen to the Sovereign, not while he or the other Guardians were alive and had anything to say regarding the situation. Not for the first time he wondered how Regar had even become the First Counselor of the Cadre. He had also served in the Unified Armed Services, but by all accounts his record had been less than sensational. Having attained the rank of Captain, his career had stagnated and he made the move to the administrative side of the Alliance as soon as possible. From what Dragar had been able to learn, Regar had always desired to work within the bureaucratic infrastructure of the massive Alliance; the military had merely served as his means of achieving that goal. According to the traditions of the Alliance there was nothing wrong with that, but Dragar was beginning to wonder whether or not that policy might be reexamined given the way things seemed to be working out.

During the extended absence of Sovereign Sayoose the First Counselor seemed to have forgotten that his role was supposed to be that of an Advisor, not leader; a fact that seemed to have slipped the mind of the ambitious bureaucrat. Dragar shook his head again at the memory of their last encounter; still, at the time he had believed the man to be mostly harmless, but he had been rubbing the Prime Guardian the wrong way, never a wise when you knew with whom you were dealing. Fortunately, for First Counselor Regar, he had recalled that Dragar was not only the Sovereign's Prime Guardian, he was also her First Advisor, a position which afforded him extraordinary access and privilege. Crossing him was never a judicious thing to do, especially when it came to the safety and wellbeing of the Sovereign. Now, having received the message from Fleet Commander Marshal Salzat and the First Counselor's blatant attempt to usurp the authority of the Sovereign, Dragar was seriously beginning to wonder just how far the man could be trusted. Based on the message the Sovereign had entrusted him with it seemed obvious that she no longer trusted her First Counselor.

It was time to make contact. As soon as Dragar initiated the transmission Helios-2 responded. Brem's rich baritone came through the receiver implanted behind his right ear as clearly as though the faithful Tactical Sergeant were standing right next to him, "What news, Commander, do you need us to come there to rescue you?" his deep voice sounded mildly concerned. Dragar knew it was all feigned; both Brem and Pertu knew that he was more than capable of taking care of himself, even on a planet as primitive as this, "Yeah, the Captain and I were beginning to wonder if it was going to be necessary to send a Tracker after you," he grunted, "or if we would have to call in the Fighting Fifth, to rescue your sorry ass," the sound of laughter came roaring into his ear. Dragar winced at the mention of the Fighting Fifth, his old battalion, which he had commanded for over five thousand years.

Dragar bristled at the thought of a Tracker being sent after him. A Tracker Device, or an ATD, as it was known in the Corps, was an Automated Tracking Device that could be launched from the ship. After entering the atmosphere an ATD would seek out whatever it had been programmed to find; Trackers could also be used to survey the planet until it was time to return to their launch point or base of operations. Trackers were equipped with a power unit that provided them with enough energy to last up to thirty days, though the duration of their missions rarely required that much energy. Dragar grunted at the thought of having one of the head-sized devices searching for him. Besides, he was not lost, nor did he need to have any of Brem's toys running after him.

"No," he replied quietly, "there's no need to send in the Fifth, and unless you want me to have some target practice, I don't need any Tracker either," he gave a mirthless laugh, "unless you step your sorry ass down here," Brem's laughter was stifled at the jibe. "I'm reporting in that the Sovereign has been located; contact has been initiated."

This time it was Pertu who responded, obviously not willing to suffer through any more of Brem's shenanigans, "That's great news, Commander," she said, her raspy voice filled with enthusiasm, "when do we transport the two of you up and return to Felis Prime?" her voice registered the typical impatience of a pilot who became easily bored with the routines of maintaining an orbit rather than hurtling through space at seemingly impossible speeds.

"Not just yet, I'm afraid, Captain Pertu," Dragar replied formally to show her this was about business and he was not joking around. "Sovereign Sayoose is safe," he continued, maintaining the seriousness of his tone, "but, for the present time, she wants to remain on this planet," he struggled with whether to reveal anything about her physical transformation, or her decision to play the part of a companion animal to a human, but decided against it, continuing with his report.

"She would like you to convey a message to Operations on Felis Prime, to be delivered directly to the Cadre: first, inform them that the Sovereign is fine; she also has instructed that the Cadre is hereby ordered to aggressively defend each and every Protectorate, and every Alliance member, regardless of the cost," he paused for a second, "is that understood?"

"Yes, Commander," Pertu replied, her voice upbeat again. She was about to ask another question, but Dragar cut her off before she could say anything.

"There's another message," Dragar continued, his voice conveying the weight of the message. "This one is to be sent to Fleet Commander Marshal Salzat, and is a Priority One, Eyes Only Fleet Commander Message." Dragar dictated the message that the Sovereign had given him to deliver and both Captain Pertu and Tactical Sergeant Brem responded with silence. They could not believe that the Sovereign had essentially ordered the Fleet Commander to ignore any communications he might receive from the Cadre. It was an unprecedented move, but at the same time, it seemed completely reasonable considering the last message the Marshal had sent that had originated from the First Counselor of the Cadre.

"First Counselor Regar is up to something," Brem whispered to Pertu.

"That's not your problem right now, soldier," Dragar hissed, smiling to himself. He knew that his friend had forgotten that the channel on the communication system was still open.

"Sorry, sir," the chastised Tactical Sergeant replied, "I only meant ..."

"I know what you meant, and I want to wrap my hands around his throat to, but we have a job to do, right here, and that's protecting the Sovereign. For now, I'll be remaining down here, close to her; there's no perceivable dangers in the area. There are relatively few people in the vicinity, and there are no buildings nearby, so I should be fine. I don't think the two of you need to be hanging around up there; I can remain in contact as required..."

He was about to go on, but Brem burst in, the chastising he had received a moment ago clearly forgotten, "Now you just wait one second, Commander," he barked out, sounding like the Tactical Sergeant that had earned so much respect in the Corps for so many years, "If you think we're just going to leave both you *and* the Sovereign on that primitive planet, just because you *think* there's no danger, well

... you've got another thing coming my friend. Remember, you weren't the only Guardian to serve in the Corps," he grunted as finished.

Nothing more needed to be said: no member of the ASCAR would knowingly abandon another member, even at risk to their own life and limb. As Commander of the Guardians Dragar was impressed at the fierce loyalty his team displayed for one another; he knew that each member would do anything in order to save the life of one of their comrades, not to mention what they would do for the Sovereign. Brem had risked his life more times than could be counted while in the Corps, having been recognized for his heroics by being awarded the coveted Golden Cluster, with Distinction, on four separate occasions. The citation was given to anyone within the Unified Armed Services who displayed distinguished bravery in the service of the Alliance. It was the highest military honor that could be awarded, below the Beryllium Cluster, which was awarded for extreme valor and heroics, though it was usually presented posthumously.

"Alright," Dragar replied, slightly exasperated, "look," his voice grew a bit softer, "remain in orbit, for now, just make sure you remain shielded. From what I've seen from down here, this planet may be closer to being fully technically developed than our sensors led us to believe from our ..."

Brem's voice cut him off, "Commander, there's some sort of aircraft approaching, vector 270 degrees, altitude of fifteen Krenar, speed ..." the pause was short, but long enough for Dragar to extract his monocular from the breast pocket of his uniform and aim it in the direction of the approaching aircraft. "By Caiphus, it's speed is *nine hundred Krenar*," Brem whispered into the receiver, sounding amazed at what he was monitoring from the ship.

It was easy to see the speeding aircraft through his monocular as it tore through the clear blue sky. Dragar guessed by its size and speed that it was of some military variety as he looked up, seeing the twin contrails from the engines as the plane raced across the sky, breaking the sound barrier in the process. He flinched as the shockwave reached his ears.

"Whatever that was, it wasn't about us," Dragar commented quietly. As he finished the door of the building burst open and he watched as the woman raced out onto the porch to stare up at the sky for a moment. She seemed upset at the noise the aircraft had made. Dragar could only imagine what the shockwave must have felt like inside the building and wondered how the Sovereign was enjoying the planet now.

"How do you know it wasn't about you?" Brem challenged.

Replying quietly, "Unless they have scanning equipment at least as sensitive as ours, which I doubt quite sincerely," this elicited a grunt from Brem, "that aircraft was definitely going somewhere, and we just happened to be under its course. There have been other aircraft, but at much higher altitudes. But, what just flew overhead might challenge one of the old Ripper Class fighters, with Brem flying, of course," he laughed quietly, slipping the monocular back into its pocket in his uniform.

Ripper Class fighters had been a mistake from the beginning, but they had performed well in space. It was only when they entered the atmosphere of a planet that the fighters began to fly as though they were dragging thousand ton anchors. Their maneuvering ability was greatly reduced and the aircraft had tendencies to stall mid-flight, which was a critical problem with their design. Stalling, accompanied by an annoying tendency to fall from the sky, was the last thing a pilot wanted to experience while flying over an alien landscape. It did not take long before the Alliance decided to completely replace the Ripper Class with an entirely new class of fighters, many of which were still in use as trainers.

"Oh, you're hilarious, Commander," came the gruff reply from Brem, "I've flown those Rippers; I'll show you what I can do with one," he was ready to rage on but Dragar cut him off.

"Relax, I'm only kidding," he chuckled again, "just send those messages to Operations and Fleet Commander Salzat. I'm going to keep my eyes on the Sovereign." He thought for a moment, considering some of the things they had discussed, and what they had not discussed, then added, "On second thought, I don't want you in orbit after all, I want you to carry out a patrol to the edge of this galaxy and ..." he paused, referring to the information on his wrist device which contained data about the other Green Zone planets in the Sector, "make sure there isn't anything going on with any of the other Green Zone planets in this Sector." Dragar paused for a moment as he looked again at the building, thinking he had seen some more movement, but there had been nothing. Tanya had closed the door and everything was secure.

"Maintain shielded status and radio silence once you leave orbit, unless using coded contact with me or Operations on appropriate channels. Make contact at standard intervals; is that clear?" This time there was nothing for Brem or Pertu to argue with; he had issued an operational order, something they were sworn to uphold. If the Sovereign was safe, which Dragar had indicated she was, they had no reason not to obey his command.

"Yes sir," came the curt reply from Pertu, "we'll send the messages immediately," she paused for the shortest moment, "will notify as soon as Ops responds and depart once we've reported back to you."

"Thank you, Captain," he replied, smiling. He knew that it would not take too long for the message to be received by Operations at the Communications Array on Felis Prime. If he knew Administrator Marta well, and he did, she would hand-deliver it to First Counselor Regar herself, considering it had information pertaining to the wellbeing of the Sovereign. They would likely reply within the hour, if not sooner. Looking at the chronometer on his wrist device, he figured he would not have long to wait before the reply was received through Trans-Space.

"Thank you, Captain. Dragar out."

Dragar returned his attention to the building containing the Sovereign. It seemed to be constructed of hardened brown and black objects, arranged in an attractive interlocking pattern of rows. An occasional window was scattered around each side of the structure, and there was one front and one rear door. From his vantage point he was only able to observe the front door, but he had a view of the back door through a small camera he had placed on the fence that wrapped around the backyard, allowing him to see the entire back of the structure from the small view screen on his wrist device. Looking in through the side window, into what was the living room of the house he was able to clearly see the Sovereign, curled up on the lap of the young woman, sleeping contentedly. Dragar was confused as to the nature of the strange relationship between the Sovereign and this young human, but he had to respect her wishes. If this was how she wanted to spend her time away from the Alliance, who was he to say otherwise?

(*|*)

When Dragar had been appointed Prime Guardian to Sovereign Sayoose they had spent many hours getting to know each other, which included his learning about her origins and abilities as a genomorph. She had been an easy woman to become friends with right from the start of their relationship. Her gregarious character made it seem to those who were introduced to the small, dark skinned woman with captivating eyes that they were long-lost friends from the moment they had been introduced to the Sovereign. Even though she stood only a few fingers taller than five feet in height, coming to just about the middle of the imposing chest of her Prime Guardian, her personality both illuminated and captivated any room she entered. Every eye would be on the Sovereign thanks to the intense magnetism of her personality and every conversation taking place would stop in order to hear what was on her mind whenever she spoke.

Her main popularity, however, did not come from the way she dominated conversations but rather from her ability to listen. Sovereign Sayoose would meet with people and listen to what they had to say, even if their opinions differed from what she believed. She would always say, "One cannot grow unless your mind is opened to hearing the ideas of others." Even before Sayoose had been selected to be the Sovereign of the Alliance Dragar knew that Sovereign Martok had leaned on her wisdom far more than that of any of his other advisors. Sovereign Martok had also relied on the advice of his own Prime Guardian, an impressive man named Tallis who had been killed after saving the life of the Sovereign. It was after that incident that the Sovereign had decided it was time to retire. Regardless the amount of advice he had received from Tallis, Martok never appointed him his First Advisor. That post had been created by Sovereign Sayoose, specifically for Commander Dragar.

During their numerous long meetings and private conversations, after Dragar had been selected to become her Prime Guardian, and many years later her First Advisor, Sovereign Sayoose had been candid about her past and her nature as a genomorph. While numerous variations in the humanoid genome were not unheard of, the shapeshifter, or genomorph, was without question, the most unique genomic variations to have evolved within the constraints of the human genome on any of the planets currently within the Alliance. Sovereign Sayoose hailed from Tarlos II in the Cara Nebula, located in Sector 0001, the same Sector in which Felis Magoris was located. It was one of the oldest members of the Alliance, with many of its Citizens serving in high-level Administrative positions thanks to their highly developed analytical skills.

Only those born on the southern continent of Waylacor had the ability to shapeshift, and it seemed to be an ability unique to that one planet. When a female genomorph had children with someone born from another part of Tarlos II, or anywhere else, the child might inherit limited abilities to shift, allowing themselves to alter their appearance in small ways, but they would not inherit the full abilities of the original parent. After that, the abilities would be diminished after subsequent generations, until they were completely eliminated after four or five generations, but shapeshifting fathers did not confer their abilities to a non-shapeshifting mate.

Perhaps the greatest advantage genomorphs possessed was their ability to live far longer than any others thanks to their ability to completely regenerate their cellular structures at far greater rates than any other humanoids. This ability had been discovered several millennia before and, since then, had been regularly exploited as a means of extending the lives of those living on the continent to such an extent that Waylacorians had begun limiting the number of offspring they produced in order to avoid overpopulating their beautiful continent.

At the same time, the Sovereign had confided in Dragar, thanks to their extended life-spans it was possible for a Waylacorian female to bear a child at virtually any time during her life, until the aging process began to manifest itself in such a way that it became impossible for them to safely carry a child. Age was an inevitability, even when life was as prolonged as it was for those who were born on Waylacor the Sovereign had told her Guardian, but for a genomorph like herself, now entering her 1,000th century of life, the worst parts of the aging process were not expected to begin expressing themselves for several more millennia, especially if she continued the 'therapy' of spending time as another creature every several centuries, which substantially extended her lifespan.

It had been thanks, in part, to the discoveries made through the Waylacorians and their abilities to slow their aging processes that Alliance scientists had developed the Advanced Genomic Manipulation Program, which ultimately helped trillions by eliminating disease and the ravages of age from the human genome. That alone demonstrated one of the benefits of being a member of the Felis Alliance: when signing a treaty to join the Alliance your planet became part of something far greater than it would have ever been on its own, which included having access to the advantages of medical and scientific discoveries that existed on worlds in Sectors scattered across the known universe.

Dragar smiled to himself as he recalled his introduction to the Sovereign. He had to admit, it had all seemed outrageous to him at the time: how could this small, young-looking woman possibly be over 100,000 years old? He had, of course, heard of Tarlos II, as had most people in the Alliance, but few ever encountered the shapeshifters, or genomorphs as they preferred to be called. Information regarding their lives, and their lifespans, was held as closely-guarded secrets by those who hailed from Waylacor. Dragar had considered it an honor to have been taken into her confidence so easily, but Sovereign Sayoose was like that, and it helped their friendship develop into something which he cherished. All the more reason why he was so confused about the Sovereign's reasons behind leaving Felis Prime without having confided in him or the other Guardians regarding her concerns about the First Counselor.

Had the Sovereign expressed a desire to leave Felis Prime for a vacation or any other reason Dragar would have done anything for her in order to honor her wishes. That was his job, as a Guardian, as well as that of Pertu and Brem, now orbiting above the planet in Helios-2. All she had to do was ask and they would have taken her anywhere in the universe, anywhere except Ursus Minor, the home world of the Ursus Consortium, or any of the planets under their control. Even so, Dragar had seen how much the Sovereign had been pained by his concern for her, which had warmed his heart. It was impossible to be angry at such a wonderful woman, even if she had gone through so much effort to elude their protection.

He returned his attentions to the building where the Sovereign was, looking through the window and watching for a few moments as she sat on the couch next to the human female. He could not help but smile as the single most powerful individual in the known universe opened her eyes and seemed to look directly at him; she then stretched and let out a big yawn, then rolled onto her back, allowing the human to stroke her exposed belly. Dragar shook his head in disbelief as he prepared himself for a long period of vigilance. His training had prepared him for this sort of thing; discomfort was of no concern to him, nor was being cold: the only thing that mattered to an ASCAR commando was fulfilling their mission, for which Dragar was eminently prepared. Having to spend time in a tree was merely something he would have to do in order to accomplish that mission.

CHAPTER VII ~ VACATION

"Anyone with a desire to become a member of the ASCAR, the Alliance Special Combat Armed Response Corps, required a level of commitment that was often tested to the extreme. Initiates were required to demonstrate uncommon capabilities with all weaponry, demonstrating proficiencies on each weapon system used within the Corps, the training for which was only available to Initiates who were training to become members of the Corps. What the Corps valued above everything else, even beyond Initiates becoming superbly trained warriors and being prepared for any contingency that may arise in battle, was that their commandos possess uncommon minds: it was always understood that nobody was expected to go into battle as a mindless automaton; the Corps did not use fighting machines.

"If the Unified Armed Services had desired to use fighting machines, or Synthetic Intelligent Living Systems as soldiers, or commandos, they had that option and could have done so, but it had been decided that SILS were not permitted to carry weapons or serve in the UAS: only humans could serve. Those who had completed their training to become members of the Corps were considered too valuable to lose their lives through blindly accepting irrational or inappropriate commands when reasoned thought might well have saved their lives. Commandos received extensive training and knew they had the right and responsibility to question any situation and order which they believed might ultimately endanger their lives and the lives of those under their command.

"Of course, the Chain of Command was still considered sacrosanct, but nobody wanted to see a Platoon, or worse, lost due to some idiot having issued some orders that their Sergeant knew to be poorly

conceived, and which should have been questioned or
countermanded from the start. By not blindly following
orders, both throughout the Unified Armed Services, and
especially in the Corps, many valuable lives had been
saved."

[...]

Excerpted from: *Warriors with Minds: the*
Alliance Special Combat Armed Response Corps, by
ASCAR Commandant Llashar, Director of ASCAR Training
Facility, Tarak III.

(*|*)

Neither Pertu nor Brem were pleased with the idea of leaving
orbit now that the Sovereign had been found, but Commander Dragar
had not only insisted, he had issued a direct order. As their Commander
that meant there was nothing they could do but obey, particularly if
they wanted to avoid his wrath, and nobody wanted to incur the wrath
of Commander Dragar. Of course, they could disobey the order if they
had reason to believe there was a compelling reason for them not to
follow his command, but the Commander Dragar knew better than to
issue reckless commands to his comrades. He had been one of the most
decorated commandos in the history of the ASCAR, having been
awarded the Golden Cluster, with Distinction, on two occasions, as well
as the Bleeding Heart, for being injured in the line of duty, on three
separate occasions. On top of that, he was the only member of either
the ASCAR, or the Unified Armed Services, to have ever been awarded
the coveted Beryllium Cluster on *two* separate occasions. It was the
highest honor that could be conferred upon any soldier within the
Unified Armed Services, and was most frequently awarded after the
death of the individual.

One such example was Lieutenant Commander Tallis, the Prime
Guardian of Sovereign Martok; he had been posthumously awarded the
Beryllium Cluster after saving the life of the Sovereign. Thanks to the
security briefings he had received before the conference began, when
an assassin from the Ursus Consortium infiltrated a conference the
Sovereign had been attending on Altus 9 Lieutenant Commander Tallis
had been able to recognize the man, and had been able to save the life
of Sovereign Martok. Even though the Sovereign had been seriously

injured by the blast of the plasma grenade used in the attempt on his life there had been no question in his mind that had it not been for the heroic act of his Prime Guardian, who had exposed himself to the brunt of the blast, Martok would have been killed.

Several members of the Sovereign's Guard joined Prime Guardian Tallis, who was now injured as well, but not willing to give up pursuing the man who had tried to murder the Sovereign. As they raced through the bowels of the conference, pursuing the would-be assassin, they were all subsequently killed when the man unexpectedly detonated a secondary explosive device, killing everyone that had been pursuing him. Being captured by the Alliance had not been something the man was willing to face and it made little difference to him how many lives were destroyed in the process; that was the way of the Consortium. Unsurprisingly, Factotum Effris Mar disavowed all knowledge of the attempt on the life of Sovereign Martok and refused to discuss the matter.

During the presentation of his second Beryllium Cluster, Sovereign Sayoose had declared that Commander Dragar was, "A genuine hero." She went on to call him, "A living treasure of the Felis Alliance. He is a soldier to whom our children may look up to as an example to follow, knowing that he exemplifies the finest tradition of what the Felis Alliance stands for, and all that it represents."

Commander Dragar had been offered numerous promotions throughout his career, but all they would have done was take him away from what he loved the most, commanding the men and women he had trained with every day, for thousands of years: commandos he had fought and bleed with; commandos he had sworn an oath to die with, if necessary. In the end there had only been one offer which Dragar had found he could not refuse, even though he did not want to leave the command of his battalion. Dragar decided to take on a different challenge, accepting an offer that had been made directly by the Sovereign herself. He decided to join the one group within the Alliance considered even more elite than the Corps. He accepted the Sovereign's offer to become her Prime Guardian. Dragar knew that he would still be able to draw upon his battlefield training, and he still had the power to command, though he was now in command of a much smaller group than the battalion of one thousand ASCAR commandos he had led on so many occasions.

As Prime Guardian he also had operational command over the Sovereign's Guard, the platoon of ASCAR commandos tasked to provide the outer ring of protection for the Sovereign. Protocol may have afforded Dragar the authority to command the Sovereign's Guard but he preferred to leave the operations of the platoon in the capable hands of their commander, Lieutenant Kar. When he had assumed the position of Prime Guardian the Lieutenant had enthusiastically welcomed Dragar into his new role, introducing him to the platoon and acquainting him with the others to such an extent it felt as though he had been part of the team for ages. He was also able to clearly appreciate how much esteem the team had for their commander, and he had no intention of shaking things up just so he could bark out a few orders every now and then. Lieutenant Kar, or 'LT', as she preferred to be called, understood that her authority did not extend to the Guardians, and she was aware that Commander Dragar could issue an operational command at any time if the security of the Sovereign was involved.

As a fellow ASCAR commando Dragar recognized that the LT knew her role; if anything came up that she was unable to handle, something he knew was highly unlikely, the first thing she would do was turn to her superior for assistance and Dragar would be there to provide anything she needed.

Everyone who worked with Commander Dragar understood that there was one important rule to obey: it was so important they half-jokingly dubbed it, *The First Rule*. If you wanted to survive, all you had to do was avoid Dragar's wrath. Now that Captain Pertu had something specific to do she did not feel so helpless, and knew she was much further from incurring his wrath because of her insolence, but she was still in a foul mood. She waited, somewhat impatiently, while Brem contacted Operations through the Trans-Space transmitter and delivered the report regarding the Sovereign. Trans-Space communications did not take much time, being dramatically faster than normal radio transmissions, which would have taken thousands of years of years to reach the antennas of the Communications Array on Felis Prime.

It took Brem all of seventeen seconds to transmit the messages that Commander Dragar had relayed from the Sovereign to Operations on Felis Prime and then to Fleet Commander Marshal Salzat, on his flagship. Now they just had to wait for the response from Felis Prime before they could do anything else. An acknowledgment of the transmission would be sent as soon as the message had been received, but that would only be the beginning. A full response could only come from the Cadre, which meant the two Guardians would have to wait until the message had been personally delivered, read, and a reply had been formulated and transmitted back to them, which might take up to an hour. It was something Pertu did not particularly feel like waiting for at the moment. Brem could sense her restlessness from his position at the Tactical station.

He cleared his throat, the sound of which filled the cabin of Helios-2, eliciting a glare of disapproval from the Captain as Brem prepared to address the restless pilot, "Might I make a suggestion?"

Brem's voice had barely been above a whisper, but it still managed to sound too loud in the confines of the ship to Pertu. She turned to face him, her black eyes boring into the thick-set man, "I'm not in the mood for any of your nonsense right now, Sergeant," she rasped, her voice strangled and pained. Whenever Pertu was under a great deal of stress or unduly upset the injury to her vocal chords became exacerbated, making her already gravelly voice sound even harsher. She was aware of it, and it annoyed her tremendously, but there was nothing she could do to change the fact that her injury had damaged her vocal chords.

She had been warned while she was undergoing her rehabilitation that stress would make her condition worsen and been told to try and avoid getting upset too much, but the advice had been laughable at the time and all the more ridiculous now that she was a Guardian. For those in the military stress was part of the job, and for the Guardians, it was simply an everyday occurrence. A day without stress meant you were not doing your job.

Pertu remembered being told by her doctors that military flying was difficult work and becoming excited involved having the system flooded with powerful hormones that caused the body to experience both physiological and psychological responses to the stress; this was one of those times. If ordinary military flying, if there was such a thing, could make her damaged voice worse, having become a member of the Guardians and the pilot of the Sovereign's vessel had certainly added even more stress to her life. In truth, she had welcomed the challenges. It was something Pertu had been learning to live with, even if it had not been an easy path to navigate.

She was certainly not about to accept an MRe over a damn sore throat. *MRe, not for me*, she thought to herself ruefully, while considering the medicated lozenges in the pocket of her uniform. MRe was the term used by the Alliance for a Medical Retirement that could be requested when someone had an injury that was too difficult for them to work through. There was no shame in requesting one, and there would be no question about her request being accepted if she had decided to retire, but she was an elite pilot: that was all she had ever wanted to be, and she was now commanding the best ship in the fleet as part of the most elite unit. She glared at the Tactical Sergeant who was still looking at her, a questioning look on his face.

Brem held up his hands, "No, no," he said, disarmingly, "I promise, no nonsense," he flashed her a mischievous smile that had the desired effect. Pertu visibly relaxed, which was quite a bit easier since deactivating the artificial gravity of the ship that she had used to help Commander Dragar move to the aft section without having to float. As enjoyable as it was to perform spins in Zero-G, it was far easier to be able to walk around on a ship with an artificial gravity field activated.

Even a slight gravity field, scientists had found, also aided in the leeching of calcium from bones, which could lead to serious issues for those who found themselves on long missions in space. For that reason, the longer the mission, the higher the artificial gravity would be set on the ship. For anyone onboard a ship like the BC-Orono-001, the flagship of the Alliance, or any other Alliance ship that spent months at a time away from spaceport, it would feel as though they were on Felis Prime: the gravity settings were identical, being set at ninety-seven percent that of Felis Magoris.

Pertu looked at the smiling face of the Tactical Sergeant, "Go ahead," she croaked, grimacing at the sound that came out of her throat. She finally fished out the small packet of medicated lozenges from the side pocket of her uniform and popped one of them into her mouth. She smiled as the relief instantly numbed the discomfort in her throat, momentarily distracting her. They were dispensed from the Rehabilitation Pharmacy on Felis Prime whenever she needed them and were the only things that provided relief from the near constant pain she still experienced from her injuries.

While a single lozenge was able to calm the burning pain for about eight hours, they could not do anything to restore the sound of her voice. For all the medical advances that had been made by the Alliance and their ability to radically extend lifespans, the deleterious results of the accident, unfortunately, had resulted in permanent injuries. At least she was able to get rid of the pain relatively easily, without having to resort to using the heavily sedating medications they had used when she had been in the Healing Center during her recovery. When she had first arrived there the pain had been unbearable, until they had given her the medication to numb the pain. Now all she needed were the lozenges. It was hardly the debilitating disability that some soldiers had ended up with after engagements with the Consortium. Pertu knew that she had been lucky; her injuries could have been much worse, she might have even died had her piloting skills not been what they were: under the circumstances, she was willing to live with the sore throat given what she had gained as a result of the injury. After all, she thought to herself, it had led to her becoming a Guardian.

Brem continued to smile, "What I was going to suggest," he began, his voice uncharacteristically calm and quiet, "was that you begin going through the system checks that will have to be done before our departure," he nodded toward her console, "that might take your mind off of the waiting we're going to be doing," he winked, allowing his gaze to settle on the series of screens and switches that made up the Automated Control Command module that was so critical to the running of the ship.

Pertu stared at Brem for a moment without saying a word, then smiled, "Thank you," she finally said, her voice a bit less strained as the lozenge relieved her discomfort. Without another word she swiveled her seat and faced the helm, beginning the process of going through the various checklists that would ensure that Helios-2 was ready to depart as soon as the reply from Ops had been received. She still was not pleased with the idea of leaving Commander Dragar alone planet side, but at least she was not sitting around, doing nothing.

(*|*)

Helios-2 had been designed to be commanded and flown by a single pilot, though having the other Guardians on board, both of whom were qualified pilots, meant they could assist with any issues that arose during a flight. With the advanced technologies that had been built into the ship's systems, the assistance of the other Guardians was rarely necessary. An A-ConCom was far more than a glorified Auto-Pilot, it was the equivalent of an accomplished co-pilot; a co-pilot that could, should the need arise, assume all functions of the ship should the pilot become incapacitated, or only momentarily should they be required to turn their attentions onto other matters, even for the shortest time.

All bridge commanders were fitted with a specially designed

halo device that interfaced with the A-ConCom and allowed the ship to monitor the thoughts of the pilot. Once activated, the halo device allowed the pilot to make inputs into the system directly through their neural connection, using the various screens and switches as a secondary form of input, or in the unlikely event of an interface failure. One of the few times it was necessary for the pilot to physically touch the controls was to manually key course information into the Navigational Controls, which had been created as a safeguard against the device picking up a mental artefact manifesting itself in erroneous digits during the transfer process.

During the testing phase of the interface it had been determined that when someone was thinking about a string of integers to be entered into the Nav Con, even if they were focusing clearly, they might inadvertently transpose one or two of the numbers, or substitute similar numbers with letters, which could send a vessel to an entirely different part of the Sector if the coordinates were not properly confirmed. By entering coordinates manually and confirming them before they were locked in no mistakes were made, and the halo devices had ultimately greatly increased the proficiency of pilots.

Pertu did not mind wearing the device at all and felt odd when she did not have the thin ribbon perched on her head. It was barely as wide as her index finger and went entirely around the circumference of her head, being covered by her short hair. When it could be seen it looked as though it was glowing with energy, but that would have been an inaccurate way of looking at the device which had no internal power source. All of the power for the halo was provided by the ship and its systems which provided a field of energy throughout the entirety of the vessel, making it possible for the pilot to remain in control of the bridge even if they had to leave the bridge.

Most importantly, since the halo device was allowed the ship to monitor the brain of the pilot, it was possible for the A-ConCom to tell the instant the pilot took their attention off of piloting the ship for any reason. If a situation where they might be engaged in a battle the system would allow the pilot to focus their attention on the weapon systems while the A-ConCom dealt with evasive maneuvers, and the pilot knew they did not have to worry about anything because they were able to maintain complete situational awareness thanks to the neural connection they had through the halo device.

After completing her checklists, Pertu saw that the reply had still not arrived, so she decided to do a Series One Maintenance Check, which could be accomplished automatically, from the helm. Maintenance Checks were normally done while the ship was in spaceport, but they could also take place while the ship was in a stationary orbit. As she suspected everything came out ten by ten, the best possible result. Pertu was not surprised; Helios-2 was the best-maintained ship in the fleet, which was not unexpected considering who it had been designed and commissioned to carry. Just as the Check was being completed Pertu's sensitive ears picked up the soft chime coming from Brem's station: the reply had just arrived.

"Well?" she asked, turning to the thickset Sergeant, "What did they have to say?" Brem waved her off as the response was still coming through on his headset. She blushed at the rebuke, realizing that her impatience was not going to get her anywhere.

"You," Brem began, unusually calm, "need to relax." He laughed, "First of all," he continued, his voice becoming a bit more serious, "the First Counselor of the Cadre has indicated that they will be ordering the dispatching of appropriate forces to guard all Protectorates, as per the Sovereign's orders, immediately," Pertu nodded as she heard this. Of course, she thought to herself, somewhat bitterly, the Cadre should have been doing that from the beginning, but, she reminded herself, she was a Guardian, not a member of the Cadre. "Secondly," Brem continued, looking toward Pertu, "uh, well," he paused as he looked down at the datapad, "they want to know why we're not returning ... immediately, with the Sovereign," he smiled, "I really don't know how to reply to that."

Pertu looked at her colleague for a moment before replying, "Well, you don't suppose we could ask our talkative Commander about that, do you?" Brem's face reddened at the suggestion. The last thing he wanted was a confrontation with Dragar, even if it was over the relative safety of Comms. Pertu laughed at his obvious discomfort.

"Don't worry my big hero," she said, trying hard not to laugh while managing to sound as calming as she could manage, "I'll talk to the mean Commander for you," she giggled, sounding as girlish as she could with her rasping voice, "will that make you feel better?"

Brem did not even jump at the mocking, he just handed Pertu the headphones for the communications console and moved out of his seat to allow her access to the controls, "Thanks," he muttered, as he maneuvered himself toward the aft section of the ship, moving to the Waste Disposal Unit. "This stuff makes my stomach upset," he complained as he began to slide the door closed to relieve himself.

Pertu looked toward the WD Unit and called after him, "Don't forget to activate the air filters! Last time your stomach was upset it smelled like a Verkallian Tarvok had given birth to a dozen kits in there," she paused, swallowing against the pain in her throat. "What in Caiphus have you been eating lately?" She could hear him laughing as the door hissed shut. As she sat down at the Tactical console she could see a yellow light on the Master Control Panel at the helm blink on, indicating that Brem had indeed activated the air filters, causing her to smile to herself as she reread the message Brem had transcribed from Operations. For a moment she considered activating the auxiliary air filters using the halo device, but she had more important things to attend to at the moment. Besides, she thought to herself, the regular air filters were more than sufficient to deal with whatever the Tactical Sergeant had been eating lately. At least, she hoped tha was the case.

Pertu returned her attentions to the console and put on the headphones so she could contact Dragar. She was not about to start making things up to Operations as to why they were not returning with the Sovereign. "Guardian One, come in; Commander Dragar," she called, and was pleased to hear his familiar response right away.

"Dragar," he replied, "What's going on, Captain? Have you received a reply from Ops?" he sounded almost relaxed.

"Yes sir, it just came in, and they're requesting some clarification. They've inquired as to why we aren't returning immediately with the Sovereign. Also, the Cadre has acknowledged that they are dispatching appropriate forces to guard all Protectorates and member planets." Pertu waited for a response, not wanting to say anything inane that might upset the Commander. She knew it was not easy for him to be as close as he was to the Sovereign and not be able to bring her home, but it was not as though he could just snatch her against her will. They would all be executed for doing something that brazen, right after being hailed as heroes for returning her to Felis Prime, all things being equal, Pertu preferred not being executed.

She could hear Dragar sigh through the open channel and realized the toll this mission was taking on her commander, "Yeah," she heard him say, "like those useless fools couldn't have ordered the mobilization of forces to those planets before it got to a point where things became dangerous." Pertu was about to respond but decided she would be throwing fuel on a dangerous fire.

"Look, Pertu," he continued, his voice now sounding a bit tired, perhaps even haggard, "I want you to convey to Ops that the Sovereign has decided that right now she requires some time away and, for the next little while, we don't know how long at this time, she will be remaining here, on Terra," he paused for a moment. "That's the best answer I can give you for now," he paused for a moment, then added, "confidentially, there's something else going on that she alluded to, but I'm not sure what it is at this point. When I know, you'll know, but that's just between you and me, and of course the other guy up there with you," he gave a snort, the closest he could get to a laugh at that moment.

"When you receive a response, let me know; then," he continued, "I want you to begin your patrols to the other Green Zone planets in this Sector. Remember," he added before Pertu could interject her objections to his previous command, "I don't want anyone to see you, not even other Alliance ships, I just want to know what's going on out there. If the Sovereign is going to be down here I want to know about everything that's going on around us." He paused for a long moment, "Pertu?" he finally asked.

"Yes, Commander?" she asked curiously, leaning toward the tactical station.

"Be careful," there was genuine concern in his voice as he spoke, and Pertu knew enough not to say anything else. Dragar spoke only when necessary, otherwise, he kept his counsel to himself.

"I'll send the reply immediately," she responded, "and will report back as soon as a response is received," she paused for the shortest breath, "I'm pleased to report that we're ready to depart," she paused again as the door to the Waste Disposal unit slid open and Brem stepped out, looking as though he had lost his lunch.

"At the suggestion of Tactical Sergeant Brem," she gave him a warning glance, indicating that he would regret saying anything, "I ran all the pre-flight checks and even decided to run a Series One Maintenance Check: everything came back ten by ten; all systems are checked and primed." She was trying to sound enthusiastic, but thought it came out sounding too forced.

"Excellent, Captain," Dragar replied, genuinely pleased with her efficiency. "In the meantime, I await your response. Dragar out."

As the transmission ended the sun was beginning to set, but that meant nothing to Dragar; he could sleep easily enough in the shelter of the tree, nestled in the large branch he had been sitting on for the past few hours. He had no need of a sleeping bag or extra clothing thanks to the design of his Guardian uniform. Like many things used by the Unified Armed Services, the Guardian uniform was a modification of that worn by the ASCAR, which allowed commandos to spend months at a time dug into a position without having to worry about being relieved. It had multiple layers which provided protection from both extreme cold or heat and allowed the garment to be worn continuously for several months before it needed to be changed thanks to a self-cleaning system that recycled all the moisture collected from the wearer that would be filtered into potable water while solid wastes were transformed into a powder that could be disposed of when convenient. He smiled to himself as memories of previous campaigns came to mind as he inflated the collar behind his neck to provide a makeshift pillow for himself, but the smile disappeared as the communicator on his wrist vibrated, indicating an incoming message from the ship.

"Dragar," he replied quietly, the sun had now dropped completely below the horizon, leaving the area in total blackness. As he looked into the night sky he was almost certain he could see the spot where Helios-2 would be orbiting, though he knew that was impossible since the ship was in such a high orbit and shielded from view.

"Hey boss," came the gruff voice of Brem, his stomach now settled, "I was able to wrestle the controls of the radio back from the Cap," Dragar heard the sound of a loud slap come through the transmission. "Uh, right," he continued sheepishly, "anyway, Ops replied a moment ago: apparently they don't have anything to say about the Sovereign wanting to take a vacation. Their exact words were, and I quote, *'You are to remain on station and provide Sovereign Sayoose any and all support she requires, providing her with transport back to Felis Prime the moment she decides she has had enough of her vacation,'* unquote; and that, quite frankly, is all they had to say."

Dragar waited for his friend to finish, "Excellent," he replied, "that's just what I expected from them: nothing. Now it's time for the two of you to go inspect the other Green Zone planets in this Sector. I'll still be in communications range if anything happens, so you won't have to worry about anything, and the Cadre should have the backup ships here shortly, in case something does come up."

Brem, who had known the Commander for far longer than Captain Pertu, was less afraid of incurring his wrath and started to object when Dragar interjected, "There's nothing for you to worry about, old friend, I didn't come down here unprepared," he let out a small chuckle.

"You didn't?" Brem asked, incredulously.

Dragar laughed again, "Of course not, you silly Grunt! What kind of commando would I be to go on a mission without my Battle Pack?"

"Battle Pack?" Brem was totally surprised. He had not seen the Commander take a Battle Pack before leaving the ship.

"You should know by now that I stow my Battle Pack under my seat," Dragar chided, as though it was something Brem should do as well. He knew the stocky Tactical Sergeant had his Battle Pack stowed in the munitions locker near the LDMT, used to transport them to the surface of the planet. "I put it on before walking to the LDMT, before you even sent me down here. I've got a full complement of weapons; all are fully charged and T-rated." Hand weaponry used by the Alliance was based on pulsed-plasma technology that ran on slow-draining, rechargeable power sources. Each class of weapon was rated from A, for least lethal through T, the most lethal variety.

"Well, spill it," Brem said, impatiently, "what do you have?" he asked, not fully convinced his friend was adequately protected.

"Really?" Dragar asked, impatient at the interrogation, "Well, for starts, I have my T-17, how does that strike you? If any threat comes within two Krenar I will be able to vaporize them," he heard Brem let out a grunt and laughed. T-17 Plasma Rifles were the weapon of choice for any ASCAR commando. It was the most versatile of the plasma rifles as it could fire up to fifteen multiple pulses per second, which would reduce a stone wall to a pile of smoking rubble in seconds; it was also effective as a sniper rifle, capable of firing with incredible accuracy and tremendous range.

"What else?" Brem asked, knowing the rifle would not have been the only thing the Commander had in his Pack.

"Would you be satisfied to know that I also have a -77 with me?" Dragar laughed, referring to the PPD-77, the hand-held version of the Plasma Rifle. It could do virtually everything the T-17 could, but had a variable setting, allowing it to cycle from non-lethal to fully lethal.

"Yeah, great," Brem responded, still annoyed, mostly since he knew he would be stuck in Helios-2 and not get a chance to join his friend on the planet. "You just make sure you keep it set on Level-T, I don't want to have to go down there to recover both you *and* the Sovereign," it was impossible to conceal his annoyance, but Dragar took it in stride. "What else do you have?"

Dragar could not resist the opportunity to tease his old friend, "Aw, you don't want me to stun some of these creatures?" he laughed, for a few seconds, then abruptly stopped. "I'm just kidding," he quickly added, before Brem could reply, "as a matter of fact, I also have two dozen Shadow Makers, which I certainly hope I won't have to use. Quite frankly, old friend, I don't want to have to use any of these," his voice had lowered to a near whisper as he saw the door to the building open and the woman emerged. "Subject moving. You have your orders. Dragar out."

He watched as the woman brought what appeared to be a small bag out of the building and placed it in a metal canister at the end of the walkway, near the roadway. She seemed to look right where he was sitting, in the curve of the branch in the tree, but he knew his shield rendered him invisible to humans. At the same time, she continued to stare for several long seconds, making Dragar wonder if she possessed some special talents or abilities to perceive things they had not taken into consideration. It was not impossible with underdeveloped examples of humans, Dragar knew, though it was unlikely.

After another several breaths she finally looked away, scanning the rest of the tree as though she was looking for some animal or bird. She then looked up at the stars for a few moments, seemingly enjoying the view of the clear night sky, before turning and walking over to her car where she retrieved something before returning back to the building, where he heard her close and lock the door. Dragar took a slow deep breath as he watched and saw the light over the door turn off. It looked as though things were settling down for the night inside the building.

His wrist was vibrating, "Yes," he replied, "I'm still here; the human came out of the building."

"House," Brem corrected, "it's called a house, I've been monitoring their transmissions. They live in houses; they work in buildings."

Dragar grunted, "Fine … house, whatever."

"Shadow Makers?" Brem asked, wanting to continue the conversation.

"Yes," Dragar responded, "two dozen. Believe me, I'm more than armed enough to deal with an army of these humans." Dragar did not sound boastful, he was merely stating a fact. As a grenade the Shadow Maker had a blast-zone of about fifteen feet and would turn anything within that zone into a shadow, but the advantage it had over other grenades was its size, and that it made virtually no sound when it exploded. They were only about the size of a marble, and only made a soft popping sound when detonated, which was why the Corps preferred them over the other grenades that had been developed. He did not have to worry about running out of ammunition with either the T-17 or the PPD-77: their power cells could stand up to being used constantly for up to five months at a time, which would have to be one intense battle. Even the suspicious Brem had to admit that the Commander was well prepared considering the types of weaponry on this planet.

He looked into the sky once again, picking the spot where he thought the ship was orbiting before speaking again, "Brem, put me on the open channel," he said, so that what he said would be heard by both Guardians onboard Helios-2.

"Channel's open, Commander," Brem replied, without hesitation.

After a short pause, Dragar addressed the two Guardians, who also happened to be his dearest friends, "I just wanted the two of you to be careful. Be safe, and don't take any chances. Sovereign Sayoose said there was something else going on, but she wasn't able to tell me about it just yet; I have a feeling that we're going to be getting the cold shoulder from the Cadre, but I might just be showing my feelings toward First Counselor Regar. Otherwise, why would the Sovereign have had us send that message to Marshal Salzat? If you were to ask for my impression of the situation, I would have to guess that … well, let's just say that I'm not expecting the First Counselor to live up to what he said in that message."

"But …" Pertu tried to interject.

"All I'm saying," Dragar continued, "is that for now we should assume that we're the only Alliance presence in this Sector, alright? If necessary we can call on Salzat, but not just yet. Is that understood?"

There was a long silence from the ship before the two Guardians replied, in unison, "Understood, Commander." His message had been heard, and understood.

CHAPTER VIII ~ COMMUNICATIONS

"Once a planet succeeded in traveling beyond their planetary system it was the policy to offer them an opportunity to join the Alliance. Socioeconomic situations on each planet were taken into consideration, but there was not usually anything that could not be resolved through reasoned, peaceful negotiations with representatives of the planet. What the leaders ultimately recognized was that their planet had far more to gain by entering the Alliance than by rejecting the offer. At the time of the offer they were also made aware of the existence of the Ursus Consortium who would, undoubtedly, be vying for the planet's resources should they fail to sign a treaty with the Alliance. On the rare occasion that the leaders of the planet decided to seek out membership with the Consortium, the Alliance left and never looked back. As the Head Negotiator for the Alliance would say in such cases, 'No great loss.' Such planets, if they actively sought out the Ursus Consortium, were of no interest to the Alliance."

[...]

Excerpted from: *A Brief History of the Felis Alliance,* by Sovereign Sayoose

(*|*)

While the transmissions were being exchanged between Helios-2 and Operations on Felis Prime, a single patrol ship flying through deep space near Felis Magoris received decoded copies of the messages from an unregistered transmitter on Felis Prime, which they immediately sent on through the Subspace Communications Web of the Consortium to Sector 1009, the home world of the Ursus Consortium; the response they received was unambiguous:

"Transit directly to planet Terra, Sector 0107. Coordinates in database. Avoid contact with any Alliance ships: maintain close

surveillance on situation on the planet. Upon arrival, deploy STAWS Fire Team for Cleansing Operation: leave no Alliance personnel alive. Reinforcements will be dispatched accordingly. Supreme Leader, FEM, UC."

While considered a patrol ship, the GAF-Tralta-9 was still a fully armed Battlecruiser, and was armed accordingly. Although Captain Tiernat had great confidence in his crew and knew that the ship itself was more than capable of fulfilling any mission that it had been tasked with, he was not thrilled with the prospect of doing something that might lead to an overt war with the Alliance. He had engaged in battles before, to be sure, but he had seen the Alliance messages that had been sent to Factotum Ebla Mar: he knew that he was being ordered to kill the Sovereign of the Alliance. Had the Factotum lost his mind? Of course not; Tiernat purged the thought from his mind before any sign of weakness could be seen by one of the ambitious members of his crew who would be more than willing to have him removed from duty at the first sign of him wavering under the stress of command. Captain Tiernat looked at the display of the vast field of stars in the galaxy that the ship was approaching, traveling just below the speed of light.

"Prepare for a transit through Light Drive," he announced, sending the command to the Engineer who quickly began the process of spinning up the engines, generating the field necessary to propel the ship through the dimensional barrier required to break through the speed of light. "We'll be arriving at our destination in about," he paused to look down at the panel next to his command station, "fifteen hours. Then we'll be employing our Standard Drive from there," the ship jolted for a second as it made the transition into light speed and after an uneventful journey emerged just behind the planet Jupiter, shielding them from any Earth-bound observatories while the ship modulated its shields to match the wavelength of the light in the area.

"Alright," Captain Tiernat announced, having returned to the bridge, "I need any damage reports made immediately to Ship Supervisors; maintain all bulkheads at Level One Priority Seal while we transit to Terra. Time of arrival at Terra using Standard Drive?"

He turned to his Nav Officer who responded immediately, "Three days, Captain."

(*|*)

As Captain Tiernat was guiding the GAF-Tralta-9 toward Terra the Communications Administrator on Felis Prime was sitting at her console, reading the message that had been received and decoded from Helios-2, which had been marked with the classification EOC, or Eyes Only Cadre. Knowing the importance of the message Marta decided to personally take it to First Counselor Regar. First Counselor Regar was alone in the private chambers usually used by the Sovereign, but which he had taken to using in her absence. It was a long walk from the Communications Array to the Sovereign's chambers, on the rim of Felis Prime, but Marta enjoyed the sights and sounds of the bustling orbiting city and quickly found herself standing outside the double sliding doors of the chambers. She knocked on the frame of the doors, waiting for an invitation to enter. The doors slid open and the tall Regar said, "Enter," in a soft voice, without looking toward her.

"First Counselor Regar," Marta began, as she approached him, "I have news regarding the Sovereign," her voice had been upbeat and jovial, which was not unusual for the Communications Administrator, but in this case she had a legitimate excuse for sounding so cheerful.

Regar spun around too fast, almost falling over in the process, for a second there was a near crazed look in his eyes, but it disappeared, quickly replaced by one of concern. "What news?" he asked, trying not to sound overly desperate. "Is she alright? Where has she been? Is she on the way back to Felis Prime?" He seemed genuinely eager to know of her wellbeing, which made Marta momentarily regret how she had thought of the man on a few occasions; the First Counselor was not her favorite person.

Marta smiled disarmingly, "She's fine," she said, "she's on a planet called Terra, a Protectorate, she was found by the Guardians," at the mention of the Guardians Regar looked deflated, but he quickly brightened.

"Ah, how lucky we are for the Guardians," he tried to sound upbeat, but it came across sounding stiff. "Tell me more," he encouraged, and Marta filled him in on all of the details from the message, including the orders from the Sovereign to deploy Alliance forces to aggressively guard the Protectorates and member planets.

Regar listened to everything the Communications Administrator had to report and considered his response carefully, looking at the shaded windows that gave a wide vista of the crowded space around Felis Prime, "This is indeed excellent news, Administrator Marta," he began to respond, his tone as pleasant sounding as he could make it, "but we must be careful about who hears about this, particularly since the Sovereign is still absent," the Administrator nodded in agreement, though she looked dubious. Regar pressed on, "What I'd like you to do, if you don't mind, is to personally send a reply," he stared at her intently, but he seemed sincere.

"Of course, First Counselor Regar," she replied, nodding eagerly.

"Excellent," he turned away from the Administrator, "please inform the Guardians that their message has been received and the Cadre is taking all appropriate actions," he seemed to hesitate for a moment, "we would also like to know the reason for the delay in their return with the Sovereign." He looked out at the crowded space around Felis Prime again, watching as a small shuttle wove its way between two larger ships as it transited toward Felis Magoris. He turned back to face the Administrator, "I trust that nobody else has seen this message and that you are able to keep these transmissions to yourself?"

She blushed at the intensity of his glare, "Of course, First Counselor," she replied, looking down to avert her gaze, "only one of the Comm Personnel saw the original transmission, and she has EOS clearance," the Administrator was referring to the highest level of security clearance for Communications Personnel, *Eyes Only Sovereign*, indicating messages directed specifically to the Sovereign. "Her Console will be the one that receives any further communications from Helios-2, and she reports directly to me," she paused for a breath before continuing. "Besides, as you are well aware," she was now looking directly at the First Counselor, her pulse quickened at having to defend her personnel, "my Communications Officers are sworn to secrecy: they would *never* reveal any of the messages received through the Array, especially something sensitive that might threaten Alliance security. We haven't had a security breach in Communications in several thousand years, and the last one was so minor it was hardly worth mentioning."

Regar nodded, realizing his tactic in trying to intimidate the Communications Administrator had been a mistake and returned his attentions back to the tall windows of the chamber as though he was searching for something only he could see, but it was his way of ending the meeting. Without saying another word, Administrator Marta turned and left the dimly lit chamber, pleased to be away from the First Counselor. Something about the man left her feeling unsettled, though she was not able to identify anything specific; he just bothered her. At least she had delivered the message from the Guardians, she thought to herself. Now that he knew, First Counselor Regar would pass the information on to the rest of Cadre and they would do what the Sovereign had requested. As Marta walked down the long hallway from the chamber back to the Communications Center her mind replayed their conversation: something was troubling her.

She knew that Sovereign Sayoose had been absent for three years, and the Cadre had been making various excuses to explain her absence while ruling in her absence. They were unable to do anything beyond the small, administratively necessary things, but, it turned out, they had more than sufficient power to run the majority of the Alliance's functions, unless any crisis had developed, which had not happened, grace be to Caiphus.

Anything that the Cadre could not handle was simply pushed aside, but that was not unusual for the Alliance given its massive size. Due to the complexity of the bureaucracy in the Alliance it routinely took many months, if not years, before major decisions were made, so it was not unusual to have some issues set aside before they could be resolved, even while the Sovereign was present. Having this done in her absence was hardly noticed by most people.

At the same time, now the Cadre knew the Sovereign was safe, that she was potentially on her way home, why would First Counselor Regar not want anyone else to know? Marta had wanted to ask, but did not want to seem as though she was being impertinent by questioning the wisdom of the First Counselor. As First Counselor of the Cadre his opinion carried more than a bit of weight within the Alliance.

Marta was not sure what to think as she returned to her desk in Communications and began sending the reply to Helios-2 from First Counselor Regar, but there was one thing that she knew for certain: if anything did happen to the Sovereign, the First Counselor's name was *not* the one most whispered when people spoke of possible replacements for the Sovereign. It was one of the reasons why Marta felt so troubled by how she felt after her brief meeting with him. She simply could not get rid of the impression that there was something off about the man. If he was ambitious, which was the impression he gave to those around him, he surely had to know that he had reached the apex of his career as First Counselor. It was hard to deny his ambition, Marta thought to herself given the way the man had brazenly taken over the Sovereign's chambers in her absence.

It was as though he expected her not to return, though nobody had even suggested such a possibility. Before Prime Guardian Dragar had located the beacon of the Sovereign the suggestion that she might not return would have been met with a vehement response to the contrary. Marta had known that Dragar was not about to give up on his mission to locate the Sovereign, and she knew that the First Counselor would have also been aware of his commitment to his mission.

At the same time, there was no chance that the Stellar Mining Bureau would select First Counselor Regar to replace Sovereign Sayoose. One thing was certain, Marta thought, when the next message from Helios-2 was received she was going to send it directly the First Counselor, without going to see him herself.

A reply from Helios-2 came within a few minutes and Marta immediately routed it to First Counselor Regar. She had to smile at the thought of the Sovereign not wanting to come home from her 'vacation' just yet. She thought to herself, *Sovereign Sayoose more likely doesn't want to come home to deal with First Counselor Regar*, as the response from the First Counselor appeared on her console. Apparently he was also uninterested in speaking with Administrator Marta. She smiled as she read the brief response and immediately sent it off to Helios-2: *"You are to remain on station and provide Sovereign Sayoose any and all support she requires, providing her with transport back to Felis Prime the moment she decides she has had enough of her vacation."*

Marta thought about Prime Guardian Dragar, her friend of many years, *as if he'd do anything less than that*; the absurdity made her laugh for the first time in a quite a while.

Before her shift ended, several hours later, Marta decided to examine the logs of outgoing messages and noticed that the logs of military communications did not include any new orders from the Cadre to send Alliance forces to guard the Protectorates, or any of the member planets, as the Sovereign had ordered. Marta thought to herself that more than adequate time had passed since the first message had arrived for First Counselor Regar to have convened a Special Session with the Cadre, what were they waiting for, or what was *he* waiting for? She checked another transmission log to confirm her suspicions, but nothing had been sent from the Cadre. First Counselor Regar had received the initial message over five hours ago: what in Caiphus was going on, Marta wondered as she secured her terminal, shutting things down for the evening.

(*|*)

First Counselor Regar had left the Sovereign's chambers after his surprise visit from the annoying Administrator Marta had concluded. He returned to his own private chambers, locking and sealing the doors behind him to ensure his privacy. Turning to the window, he resumed gazing at the traffic flying around the orbiting city. It was not as impressive a view as what he had in the Sovereign's chambers, but he could never bring himself to sleep there.

Not yet. Not until everything had been accomplished.

A hissing sound reached his ears and his body tensed for the briefest instant, then began to relax as the familiar scent of perfume reached his nose, reminding him of the first time he had smelled that aroma; it had been the sound of the sliding door connecting the adjoining sleeping chambers. Two delicate hands reached around from behind and began to slowly massage his chest, stroking both his stomach and abdomen in a circular fashion. One hand slowly pulled his long robe off his shoulders, while the other turned him around. His eyes had closed as he savored the moment, but he opened them to drink in the beauty of his wife, Lareena, as she seduced him once again.

It seemed as though she repeated this routine every single night, or some variation of it, not that Regar minded. It was one of the things he truly adored about Lareena; she was a self-described sensualist who happened to delight in both giving and receiving pleasure. They had now been married for one hundred and thirty-nine years, without doubt they had been the best years that Regar could have ever believed possible. He had never imagined finding a wife like her, not even a man in a position with as much power as he commanded.

Men like Regar were usually so dedicated to matters of business, far too concerned with the advancement of their careers to focus on relationships, but Lareena had other ideas about the priorities of life. When Regar had been on a trip to one of the moons of Altus 9 for a conference on Alliance governance they met after the first session of the conference, and the two became inseparable. It was as though they had been meant to be together.

Now, as he lay in her arms, breathing in the intoxicating scent of her perfume, Regar found himself carried away in an erotic fantasy that was simply too good to be believed. No man should live a life as wild as this and not be able to boast about it to his friends, he thought to himself, as his body reveled in the pleasures he was experiencing, but he knew that the only taboo existing between the two of them was that what they did behind the closed doors of their chambers was their secret, and theirs alone.

It was not much of an issue for the First Counselor considering that he despised the other members of the Cadre, and he knew that the feeling was likely mutual on their part. Outside of his professional associations with people who were cordial toward him because they wanted or needed something from the First Counselor, he had virtually no close friendships with anyone on Felis Prime or Felis Magoris. He did not mind, though, that just left him more time to be with his wife.

As the scent of the perfume continued to entrance him the thought occurred to that it was odd, as another jolt of pleasure shot up his spine, Lareena never even wore perfume, unless it was for … *this*; he gasped for breath as she resumed her ministrations, bringing him to an explosion of pleasure quite unlike anything he had ever experienced, at least, not since their last episode together. His mind wandered as the seemingly endless pleasures continued.

Regar knew that afterwards, once every physical urge had been utterly satisfied to the point that his mind felt as though he had just returned from a month-long vacation, they would talk to each other about his day. He would tell her everything, from the most insignificant details to the news he had received regarding the messages about the Sovereign. He would also tell her about his meeting with that annoying woman, Administrator Marta, and the response he had sent back to Helios-2, as well as anything else that came to mind. It was the way they had been doing things since the beginning of their marriage. Regar had always been surprised by the fact that Lareena was seemed so captivated by his work. He was also impressed by how good a listener she was; she never interrupted him as he recounted his stories, unless it was to ask a question for more details. Regar always found himself to be willing, and quite eager, to provide the extra details, even as the residual scent of the perfume lingered, urging him to continue speaking, pouring out his heart to the woman he loved with all of his heart.

(* | *)

Tanya was certain that she had heard a sound coming from the direction of the great oak tree beside the driveway of her house while she was taking out the garbage. When she looked at the hulking tree in the failing light of the day she could only see shadows. There were some movements but they came from the slight breeze rustling the branches and leaves of the tree, which had been there since before the house had been built, several years before her grandparents had purchased the property.

She half expected to see a raccoon staring back at her, or perhaps an owl, but there was nothing, just the empty tree. Tanya shrugged her thin shoulders, then gazed at the canopy of stars above her, imagining how incredible it would be to travel out there, exploring the great vista of space. She went to retrieve her purse which she had left in the car after returning home from the Vet's office earlier in the day. Once she had retrieved it she locked the doors and returned to the house, looking back at the tree as though something was beckoning to her from within the collection of branches, but she was still unable to see anything. There were no other sounds to be heard except for the sporadic chirp of crickets, calling to each other from the field across the road, but Tanya was still convinced that she had heard something. She also had the uncomfortable feeling that she was being watched, but she knew this was impossible since their house was miles from their closest neighbor. Once again she reminded herself that she was in desperate need of a vacation.

Sayoose was sitting by the door, waiting for her when she came back into the house. She rubbed up against Tanya's leg, purring loudly, as though she sensed how disquieted she had felt and needed some comfort. Tanya giggled at the sensation on her bare leg and bent over to scoop up the tuxedo cat. Walking over to her favorite chair in the living room, Tanya sat down, folding her feet under her and placing Sayoose gently on her lap. Sayoose seemed quite content with the situation, allowing herself to be placed into the position, after which she immediately went to sleep. Tanya noticed that the cat would occasionally lift her head to look through the window, as though there was something in the tree that she could also see, something she seemed to look at every time she looked out the window.

During the day Tanya continued to work on her writing while Sayoose spent her time either by her side, enjoying the music, or sleeping and playing with whatever struck her fancy. She also spent some of her time sleeping next to Gramps, especially when he was reading his newspaper, knowing that he also enjoyed her company. Throughout all of it, Dragar continued to stand watch, feeling as though he was beginning to lose his mind as he observed the single most powerful being in the universe living her life as a companion creature. If the woman the Sovereign was sitting next to only knew who she was playing with, Dragar thought to himself, grinning wryly, she would fall over in shock. He was about to return to the oak tree when his wrist device vibrated, indicating an incoming message from Helios-2.

As soon as he was away from the building and back in the tree he responded, "Dragar here, what do you have?"

There was a short pause in the response, indicating that the ship was not in orbit over the planet, "Commander," came the familiar voice of Brem, "we're near a Green Zone Protectorate near the edge of the Sector and well, sir," the Guardian sounded hesitant, "there are Consortium vessels present; they may be making a move." Dragar felt his pulse quicken. If the Ursus Consortium was operating within this Sector no planetary system was safe, particularly the one on which the Sovereign was located.

Brem continued, "I'm counting three Battlecruisers, four Star Cruisers, and two Carriers, and I believe there are even a few Battle Transports planet side," his voice sounded strained. It must have been extremely difficult for the Guardian knowing he was not able to do anything for the Protectorate planet.

Dragar was ready, "Contact Ops immediately; tell them what you've told me and give them my recommendation, which is that the Cadre immediately dispatch five Battlecruisers, five Carriers, and five Battle Transports, with a total of ten brigades of the ASCAR. If that isn't enough, double the forces; is that clear?"

Brem was nodding his head when he realized that the Commander could not hear him, "Yes ... yes sir, but, but," he paused, "what if they don't accept your authority, sir?" It was a legitimate question, for which Dragar had been prepared.

"Remind them," he said, his voice filling with genuine anger, "that I'm the Sovereign's First Advisor, and am in close contact with her while she's on her vacation," he paused for a second as he looked through the window at the Sovereign, sitting on the woman's lap in the form of the cat. Well, it was mostly the truth: he was close to her, he just was not speaking to her on a regular basis. "This is what I would advise her to do," he continued, "more importantly, it is what the Sovereign has already ordered the Cadre to do; is that clear?" This time Dragar was the one nodding.

"Yes sir," the transmission went dead.

"What in the name of Hydra is going on out there?" Dragar muttered to himself as he lowered himself from the tree again, walking around the property to ensure that there were no immediate threats. He had been doing this since he had arrived, but the only thing he had encountered had been a family of squirrels, which had not been intimidated by the imposing Guardian, as well as another cat, who seemed less inclined to be friendly toward him than the Sovereign. When he approached the creature he was surprised to find it arching its back and hissing while flashing its claws in the dim light of the early evening.

"Lovely planet you've chosen," Dragar muttered as the feral cat leapt into the night, knocking over a flowerpot on the porch in the process.

(* | *)

Administrator Marta had only been on duty for a short time when the urgent message with the recommendations from Commander Dragar arrived. She immediately contacted First Counselor Regar, hoping she was not interrupting him, even though it was an urgent matter. His face appeared on the view screen, obviously displeased at the disturbance, "Administrator," he said acerbically, "what may I do for you now?" his voice rang out through the small speakers on her desk, not concealing the contempt the man felt for the Administrator. She shuddered at the tone of his voice, but it only reinforced what she had initially felt about the man.

"First Counselor Regar," she began, tentatively, "an emergency message has been received from Helios-2: they're reporting several Consortium vessels threatening a Protectorate at the edge of the same Sector on which the Sovereign is presently on is located. As First Advisor to the Sovereign, Commander Dragar has recommended that the Cadre order the following forces be dispatched to prevent the loss of the planet: five Battlecruisers, five Carriers, and five Battle Transports with a total of ten brigades of the ASCAR. He added that if these forces were insufficient, they should be doubled; he also wanted to remind the Cadre that the Sovereign's orders to guard the Protectorates had been quite explicit in her previous message." She took a deep breath, trying to calm her heart which felt as though it was about to burst.

There was a long pause before the First Counselor replied, but his face went through several contortions as he seemed to consider what he was going to say in response. "Thank you, Administrator,"

Regar finally replied, quite sanguinely, "I'll convene a Special Session of the Cadre immediately," the view screen went black without another word from the First Counselor of the Cadre.

Marta had an uneasy feeling about her exchange with the First Counselor of the Cadre and she turned her attention back to her console. After considering the situation for a moment she decided to call up the logs of military communications for the past two days, since her last encounter with First Counselor Regar. Once again she was searching for any orders to send Alliance vessels to Protectorates, but none had been issued. First Counselor Regar was obviously not following through on the orders from the Sovereign, or was it the entire Cadre? Something was definitely wrong, but what could she to do about it, Marta asked herself.

She decided that there was enough evidence regarding her suspicions that she should risk warning an old friend that they might not be receiving as much help as they were expecting. Marta composed a short message to Commander Dragar to inform him that their messages had been received, but that was all. She added, as cryptically as she could, that Dragar should, *"Expect a great deal of loneliness in space."* It was the most she could say without risking discovery from someone who might be sympathetic with the First Counselor. One thing that Administrator Marta was not skilled at, she reminded herself, as she deleted the records of her transmission to Helios-2 from the Root Directory of all communication activities for the day, was deception. Somebody would have to have clearance beyond hers to restore the logs, which would take no less than a member of the Cadre.

(* | *)

Even as the Communications Administrator was beginning to suspect that something was amiss with First Counselor Regar and the Cadre the first ships of the Galactic Armed Forces were beginning to make the transition to sub-light speed as they entered what humans on Earth referred to as the Milky Way. A veritable armada of Consortium vessels had been summoned from every part of their territory once Factotum Ebla Mar had received the news that the Sovereign of the Felis Alliance was somewhere on the planet identified as Terra.

Nothing would have made the twisted leader of the Ursus Consortium happier than seeing his rival eliminated, and he did not care about the cost. If innocent lives were lost along with that of the Sovereign, so be it; they would be remembered as martyrs of the Consortium. Their names, Mar had laughed to himself, their names would be as insignificant as their lives had ever been. If a thousand, a million, or even more innocent lives were lost it was nothing to a man willing to send his own soldiers to their deaths as easily as anything else he did during the day. Death meant nothing to Factotum Ebla Mar; it was, as he often said, *the cost of doing business*. If that resulted in the ultimate defeat of the Felis Alliance, let the blood flow like a river.

Few people realized that Factotum Ebla Mar had tried to have the Sovereign assassinated once before, but the attempt had been a miserable failure. Things could only have ended worse had the assassin revealed his close connections to Mar.

Things would be different this time, Ebla Mar thought to himself as he sat behind his imposing desk. His office was where he spent the majority of his time. He rarely left the comforts of his office unless he was conducting some sort of inspection or meeting with someone important who could not meet him at the Factotum's Palace. In such cases he would grudgingly make the concession of leaving the comforts his office and the Palace afforded him, but would return to them, and the safety they provided, as soon as possible. Outside of being in the office, he spent his time in his equally luxurious private chambers, which he retired to at the end of the day.

After spending much of his youth wandering the streets in the Fourth Quarter of the city of Hydra, running with the *Gujos*, the last thing Mar wanted now was any reminder of poverty in his life. Everything about the Factotum's Palace, and the office, reeked of luxury. From the rich paneling on the walls, the hand-woven carpet, to the jewel-encrusted mosaics that had been hung on two of the walls. It was one of the most ostentatious displays of wealth one could find, and it had been designed to intimidate anyone who had the misfortune of having to visit the leader of the organization. Those who saw the desk were reminded of the helm of a ship, which was precisely what it was designed to resemble. It had a built in computer system, directly connected to the Consortium's Main Frame, providing Mar with instant access to everything within their libraries and databases at the flick of his finger. It was also setup with an optical system allowing him to glance at a screen to access files, without having to use one of the keyboards on the desk. All he had to do was open a new window on one of the four monitors on his desk and he could find anything relating to the Consortium in a matter of seconds.

Factotum Mar smiled maliciously as he reviewed the intercepted messages and responses that had been transmitted between Helios-2 and Felis Prime. He could see that things were going precisely as planned. All of the transmissions in the world were not going to get them any help. He began to laugh quietly to himself as he typed out a brief message which was sent to several of the Vessel Commanders of the Galactic Armed Forces. Once the orders were given, once the plan was in motion, it was only a matter of time before the Sovereign would be dead and the Consortium would assume its place as the dominant force in the universe.

When Factotum Ebla Mar had discovered that the Sovereign was on Terra he made certain to order the GAF-Tralta-9 into a position to take advantage of the situation. Sending a STAWS Fire Team down to the planet to assassinate the Sovereign was a natural extension of the plan, even if the end result might result in an all-out war between the Consortium and the Alliance. That was simply the cost of doing business. Mar also knew that whoever took over for the deceased Sovereign might not be so likely to prosecute a war against the Consortium, not if his plans came to fruition.

Mar reflected on the five-member Fire Team assigned to the Battlecruiser; the STAWS were the Special Tactical and Weapons Specialists Corps, they were all highly trained commandos and were the Consortium's equivalent of the ASCAR. STAWS commandos would do anything necessary to fulfill the needs of their mission, even if that meant dying in the process. Mar also knew that one STAWS Fire Team was more than what was needed to deal with any number of Guardians who might be protecting the Sovereign; thanks to the transmissions he had received from his informant he was quite cognizant of the fact that only one of her precious Guardians was with her. It would make no difference to the commandos that the one remaining Guardian happened to be Commander Dragar, Factotum Mar thought to himself; he had every confidence in the superiority of the STAWS Fire Team and their training.

At last, Ebla Mar thought to himself, the Sovereign's days were coming to an end.

CHAPTER IX ~ FELIX TANGO

"My thoughts on leadership may be summarized in a simple dictum: 'Those who resist your authority should be eliminated with extreme prejudice, before the virus of their resistance spreads to others.' If this philosophy guides your leadership you shall encounter the successes enjoyed by Factotum Effris Mar, my grandfather. When he led the Ursus Consortium he refused to allow the vagaries of sentimentality to pollute his judgement with meaningless emotionalism. Once those resisting your authority have been expunged from society, with the greatest possible violence if necessary, the remaining population will quickly fall into place. This is the best way to maintain your position of power over the population, while maximizing control over law and order."

Factotum Ebla Mar, Supreme Leader, Ursus Consortium: *Notes to Posterity*

(* | *)

Captain Tiernat looked across the bridge of the Galactic Armed Forces Battlecruiser Tralta-9 at the stunning blue planet over which they were now in high geosynchronous orbit. By nature, he was not an overly sentimental man, but as far as planets went, Terra seemed to be a nice enough place.

It would not be that way for long, he thought to himself as he signaled for the STAWS Fire Team that had been selected for this mission to report to the bridge. Members of the Special Tactical and Weapons Specialists Corps were the elite commandos of the Galactic Armed Forces, trained to do the 'dirty work' of the Consortium, which was where their motto came from: they called themselves the Consortium's *Clean-up Crew*. If you had a mission done and there were any concerns, you sent in the STAWS; that usually meant success since the STAWS were the most elite representatives of the GAF, as well as the most capable.

Captain Tiernat looked up as the Fire Team entered the bridge and smiled grimly as each member of the team snapped to attention, delivering a perfect salute in the tradition of the Galactic Freedom Forces. Their right arms were raised at a perfect 45-degree angle directly in front of their bodies, their fists tightly clenched. At the end of the salute their extended arm would bend at the elbow, allowing their clenched fist to touch the center of the chest. Captain Tiernat returned their salutes, nodding to the group in greeting.

He signaled for them to stand at ease, "Good day, gentleman," he began amiably, then added, "lady," as he nodded toward Sergeant Candille, one of the few female members of the STAWS. "Please, follow me to the War Room," his clipped accent cutting the words short as he gestured toward the sealed door to his left, directing the five commandos to follow him to a specially shielded room reserved for confidential briefings, situated behind the main bridge, next to the Captain's Ready Room.

Once the door to the War Room was fully sealed and the Fire Team was seated around the large table Captain Tiernat began to speak, gesturing toward the view screen at the front of the room which everyone could see from their seats, "As you may have heard from rumors circulating on the ship," he began, his voice quiet but strong, "for the past three days we have been travelling toward a special destination. Well," he looked at each one of the five commandos looking back at him, "we have now arrived and are in orbit around what has been declared a Protectorate of the Felis Alliance," he watched with some satisfaction as the five commandos before him began to look slightly uncomfortable. It showed that his crew had not, in fact, been spreading rumors, which was always a security issue for a Captain in command of a warship. Seeing that the Fire Team was unaware of where they were meant that they had been left alone during the journey, just as they should have been.

"But that's not the reason you're here," he continued, making eye contact with Lieutenant Zarrs, the Team's commander, who nodded back at the Captain, encouraging him to continue.

"Your mission," Tiernat pressed on, his voice growing a bit softer, as the view screen changed, "is to eliminate an enemy of the Consortium." This time it was impossible for the Fire Team to hide their surprise, as they saw the image of Sovereign Sayoose displayed on the screen. "Yes," Tiernat confirmed, "you are being sent down to eliminate the Sovereign of the Alliance."

"You mean assassinate her," came the gruff response of Lieutenant Zarrs, whose face had darkened considerably. "Damn it, Captain," he said, slapping the table with enough force to make the Captain jump in surprise, "we're soldiers, we're *not* assassins; we have a code of honor." He crossed his arms over his impressive chest and sat back as Sergeant Candille gently patted his shoulder to calm him.

A thick silence settled over the group. Captain Tiernat seemed unwilling to continue while there was so much anger on display and the team unable to fully express their anger without becoming violent. This was, after all, what they were trained for: they had trained for any contingency, even if they had not been trained to be assassins, it has always been something they knew they might be called to do at some point in their careers.

After several long seconds the soft voice of Corporal Vontic broke the silence, calming the situation, "Look LT, we all know this isn't what any of us wants, but you also know that we're all sworn to follow any orders we've been given," this elicited a grunt of displeasure from the Lieutenant. "But," he pressed on, "as long as we're not being asked to commit an act which we know is a direct treaty violation, or something that puts the lives of noncombatants in harm's way, then we're able to follow those orders freely, and without restriction," he paused to consider his words. "You know as well as anyone that if the Sovereign were on Felis Prime and we made it through their defenses we would take her out without hesitation, correct?" Vontic looked directly into the eyes of the Lieutenant, challenging him to answer, but he was rewarded with a cold glare and silence.

"Yeah," Lieutenant Zarrs nodded, "you're right, I still don't like it. Not one bit. You can't possibly believe that they've allowed the Sovereign to remain down there unprotected, do you?" Lieutenant Zarrs looked accusingly toward the Captain.

Captain Tiernat nodded, "Had you allowed me to continue, Lieutenant," he said, unphazed by the interjections, "I would have told you that the Sovereign is, in fact, guarded by one of her Guardians," the Fire Team groaned at the mention of the Guardians. They were renowned as the finest bodyguards, and were highly respected. Lieutenant Zarrs did not relish going up against them, not even one of them. Tiernat continued, "I can also report that their ship has been sent on patrol. However, because of its shielding we can't track her," he sounded frustrated, "on the planet, however, the only Guardian that remained with the Sovereign is ..." he looked at the datapad on the table, "her Prime Guardian, Commander Dragar," he turned to the Lieutenant, "have you heard of him?"

Lieutenant Zarrs was unable to reply only because Sergeant Candille reacted faster, "You've got to be kidding?" her voice was not panicked, but contained a note of serious concern. "Are you aware of who Commander Dragar is, Captain? He's not *just* a Guardian, he's one of the most decorated soldiers in the history of the Alliance," the Sergeant had a look somewhere between crazed and awed, "Dragar has earned, and I do mean *earned*, three Bleeding Heart citations, for being injured while in combat. Consortium forces tried to kill him on three occasions and failed; each time, he slaughtered those sent against him." She looked into the eyes of the Captain, "Do you know what it takes for someone to be awarded the Golden Cluster, *with Distinction*?" she asked, glancing around the room.

Nobody knew, so she pressed on, "The Golden Cluster, with Distinction, is the second highest citation awarded by the Alliance; it's often given posthumously, for acts of extraordinary heroism and valor in the face of impossible odds in battle. Commander Dragar has been awarded this citation twice. First, for single handedly holding off a battalion of STAWS commandos, 500 of our best, while the wounded of his own battalion could be evacuated, allowing fresh troops to be brought in to reinforce their position, which the Alliance then recaptured and won as though they were being led by a machine, not a man. Dragar was also injured during that battle, but that didn't even seem to slow him down," she glanced at the Captain, but he remained silent, nodding for her to continue.

"His second Golden Cluster came from a campaign you might have heard of," she smiled grimly, "it took place on Silas 8," she seemed pleased as the Captain's face showed that he recognized the name of the campaign. Every cadet in the Galactic Armed Forces studied the Silas 8 campaign, and one of Tiernat's ancestors had been commander of a Cruiser during the battle; it had been an older class ship but was solid enough. They had been ordered to the Silas system to support mining operations undertaken by the Consortium. Unfortunately, before leaving the Halol system they discovered that things were not exactly as they had been briefed on when they arrived.

Most importantly, the Silas system contained a Green Zone planet, which the Felis Alliance had declared a Protectorate. Silas 8 was already an extremely advanced planet, at level GZ-9, and had made their first flights into the space around their system and there were many satellites orbiting the planet. While their spacecraft had not yet approached the speed of light, their progress was impossible to deny. As soon as the Consortium vessels arrived in the Silas system the Alliance had realized that they had chosen to set up operations in an inhabited system. His ancestor, Commander Tiernat, and his cruiser, the GAF-Topaz-33 were far from the only ships sent to the system, and several contingents of commandos and regular forces had been sent down to Silas 8 as well, but the Alliance had been ready for their arrival.

Before Commander Tiernat had been able to even prepare his ship and crew for their first battle drills the Alliance's ships arrived in force. Battle Transports arrived first, escorted by Battlecruisers from the opposite side of the planet which allowed them to deploy their troops without any Consortium vessels observing the operation. Then, the rest of their forces arrived, to deal with the Consortium vessels in the system, including those attempting to mine the sun of the Silas system.

Commander Tiernat's ship had been one of the first destroyed. GAF-Topaz-33 was ripped in half by a weapon the Commander never even saw, exposing the ship's core to space, venting their precious atmosphere so that the only crew members who survived were those in areas behind sealed bulkheads. Only those in engineering, communications, and weapons control made it to the egg-shaped life-pods, which were automatically ejected from the dying ship, sent to float in space where they orbited until they were picked up by a Consortium Battlecruiser answering their distress beacons. Commander Tiernat died on the bridge of his ship, along with his entire bridge and command crew.

Captain Tiernat was familiar with the general facts regarding the Battle of Silas, but had no idea as to how Commander Dragar had earned his commendation at that battle. He looked at Sergeant Candille who began to recount the story, "Several STAWS battalions were deployed to the surface," she began, leaning forward. "Captain Felgarz had ordered the lead battalion to take up a position outside one of the main cities on the planet, preparing to enter after the sun had set, hoping to take them by surprise, but they never made it that far," she was shaking her head as though she were reliving the event herself rather than recounting something that she had studied.

"As the sun began set behind the mountains the battalion could hear the first sounds of plasma rifles firing in the distance, but nobody knew where they were coming from. Well," she let out a nervous laugh, "they found out soon enough. One minute their rear flank was guarded by regular GAF soldiers, the next, they had," she snorted, "I don't know how many battalions or brigades there were of the ASCAR pursuing them, and pursue they did! Or STAWS commandos fought back, but they were no match for their weapons or their numbers," she looked down, as though in shame at a loss that had taken place many years before her birth.

She looked up again, "At one point the entire command staff of the STAWS was wiped out by a single sniper; they were being picked off with impunity. He was in a position that couldn't be approached and was perfectly defended; anyone who tried to approach was cut down faster than you could blink. One General, a Major General, three Colonels, two Majors, four Captains, and seven LTs were taken out by this one Alliance sniper before a call to retreat was finally issued. By that time the mining operation had been completely shut down, destroyed by the Alliance, and our forces were in tatters, practically beyond salvaging." She sounded as though she had just returned from the battle, physically drained by the conflict.

"Our forces were beyond decimated," she continued, "we'd been well and truly routed. We'd suffered nearly seventy percent losses, unprecedented for the Corps, and the man who led it all, well ... you know him as Commander Dragar, now working as the Prime Guardian of the Sovereign. He received not only his second Golden Cluster, with Distinction, but it was for that battle for which he was awarded his first of two Beryllium Clusters, the highest commendation awarded to any member of the Unified Armed Services of the Alliance," she was about to continue but the Captain raised his hand to silence her.

"That's quite fascinating, Sergeant, and I'm certain we're all delighted that you have such a wealth of information about your opponent," he looked at her with his head tilted to the left, "how is it, by the way," he asked, his voice taking on a slightly condescending tone, "that you happen to know so much about this particular Guardian? I don't recall there being all that many documents floating around the Consortium's Intel Service regarding the personal history of Commander Dragar."

Sergeant Candille blushed at the comment, but Lieutenant Zarrs jumped in to answer, "Sergeant Candille has a unique talent for squirrelling out information about anything," he winked at the Sergeant, "and anyone she happens to find remotely fascinating," he looked into the Captain's eyes. "Believe me, Cap, if she's posted somewhere, Sergeant Candille makes it her business to find out anything and everything she can about the ship she's on, as well as its crew," he looked around the War Room, smiling at the other members of the Fire Team who were each nodding in agreement. They had all come to respect the Sergeant's abilities to ferret out information from the Consortium Database and had each turned to her at various times to find out something pertaining to their missions.

"In fact," Lieutenant Zarrs continued, I'm fairly certain that Sergeant Candille could tell us all a thing or two about you, and this ship as well," it almost sounded like a taunt, but it had been meant in good nature. Captain Tiernat, however, refused to take the bait. He merely nodded and returned to the matter of the briefing.

"Fine," he said curtly, turning back to his briefing notes, "this is what we know about where the Sovereign is located," he pointed to the view screen and an image of a small building situated at the end of a long, isolated driveway came into focus. "As you see, the advantage is that there are no other dwellings nearby. There shouldn't be any difficulties involved in your assault on the target," he glanced toward the Sergeant, "not even from your amazing Commander Dragar." This earned him a derisive snort from the commando as she turned her attentions to a knife on her harness, ensuring that it was firmly attached to its scabbard. She seemed satisfied with the weapon and returned her attention to the briefing.

"It won't matter how isolated the Sovereign is," she said, her voice barely above a whisper. Every eye in the room was on her as she spoke; her words measured and deliberate, "If we're not absolutely perfect, if we make even the slightest miscalculation, we won't get within a Krenar of that building," she looked around at the commandos she had been training with for the past several months, seeing the look of trepidation on their faces. "I can guarantee that even on his own, Commander Dragar will have arranged a defensive perimeter that will not be easily breached. Not even by us," she gestured at the four men around her who were, without question, the best she had ever worked.

"We can deal with it," Private Anju blurted out excitedly. His specialty was hand-to-hand and general weapons and they liked to joke that Anju could find a way to kill someone with a blade of grass, which was not really an exaggeration. He was also a wizard when it came to explosives, both making things blow up and stopping them from doing so, an extremely handy skill to have when engaging an adversary as worthy as the Alliance, or ASCAR commandos. Unfortunately, he had an exaggerated sense of his own abilities, which Sergeant Candille knew would get the young Private into serious trouble at some point in time.

"We'll know soon enough," Candille replied, and the rest of the team nodded soberly.

Captain Tiernat cleared his throat to regain control of the briefing and the five commandos immediately returned their attention to him, "To give you the best chance at success it has been decided that you not be sent down to the surface wearing your uniforms," he said, calling up another image. "We found samples of what they wear from monitoring satellite transmissions and have created outfits that will allow you to blend in with any indigenous population you may encounter," he was pleased to see that even the doubtful Sergeant Candille seemed impressed with the plan. "These are what you'll be wearing," the image showed a man wearing leather leggings and tunic, along with calf-high boots with an embroidered design down the front. Each image showed the men wearing long cloaks, with hoods, while the women were wearing floor-length dresses, along with cloaks that also covered their heads.

"As you can see," the Captain continued, "these outfits should allow you to conceal your weapons quite effectively, and you will look exactly like one of the planet's inhabitants."

Captain Tiernat truly believed the Fire Team had a decent chance at succeeding in their mission, though he was still not sure what the ramifications might be for the Consortium in the event of their success. He was not privy to whatever else Factotum Ebla Mar might be planning for the Felis Alliance, all he had been told related to this particular mission. One thing that Captain Tiernat did know was that it was unlike Factotum Mar to start something without having fully considered the consequences of his plans.

"Your outfits are waiting for you in your training area; you depart in your shuttle in two hours, understood?" Nobody had any objections or questions.

They had been continuing their training and resting while traveling to the Terran system and were now anxious to get down there, even if that might mean facing the legendary Commander Dragar. After nodding to the group the Captain gave them a crisp salute, which was immediately returned as they leapt to their feet, "Excellent," he said, nodding to Lieutenant Zarrs, "I wish you all good luck and success; I'll see you when you return," he smiled at each one of them. "You'll all be heroes of the Consortium." He waited for a reply, but none came. "Dismissed," he finally said, a bit confused at the sudden change in the mood of the group. He decided they were simply focusing their energies on the task ahead of them; STAWS commandos were unlike other members of the crew, and were given more latitude as a result of their exceptional skills.

Once dismissed the Fire Team silently filed out of the War Room. As they were walking back to their training area, where their bunks were also located, just aft of the shuttle area, Private Tayko whispered, just loud enough for his friend, Private Anju to hear, "Anju, Did the Cap just jinx us … I mean, you've *got* to be kidding, *Hero* of the Consortium, right?"

"You got something to say, *Private* Tayko?" Lieutenant Zarrs practically shouted at the man, his voice easily penetrating through the loud hum of the passageway.

Everyone stopped walking, "No sir. I mean, well," he hesitated, "I was just saying, well …"

"You believe that the Cap jinxed us, am I right?" the Lieutenant prompted, his voice less harsh now that they were no longer walking through the passageway.

"Yes sir," the two Privates responded, in chorus. Even Sergeant Candille was nodding in agreement as they approached their training area, just above the engineering section.

"Look," Lieutenant Zarrs said, "I'm not thrilled with this anymore than you are, but this is the mission we've been dealt, alright? Yes, Cap might be an idiot, but he's a good egg. We've been given a shit mission … again. That's what STAWS gets: the shit missions. You knew that when you signed up for the Corps. We're going down there, and we're going to do what we've been ordered to do, and then we're going to get out," he looked directly at the Sergeant, "and I don't give a crap about Commander Dragar and his damn awards and commendations. He's also going to die, is that understood?"

The four other members of the team replied as one, "Yes, sir." Lieutenant Zarrs turned to Corporal Vontic, and looked directly into the eyes of the commando.

"You alright with this, Vontic?"

"As I said earlier, sir … so long as the orders don't ask us to violate any treaty, we're cool," the commando responded quietly.

Lieutenant Zarrs nodded, looking down at his boots as they

began walking again. He loved his boots and was annoyed that he would not be able to wear them on this mission. "Look," he said, keeping his voice low, "we all heard what Candy said," he nodded toward Sergeant Candille, who frowned. Her name was not that difficult, she thought to herself, that it required such a stupid nickname.

"You know as well as I do that facing Dragar has to be one of the stupidest ideas that Central Command has come up with since," he paused, "well, I guess since the debacle in the Silas system," the others were nodding in agreement. That conflict had ultimately led to the Callisto Treaty, declaring that the mining of any sun within an inhabited system was strictly forbidden.

Lieutenant Zarrs also knew that the Consortium had attempted to violate that treaty on more occasions than he could count, but the Alliance had always been there to thwart their efforts. However, he was a soldier, sworn to defend the Consortium. His job was not to apologize for their actions, and that was exactly what he was going to do: defend it, and carry out his orders, even if that might result in an all-out war between the Consortium and the Alliance. That was something the Factotum would have to consider, he thought to himself. Of course, if the result was a war it would be his friends, his comrades, who paid the heaviest price by having to face the Alliance in battle. He knew that it would not bother Factotum Mar if any of them were killed, and that did bother him, but only for a moment.

He allowed his mind to flit over the question of how many lives might be lost in the event the Consortium went to war with the Alliance as they arrived at their training area, but quickly brushed aside the thought. This was not about morality or ethics, he reminded himself, it was about following the orders that had been issued to them by their commanding officer, regardless of how much of an idiot he may have been, orders that had originated from the Supreme Leader of the Consortium. It was also about being the soldier he had trained to be, and that was exactly what he was going to do, even if he lost his life in the process.

Zarrs did not want to die; none of his team did, but he also knew that they had been trained to the point that death was something that they did not think about. Completing their mission was more important than the personal cost. With less than two hours to go before the Fire Team was scheduled to take their shuttle down to the planet he still had several things to do to prepare for their departure. First he would have to figure out how to conceal his weaponry within this strange Terran clothing, he thought to himself as he wrestled on the leather boots he had been provided. He then began examining the numerous deep pockets in the cloak he was supposed to wear, filling them with the various weapons he was planning on taking on the mission.

(*|*)

After the sun had risen over the horizon Dragar had once again resumed his observations from his post in the oak tree, watching the window on the side of the house while keeping an eye on his wrist monitor to ensure there were no disturbances around the perimeter of the property. From his vantage point he observed the Sovereign sleeping on the couch, curled into a tight circle next to the female, who was reading a book. That was all the Sovereign seemed to do, Dragar thought to himself. Well, not entirely; she ate her breakfast and allowed the human to rub her belly for a while, then she would lie down and sleep for several hours while the female went about her business, he smiled to himself, thinking about how easy it had been to protect her while in this form.

Sovereign Sayoose would usually remain next to the woman, but she would still be sleeping. He could not imagine how she managed to spend so much of her time asleep. Of course, there was also the music, which Dragar could hear thanks to the micro-transmitter he had placed in the house during his inspection. Lovely stuff, he thought to himself, and the Sovereign obviously enjoyed it tremendously as well. She made a point of turning on the device that played the music when the woman was not at home, and somehow convinced the old man that he had done so, simply by staring at him with her mesmerizing eyes.

He would have to ask if that was the reason she had chosen this planet; he knew that music was one of her great loves and interests. Sovereign Sayoose had pursued degrees in both Art History and Musical Composition before entering the military, so it was no surprise to see her enjoying the works of the composers from this planet. Dragar had to admit that for such a primitive world their cultural works were quite admirable. That must have been why she chose to come here, he reflected, watching as the human gently stroked the back of the Sovereign while listening to the *String Quartet*, Opus 130, by a composer named Beethoven. As the music filled his head through his implanted receiver he marveled at how beautiful it sounded. Not for the first time, Dragar thought to himself that this was definitely a culture worth exploring.

Given how hard the Sovereign worked, often for days on end without rest or sleep, he imagined she could easily spend quite some time enjoying doing almost nothing but sleeping; that made the choice of this cat creature seem like quite an appropriate selection given their proclivity for spending so much of their time asleep. At the same time, he was well acutely aware that the Sovereign would not be wasting her time while lying around: she had one of the keenest minds; even without the assistance of a data pad or other devices, she was undoubtedly working on any number of projects which she would be able to down-line from her memory once she returned to Felis Prime and was able to connect to a computer using a Neural Interface. He quietly laughed to himself at the thought of her returning to Felis Prime with a dozen or so new volumes to contribute to her already impressive collection of works. Well, they would find out soon enough, he thought to himself.

Dragar remembered the first time he watched the Sovereign use the Neural Interface; she had told him that she had been working on a few things, and felt it was time to finally get them out of her head. One of the things had been a completed draft of the history of the Callisto Treaty, which the Alliance and the Ursus Consortium had struggled over for several years since the battle on Silas 8, while Dragar still commanded the Fighting Fifth. Once the Neural Interface was activated the Sovereign was able to down-line what she had created in a manner of seconds. Instead of having to write things out they were there, complete: just as they had been conceived.

It was an especially popular device for writers and composers who would work on their books or compositions and then, after having fully conceived the work in their mind, could then down-line an entire work, making any changes where necessary to clean things up once they had been entered into the computer. It made the process of creativity faster by several orders of magnitude, opening the doors of creativity in ways that had simply not been possible before. Of course, some things were still done the old fashioned way, but even then, there were ways that the new technologies were able to assist: painters were able to visualize their works and have realistic mock-ups created in a matter of seconds, which could then allow artists to transform them into posters, etchings, or lithographs. Sculptors were able to employ the technology to guide computer-aided carvers into releasing their designs from whatever matrix they chose to work; the vision still had to exist within the mind of the artist in order for the creation to be born, but the creative process had been made far less cumbersome. Art, and its creation, had flourished throughout the Alliance since down-lining technology had been invented, opening up a new age of culture and creativity that had never before been seen by humanity. A golden age of humanity and the arts had truly arrived, the fruits of which were being enjoyed by all.

Humanity had been truly liberated. Thanks, in part, to the Neural Interface, but also as a result from being freed from the drudgeries of manual labor, thanks to the creation of Synthetic Intelligent Living Systems, which now worked in virtually every position once undertaken by humans. SILS provided humans the ability to spend their extended lifespans in far more enjoyable pursuits. Save for doing something that required them to kill, or a task that involved creative or interpretive work, SILS were capable of doing virtually any task within the Alliance, leaving much less that humans were required to do in order to maintain their civilization. It had been decided that the administrative work of the Alliance itself was something that should be done exclusively by humans, though there were some SILS who worked as assistants. Emergency medical personnel were also human, considering they were required to make creative decisions regarding the diagnoses of illnesses, as were lawyers, who had to interpret the laws, which required skills the devices were not equipped to make, but SILS did work alongside doctors and nurses in hospitals, performing routine procedures. SILS had made the Alliance as close to a true paradise as one could have imagined; they were heralded as truly wondrous creations.

Unfortunately for the female in the house with the Sovereign, Dragar thought to himself as he watched her take some plates into the kitchen, there were no SILS to assist her while she cared for the Sovereign during her vacation; she had to do all of the work for herself. As Dragar watched the Sovereign sitting on the couch he imagined that she might be writing another installment of her memoirs, or something having to do with the history of the Alliance, or both, or many other things; she was certainly capable of doing that, and more. Or, he smiled to himself, she might just be relaxing; he would not hold it against her for wanting to take some time to give her mind a break, particularly after all she did on a regular basis.

An unusual sound in the distance caught his attention, making him forget about his speculations regarding what the Sovereign might be doing during her periods of relaxation. He had been in this location for enough time to learn the indigenous sounds of the place and there was definitely something wrong. Something off to the north-west had made a sound that he had not heard since arriving on this planet, though it was a sound that he had heard before. He instantly recognized the faint sounds coming from the engines of a Class-2 Consortium shuttle. A small transport shuttle was landing.

"So," he muttered to himself, "it begins." Dragar quickly checked the status of his weapons, making sure their power-cells were fully charged, and took out the small pen-sized monocular from his breast pocket. He pulled on it, elongating it, and placed the widest end over his right eye. Closing his left eye, he aimed it toward the direction of the sound; he was looking directly down the road the human had to drive up in order to approach the house, but the sound had originated deep in the field. He could just see the top of the shuttle as the five-member Fire Team worked to cover it with the surrounding vegetation. He let out a small chuckle, "Don't worry, my friends," he whispered, "you won't be needing that anymore."

He lowered himself from the tree and disappeared into the grass, still wet with the early-morning dew.

(*|*)

"Don't ya' think it's already covered enough?" Private Anju grumbled, annoyed at how difficult it was to cut the tall stalks of corn from the ground in order to cover the profile of the chunky shuttle.

"Just keep covering until you hear otherwise," Sergeant Candille replied, as she slashed at another few stalks with her razor-sharp knife, being careful not to slice the leg of Corporal Vontic, who was working alongside her, swinging his own knife with military precision. "We still need several more stalks, then we'll be fine," she said, her breath growing heavy from the exertion as she handed her harvest to Private Anju, who carefully placed the stalks so that the shuttle was becoming obscured from sight in the field. After another few minutes it would be as though it had never been there.

As Sergeant Candille continued working she realized that the gravity on this planet was a bit heavier than what she was used to, but it was nothing the team would not be able to adapt to quickly enough, but it was making their work more difficult, making them take more time than they had expected. Fatigue might become an issue if they had to face Commander Dragar, Sergeant Candille thought to herself, since he had already been on this planet for a few days and had undoubtedly adapted to any gravitational differences between here and Felis Prime. She silently cursed Captain Tiernat under her breath for not having had the foresight to tell them about the gravitational differential on this planet. It was just like the Consortium to send in their troops without all of the information they required to meet their adversary.

After concealing their shuttle, the Fire Team walked through the field and joined their Lieutenant, who had gone to the road, looking for signs that anyone had seen their arrival. "I think we're okay," he said, nodding to the others, "that's the direction we're supposed to go, but," he hesitated, looking around at the vast nothingness around their position. As the Captain had pointed out, there were no other buildings within line of sight, except for one old, decrepit barn, far to the west of their position, but it was obviously deserted; it was clear that nobody lived there: you could see clear through the abandoned structure from the road.

"You want to go around and approach from the other direction," Sergeant Candille said, before Lieutenant Zarrs could complete his thought. Their plan was to circumvent the house and approach from the road, from the opposite direction, from a wheat field growing next to the property adjoining their target.

He nodded, "Exactly," he said, "I don't know where he is, but Dragar is out there, and there's no reason we have to make this any easier for him, right?"

"You can also be sure that he's already acclimatized himself to the …" Candille started to say, but the Lieutenant silenced her with a raised hand, glaring at her in a menacing manner.

"I really don't need to hear anything else about the amazing Commander Dragar, Sergeant, is that understood?" Zarrs sounded far angrier than she had ever heard, making Candille genuinely concerned that the man might strike her.

She nodded, silent for a moment, then whispered, barely loud enough for him to hear, "Understood, sir."

"Good, now let's get moving. Step lightly," the angry tone was gone, but his eyes still possessed the shadow of what had been there only a moment before.

Each member of the Fire Team nodded, perhaps a bit reluctantly, as they turned and began trudging through the field, single file, each one dragging their feet as they tried to acclimate to the heavier gravity of the planet.

(*|*)

Dragar had established his defensive position well away from the house, and was watching the small group when he decided to contact Helios-2. One thing that he knew was that they had not flown here from the Ursus system in that shuttle. "Helios-2, come in; this is Guardian One," he began, barely above a whisper. He knew the transmitter would carry his voice as clear as if he were shouting, "Reporting situation with presence of potential F-T; I repeat, a potential Felix Tango targeting object of my attention. Recommend you return immediately to find and eliminate source of this threat. Maintain silence. Will update when possible. Guardian One, out."

He knew the message would make the other two Guardians sick with worry, but it could not be helped. Helios-2 was more than capable of taking care of any Consortium vessel, especially with surprise on their side, and there was no way that Dragar wanted to let the Consortium get away with sending a squad of assassins without paying the price. Dragar was not surprised that a Fire Team had been sent to assassinate the Sovereign, but he was surprised that they had arrived so soon after the Guardians had located the Sovereign. His mind was going over the messages that had been exchanged between Operations since they had arrived and he was beginning to think about what the Sovereign had mentioned about there being *more to this* when he had first encountered her at the clinic.

Now he was wondering if that might have anything to do with the possible presence of a betrayer within her Cadre. It was an unthinkable situation, yet the evidence was currently stalking through the field, seemingly ready to kill the Sovereign once they had the opportunity. As he adjusted his position to ensure he had an unobstructed view of the approaching group Dragar felt the vibration of his wrist device indicating an incoming text. He looked at it and smiled as the text scrolled by on the device: *"Guardian Two received and understood. Helios-2 returning, shields on. Weapons armed and ready: all systems primed for engagement. Guardian One: stay safe. Guardian*

Two, Over."

Dragar felt a pang of the deep love he felt for his crew; he may have joked around and harassed them, especially Tactical Sergeant Brem, but they were great friends, and would give their lives for one another in an instant. With a lump in his throat the big Commander whispered a response, "Guardian One, received. You are weapons free: I repeat, weapons free. Thank you, and stay safe. Guardian One, over and out." Nothing else needed to be said, nor would be. Not until the mission had been concluded. If they failed, he would never know. If he failed, he shook his head: he could not allow the thought to enter his mind as he once again raised the monocular to observe the progress of the Fire Team as they marched away from the shuttle.

"So predictable," he whispered, as he settled into the glare of the early morning light, his T-17 Plasma Rifle was aimed at the group as they moved through the fields toward the house, but Dragar wanted to give them a sporting chance. He also wanted confirmation from Helios-2 that there was a Consortium vessel in orbit overhead. That would be all the proof he needed. After all, they could have been from a ship that had to be abandoned, resulting in their shuttle landing on this planet. *Sure, and I'm going to be the next Sovereign,* he thought to himself.

His wrist device vibrated, indicated another incoming text from Helios-2. He looked down as the text scrolled across the screen and his heart speed up a bit as he realized there would be some killing. Helios-2 had arrived on station and identified the GAF-Tralta-9, a Consortium Battlecruiser.

Even though they had their orders, Dragar quickly replied, "Guardian One received. Maintain defensive shields; drop stealth and engage. Plasma torpedoes and Canons. Over and out." It had not been necessary for them to contact him, but no Alliance ship wanted to fire first in any engagement. Revealing their presence to the Tralta was a calculated move designed to draw the fire of the Battlecruiser, and he knew it would work. If the Captain of the Consortium vessel suddenly saw an Alliance vessel sitting in front of them they would immediately fire upon them, but it would be too late: as soon as they made the move to arm their weapons, something the A-ConCom of Helios-2 would immediately detect, Captain Pertu would have the weapons-systems of Helios-2 shred the Battlecruiser. Plasma torpedoes were the most advanced weapons on any Alliance ship, and had destroyed many Consortium vessels. Nothing could withstand the force of the weapon, and the last thing a Consortium Captain would be expecting would be for a ship the size of Helios-2 to fire a weapon usually reserved for something several times their size. Unfortunately, Dragar thought to himself, that Captain had sent down a team to assassinate the Sovereign. He was not about to allow them to go home; they had committed an act of war.

Dragar turned onto his back for a moment and trained the monocular directly overhead at the morning sky, trying to see what he knew was out there, high in an orbit over the planet. He knew he would not be able to see the Consortium Battlecruiser ripping apart after the Class T Plasma Torpedo and Plasma Cannons of Helios-2 tore several cavernous holes and gashes into their hull, destroying their structural integrity while venting their precious atmosphere to the vacuum of space. If they were lucky, he thought to himself, some of them might have been able to get to the escape pods; if not, too damn bad.

"That's what you get for trying to kill the Sovereign," he whispered, under his breath, as he returned his attentions to the Fire Team.

By the time he rolled back onto his stomach and relocated the Fire Team his wrist device was vibrating. He knew what the message would be, but looked anyway, nodding as the text scrolled across the screen, *"Mission accomplished. No escape pods visible. Guardian two, over and out."* Dragar smiled grimly to himself. Brem knew better than to wish his commander luck when he was on mission: it was not only bad luck, it was rude. Commandos trained, and they trained hard. They relied on well-honed skills, not luck.

"Any soldier that relies on luck may as well be dead," they were be told during their training to become part of the Alliance Special Combat Armed Response Corps, and it was true. "Luck favors those who lack skill and training. Those who were prepared, who had trained for every contingency, did not require luck." He remembered the words of one of his Drill Sergeants, a tough Ionian woman who had worked the grunts through their paces from dawn to dusk. She would say, "If you think you require luck to be a good soldier, get your sorry ass off my team: I don't want to be anywhere near you when you get your head blown off!" They were words he had lived by for five thousand years as a battalion commander, and they had served him well then, and now. Skill was his stock in trade; luck was for losers.

Dragar took a final look through the monocular and muttered, "Still all five in a row, you're just making this too easy, aren't you?" He flipped the switch on the T-17 to single shot mode, turning it into a sniper rifle. It would be silent and the pulse of plasma would be impossible to see in the early morning light. He carefully sighted the weapon's viewfinder on the last man in line, took a few long, slow breath, to slow his heart rate and brought it down to about 30 beats per minute; once he was ready, he gently depressed the trigger. None of the others reacted as their comrade's head disappeared in a cloud of vaporized bone and flesh as he fell backwards into the wheat field. He then re-sighted on the next man in line and, after another breath, pulled the trigger. This man also fell backwards, allowing Dragar to immediately move the crosshairs onto his third target, and pulling the trigger. Dragar cursed quietly to himself as the man fell forward, knocking into the only woman of the group who had been walking behind the man leading the team.

Sergeant Candille instantly dropped to the ground, covered in the blood of Corporal Vontic. She turned to find Lieutenant Zarrs but he was gone. After a few seconds she saw that he had begun crawling toward where he thought the shots had come from.

"LT, what are you doing?" she hissed, trying to remain concealed within the dwarf wheat they had been walking through.

"I think I know where he is," came the reply from Lieutenant Zarrs, he had turned toward Sergeant Candille, beckoning for her to follow. "If we can get behind him …" he started to say when his head disappeared in a cloud of blood, vaporized bone and brain matter. Sergeant Candille did not scream, even though she was terrified. She knew she was facing Commander Dragar, and did not expect to receive any mercy from the greatest warrior the Alliance had ever produced.

"Do not move," she heard a deep voice say, as the shape of the Guardian shimmered into view, several paces from the body of the fallen Lieutenant. Candille looked at Dragar, then back to the Lieutenant with a puzzled look on her face. He smiled at her, "You have a question?" he asked, almost casually.

"It's nothing, really," she began, "I just can't figure out how you were able to take that shot … and, if you don't mind my asking, when did you see us coming?" she sounded genuinely deflated at having been so easily captured, even after pointing out how exceptional their opponent was to the others, including Captain Tiernat.

Dragar smiled, "To answer your second question first," he began, "I saw you from the beginning," she looked shocked, but he just nodded, "the sound of your shuttle's engines flying through the atmosphere of this planet created a sound quite unusual to the sounds

I'd been hearing since my arrival; there aren't any aircraft with engines quite like a shuttle on this planet. Also, the shuttle created a localized pressure wave when you landed, which I observed from the vantage point I had taken up near the house," he was pleased to see that she was completely demoralized.

"As for your first question," he continued, "I took that shot," he gestured to the body of the Lieutenant, "from up there," he pointed to a position about fifty paces in the air, and then began to levitate into the air without a sound, aiming his plasma rifle simultaneously. Once he was in position he activated his shield and disappeared, as though there had been no sign of him in the first place.

Before Sergeant Candille could say another word Dragar turned off the shield, but he was no longer in the air: he had repositioned himself. He was now right next to the Consortium commando, which surprised her enough that she tried to jump to get out of his way. Dragar quickly grabbed her left arm, holding her firmly in place. He then had her disarm herself, being sure to account for every blade and explosive that a commando would normally have. Once she claimed to be finished he had her strip down to her undergarments, and searched her clothing, finally frisking her, at which point he found another knife and plasma pistol, which he kept, before allowing her to dress. Instead of being upset at finding the concealed weapons Dragar seemed genuinely impressed.

"What are you going to do with me?" she asked sheepishly, surprised to still be alive.

"What would you *expect* me to do? Release you so you might try and complete your mission? Allow you to return to your ship?" he glared at her for a moment before relaxing. "Would you be surprised to learn that the Tralta has been destroyed?" Dragar asked, but there was no response from the woman, she just stared at him.

"You won't kill me, Commander," she said, her voice softer than it had been. "That's not your way."

Dragar seemed surprised, "What in Caiphus do you mean, *that's not my way*? What do you know about my way? Who *are* you?" he moved a step closer to her, but not close enough to be struck by any surprise attack she might launch. He was keenly aware of the abilities of STAWS commandos.

"My name is Sergeant Candille, Commander Dragar," she began tentatively. "I am someone who has admired your career for an extremely long time, and I've wanted to meet you, to tell you how much

166

I admire ... how much I respect you. I joined the Corps, the STAWS, only because I was born in the Consortium and could not join the ASCAR, but that's only because of where I lived," she was speaking faster now, her words full of passion. "We studied our so-called enemy, and that's where I heard about the great Commander Dragar; I discovered that you could be a military leader, that you could be a commando, without being cruel. I learned that you could command with honor, and that you could lead both men and women with dignity ... that you could serve your leader with a heart that was full of something that I did not have, simply because I had been born on a planet in the wrong planetary system," tears were rolling down her cheeks as she looked into the eyes of the big commando.

"When I learned of how you and the ASCAR dealt with the STAWS on Silas 8 I knew the Consortium was in the wrong, just as I knew that we were violating the Callisto Treaty when we were given our orders to come here today, despite what our stupid Captain and Corporal Vontic may have said to the contrary, but please, Commander," she looked directly into his eyes, "let me make up for this. Please, let me join you: there are many things I can tell you. Things that you could learn from me about the Consortium's military strength and operational readiness, as well as their plans for this system."

Dragar looked at Candille for a long moment, his arms crossed over his chest. He had scanned her body and could see she was not concealing any electronic or microscopic devices which could be used by the Consortium to spy on them; had she been she would have already been dead. There was no question of weapons, although by virtue of her being a member of the STAWS Corps she was an extremely well trained commando, which meant she could kill with her bare hands as easily as someone could have a drink of water. At the same time, Dragar thought to himself, she seemed sincere, and if she was, how could they pass up the opportunity to learn something about the Consortium from someone who had been so deep within the military. Besides, she had not even flinched when he mentioned that the Tralta had been destroyed, which meant she was either the best actress in the universe or truly sincere about defecting.

He turned to face her, uncrossing his arms, "I don't have to warn you," he began saying, but she finished the thought.

"You'll kill me if I try anything. Yes sir. Understood clearly, sir."

He looked at her, his head tilted to the left, "Alright, first thing, you don't call me 'sir', you're not a member of the Alliance military," he winked, "yet." He crossed his arms again as he looked at her outfit, "Secondly, what in Caiphus are you supposed to be wearing? You look like something out of a bad dream from another century."

Candille looked down at her colorful skirt and laughed at how ridiculous she must have looked, "Don't worry," he said, "I'm pretty sure Captain Pertu has an extra uniform that should fit you on board Helios-2. They'll debrief you when you get onboard, but remember," he held up a large index finger to caution her, "any funny stuff and I'm quite certain Tactical Sergeant Brem will toss you out the airlock, is that understood?"

She gulped, nodding her head. "I assure you, Commander, I will not let you, or Sovereign Sayoose, down."

Dragar looked at her and then took her hands in his, which seemed dwarfed, "I assure *you*," he said, his voice taking on a note of deadly seriousness, "should anything untoward happen on that ship while you're onboard, I shall hunt you to the ends of the universe," he pulled her close enough so she could smell his breath, "is that clear? I am giving you the gift of your life today; I have never regretted giving someone a gift in the past: don't make me regret giving you this one today." He surprised her by kissing her, extremely gently, on the right cheek, and then he released her hands. She took a step back, nodding silently while she blushed furiously at the unexpected moment of intimacy. For the first time since she had begun studying the character of Commander Dragar and now having met the man, Sergeant Candille realized that here, in the flesh, he was far more alluring than she ever could have imagined.

Dragar took another long look at her, realizing for the first time how truly attractive the young woman was; she had auburn hair, clipped short as was the custom with most commandos, but it was her eyes that captivated Dragar. They were intense, green eyes that seemed to shimmer, even in the early morning light.

"You won't regret your gift, Commander," she whispered, her voice thick with emotion, as another tear streaked down her cheek.

He gently wiped away her tear, surprising himself with the overt gesture of intimacy. Shaking his head, he turned his attention away from her for a moment and spoke into his wrist device.

After speaking to Helios-2 Tactical Sergeant Brem activated the Long Distance Matter Transporter, bringing both Dragar and Candille up to the ship. As they materialized on the LDMT pad Candille was unsurprised to see they were being greeted by a young woman aiming a

Plasma Pulse handgun at her, "Just stand where you are," she said, as the sound of the scanner confirmed what Dragar already knew. "All clear, Commander," she said, lowering the weapon and placing it into a holster strapped to her right leg.

Dragar turned to Candille, "I'm sure you understand, given the circumstances," she interrupted him before he could continue.

"Commander, I'd have been shocked if you had allowed me aboard the Sovereign's ship without going through some sort of scan. Believe me, things are different in the Consortium, but," she laughed, "security is still security." This earned her a grunt of approval from Brem, who was looking at her appraisingly.

"I can see why you didn't have the heart to shoot her, Commander," he chuckled, as he moved around to the back of the cabin, earning a glare from Dragar. He ignored the jibe and turned his attentions back to Pertu.

"Thanks, Captain. What's our status?" Dragar asked, as he guided Candille off of the LDMT pad toward the passenger quarters of the ship. "Captain Pertu has left a uniform for you, as well as some other things you might find useful. We'll get to your debriefing in a while. I'll be going back to the planet shortly so, if I don't see you before, thank you for your offer of assistance, and please," he looked into her striking eyes, "remember what I said."

Candille nodded and allowed Brem to lead her to the quarters that had been assigned to her. Dragar turned to Pertu, who handed him a datapad with the status report of the ship. "All systems optimal, Commander, they barely managed to get a shot off when we turned off our shields; I mean, they fired, but not really at us," she smiled, "it was as though they were shooting at phantoms." She laughed. "Of course, that may have been because a certain Tactical Sergeant who should remain nameless," she glanced toward the direction Brem had gone, smiling, "and silent, had hacked their tracking systems to make it look as though there were twelve of us attacking, but," she giggled, which resulted in a croaking sound, "I can't be certain."

Dragar shook his head, "Excellent work, really, outstanding." He turned as Brem re-entered the bridge.

"What're we supposed to do with that one?" he jammed his thumb toward the aft section of the ship.

"You're supposed to debrief her," Dragar replied, almost in a whisper. "She's a STAWS commando, a Sergeant. She knows plenty, and she wants to help us: she always wanted to be part of the Alliance, and I

169

believe her. Be gentle, but don't forget, she's also commando. Don't let your guards down," they both nodded in agreement. "In the meantime, I must return to the Sovereign; I know they only sent one team, and they didn't know about the change in her form, but I still don't like leaving her alone. Besides," he sighed, "I've got a bit of a mess to cleanup. Wouldn't do to have a Consortium shuttle be discovered by these people." Both Brem and Pertu nodded in agreement as he returned to the LDMT pad. Brem activated the device as soon as Dragar gave the signal to be sent back to where he had left from a few moments before.

After collecting the weapons that Sergeant Candille had left behind he moved the bodies of the four others into one spot and carefully tossed a single Shadow Maker grenade onto the pile, instantly eradicating any evidence of their existence. No memorial would be erected to these soldiers, he thought to himself sadly, only a shadow which would eventually be replaced by a new growth of wheat. He then jogged through to the cornfield, to the site of the shuttle and repeated the process, leaving a perfectly formed circle burned into the field where the shuttle had been.

Once all trace of the Fire Team's attempted attack on the Sovereign had been eradicated Dragar returned to the oak tree next to the house and resumed his silent vigil, looking through the window at the form of the Sovereign as she slept, blissfully unaware of everything that had transpired.

CHAPTER X ~ EXCURSION

"Planets that found themselves in the unenviable position of being in one of the adjacent Sectors to the one containing Ursus Minor, the home world of the Ursus Consortium often became targets for the power-hungry company, regardless of their interest in joining. It was never a matter of choice, but rather whether a planet possessed something the Consortium desired or required. Be it a particular resource, slaves for their industries or processing facilities, or something else entirely, forced membership eventually led to the spirits of those living on these planets being extinguished under Consortium rule and the inhabitants losing all hope of living under the banner of freedom.

"Precious few ever found their way from a Consortium controlled planet into an Alliance controlled territory, but it was known to happen on occasion. When it did occur, the people who escaped from the Consortium were referred to as 'Converters' for having converted from one system of life to another. Without exception, Converters were the most appreciative of Alliance Citizens; more than anyone else, they recognized how much they had gained within the Alliance, and what it meant to live under the crushing oppression of the Ursus Consortium."

[...]

Excerpted from: *A Brief History of the Felis Alliance*, by Sovereign Sayoose

(* | *)

Lareena slowly turned over on the bed, stretching sensually, making sure that Regar was watching as her diaphanous bedclothes slipped off of her finely sculpted body, leaving her completely naked. Her vanity was as highly developed as her desire to be noticed by members of the opposite sex, which was something she knew drove her husband mad with jealousy, though he managed to contain his feelings thanks to the knowledge that Lareena only wanted to be seen and acknowledged for her ravishing beauty; he knew that it never went beyond flirting. Regar was consoled by the fact that Lareena was equally interested in having women notice her, she seemed to take as much pleasure in the looks appreciative looks she received from women as from men wherever they went as a couple.

At first Regar had been bothered by his wife's overt sexual appetite, but he grew accustomed to her salacious tendencies. It had been, after all, her beauty and intense sexual appetite that had brought them together. How could Regar despise what was ultimately his wife's greatest asset? Just looking at her, as she lay exposed on the bed, drove any thought of jealousy from his mind as blood rushed away from his brain. Lareena was the only woman he had ever genuinely loved, though he sometimes wondered to himself if the intense feelings he was experiencing were more lust than true love; truth be told, he was not sure; he also did not care.

Regar knew that the moment he had first seen this enthralling woman, staring back at him from across the reception hall after the first day of the conference on Altus 9, the only thing that he had thought was that he wanted was to possess her. He was well aware that what he had been feeling at that moment had been unabashed lust, but she had responded to it as though she had read his mind. At some point, he was sure, that feeling had translated itself into love. He was certain of it; at least, he thought it had. After that she had gone back with him to his room, something that Regar had not thought possible. Still did not think was possible sometimes, even though they had been married for so long.

On that first night at the conference, he had breathed in the scent of her perfume and felt as though he had been in love with her for his entire life. She allowed him to do things that night that he had only dreamt of, that he had only fantasized of, and after that, they had been inseparable. He believed he was in love, but whenever he saw her, felt her body pressing against his, and tasted her flesh, he knew it was deeper than love; it was something unrestrained and animalistic taking control of his body as his base emotions bypassed his mind ... though he was certainly not going to start complaining. Certainly not right now.

Even as he once again felt himself drawn into her hypnotic control there was that heady perfume which she only wore for him.

Then he fell into the gaze of her crystalline green eyes where he always seemed to lose himself. He hardly remembered a moment during their marriage when it had been necessary for him to initiate a sexual act, but that hardly mattered. He shook his head in pleasure as he was once again engulfed by her soft flesh; how could something like that make a difference when it was so wonderful? All she ever seemed to want was for him to be thoroughly satisfied. Since they had met their nights had been filled with passion, consummated over and over again, something akin to the erotic fantasies of some naughty schoolboy, though it was far more than even that, he realized. He was given the most beautiful body to conquer, to ravish, to do with as he pleased … or, he had to ask himself, was that really what was happening? As he was still being overwhelmed, not for the first time, with paroxysms of pleasure Lareena casually slipped out of the bed. She covered herself with her flimsy robe, then glided across the room into the bathroom, knowing that the hungry eyes of her husband were taking in her every move before sliding the door shut behind her.

It was virtually the same scenario every time, but Regar was used to it now; Lareena would go clean up or 'refresh herself' as she said, then return to their bed and they would resume their lovemaking until he was too exhausted continue, except for talking, which he seemed to do far more with Lareena than anyone else he had ever known. Nobody had ever seemed more genuinely interested in his work, which had definitely been part of the attraction when they had first met. Well, that and her astounding body, of course. It would have been impossible for him to have *not* noticed her body, Regar thought to himself as he once again felt himself becoming aroused under the sumptuously soft sheets. Thinking of the swell of her perfect breasts, her aristocratic nose with arching eyebrows, and her luxuriously long, brown hair; she would always correct that it was brunette, cascading down her back, almost to her buttocks.

First Counselor Regar thought of the first time he had ever seen Lareena. It had been while he was visiting Altus 9, a colony on the second moon of Artunal, for a conference on issues pertaining to Alliance governance. As he had expected, it had been a shockingly boring event, but he had been sent by the Sovereign as her representative from the Cadre. After the first session of the conference he was having a drink at one of the gatherings and his eyes meet those of the most incredible women he had ever seen, standing on the opposite side of the room, staring back at him. Her name, he discovered, was Lareena.

He also discovered that she had been attending the conference as a delegate from … the odd thing was, he could never remember what planet she was representing, but it made no difference to the First Counselor. When he offered her a drink, to his utter surprise and joy, she accepted his invitation. After that drink, which led to a meal together and a long evening of conversation, they finally ended up in his room, and had inseparable since then, spending the remainder of the conference together. After the conference ended she returned to Felis Prime, and had never left. Ultimately, he had been thrilled he had attended. It had never seemed odd or even occurred to the First Counselor that this woman he had just met and fallen so deeply in love with had been at the conference as a delegate from a planet of the Alliance to which she had never once returned, or even mentioned.

From the moment they met he knew that he was in love. Perhaps he was only enamored with the idea of being in love, perhaps he was in love with her; he knew for certain that he was, at the least, deeply in lust. He had never encountered a woman who had been so willing to open herself, her entire body, to someone like him. Regar had long given up on trying to differentiate between love and lust. He was certain that he loved Lareena; he was equally certain that every fiber of his being lusted for her as well. Regar maintained no illusions about himself; he realized he was not overly attractive, even though he held an important bureaucratic position. He knew that many believed that power was an aphrodisiac, but with a smile, or less, Lareena could possess any man she desired. She was attractive and intelligent, yet she had chosen him; not only that, she had given herself to him freely, and continued to do so, with an exuberance that took away his breath.

He could still remember their first night together in his bedroom of the Conference Center: it was a memory he could never forget. Lareena had emerged from the bathroom of the room Regar had been staying in wearing nothing but a silky scarf and the most enticing perfume. It was the perfume she always wore when they were alone. It had the effect of a magical elixir on him, never failing to arouse him to such a degree, he felt as though he was being overtaken by a wild-man dwelling deep within him, struggling to escape. Every time she wore it Regar felt as though he had been transported into an entirely different dimension. Here he was, alone with his precious Lareena.

He had done things that first evening that he had never even imagined possible, things he had not dreamed were acceptable between a man and a woman, and she not only allowed him, she had *encouraged* him. When he thought they were finished, she simply rolled over and beckoned him to continue, which he did with a fervor he had not thought possible. In the morning he had been terrified that she would be offended by how he had acted, that she might have contacted one of the Enforcement Officers to report him for having brutalized her throughout the evening. Had that happened, he was ashamed to remember, he would have had no defense. She may not have objected, at the time, but he had not even tried to be gentle. He had left her bruised, and he was sick to his stomach with regret, thinking that he had ruined everything.

But, that had not happened. Lareena had not called for help and had not left: she was still there, next to him, as naked as the day she had been born; the perfume was as intoxicating as it had been the night before. With a few gentle words of encouragement, to convince him that she had not been offended by his aggressive attentions, she offered herself to him and they started all over again, though this time Regar made a concerted effort to be gentler, to which she responded by redoubling her own efforts in the consummation of their relationship. Even with this gentler approach during their first full day together, there were moments when Regar feared he might have either hurt or offended the delicate Lareena who seemed so vulnerable as they immersed themselves in passion. Her gentle touch assured him that neither was the case, as they continued to relish the touch of each other's flesh throughout that day, into the second night. They missed every session of the conference that day, spending it in his room, but mostly in bed, as they celebrated the birth of their new relationship. He could hardly keep himself from smiling like a giddy adolescent when, on the third day, they managed to return to the conference for which they had travelled to Altus 9 in the first place.

Regar watched as Lareena returned from the bathroom, walking in a manner that made it impossible for him not to notice the sway of her hips beneath the gossamer robe that did little to cover her nakedness. She then slipped back onto the bed they shared and began the familiar gyrations she performed, what she euphemistically called her *dance of love*, as she made herself comfortable, casting off the robe to fully reveal her nakedness to her husband who was now practically salivating in the anticipation of what he was about to experience.

He could not help but marvel at how her breasts seemed to defy gravity regardless of her position; they always maintained their perfect shape, and he knew they were neither artificial or enhanced. Even with the abilities that the Alliance possessed to slow the aging process, Lareena was a woman seemingly without age, a woman for whom sensuality meant something an entirely different thing than what it might to another person.

Before having met this amazing creature, Regar sometimes chided himself at how he thought about his wife, but there were times when she defied being referred to as a mere human; indeed, she was an exotic creature, a creature wholeheartedly dedicated to the art of love and sensual pleasure, Regar would have never considered the idea of indulging in a romantic dalliance in the middle of the day. Now it was a regular occurrence, and he did not even have to initiate the action. All that was required was for him to be there and she would sense his desires; she would be naked within seconds, doing things he had only ever imagined before they had met.

Then there was that intoxicating perfume: as soon as Regar had one hint of its aroma he was carried away on an erotic journey that seemed endlessly fulfilling, something unmatched by anything he had ever envisioned before meeting this incredible woman. Even now, as he watched her body moving next to his, he could feel his desire growing and he knew that she would once again be his; he knew that the ritual of his dominating her would be repeated, as it had almost every morning since their first meeting, and marriage, making him feel like the most virile man in the universe as he once again conquered the most erotic creature he had ever encountered.

In the many years of their marriage Regar had also changed. After almost one hundred and forty years with this incredible woman, a woman he was certain he adored, he was no longer concerned that his ministrations had become more violent, more forceful, and had started affecting his wife. Lareena never uttered a word of complaint or intimated that he had hurt her in any way, but since the departure of the Sovereign from Felis Prime Regar had become more forceful during their sessions, as though he somehow had something to prove. He was unsure whether it was to Lareena or to himself, but the violence was there nonetheless, and it was beginning to scare her. What Regar would never know, could never know, was that Lareena would endure anything. It was not out of her love for him but rather a motivation that she could never reveal, though she was quite certain that he had figured out her motivations after so many years together. If he had, she thought to herself, he had never once revealed his suspicions to her, although his increasing level of violence might be a sign of his unconscious resentment. She could not be sure, and it was something that they could not discuss.

To Regar, however, it all seemed like a dream, but this was what had become his life, and it was something he would not trade for anything. Lareena only asked for one thing from him, and it seemed so trivial when he thought about it: she wanted to know everything. Not just about his day, but every detail relating to what he did throughout his day, from the moment he left their chambers until the moment he returned. She wanted to know about who he had spoken to and what had been said; what messages the Cadre had received, and the replies they had dispatched. At first it had seemed odd, perhaps even silly, but he realized that since Lareena did not enjoy leaving their quarters while she was alone, she needed to be entertained. Living with the First Counselor of the Cadre made her feel powerful; she merely wanted to know what was going on in the Alliance: what better way of finding that out than by hearing about it from her own husband, a man who was one step away from being the Sovereign of the Alliance?

It was the least he could do for someone who provided him with so much pleasure. After all, what harm could there be in telling his wife what he had done at the office?

(*|*)

Sergeant Candille was sitting in the seat that Commander Dragar had occupied during their flight to Terra, wearing the uniform that Captain Pertu had provided. They were identical save that Pertu had removed the insignia and unit markings, making it an unmarked UAS uniform. It was still a radical improvement over what she had been wearing on the planet. Fortunately for Candille, the uniform fit her quite well as she was virtually the same size as Captain Pertu. Tactical Sergeant Brem was still looking at her with some degree of distrust, but after several hours of debriefing the young woman he was beginning to change his views.

"Let me get this straight, Candy," he asked, causing her to sigh. It never failed; as soon as someone met her, especially another commando, they instantly began calling her Candy as a nickname. She supposed it was better than some other options they had used in the Corps, but still, Candille was not such a difficult a name for people to say.

"You're telling us there's someone on Felis Prime funneling information directly to Factotum Mar?" he shot a glance over to Captain Pertu who had a look of disbelief on her face. That level of betrayal was unheard of in the Alliance. "I'm sorry," he continued, "but you're going to have to do better than that. We need more."

"Yes, Sergeant Brem," she began

"Tactical Sergeant," he grunted, then smiled.

Candille stared at him for a moment, nodding, "My apologies, *Tactical* Sergeant Brem. Yes, it's the truth," her voice was stronger now, building in confidence. "How else would you explain that we knew that the Sovereign of the Felis Alliance was on Terra?" This earned her another grunt from Brem and a groan from Pertu, but he encouraged her to continue.

"Look," she said, "you just destroyed the Tralta, a ship I'd served on for three years. I knew most of its crew and the only thing they ever did wrong was follow the orders of Factotum Ebla Mar, a madman. Other than that, they were all good soldiers. They were just trying to serve the Consortium; remember," she added softly, "in the Consortium you don't usually have a choice when it comes to serving in the military. Anyone who is considered strong enough from certain planets is drafted into the Galactic Armed Forces."

This earned another grunt from Brem, but his tone had softened. He had known about the Consortium's draft, and it troubled him deeply. He never felt good about having to kill someone who had been forced to fight for something that they did not believe in but had been forced to under pain of imprisonment or even death. If only Factotum Mar had not been trying to defeat the Alliance he might be satisfied with a smaller military force, but the only way the GAF could pose a threat to the Alliance was by forcing every able-bodied person into service; even then, the Unified Armed Services had no difficulty in deflecting any attacks from the Consortium.

Seeing the conflicted look on the face of the Tactical Sergeant, Candille continued, "I know," she said, holding up her hand, "when Captain Tiernat gave our Fire Team the order to go down to the planet I knew it was a violation of the Callisto Treaty, but Corporal Vontic and my LT tried to convince us that it wasn't ... well, they paid for that mistake, didn't they? I'm not going to defend what happened down there," her voice rose in pitch and she slapped the arm of the chair she was sitting in, "I'm trying to tell you that we had solid information, decoded transmissions from the Alliance, telling us where the Sovereign was located. I've been in the STAWS long enough to know that there's a real problem in the Alliance, and I don't want it to get any worse. Please," she was almost in tears, "I despise Factotum Mar and I want to see him stopped: the people of the Consortium have suffered tremendously under the rule of him and his family. Now, after trying to assassinate the Sovereign, that was never what the STAWS was meant to do; I was trained to be a commando … not a murderer," now she was crying, and both Brem and Pertu watched as her shoulders shuddered and the tears coursed down her cheeks.

After a several long seconds Brem reached over and patted her on the knee, "It's alright, Candille," he said, his voice uncharacteristically soft, "really. Nothing's going to happen to the Sovereign as long as we're around, and I can guarantee that whoever has been leaking information to Factotum Mar," he grunted, "well, they're going to wish they'd never been born," he looked over at Captain Pertu, "right Cap?"

"Damn straight, Sarge. You nailed that one. Nobody betrays the Sovereign," her voice was as strong as he had ever heard it, filled with the wrath of a soldier that wanted to take her anger out on an adversary she had yet to identify, but knew was out there, stalking her position. "By Caiphus, when we find out who this spy is, they'll pay for their deceptions," she let the thought hang, as she handed a cloth to Candille to wipe away her tears.

Candille had composed herself somewhat, and was encouraged by the kind treatment she was receiving from the two Guardians, "I might be able to help figure out who the spy is," she said, hopefully.

"How so?" Pertu asked, leaning forward.

"Well," she continued, "as it happens, in a security briefing, several years ago, we were told about an operative who had been connected to a bureaucrat of the highest levels in the Alliance. The thing is," she blushed, "I actually knew who that operative was, I mean, I didn't know them personally, but I'd met her sister once, her twin sister. We're both from the same home world, Ursus Minor, and were both born in Hydra, the capital city. You see, the woman happens to be a distant relative of Factotum Mar, which allowed her some small privilege, including access to stolen medical technologies from the Alliance, which has greatly extended her life, but, in the end, it didn't serve her as well as she'd hoped. Because of her extreme beauty Mar decided to take advantage of this, hoping to capitalize on her looks in order to entice an Alliance figure into a situation he could profit from, which she apparently succeeded in doing," she looked down at her hands.

Sergeant Brem whispered, "Her name, Candille, what is her name?"

She looked up, meeting the kind, blue eyes of the Tactical Sergeant, "I heard her sister refer to her as Laranna," she said, "but ..." she paused, "a transmission record I once found referred to her as Lareena. She had travelled to a colony on the second moon of Artunal, Altus 9, in Alliance territory, to attend a conference, over one hundred years ago."

Both Guardians gasped: they had both met the wife of First Counselor Regar, as had Commander Dragar and the Sovereign. None of them would have guessed in a thousand years that she was in any way related to Factotum Mar, or that she was working for the Consortium, but how could they deny what Candille had told them? If she was, in fact, from the same home world, that would be damning evidence indeed. But what of the First Counselor? What role did he have to play in all of this; surely Lareena could not have access to confidential transmissions without the assistance of her husband. It was devastating to consider the implications. There was no question that they would have to discuss it with the Commander.

Pertu was about to say something when an alarm went off at the helm. There were ships approaching Terra at the speed of light, and their transponders indicated they were not from the Alliance. She quickly ensured that their shields were fully engaged and everything was as it should be after their brief engagement with the Consortium Battlecruiser, which had not taxed their systems. Still, it could not hurt to check things; Pertu was never one to leave things to chance, which was why she was considered one of the best pilots in the Alliance. She scanned her monitors for more information and let out an oath to Caiphus under her breath.

"What's going on?" Brem asked, turning to his tactical sensors, hoping to see something for himself. He too let out an oath, "Caiphus be Damned, is that what I think it is?"

"It certainly is, my friend," Pertu replied softly.

"What?" Candille asked, craning her head to get a look at Brem's sensors, "what's going on?"

"This system is about to get a lot more crowded," Pertu answered, as her hands flew over the helm controls. "According to my sensors at least three Consortium mining vessels, accompanied by several Battlecruisers, are approaching at just below the speed of light; it looks like they're transitioning just behind the first planet of this system. I think they're planning on mining this system's star."

Brem was already transmitting a message to Commander Dragar while Candille sat stunned into silence.

(* | *)

Dragar had just completed an inspection walk around the property and was once again ensconced in the large branch of the oak tree near the house. He was watching the Sovereign eat something called tuna salad with the two humans, which made the Guardian's stomach growl at his own hunger. Watching the Sovereign and the two humans eat reminded Dragar of the one thing he did not enjoy about long missions: having to rely on the nutritional supplements developed to be used by Unified Armed Services for long missions. They provided everything anyone required to fuel the body, but they did nothing to satisfy the desire to dig into something tasty. All the little red pills did were provide caloric energy and balanced nutrient supplements so that his body would function at an optimal level throughout the duration of a mission. Dragar had once survived on the pills for six months without having a morsel of real food, but he still preferred the real thing when it was available. The Guardian was thinking to himself that some of that tuna salad was looking really tasty, and he had no idea what it was, when the vibration of his wrist device snapped him out of his reverie.

"Dragar," he replied, pleased for the distraction, "so, have you sent our guest into orbit yet?" he asked, half-jokingly. He was confident that the former Consortium Sergeant would turn out to be an excellent source of information.

"Hardly," Brem replied curtly. "In fact, you're not gonna believe what she's told us. But," he paused, "that's not why I'm contacting you, Commander," Dragar immediately sat up; Brem was referring to him by his rank which meant something serious was occurring.

"What's going on? Is there another team on their way?" Dragar asked, concerned another Fire Team, or something worse, might be after the Sovereign.

"No, there doesn't seem to be anything coming your way, but sensors have picked up several vessels entering the system, and we've identified at least three of them as mining vessels," there was a short pause. "Commander, they're transiting toward the sun," Brem finally added, his voice full of concern. "They're accompanied by several Battlecruisers, perhaps three, maybe four; it's difficult to tell as they're in close formation and haven't made the transition to sub-light. Looks like their transition point will be the planet closest to the sun. Requesting your orders, sir."

Dragar had to smile to himself, even though the news was bad, this was the way they had been trained: the chain of command was sacrosanct, inviolable. One did not go off and do their own thing just because they felt like it; especially not when their commanding officer was guarding the Sovereign down on the planet. After considering the situation for a few seconds Dragar understood why the Sovereign had chosen this planet, and knew exactly what had to be done. He also knew why she had been so willing to allow him to remain with her; she had been expecting this right from the beginning, this or something like it, and now that it was happening, it was time to act quickly.

"Alright, Tactical Sergeant, this is exactly what I want you to do," Dragar began, "I want you to listen carefully, and follow these instructions to the letter," he said, explaining his plan.

By the time he had finished his explanation he was sure the surly Tactical Sergeant would have something to say, but he merely grunted appreciatively, "Got it, Guardian Two, out."

Pertu looked over her shoulder at Brem and asked, "Everything alright?"

"You wouldn't believe me if I told you," he replied, as he sorted out what Dragar had recited, preparing his first transmission to Felis Prime. "Listen carefully and it should all be clear in a few seconds," he said, as he entered the appropriate codes to send a transmission to the Communications Array.

"This is an EOC Priority One Message from Guardian One, I repeat, this is an EOC; Eyes Only Cadre, Priority One Message from Guardian One to Felis Prime: request immediate UAS fleet support for the Terran system. Consortium mining vessels and an unknown number of Battlecruisers are presently transiting to the Terran star with the intention to begin mining operations and must be stopped immediately. This is a Priority One request: Sovereign Sayoose is on Terra and is in imminent peril. Repeat: fleet support required for Terran system immediately. System Sun in imminent peril from Consortium mining vessels and Battlecruisers. Message Ends from Guardian One, EOC." Brem looked over at Captain Pertu who was staring at him with her mouth open.

"Is that what Commander Dragar wanted you to send?" her voice croaked, prompting her to reach for another lozenge.

"Word for bloody word," he replied, "but wait, you haven't heard anything yet. Dragar suspects there won't be any help coming from the fleet," Candille gasped, causing the two Guardians to look at her.

"Well, what would you expect from your spy?" Brem asked pointedly, turning to look at her. "We suspect that it goes deeper than Lareena, Candy," he shook his head, "we've made other requests, and they were returned with … well, with static. When your ship arrived we had already seen some Consortium ships around other Green Zone planets in this Sector, and had received a message from Felis Prime that we wouldn't likely be receiving any help. Apparently, the Cadre had not been sending out any of the help the Sovereign had ordered," he shook his head in disgust. "Lareena may have been sending some messages to Factotum Mar, but she isn't the only one pulling strings in the Alliance right now. We have to do this to find out exactly what's going on and gather the evidence the Sovereign needs to flush out the Verkallian Tarvok hiding amongst the Torgons."

Candille looked momentarily confused at the reference to the Verkallian Tarvok, a creature indigenous to an Alliance planet in Sector 1009 that could clear a room with its dreadful odor, but she had heard of the Torgons, which were famous for having the sweetest dispositions of any companion creatures, though she had never personally seen one; the Consortium had never had any success in importing the peaceful creatures. On the one occasion that the Paragon, the Premier of the Stellar Mining Bureau, had managed to bring one of the creatures back to his palatial estate in the capital city of Hydra the poor creature had allowed itself to die of starvation rather than remain in that environment.

Brem was already preparing his next transmission and had made the appropriate settings to the transmitter, *"This is an EOF Priority One Message from Guardian One,"* he began again, *"I repeat, this is an EOF; Eyes Only Fleet Commander, Priority One Message, from Guardian One to Marshal Salzat, Battlecruiser Orono-001: Sovereign in peril; Terran system under attack by Consortium Battlecruisers and mining vessels intent on mining system sun. Report all due haste. Repeat: Sovereign in peril; Consortium attacking. Please report soonest. Message Ends from Guardian One, EOF."*

Pertu could barely contain herself, "You might have mentioned that you were contacting him before," she practically hissed, trying not to strain her throat. Marshal Salzat was in command of the Flagship of the Alliance, the impressive Battlecruiser Orono-001. More importantly, the Orono was always accompanied its Battle Group, two other Battlecruisers, two Cruisers, one fully equipped Carrier, with four wings of one thousand interceptors, and two Battle Transports, each of which was capable of carrying two regiments of UAS troops. In the case of Salzat, however, he always had one regiment of the ASCAR: 7,000 of the best commandos in the Alliance, each one ready to be deployed at a moment's notice, and they had just been summoned to protect the Terran system, and the Sovereign, from the Consortium.

"I was doing exactly as our Commander ordered," Brem replied, turning back to his controls. An acknowledgment was already coming back from Felis Prime acknowledging receipt of the message.

Administrator Marta had, once again, broken protocol with her standard response. Instead of sending a standard acknowledgment that the message had been received her response read, *"Priority One Message, EOG; Eyes Only Guardians, EOC Message received: Guardian One should expect to receive a great deal of interference before you receive any other assistance. Administrator Marta sends regards. Priority One Message Ends, EOG."* Brem read back the response to Pertu and Candille in disbelief, but he had to admire the fortitude of the Administrator. She was never one to pull punches, telling things as she saw them: she also could not stand duplicity, and had been the first of them, besides the Sovereign, to detect something rotten within the Cadre.

Brem quickly relayed the message to Dragar, knowing exactly what the Commander's response was going to be, as did Pertu, who was already going through the necessary pre-flight checks, "Yes sir," Brem replied, "we're ready to leave orbit. Don't worry, by the time Marshal Salzat arrives there won't be anything but pieces for him to pick up."

"Look," Dragar replied, his tone serious, "I don't want any heroics up there; this is a blatant violation of the Callisto Treaty; there's no reason for you to reveal yourselves before you fire. If there's even the slightest indication that they're preparing to mine the sun you are to fire for effect. Is that clear? *Fire to destroy those ships.* You are to go in weapons hot and free: I don't want anything going to chance here. No mistakes," there was a pause, "how's our new friend doing?"

Brem laughed, an unusual sound coming from the plug-like

man, "Fitting in just fine, Commander. Pertu's uniform fits her like a glove. In fact, she's strapped into your seat and is ready to ride into the show, right up front with us," Dragar was not sure he liked the idea of the former Consortium Sergeant sitting on the bridge of Helios-2 while they flew into combat against other Consortium vessels, but the alternative was having her in the aft section of the ship, where she would be alone and unobserved, and might be able to do something that could jeopardize the mission.

"All right," he replied, "just make certain she remains strapped in, is that clear?" Brem understood completely. He knew exactly what Dragar had been thinking and had considered it himself. He definitely preferred having the former Consortium Sergeant up front with them rather than somewhere in the back. Besides, she was a lot easier on the eyes than the Commander was, but he would never say as much.

"Yes, sir," Brem responded, then added, "take a look at this when you have a moment," and he transmitted the information that Candille had given to them to Dragar's wrist device.

"Hold on tight," Pertu said, looking over her shoulder at the others as Brem finished the transmission, "this isn't going to take that long. Our Star Drive will have us in orbit around this system's star in less than 45 seconds," she looked at the helm display for a second, then asked, "ready?" After confirmations from Brem and Candille she activated the Star Drive and Helios-2 slipped out of orbit and reappeared between the orbits of the sun and Mercury, giving the crew a perfect view of the three Consortium mining vessels and four Battlecruisers. Each of the mining vessels were beginning their surveys of the sun's outer corona, but their intentions were obvious from their positions in orbit over the star: they were preparing to begin mining operations, which would lead to the end of all life on the planet Earth, including the deaths of the Sovereign and Commander Dragar. Brem was already transmitting their status back to Commander Dragar.

Even before appearing in orbit near the Terran star the A-ConCom had activated the ship's Temporal Compensator, which prevented it from experiencing a slowing of the localized time stream, or a temporal displacement within the ship resulting from their proximity to the star and the massive gravimetric forces being exerted by the stellar body. Power for the Temporal Compensator was diverted from the ship's Star Drive. This served to create an inverse graviton field which offset the extreme gravitational forces exerted by any celestial body, or singularity, that a ship might encounter which was powerful enough to interfere with their localized time stream. This prevented the ship from experiencing any undue dilations of their own time stream as the flow of time, relative to where their point of origin, would have been significantly slowed as they advanced toward a source of gravity such as the stellar body they were now approaching.

If the ship flew closer to a star without the benefit of a Temporal Compensator they would find themselves greatly affected by the star's intense gravitational forces, subsequently moving slower within their own time stream relative to their point of origin. This dilation made coordinating activities with other Alliance planets virtually impossible, particularly where their time stream was adversely affected every time they ventured close to a star or massive gravity source such as a black hole or even a micro-singularity.

With Commander Dragar remaining on Terra while Helios-2 travelled near the system's star, the dilation would have resulted in several months or even years having passed for Dragar while only a few minutes would have passed for the individuals onboard the ship. Temporal Compensators were also activated, automatically by the A-ConCom, whenever the ship travelled near to or faster than the speed of light using the Star Drive since this would also result in a similar dilation of the local time stream within the ship, making it impossible for them to return to their point of origin without observing substantial passages of time upon their return.

Since the Consortium had not developed the same technology as the Alliance they used different tactics to deal with the temporal distortions. As a result, their mining operations were mostly carried out remotely in an attempt to minimize their exposure to temporal displacement as the ships controlling the mining vessels maintained a much higher orbit from the star being mined. This lessened the effects of the temporal dilation, but it was not able to fully eliminate the effect completely. As a result, there were still delays between the signals being transmitted between the ship controlling the mining vessel and the receiver near the stellar body due to the temporal anomalies, but the alternative was to have crews on the mining vessels returning to their point of departure only to discover that everyone they had known when they had embarked had aged dramatically, or died, as a result of the temporal displacement they had experienced.

Thanks to radio technology the Consortium had managed to steal from the Alliance it had been possible for them to develop a means to compensate for the temporal differential by broadcasting boosted signals through local subspace, enabling them to maintain control over their mining vessels with only the slightest delay. At the same time, they had developed their operations to a degree that the majority of their stellar mining consisted of pre-programmed routines requiring minimal intervention from the monitoring ship. Vessels of the Galactic Armed Forces, on the other hand, often found themselves directly exposed to the temporal distortions as they were forced to fly perilously close to the gravitational pull of an alien sun. This was especially true now as they tried to protect their mining vessels from the single Alliance ship they knew was in the Terran system while additionally acting as the controllers of the mining vessels. It was a risk that Factotum Mar had believed was worth taking, even if it resulted in the crews returning to their homes several years after they had departed. Considering the wellbeing of his troops was never something that entered the mind of Factotum Mind when issuing orders; his only concern was the potentiality for success.

(* | *)

Knowing that Consortium mining vessels had entered the Terran system and were attempting to mine its sun was wreaking havoc on the nerves of the Prime Guardian, but he could do nothing about it from his current position. It did not help that the mining vessels had been accompanied by several Battlecruisers, but Dragar had supreme confidence in his team. Even without the support of other Alliance vessels, Helios-2 was more than capable of dealing with any number of Consortium warships. They had, after all, managed to destroy the GAF-Tralta-9 without its weapons even coming close to harming the nimble craft, but it still bothered him to be planet side when his team faced danger. It was his nature: when there was action, that was where he wanted to be, even if that meant risking his own life.

Of course, he thought to himself, were he on the ship with his colleagues, not to mention their passenger, former STAWS Sergeant Candille, there would be little for him to in any battle. Helios-2 had been efficiently designed to be commanded by a single pilot, and Captain Pertu was that pilot; she was more than capable of dealing with any contingency without having her Commander breathing down her neck or barking out orders. In fact, he knew that she was probably better off without him on the bridge, scrutinizing her every move. While Pertu was not prone to anxiety during an operation, in situations like this the last thing she needed was to be worrying about what her commanding officer was thinking while she was contending with several enemy vessels. If Commander Dragar knew one thing about Captain Pertu and her skills as a pilot it was that when it came to commanding Helios-2 she would never take any unnecessary risks or endanger the ship and its crew.

No, Dragar conceded, frowning as he surveyed the house in which the Sovereign was residing, everyone was better off with him right where he was, which was all the more frustrating for the former commando. As he watched the Sovereign sleeping on the couch he saw that caretaker and the old man were preparing to leave the house. He could hear through the transmitter that she was taking the old man to a doctor's appointment in the town where the veterinary clinic was located. Dragar smiled at the thought; this would provide him with an opportunity to speak with the Sovereign while they were away from the house. Lowering himself from his position in the tree the Prime Guardian stood beside the front door, and patiently waited for the two Terrans to leave so he could slip inside and confer with his charge.

As the door was opened Dragar knew it would be easy for him to enter, while they were leaving, but he did not want to be detected in the process, and the old man was walking slower than usual. Instead, he decided to wait until after the two Terrans had left, not wanting either of them to notice him passing them through the open door. While he waited, Dragar read through what Brem had transmitted to his wrist device and nearly screamed in rage.

"Don't you be rushing me," he chided his granddaughter, "my hip's been bothering me since the damn weather turned. Can't stand the pressure, ya' know," he groused as he leaned heavily on his cane to step down the front steps, approaching the little red in front of the house.

"Who's rushing?" Tanya replied, almost in a song, "I only said we didn't want to be late for your appointment; that's why we're leaving a few minutes early," she gave a soft laugh as the old man grumbled something under his breath as he limped toward the car and tried to open it while Tanya locked the door to the house.

"It's locked!" he cried out in frustration. "Why'd youse lock the damn door way out here?"

"Sorry, Gramps," she replied, turning her attention away from the house for a moment, leaving the door open. As she did she hit a button on her key-chain, causing the car horn to beep once as the doors unlocked, "It's an old habit from living in the city."

"Damn city," he grumbled, almost under his breath as he pulled open the door and began folding himself into the small car. "I still don't understand why you couldn'a bought a full-size car," he shouted through the still-open door, as he adjusted his tall frame in the compact seat.

Tanya laughed as she turned her attention back to the front door, pulling it shut and locking it, "Oh Gramps, you know you love this little car; it gets great mileage, and it's all that either of us need. Besides," she said as she climbed into her own seat and closed the door, "you're just in a bad mood because you have to see Doctor Samford; you're always like this on days of your appointments."

She leaned over and kissed him on the cheek before starting the engine. She then turned the car stereo on and inserted a silver disc into the slot, "Here," she said, brightly, "I brought your favorite," and the *First Brandenburg Concerto* by Bach began to play.

His anger melted away, "You're a good girl, baby," he leaned over, smiling and wincing at the effort, kissing her on the cheek in return. "As long as we ain't goin to the damn VA. I can' stand tha' place," he humpfed in mock anger, crossing his arms over his chest as he listened to the music of Bach fill the small car. "I'll admit," he added grudgingly, "it does have a really fine stereo," he muttered as the music grew in intensity. As it did he settled himself into the seat and enjoyed the music.

Tanya grinned, ignoring his comment about the Veteran's Administration. Doctor Samford *was* with the VA, but had agreed to see her grandfather in his private office, otherwise the old man would never go to his appointments. He did go to the VA Hospital on occasion, for his heart, otherwise he avoided the place like the plague.

"Well, don't you forget it," she said, laughing again as she put the car into reverse and pulled out of the driveway. Dragar shook his head as he watched the exchange; it reminded him of the way Brem and Pertu sometimes acted, though he had never seen either of them exchange a kiss. He made a mental note to himself to mention it the next time they were snapping at each other. Once the car had turned down the country road he turned his attentions to the locked door. With a twist of his Shield device the lock opened, and he slipped in, closing the door behind him.

Sovereign Sayoose was sitting in the middle of the floor, waiting for him, "I've been expecting you, First Advisor," she said, her voice calm and measured, though higher in pitch due to her current form. "What news is there?"

Dragar noticed that there was music playing on the small stereo near where the female worked which he recognized as being by Beethoven. He had been hearing so much of the Terran music that he could now recognize the stylistic differences between several of the composers the Terran female enjoyed.

Turning back to the Sovereign he replied, "Nothing good, I fear, my Sovereign. In fact, this system is in extreme danger," he began, going on to explain the situation transpiring between Helios-2 and the Consortium vessels.

After he completed his briefing the Sovereign looked at him with her cat eyes, which Dragar found vaguely unsettling, "I am not at all surprised that Administrator Marta replied in the manner she has; she has been an exceptionally faithful supporter of the Alliance, and has always been an ardent believer of our ways. It grieves me to know that both Lareena and First Counselor Regar are as deeply involved in this as they seem to be but, I must admit, that man has always rubbed me the wrong way," she gave what must have been a cat smile, "he is far too ambitious for someone in his position. When I was First Counselor the last thing on my mind was ascending to the position of Sovereign; it was about serving the Sovereign and the Alliance. *That* is the role of the Cadre, at least … it is supposed to be. As for Lareena, I must admit, she is an enigma. I have never understood what she saw in him," she sounded both confused and grieved, something Dragar understood given the circumstances.

She continued, "I am quite certain you will receive a response from Marshal Salzat, in fact, I expect that he and his Battle Group will arrive as soon as they prepare themselves for transition," she looked into Dragar's eyes, seeking a confirmation, which he gave by nodding.

Dragar had known Marshal Salzat for several hundred years and knew the man was beyond reproach. His dedication to the Sovereign and the Alliance were without question; it also did not hurt matters that Sovereign Sayoose had personally promoted him to the position of Marshal, providing an added incentive for him to rush to her aid.

"Salzat's a good man," Dragar said, his voice low, "he won't let you down, my Sovereign."

"No, he will not," she agreed, her black tail flicking back and forth at the thought of the betrayal of her Cadre. "However," she added, "Helios-2 might have to take care of things around this system's star before he arrives," she looked down at the floor, a tinge of sadness in her orange eyes, the one characteristic that she had maintained from her normal form.

When she looked up again she said, "Commander, please send a message to the ship; inform them that they are to ensure that nothing is to be left of the Consortium vessels," for the first time since Dragar had spoken with the Sovereign she sounded genuinely angry, a difficult thing to accomplish in the guise of a cat. "Is that understood?"

Dragar stood up from his kneeling position and bowed deeply, "I've already given them their orders, my Sovereign," he replied, "the Terran system will not be in any danger as long as Captain Pertu has anything to say about the matter." She nodded, appreciating his initiative. Sayoose knew that Commander Dragar would have ordered Captain Pertu to completely destroy the Consortium ships. This attempt at mining the Terran star was an outrageous violation of the Callisto Treaty which could not be tolerated.

Once again her Prime Advisor had demonstrated his value in ways she could not begin to express. Dragar was nearly at the door when something else occurred to him and he turned back toward the cat, "In light of the Consortium's incursion into this system, I'd like to leave a comms device on your collar so you can hear me, in case of an emergency," he had expected the Sovereign to reject the idea, but she nodded her head and walked toward her Prime Guardian.

"An excellent and prudent idea," she said. "Once again I am reminded as to why I chose you to be my Prime Guardian … and my First Advisor," she purred as he bent down to attach the tiny device underneath her collar, near her left ear.

"Thank you, my Sovereign. This will also allow you to speak to me; but anything I transmit will only be heard by you. I just don't want," he was explaining, but she stopped him.

"I understand, Dragar. Thank you. I appreciate your concern. Everything will be fine. Marshal Salzat is going to arrive, and Captain Pertu, along with Tactical Sergeant Brem, will do just fine; and, by the way, I want to congratulate you on your restraint with that Consortium Sergeant: you demonstrated the fine tradition of the Corps by not taking a life when it was not necessary. We have obviously learned a great deal from her, it would seem," she looked thoughtful for a moment. "She really wants to be a member of the ASCAR?"

"Yes, my Sovereign, that is what she said."

"Well," the Sovereign replied, after a moment, "once this is over and we have returned to Felis Prime, have her memory down-lined; if everything is confirmed, I would be willing to have her transferred directly to the Home Guard," she looked into the eyes of Dragar, "if you have no objections."

Dragar smiled broadly, "I have none, my Sovereign. I believe Sergeant Candille would be a wonderful asset to both the ASCAR and the Home Guards."

"Excellent. Just remain silent about this until we have returned," she looked around the cozy house for a moment, "I fear my vacation may be coming to an end sooner than I had planned." She sighed, and turned to return to the couch.

"Yes, my Sovereign," Dragar agreed, "it certainly does look that way," he replied as he opened the door and reactivated his Shield, leaving the house as quietly as he had entered. Ten minutes later the little red car returned with Tanya and the old man.

"I can't believe Doctor Samford's office cancelled my appointment," the old man was saying as he entered the house.

"Well, Gramps, that's why we have cell-phones," she replied, trying to mollify his irritation.

"At least we were able to get some ice cream," Gramps said, ignoring her remark. He had no use for the newfangled electronics used by all the kids these days; if he was not home, he was not near a phone, and that suited him just fine.

As they entered the house he called out cheerfully, "Kitty, look what I brought for you!" He went into the kitchen and scooped a few tablespoons of the strawberry ice cream into a bowl, then set it down for her, which Sayoose began to eat with relish. She had been given this treat a few times and found it to be a delightful delicacy; neither Felis Magoris or Felis Prime had anything like it, at least not yet. That would certainly change once she returned.

(*|*)

Once Commander Dragar returned to his surveillance post in the oak tree he contacted Helios-2. Due to their proximity to the sun there was a short delay in the transmission, but the sound of Brem's voice was as clear as if they were still in orbit overhead. "Guardian One to Guardian two, situation report."

Tactical Sergeant Brem's reply came into his ear a few seconds later, "Guardian Two to Guardian One: currently on station near Terran star; situation unchanged. Three mining vessels currently undertaking close surveys of the outer and inner corona of the star, as well as its out-gasses. So far there are no indication that mining operations have begun," there was a pause, "oh, by Caiphus! One of the Battlecruisers just took off like it's ass was on fire. We're tracking it right now," the channel went dead.

Pertu's voice filled his ear, "Guardian One, Battlecruiser on course to Terra; repeat, BC returning to Terra."

Dragar could feel the blood drain from his face. A single Consortium Battlecruiser could devastate every major city of the planet from orbit without them ever having known it had been there, and there was nothing he could do about it; not from his current position.

"Estimated time of flight?" he asked, knowing it could not be less than a few minutes given their slower engines.

"Best estimate," there was a brief pause while Pertu checked her sensors, "three minutes, sir," her voice was filled with trepidation.

His heart was in his throat but he could not allow the Consortium to commence mining the Terran star. Mining a Red Giant was one thing as it would only happen if the star was located in a system devoid of life; it made no difference how the mining processes affected the star. If a young star like that of the Terran system was to be mined, drastic things would happen, almost as soon as the process began. Once the first probes from the mining vessels began injecting the preparatory elements, which served to loosen up the desired elements they were mining, the nature of the star began to change, particularly the radiation levels and wavelengths of light the star would emanate, which would begin to shift radically.

Anyone living on a Green Zone planet in that system would immediately notice the altered solar environment. Dragar knew that one of the most dangerous changes would be the increased intensity of the radioactive wavelengths, in conjunction with the changes of the star's temperature. Even a variant of a few degrees would be disastrous to the biosphere of a planet like Terra: once the mining process began the planet would be uninhabitable in a matter of weeks, which was precisely why the Stellar Mining Bureau had explicitly forbidden the mining of any star within an inhabited system. It was both unethical, and amoral.

Without hesitation Dragar issued an order, "Eliminate those

mining vessels, and the other ships, then return to Terra: best possible speed. Guardian One, over and out," he closed the channel without leaving them an opportunity to respond. He knew they had to save the billions of innocent lives on this planet; besides, the Sovereign was still safe, for now. Dragar thought to himself, as he continued to watch the house, Marshal Salzat had to be on his way by now. He would not let them down. Would he?

(* | *)

"You heard the man," Captain Pertu said, quickly running her eyes over the weapons system panel, though it had not been the first time she had checked them since arriving in orbit over the sun. She turned to the Tactical Sergeant, "So, which would you suggest first?" She knew he would advise that they attack the Battlecruisers, but she wanted to have his input, just to have him in the game. It was her way.

Brem nodded, "Big guns," he said curtly, indicating the Battlecruisers. They were their largest vessels, next to Consortium Carriers, both of which were still smaller than their Alliance counterparts. Pertu agreed completely; besides, the mining vessels had not yet begun their operations, and were completely unarmed. She also knew that the Battlecruisers were acting as their control ships since no other vessels had arrived in the system.

"As you say," she rasped, maneuvering Helios-2 around to align with two of the Battlecruisers. "Well, boys, you're just making this easy for me, aren't you?" she whispered as she fired four Plasma Torpedoes, two of which were directed toward each ship while simultaneously firing several salvos of the ship's plasma cannon. As soon as the weapons were fired Pertu engaged the Star Drive for a nanosecond, causing it to jump so that it came to rest in line with the third Battlecruiser, where she fired another two Plasma Torpedoes and another salvo from the plasma cannon.

It took less than fifteen seconds, but the three ships had been shredded by the weapons, their inner cores exposed to the intense heat and radiation of the Terran star. As far as Brem could tell, none of the crews managed to reach their escape pods, and even if they had, the intense gravity of the star would have pulled the pods into the surface of the star where they would have been engulfed in a fiery death. Dying in the vacuum of space would definitely have been preferable to being pressure cooked in the star's corona.

Sergeant Candille gasped at the ease with which the operation had taken place, but had really not been surprised. From what she had seen, Helios-2 was easily the most advanced ship she had ever been on, and she already knew that the Alliance was far more technically advanced than the Consortium. She had just never witnessed tactics like the ones used by Pertu, and was duly impressed.

"Now for the mining vessels," Pertu whispered, maneuvering and firing a single Plasma Torpedo at each ship, knowing that the massive tanks of preparatory elements would add to the explosive power of the weapon, making a second shot unnecessary. She watched with some satisfaction as each ship was inexorably drawn into the heavy gravity of the star, crushed into oblivion once their engines became unable to sustain their orbits.

"Now, let's get back to Terra before that final Tarvok manages to get there before us," she croaked, her throat hoarse from the excitement. As she engaged the Star Drive she popped another lozenge into her mouth and was instantly pleased by the relief it provided. "Estimated time of transition," she glanced at the helm, "46 seconds."

As Pertu had been taking care of the Consortium vessels the fourth Battlecruiser approached Terra in less time than they had initially estimated, but the sensors on Helios-2 warned Brem of its status from his Tactical station.

"Caiphus be damned," he proclaimed, as Pertu was about to engage the Star Drive.

"What is it?" she asked, surprised by the distraction.

"Never mind," he shouted, "go!" he was already transmitting to Commander Dragar.

"Guardian One, Alert! BC arriving on station: less than one minute! Scramble! Scramble! Scramble!"

It was the only message the Prime Guardian required to get moving, and move he did: he was out of the tree before he heard Brem utter the second *Scramble* and he ran straight through the front door of the house, without stopping to open it, causing both Tanya and her grandfather to nearly jump out of their skins. For her part, the Sovereign did not seem overly concerned, though she was not particularly pleased about not getting to finish her ice cream.

Dragar had not considered what he would do about the two Terrans, but the thought of them dying unnecessarily was something he did not want on his conscience, not after they had taken such good care of the Sovereign, but they looked absolutely terrified at the sight of this giant of a man bursting through their front door with a crazed look on his face.

"I'm sorry," he said, trying to contain himself, "There isn't time to explain, but you're all in great danger," he reached down and scooped up the Sovereign, tucking her under his arm protectively, "I'm here to protect Sover ..." he paused for the briefest instant, "I mean, I'm here to protect Sayoose, and you really need to get out of this house immediately," he was already moving toward the shattered door.

"Now, you jus' wait one second there, boy," came the surprisingly loud voice of the old man, "I ain't goin' nowhere, and you ain't taken' my granddaughter's cat with you." He was standing, holding his cane like a sword, which almost made the Prime Guardian laugh at his bravery, as untimely as it was at this point. For her part, Tanya seemed frozen in terror, unable to speak.

"Please, listen to him." the voice of Sovereign Sayoose, suddenly cut into the silence. "This is my Guardian, Commander Dragar; I'll explain everything, I promise. If he says we must leave, we must. Now."

Colonel Little looked at the cat and muttered, half to himself, "I knew it, the damn thing *can* talk ... probably been reading my newspapers too," but he had overcome the shock of the situation and was now hobbling toward the broken-down door of the house. Dragar went over and slipped his arm around the man and half-carried him out of the house while Tanya, roused from her terror, followed them, pausing just long enough to grab her laptop from her desk, along with a sweater as she left their small house.

Just as they reached the end of the driveway a pulse of light flashed from the sky, "Jump," Dragar shouted, "into the ditch," and they dove into the drainage ditch running along the road in front of the property, which was half-filled with muddy water. It shielded them from the blast as the house, the tree, and everything else for thirty feet around was vaporized by a massive explosion. Dragar looked around cautiously, then found what he had been looking for and smiled. Sovereign Sayoose was sitting on the side of the ditch, her sleek fur covered in mud and filth.

"I will have you know, Commander," she said with a sigh, "cats do *not* like water. What in Caiphus was that supposed to be," she asked, as the two humans watched in stunned silence.

"Consortium Battlecruiser," he replied calmly. "Helios-2

remained by the system's star to destroy the mining vessels and the other Battlecruisers."

That was too much for the old man. "What in the name of all that is sacred and holy are you *talking* about," he looked at the cat, "and … *you* …" he felt as though his world was spinning out of control. "A talking cat, fire falling from the sky, I suppose you're going to tell me that you're from Mars, right?"

Sayoose laughed, "No. There are no humanoids on Mars. I am from a planet called Tarlos II, it is part of the Felis Alliance and is quite a long way from here. If you would like, it would be my pleasure to take both you and your granddaughter there. You have been wonderful hosts to me for the past three years; I would love to return the favor." She looked toward Dragar, who just shrugged. Who was he to turn down a request from the Sovereign.

Tanya finally managed to speak, her voice trembling with emotion, "Wha … what … do you mean … you're … you're an *alien*?" she managed to ask, lifting her precious laptop out of the muddy water. She kept shaking her head in disbelief as she looked at what used to be the house she had spent so much of her life in; as she tried to stand Dragar pulled her back down into the ditch.

"I'm sorry, but we'd better stay low, until I hear from our ship," he said, "I don't want to take any chances. They might want to take another shot, just to make sure the Sovereign is dead."

"Sovereign? What is this *Sovereign* business?" the old man asked, slightly annoyed at sitting in muddy water. For the next several minutes, while he waited for Helios-2 to make contact, Dragar explained who the Sovereign really was, while she confirmed the salient points by adding extra information, though it seemed entirely unbelievable to the two humans. Of course, having witnessed their house get vaporized added credence to the story.

"Hold on," Dragar said, placing his index finger against his ear as the message from Helios-2 arrived. He was nodding his head and smiling as he turned toward the Sovereign, "Helios-2 has reported that the mining vessels near the sun were destroyed before they could begin their operations, and the Battlecruisers were also dispatched. They apologized for miscalculating the flight time of the fourth Battlecruiser …" Dragar paused as he listened to more of the message, nodding his head. "Fleet Commander Marshal Salzat and his forces are on station; they destroyed the Consortium Battlecruiser. Helios-2 is now in orbit, ready to transport us onboard at your command."

Sovereign Sayoose looked at Tanya and Gramps, "I cannot thank you enough for what you have done for me, except to show you things that you could never have imagined possible," turning to Gramps, she added, "as for you, I can end the pain you have been living with, and add many healthy, happy years to your life, if that is what you desire."

Tanya and Bob looked at each other, then at what used to be their house, and smiled. "I guess nobody's gonna miss us down here," Gramps said, giving the cat a toothy grin. "When do we leave? But wait," he suddenly looked concerned, "how is it that you all speak perfect English yet you're from … where ever it is you say you're from?"

Dragar laughed, "English? Is that what you call this language? It's been the official language of both the Felis Alliance and the Ursus Consortium for …" he looked at the Sovereign.

"Over five hundred thousand years," she answered, her cat voice sounding odd, but understandable.

Colonel Little looked at his granddaughter, "We're in for a real change, aren't we?"

Dragar nodded, "Actually," he continued, "we call this the *Common Tongue*, since it has been adopted by so many of the member planets," he let out a small laugh, "it also happens to be spoken by the Consortium, though that started because at one time we were at peace with each other and having a common language made doing business easier."

Sovereign Sayoose continued, her voice still high-pitched due to her being in the form of the cat, "There are some interesting reasons why it exists as a language on your planet, but I am not sure that you are quite ready to hear about the different programs the Alliance has in operation across the universe, including the seeding of planets and aiding in the development of the civilizations on many of those planets … among other things."

Dragar glanced at her in surprise, but remained silent while Tanya could only nod in response, feeling completely overwhelmed at the oddness of the situation.

"I'm sure you both have many questions, but at the moment we really can't wait around and answer all of them," Dragar added, trying not to sound impatient. "I promise, once we are safely back on Felis Prime, the orbiting city we'll be going to, there will be many opportunities for you to learn everything you could possibly want to know about the history of the Alliance, as well as many other things." His reassuring smile seemed to put the two Terrans at ease and he was pleased to see that they were satisfied with his proposal. Having just watched their home be vaporized by a weapon launched from space they were, apparently, not all that interested in sticking around in this mud-filled ditch for any longer than was necessary.

Deciding it was time to leave, Sovereign Sayoose nodded toward Commander Dragar, "Before you signal the ship," she walked over to the Prime Guardian, shaking as much of the mud and water off of her fur as she could, "I have a plan." For the next several seconds she whispered into his ear. As he listened he nodded, smiling as the Sovereign revealed her plan. After a few moments Dragar picked up the cat and signaled the ship; within a few breaths the three humans were onboard Helios-2, standing on the pads of the LDMT.

"Welcome aboard," Tactical Sergeant Brem said, looking at the mud-covered group. He was surprised when Commander Dragar set a small black-and-white creature down on the pads that looked somewhat like a Torgon with legs. "I doh …" he stammered, looking around the aft section of the ship in confusion. "I don't understand," he finally managed to say, focusing his attention at the cat as it sat there, staring at him with its orange eyes, "where's the Sovereign?"

"It's a long story, my friend," Dragar said, sighing as the cat leapt off the pads into the arms of Brem, shocking the Guardian while she purred loudly as the stocky Tactical Sergeant held her.

CHAPTER XI ~ DEATH AND DECEPTION

"Spies are ruled by a deeply-seated need to validate their over inflated sense of importance. This exists in an artificially created construct established by those maintaining psychological controls over every aspect of their lives while simultaneously exerting a form of physical domination through various methods, the most common being the use of either sexual enticement or material enrichment.

"While the means of control may take many forms, the fundamental purpose for manipulating the actions of the targeted individual is for them to become the spy, to provide information. Their ultimate mental and physical well-being is of little concern to those acting as their controls. Only the collection of information through the relationship they have established is of interest to those in positions of power over the spy. Undertaking this inauspicious work is contingent upon the spy fulfilling the elements necessary to execute their mission, especially when the spy is in a position affording them access to a person or information providing them an opportunity to betray a trust earned through a lifetime of dedicated service.

"Subsequently, spies are universally reviled, considered heroes only by those who sent them where their betrayal often leads to the loss of innocent lives. Leaders within the Felis Alliance discovered that the best way to avoid the proliferation of spies was through an egalitarian system that treated every Citizen with dignity, along with a robust security system designed to prevent the unauthorized sharing of classified information.

"Anyone charged with betraying the Alliance would find themselves before the First Tribunal, convening on Felis Magoris. As the highest Court within the Felis Alliance, the First Tribunal also functioned as

*the final Court of Appeals, constituting the final chance
for justice for Defendants who had gone through the
justice system. When pertaining to crimes against the
Alliance, or High Treason, the First Tribunal represents
the only opportunity for a Defendant to seek justice."*

[...]

Excerpted from *Justice in the Felis Alliance,* by
Justice Renata, Prime Justice of the First Tribunal

<h2 style="text-align:center">(*|*)</h2>

Administrator Marta was deeply disturbed: after carefully
scrutinizing transmission logs from the Communications Array, looking
for all transmission to any Unified Armed Services military vessels, she
was arriving at conclusions that were tremendously unsettling. Marta
had personally received and decoding the latest message from Helios-2
that reported the presence of Consortium vessels in the same System in
which the Sovereign was located. She had seen that the message
contained an urgent request from Commander Dragar for the
immediate dispatching of UAS vessels to prevent an attack against
Protectorate planets in the System, and she had personally delivered
the decoded message to First Counselor Regar, even though she knew
he had not wanted to be disturbed. Once the First Counselor read the
message his response had been that the Cadre would act according to
the recommendations of the First Advisor to the Sovereign, but that was
precisely why she felt so disturbed: Administrator Marta knew that
neither the First Counselor, or the Cadre, had responded.

According to the transmission logs no vessels from the Unified
Armed Services of the Alliance were on their way to Sector 0107 to
assist Helios-2, or to defend any of the Protectorates. Breaking with
protocols, Marta had decided to send her own message, which she had
directed to her friend Commander Dragar. She had advised him that he
should not expect much help from the home world.

Performing such an act grieved her tremendously, even if it was
ultimately in the service of the Sovereign. Marta had always considered
herself a faithful Citizen of the Alliance and believed Sovereign Sayoose
was the greatest leader they had ever had, but the current events were
driving her to distraction, making it impossible for her to function
effectively in her position. After not seeing the transmissions she had

expected to see from either the First Counselor or the Cadre in the transmission logs, Marta was now beginning to suspect that there was a genuine traitor amongst the Cadre, which not only angered her, but as absurd as the idea seemed, she had the uncomfortable feeling that the traitor might actually be the First Counselor, the leader of the Cadre.

As she continued to consider the preposterous nature of the idea Marta slowly shook her head; it was beyond absurd, she thought to herself: First Counselor Regar was not only the leader of the Cadre, he was one of the most trusted, well-respected bureaucrats within the Felis Alliance. Of course, it was much easier to respect the First Counselor if you did not know him personally; those who knew the man, as Administrator Marta did, felt differently: they recognized his overt desire for advancement, as well as his disconcerting disdain for the Sovereign, something he usually managed to hide, but it had still grown more obvious during her absence over the past three years.

Even with that evidence, while circumstantial at best, it was not sufficient to convict the man as a traitor; an ambitious fool, perhaps, but the Administrator had met many of those throughout her life. Of course, that had been before she had the evidence of the conspicuously missing transmissions to back her opinions regarding the character of the First Counselor. Based on everything she had seen, on every transmission received from Sector 0107, the Consortium was definitely making a move against the Green Zone planets in that Sector, as well as the star of the Terran system. Based on everything she had seen, and from what the First Counselor had not been doing, by ignoring the urgent requests from Helios-2, it certainly looked as though the leader of the Cadre had been carrying on a calculated campaign to leave Sector 0107 defenseless while the Consortium prepared to invade Protectorates of the Alliance.

Administrator Marta shuddered at the thought of what might have been had she not had the foresight to review the transmission logs so diligently since the departure of Commander Dragar. Or, for that matter, what might have come to pass had she not decided to contact Commander Dragar of her own volition. She knew that Dragar would not have relied solely on assistance coming from the Cadre. Marta knew Dragar too well to trust the First Counselor with the safety of the Sovereign. Marta slowly smiled as she realized there had to be more to his plan.

Knowing the importance of the Sovereign's security, Marta was unwilling to trust the First Counselor with any further communications, even when they were marked EOC, or *Eyes Only Cadre*. Oh, she would send the messages along to the First Counselor, should they arrive, Marta thought to herself, but she would also take care of the responses personally; it may have been a violation of protocol, but as the Communications Administrator she was one of the few members of the Alliance cleared to read every message, regardless of its classification. If there was a deception in play, Marta was going to ensure that nobody lost their lives on her watch.

(*|*)

Tactical Sergeant Brem had a look of shocked surprise on his face as the cat purred in his arms while it rubbed its mud-caked fur against his uniform. "What in Caiphus …" he began to exclaim, taken aback by the affectionate nature of the black and white creature. He had never seen anything like it before, though he had encountered several Torgons, which were quite affectionate. He looked up helplessly at the others as the cat continued to rub the mud from her fur against his clean uniform. As he did the young woman and old man that had been transported up with Commander Dragar were also wiping the mud from their faces and clothes with towels that the Commander had produced from one of the utility lockers.

"Don't worry about making a mess," Dragar said, as they cleaned up, "we have clean clothes you can change into and," he turned toward Brem, looking at both the Tactical Sergeant and the cat, "I believe she would be more comfortable washing off in the cleaning basin in the WD unit, don't you?"

"She …?" Brem was growing more confused by the moment. Now the old man was laughing at him at well, which was beginning to annoy him.

"Commander," he finally blurted out, "would you *please*, by all that Caiphus blesses, explain what is going on here?" As he tried to get an explanation from Dragar the cat jumped from his arms and casually walked into the WD unit, which Dragar closed behind her.

After a few seconds they could hear the sound of water running, and the sweet sound of singing coming from within the small chamber. "That …" Brem stammered, "that's the …" he looked dumbfounded as his mind tried to process the situation, but Dragar placed a finger over his lips.

"That, Tactical Sergeant," Dragar replied in a commanding tone, "is a cat," his glare ended anything Guardian might have tried to say. If he was anything, Brem he was a Guardian, a trained ASCAR commando, and a soldier first; when given an order he knew when to keep his mouth shut.

Dragar continued with the introductions, turning toward the young woman, "This is Tanya," he said, "and this is her grandfather," he was about to say more, but the old man stepped forward, extending his hand to the Tactical Sergeant.

"Bob Little," he said, flashing a toothy grin, "everybody calls me Bob. 'Less of course you're in the military, then you can call me Colonel," he looked around the aft section of the ship for a moment, "this ain't no military ship, is it?" Dragar and Brem looked at each other for a moment and smiled.

"That's going to take some explaining ... Colonel," Commander Dragar replied, offering the old man a crisp salute in UAS style.

"Damn," he replied softly, grinning, "I knew I was gonna enjoy this," he muttered, hobbling over to one of the seats where he lowered himself gingerly, sighing as he began to relax for the first time since the ordeal inside their house had begun.

For her part Tanya seemed to have been taking the whole thing in stride; having discovered that her cat could speak had been one thing; watching your house get vaporized by what was purported to be alien spacecraft was something else entirely. Now, after all of that, she found both herself and her grandfather, onboard a different alien ship. Not for the first time, Tanya thought to herself, she really needed a vacation. As she took in the scene around her, listening to the interaction between the giant man that had burst through the front door of her house and the other man, also large, but not as tall, she had the terrible fear that this was either all a bad dream or perhaps she was in the midst of a psychotic break. Could all of this be the result of a delusional psychosis?

Yes, that had to be the explanation. First, this giant of a man had burst through their front door proclaiming they were in danger, then her darling cat had actually spoken to her, telling her to trust this man, and then she had watched as the house she had shared with her grandfather had been vaporized. Yes, it was definitely a psychotic break she thought, as she watched the door where her cat had gone through open. Instead of her beloved cat, a young woman with dark skin and intense, orange eyes emerged. Her hair was black, with a shock of white in the center. As she looked at the woman Tanya had a sudden suspicion that everything she had experienced was all too real. No, she realized, she was not having a delusion or a psychotic break; but she was in the midst of something far more challenging than anything she had ever faced.

"Hello Tanya," she said, her voice soft, but commanding, "my name is Sayoose; I am the Sovereign of the Felis Alliance. Please, sit down; there is a great deal I want to tell you before we begin our journey," she turned to Dragar, "Commander, please inform Captain Pertu of my plan. Also, send your compliments to Marshal Salzat and his crews, and inform them that the Sovereign has been killed, as we discussed," she paused as Brem gasped, "and remember," she added, looking at the other Guardian from the corner of her eye, "maintain our call-sign as Helios-2: that is essential for our plan to be successful," she turned back to the two Terrans. "In the meantime, I would like a few minutes alone with our guests." Dragar and Brem bowed deeply to the Sovereign and backed away, leaving the aft section of the ship to rejoin Captain Pertu in the command section while she remained to speak to Tanya and Colonel Bob.

Sovereign Sayoose remained standing, enjoying the light gravity that the ship was experiencing since Pertu had activated the artificial gravity field, making it easier to move around without having to pull yourself from section to section. "I cannot begin to thank you for the time you provided me," she began, and proceeded to tell Tanya and Bob of her nature as a shapeshifter, explaining how being a genomorph extended her life. She then told them about the Alliance, and the advancements they had achieved, including the medical discoveries, which would allow the two of them to live many more years than they could have ever imagined.

"Colonel Bob," she continued, "you may feel old now, but I can guarantee that once you receive treatment from our scientists you will feel as though you are a new man," he looked at her dubiously, and she laughed, nodding, understanding his disbelief. "I know it is difficult to believe. Let me ask you a question: how old do you think I am?"

Tanya looked at the Sovereign, studying her perfect features, then looked at her grandfather. She shrugged, "I don't know, I'd have to say about twenty-seven, but I've never been that good at guessing ages."

Sovereign Sayoose laughed, "Well, do not be concerned, my dear, I am well beyond twenty-seven. In fact, I am currently around one hundred-and-twenty-one *thousand* years of age, but to tell you the truth, I do not really keep track anymore."

Bob let out a sound that was halfway between a cough and a snort, leading Tanya to slap him on the back several times.

"Really," she said, "it is somewhat young for genomorphs these days. Commander Dragar, for example, is fifty-six thousand years old. The Alliance discovered that age is a disease, and they found the cure for that disease," she paused, looking at the two Terrans, "I would like to offer you the opportunity to have all of the advantages of any Citizen of the Alliance, since you had to give up so much by offering me sanctuary in your home. Unfortunately, you will not be able to return to Terra, to Earth, until they are ready to join the Alliance, but," she paused, "thanks to our medical help, you should easily live to see that day, if you really do desire to return."

Bob looked at his granddaughter and took her hand in his, "Sweetie," he said, his voice filled with paternal love, "I said I'd give you the stars, if I could," he laughed, "well ..." he looked toward the Sovereign who was smiling at the two of them, "it looks like we're going to see them stars. What 'ya say?"

Tanya had tears in her eyes, but was nodding her head, "It sounds amazing," she said, "but I don't know what I'll be able to do with my computer...." With everything else that had been happening she was still concerned about her laptop, which had been soaked by the dive into the ditch. She laughed, "I really don't think my Dell warranty is going to cover me out in ..." she looked at the Sovereign, "where did you say we were going?"

Sayoose giggled, "Actually, I did not say, but it is called Felis Prime, and it is the capital of the Felis Alliance. As for your device, I believe we may be able to do something about that," Sayoose picked up the mud-encrusted laptop and placed it into one of the top lockers for a moment, pressing a few buttons on the side panel. After several seconds the sound of the fans in the locker switched off automatically.

"That should fix things for you," she said, handing the laptop back to Tanya. When she opened it she was able to turn it on as though nothing had ever happened. "It simply dehumidifies," the Sovereign explained, shrugging her shoulders, as though fixing laptops was something she did routinely. "By the way," she asked, "do you happen to have any Beethoven and Schumann on that device?"

Tanya laughed, they were her favorite composers, along with a number of others, "Oh my, you have no idea," she replied, opening up the Media Player and starting Beethoven's *Pastoral Symphony*, which she knew the Sovereign had always enjoyed when she had it playing. "I have the complete orchestral works of Beethoven, as well as his string quartets and other chamber works, all of his piano sonatas, and … well, the only thing of his that I don't have are his opera and a few minor pieces. As for Schumann, I have all of his orchestral and chamber works, as well as his solo piano works as well, and several other great composers are saved to my hard drive, including Schubert, Chopin, Tchaikovsky, Brahms, Bach, Haydn, Mendelssohn, and many others; it would take several hundred hours to listen to all of the music. We'll have a great deal to listen to, don't worry."

Beethoven's *Pastoral Symphony* filled the aft section of the ship as the sight of the Earth filled the portholes. Sovereign Sayoose smiled warmly, then stepped forward and embraced Tanya warmly, holding her close. It was nice to finally speak to the woman that had been taking care of her for the past three years, and for her part, Tanya did not seem too upset about the idea of her cat having transformed into a woman that had been alive for over one hundred millennia.

As they broke their embrace she heard the old man mutter to himself, "… Always knew there was somethin' funny 'bout that cat …" which made both woman laugh. Sayoose then led them to aft quarters so they could finish cleaning up and change into fresh clothing. Tanya was slightly smaller than Captain Pertu, but her spare uniform still fit well enough. Bob was given a utility uniform that was stowed onboard, which suited him well since he was taller and much thinner than Tactical Sergeant Brem. Brem's uniform would have definitely not been a good fit for the Colonel, and Dragar's was far too large as well. Both Terrans were quite pleased to have changed out of their filthy clothing which had already begun to stiffen from their mud bath, becoming quite uncomfortable.

(*|*)

Captain Pertu was not pleased after learning about the plan the Sovereign had conveyed to Commander Dragar. Transmitting messages that the Sovereign had been killed in the attack to both Marshal Salzat and Felis Prime seemed tremendously risky to her, though she had to concede that she did not have any ideas which might be more effective. She hated to admit it, but the more she considered the idea, the more it all made sense; that still did not mean she had to like the idea.

No: she would not like it, not one bit, and she was not afraid of voicing her opinion. Until, of course, the Sovereign walked onto the bridge, "My Sovereign," Captain Pertu practically croaked, overcome with the emotion of seeing the leader of the Alliance after three years, "it's wonderful to see you," she was about to say more, but the Sovereign knew the words were bringing pain to the pilot and held up her hand to silence the woman.

"Thank you, Captain, it is also good to see you," she said, her own voice quiet, she looked down at the deck for a moment, seemingly unwilling to meet her gaze, then said, almost in a whisper, "I am sorry," which Pertu immediately understood. Pertu still felt the sting of having not been asked to fly the Sovereign to Terra when she had decided to leave Felis Prime, but this was not the time for apologies. Pertu nodded, almost overwhelmed by the emotion of seeing the Sovereign safely onboard, knowing their ordeal was almost over.

"Commander Dragar has apprised me of your actions and I must say, you have acquitted yourself along the finest traditions of our fleet and I am tremendously proud of you," she turned toward the thick-set Brem, "and of you as well, Tactical Sergeant Brem. You are both exceptional examples of what the Guardians represent; you shall each be receiving tangible expressions of my gratitude upon our return to Felis Prime," the two Guardians bowed deeply toward the Sovereign, each blushing at her compliments.

An unfamiliar voice spoke from behind Dragar, "My Sovereign," the voice said softly, "if I may, it was an honor witnessing how well both Captain Pertu and Tactical Sergeant Brem dealt with the Consortium to defend this system, this planet," the Sovereign turned to face Sergeant Candille who was standing behind the seat of Commander Dragar.

"Ah yes," she said, "Commander Dragar has told me about you," the Sovereign looked appraisingly over the former Sergeant of the STAWS Corps. Sayoose knew that the Sergeant had been sent on a mission to assassinate her, only to see her entire team eliminated by Commander Dragar.

"I have to thank you as well," she said, making quick eye contact with Commander Dragar, who nodded almost imperceptibly. "It would seem that you have been of more assistance than you might imagine," she continued. "Therefore, I would like to make you an offer," she stepped forward, moving around Dragar's seat, and took the hands of the surprised Sergeant, "contingent upon one thing: upon our return to

Felis Prime you agree to have your memory down-lined," she looked directly into the eyes of the young Sergeant. "This is merely to confirm the veracity of what you have told to Tactical Sergeant Brem and Captain Pertu. If the information coincides with your briefing, as I expect it shall, I would like to offer you a position in the ASCAR division known as the Home Guard on Felis Prime, as a Converter," she paused, "unless there is something else you would rather be doing."

Sergeant Candille fell to her knees as she continued holding the Sovereign's hands, laughing as tears rolled down her cheeks, "Oh, my Sovereign!" she exclaimed, unable to contain her joy. "You've made me the happiest person in the universe, how could I ever thank you!" All three Guardians laughed at the unbridled joy being expressed by the young Sergeant.

"Well," Sovereign Sayoose finally said, releasing the hands of the Sergeant and turning to Brem while Candille tried to regain her composure, "I believe it is time to transmit some messages before we return to Felis Prime." Brem nodded as he resumed his seat and began transmitting the message to Marshal Salzat.

Marshal Salzat had been closely monitoring the situation on the large view screens that displayed all of the Green Zone planets in the Sector on the bridge of his flagship, the Battlecruiser Orono-001. His Battle Group had effectively eliminated each of the Consortium ships within seconds of their arrival, catching them completely unawares as they arrived and made their attacks over the magnetic poles of the planets, using the magnetic fields of the planets as natural shields against the sensors of the Consortium ships.

According to Consortium intelligence there was not supposed to be any resistance in this Sector; they were not expecting any Alliance vessels sneaking up on them, which only made the assault that much easier. Cleansing the Sector of the incursion took less than an hour, but that hour had left Terra vulnerable, allowing the one Consortium Battlecruiser to arrive over the planet before Helios-2 had been able to take care of the ships attempting to begin the mining of the Terran star.

By the time Salzat's flagship had arrived over Terra the single Consortium Battlecruiser had managed to fire one Plasma Torpedo at the home in which the Sovereign had been staying; it had been their only shot, but it had been enough to completely destroy the dwelling. Even as the Orono had been transiting into orbit her weapons had been trained onto the Consortium Battlecruiser, and they fired the moment their momentum allowed their weapons to be locked, destroying the

Battlecruiser before it was capable of firing a second torpedo. Unfortunately, it looked as though that first shot had been more than sufficient; the sensors of the Orono had been unable to detect anything alive within the blast-zone.

Apparently, the Consortium Battlecruiser had only required that one shot in order to inflict the damage intended by Factotum Mar; at least, that was the impression that Marshal Salzat had as he read the message he had just received from Helios-2. After the Sovereign's ship had arrived and located Commander Dragar, who had somehow managed to survive the conflagration, he delivered the devastating news that the leader of the Felis Alliance had been consumed in the explosion: Sovereign Sayoose was dead, along with the two Terrans who had inhabited the small house.

Marshal Salzat pounded his fist on the arm of his chair, "By Caiphus, you'll pay for this Factotum Mar, if I have to rip your heart out with my bare hands!" he exclaimed to the bridge crew, none of whom dared utter a word. They had heard as he read the message aloud and were each in shock. Each member of the crew had tremendous respect for the Sovereign and were now mourning her loss in silence. As the flagship, the BC-Orono-001 had been personally commissioned by the Sovereign, and many of her officers and crew had met her on numerous occasions.

Sovereign Sayoose had toured the Orono before it was officially launched, when Marshal Salzat had been installed as Fleet Commander, and during several inspections. Salzat had been a popular choice for the position, though there had been some resistance at his selection; there may have been some General officers with greater experience, but there were none with more natural talent. Sovereign Sayoose had recognized that her new Fleet Commander Marshal Salzat possessed something which all of the other candidates lacked: an intuitive ability to see a situation and discern every possible outcome. It was something that the Sovereign had counted on when she made her decision to appoint him Fleet Commander, and was something that she was counting on when she had formulated her plan with Commander Dragar.

As Marshal Salzat considered the message he had received from Helios-2 the intuition that the Sovereign had been so impressed with was bothering him. It all stemmed from the contents of message he had received, and he could not seem to get rid of the feeling that there was something wrong with the whole situation. There was no doubt that the message had been formatted exactly as it should have been; about that there was no question, but there was still something about it was that was bothering him. Something about the wording was gnawing at him as he allowed his mind to see them in his mind.

While he could not imagine how Commander Dragar had managed to survive the blast, that, in and of itself, had not really surprised him; he knew it would take more than a weapon of mass destruction to kill the former ASCAR Commander. Still, the transmission from Tactical Sergeant Brem had been extremely specific. He looked at the datapad, not wanting to trust his memory with something so important.

"This is an EOF Priority One Message from Guardian One; I repeat, Eyes Only Fleet Commander Priority One Message from Guardian One: First Advisor Dragar sends his compliments to Marshal Salzat and his crew for their fine service. It is his sad duty to report that the Sovereign, as well as two Terrans, were vaporized by the attack by the Consortium vessel. Please remain on station to continue guarding Protectorates in this Sector until further advised by Cadre. Message Ends from Guardian One, EOF, First Advisor, out."

Everything was indeed perfectly formatted, but as Marshal Salzat reread the message for the third time it finally struck him: Tactical Sergeant Brem was continuing to refer to Commander Dragar as the *First Advisor*, but with the Sovereign dead, if she *was* dead, he would no longer be the First Advisor. Commander Dragar would still be a Guardian, but it would be the choice of the next Sovereign as to whether or not he would remain First Advisor, if the new Sovereign decided to even have a First Advisor.

"Well, Caiphus be praised," he muttered, almost inaudibly.

"Sir?" Lieutenant Bacef asked, looking over from his position at the helm. "Is there something wrong, sir?"

"No, LT, nothing at all. Send a message to the Battle Group, secure channel," the Marshal said, his voice low and controlled, "they're to remain in this Sector, guarding the Protectorates as ordered."

"Yes, sir," the Lieutenant replied, turning to issue the order to Communications.

"Helm," the Marshal called out, "prepare Trans-Light Drive and A-ConCom for immediate return to Felis Prime," a few members of the bridge crew looked up in surprise, but remained silent. If the Marshal wanted to return to Felis Prime, that was what they were going to do; he was their Commander.

"Yes, sir! Ready for Pan-dimensional travel in twenty seconds," came the response from the helm. "Attention all hands, attention all hands! Prepare for Pan-dimensional travel: transiting in twenty seconds," the announcement was made over ship-wide speakers, followed by loud alarms sounding as the crew scrambled into their designated positions; they knew the drill and would be ready for the transition in less than ten seconds. Many were probably wondering what they were getting into, but they knew they would find out soon enough. As the announcement came that the Primary Activation of the Trans-Light Drive had been made the crew prepared themselves for the Secondary Activation and the transition through Pan-dimensional space. All they had to do now was concentrate on keeping their minds focused and their stomachs with them as they returned to Felis Prime. When Marshal Salzat decided to explain his actions to the crew, if he decided, they knew that he would; he was not the type of leader to expect his crew to blindly follow him somewhere without an explanation, although they would do so, without question.

(*|*)

Commander Dragar had expected that Marshal Salzat would figure out the cryptic message when it was sent, which was why he was not at all surprised to see the massive Battlecruiser blink out of orbit over Terra a few moments later. Dragar smiled to himself, knowing that the Marshal would be in place to fulfill his part of the endgame, if he was needed. Hopefully he would not be required, but with risks as high as they were, it would have been foolhardy to risk not having the flagship on their side when they returned.

"Marshal Salzat and the Orono have departed, my Sovereign," he announced, a smile creeping over his face. Sovereign Sayoose only nodded at the news, having known that her Fleet Commander would not let her down.

"Alright, Brem," Dragar continued, patting his friend on the shoulder, "it's time to send the second one."

Brem smiled, replacing his headset as he began transmitting the message.

"This is an EOC Priority One Message from

Guardian Two; I repeat, this is an EOC, Eyes Only Cadre Priority One Message from Guardian Two to Felis Prime: Sovereign Sayoose has come under attack by a Consortium Battlecruiser and has been killed. I repeat: Sovereign Sayoose is dead. Prime Guardian Dragar has survived, but has suffered serious injuries and his survival is in question. Helios-2 returning to Felis Prime immediately. Consortium vessel destroyed. Green Zone planets in this Sector in peril. Advise reinforcements be dispatched immediately. Repeat: advise reinforcements be dispatched to support Protectorates immediately. Message Ends from Guardian Two, EOC, out."

Brem looked up from the Tactical station, a wry grin on his face, "How was that?"

"Excellent," came the soft response from the Sovereign, "absolutely perfect," she turned to the others, and smiled. "Now, we shall return to Felis Prime, but I cannot walk in there like this," she said, gesturing to her humanoid body. "However, I do not think anyone would understand what a cat is, so ..." they watched as she transformed into a black and white Torgon, just slightly larger in form than that of the cat which she had lived as for the past three years.

"I believe this might be more suitable," her voice filled their minds as she now employed the telepathic abilities of the gentle Torgons.

Candille and Pertu laughed at the transformation, but Brem just grunted; he had never been particularly fond of shapeshifting, though he would never say anything out loud. He had enough trouble dealing with one physical form let alone living in any shape that popped into his head, *"Oh, Brem, you really should relax,"* he heard the Sovereign's voice in his mind.

"Hey, that's unfair!" he exclaimed, as the Sovereign launched herself into his arms, settling onto his lap. That was simply too much for Captain Pertu, who began laughing, which led to coughing spasms, causing her to pop another lozenge into her mouth to sooth the pain of the ordeal.

"Alright, you two," Dragar exclaimed, "enough," he was trying to contain his own laughter, but found the entire situation impossible. First the Sovereign had been a cat, now she was in the form of a Torgon; but, Dragar thought to himself, things could be worse: First Counselor Regar could become the Sovereign, and he had absolutely no sense of humor, the man was as dull as a stone, and apparently quite treacherous as well. Dragar turned to Pertu, "When will we be ready to depart?" he asked, trying to remain serious.

She looked over the helm controls for a few seconds, "As soon as you make certain our guests are strapped in and prepared for the transition," she replied, her voice a scratchy whisper after the coughing spasm.

He nodded, returning to the aft compartment to prepare Tanya and the Colonel, who strapped themselves into their seats after he quickly explained what to expect from their first experience with Pan-dimensional travel. Tanya looked a bit nervous but the old man just smiled, "I knew bein' abducted by aliens was gonna be a hoot," he muttered as Dragar turned to leave the two alone again, pausing long enough to give the Colonel a bemused look in the process.

He found that he liked the old man; despite how old he looked he had a fighting spirit, and a sharp sense of humor.

When Dragar returned to the forward section everyone was ready: Brem was holding onto the Torgon-Sovereign, who seemed comfortable enough on his lap. Sergeant Candille was sitting behind Dragar's station, which was where the Sovereign would have sat while in humanoid form. Once had Dragar strapped himself in he signaled to Captain Pertu that they were ready and she began a short countdown before activating the Trans-Light drive.

"Hold on, folks," she croaked, initiating the Primary Activation of the Trans-Light Drive, as she tried to clear her throat in vain. "Secondary Activation in 3-2-1," she managed more clearly, "next stop, home."

Once the Secondary Activation was engaged there was nothing for Captain Pertu to do but hang on for the ride; all of the navigational coordinates were contained within the A-ConCom, which made Pan-dimensional travel possible. It did all of the flying when the Trans-Light Drive was running. Even though Commander Dragar was not particularly fond of Pan-dimensional travel, he was keenly aware that traveling home using only the Star Drive would have taken 92 months, almost eight years, which would have been totally unacceptable given the circumstances. No, Dragar had to concede, Pan-dimensional travel accomplished in a few seconds what the older ships could only realize in months, or years. Even as his mind was reflecting on the days of slower inter-galactic travel he felt the physical discomfort from their transition as the ship emerged above the crowded orbit of Felis Magoris, the home world of the Felis Alliance.

"All systems checking out," Pertu announced, her voice still croaking from the earlier coughing fit. "As you ordered, Commander, we're still shielded. Nobody can see us. Not even the sensors on Felis Prime," she turned and smiled at him.

"How in Caiphus did you manage that?" Dragar asked incredulously, knowing that the sensor array on Felis Prime was the most advanced in the Alliance. While it was true that Helios-2 carried technology not yet used on other ships, Felis Prime was constantly being upgraded with the latest developments in a variety of different types of sensors, including radiographic and several other types designed to detect a variety of elements, none of which were supposed to be able to be tricked by vessels that may be approaching the orbiting city.

Captain Pertu smiled again, this time winking as well, "Oh," she giggled, which came out as a raspy cough, "I transmitted a subspace script to the Array, a virus of sorts," she said. "Right now, while our shields are rotating through the E to S bands all they're going to see is a bunch of dust floating around above the orbit of the city, just as they would normally see," she winked at him.

"Quite impressive, Captain," the voice of the Sovereign spoke in their minds, *"I would like to remind you to inform Administrator Marta of this, after our arrival of course,"* she added, *"otherwise she may be slightly annoyed at having had her Array sabotaged,"* they could hear her laughing, *"even if it had been for a good cause."*

"Oh, of course, my Sovereign," Pertu replied, looking into the orange eyes of the Torgon-Sovereign, feeling somewhat odd for the experience. She turned back to the helm and studied the display, "Marshal Salzat has taken up a position over the northern pole of Felis Magoris," she announced, pointing toward the massive Battlecruiser which was plainly visible over the planet. "They're not even attempting to hide their presence."

"Nor should they," the Sovereign replied, *"nobody, save for the Marshal and his crew, knows of my orders for them to remain in Sector 0107. Thanks to the message from Tactical Sergeant Brem, the Marshal discerned the importance of returning to Felis Prime."*

"Well," Pertu added, "I don't have access to their sensor array," she looked at Commander Dragar, "if they're scanning the area, which is standard operating procedure, they can definitely see us."

Dragar nodded, "Excellent," he said, "I think it's time we briefed our friend. After all, it would be a shame to have had him come all this way for nothing, wouldn't it?" this earned him a grunt from Brem, who was still holding the Torgon-Sovereign on his lap.

(* | *)

Tears filled the eyes of Administrator Marta as she re-read the message from Helios-2 announcing the death of Sovereign Sayoose. How could this be possible, she thought to herself? Not only that, one of her dearest friends, Commander Dragar, had been gravely injured and might not survive. Her heart was pained as she ran down the hallway to personally deliver the message to the First Counselor of the Cadre, tears freely coursing down her cheeks. By the time she arrived at the personal chambers of the First Counselor she had managed to stop crying, but her emotions were still in turmoil. She pounded on the door so hard she almost did not hear him ask her to enter, until Regar finally opened the door with a distinctly annoyed look on his face.

"Ah, Administrator," he said, barely concealing the contempt he felt for the woman, "what brings you here in this excited state?" he asked, as though her presence represented a distinct inconvenience. The last thing he expected was for the Administrator to burst into tears after handing him the datapad containing the decoded communication, but that was precisely what happened as she collapsed in a heap in the middle of the chambers, shuddering in tears.

He left her there, ignoring her obvious grief and distress while he read the message as though it were a list of manifests from arriving transport vessels. After a moment he looked at the crying Administrator, "Alright, Marta, enough of this," he declared, his voice devoid of sympathy, "are you certain about this message?" He was clearly more concerned with confirming the death of the Sovereign than anything else.

Administrator Marta managed to struggle to her feet and, after a few deep breaths, collected herself enough to respond, "Yes, First Counselor, it was properly formulated, and it came through on a secure channel; I decoded it personally," tears began to flow again, "it … it's true." Her shoulders were shuddering uncontrollably as she broke down again.

"Well," the First Counselor said, looking out the large windows of the chamber, "I suppose we'll have to convene a Special Session of the Cadre …" he mused, almost to himself, then turned to the Administrator, almost accusingly, "Who else knows about this? Have you told anyone?" he was glaring at her in a menacing way that made her feel extremely vulnerable.

"Nobody, First Counselor," she replied, her voice low, "it's marked *Eyes Only Cadre*, I would *never* share such a message," she insisted, sounding offended at the accusation as she wiped away the tears that continued to flow from her puffy green eyes.

Her response seemed to mollify the First Counselor who turned away from the distraught Administrator, once again focusing on the large window of the chamber. He enjoyed watching the ships as they flew past the orbiting city; it reminded him of the importance of his position as the leader of the Cadre. With a few words he could have any of the ships impounded and inspected, perhaps even destroyed if they were found to be in violation of some Alliance regulation, but it would be a meaningless gesture; the power meant nothing to him at this point. There was still so much more that had to be accomplished, and now, with that horrific genomorph dead, it was all within his grasp. With Sovereign Sayoose gone, as he had hoped she would be, as he had only dared dream a possibility, his wildest fantasies, even beyond what he experienced with his precious Lareena, were now on the cusp of being fulfilled.

He turned as he realized the sniveling Administrator was still behind him, "Is there anything else, Administrator Marta?" the contempt he felt for the woman was impossible to conceal. He would definitely be replacing her once he had taken over as the Sovereign. Yes, he thought to himself, she would be one of the first to go, especially after this overt display of emotionalism at the loss of the Sovereign. He could not afford to have people around who were that faithful to the old regime when he would be making such drastic changes to the way things were run.

He glared at her, "Well," he asked again, "was there something else you required?" He crossed his arms over his chest, not attempting to disguise his impatience.

Administrator Marta managed to get up off of the floor surprisingly fast and, after she had straightened up her short frame and brushed herself off, she answered, "No, First Counselor," her voice and emotions were now carefully controlled, recognizing that the First Counselor was no ally, "I merely wanted to personally deliver the message, considering the importance of its contents," she paused long enough for Regar to nod his head solemnly. "That was all." She glared at him, as though she were challenging him to say something about the Sovereign, but he knew better. At least, not yet. Regar was acutely aware that Sayoose had been, without question, the most popular Sovereign of the Alliance in several hundred thousand years. Anyone trying to replace her would be facing a tremendous amount of resistance, but he was willing to take on that challenge.

"Yes, well … it is indeed tragic news, Sayoose … Sovereign Sayoose was a true hero of the Alliance, her loss will be felt by all," he replied, making an attempt at frowning, but only looking as though he had indigestion. "Thank you for bringing this message to me yourself. I expect I can count on your discretion?"

She found it odd that he was once again stressing that the message remain secret. It only reinforced her suspicions regarding his character. Instead of replying she just nodded as she turned to leave; the sooner she was able to get away from the man, the better. "Excellent," she heard him say softly as she left the room, "that's just excellent." She turned to ask what he was referring to, but he had already sealed the doors behind her, locking her out.

By the time Administrator Marta returned to her console in the Communications Array she had managed to regain some level of control over her emotions, but she was still quite shaken up over both the message she had received and her encounter with First Counselor Regar. As she settled herself behind her console she noticed there was a new message, directed to her, which was quite unusual. Even more unusual was who the message was from: she had received a personal message from Fleet Commander Marshal Salzat.

As she read through the message it felt as though her heart was going to explode, and tears were once again welling up in her eyes: Marshal Salzat had returned the flagship of the Alliance to an orbit over Felis Magoris to support the Sovereign. She was not dead; he was here in an effort to prevent a coup by one of the members of the Cadre, and would soon be joined by Commander Dragar and the other Guardians. Administer Marta could feel her heart soar as she sent her reply.

"This is an EOF Priority One message; Eyes Only
Fleet Commander message, from Administrator Marta:
Received and Acknowledged. Suspicions confirmed.
Target currently in personal chambers. Message ends
from Administrator Marta, EOF, out."

It was short and succinct, but answered what the Marshal had wanted to know: had she suspected anything, and where was First Counselor Regar. She had, suspected something, and her suspicions had only grown stronger after her last encounter with the First Counselor, and he was currently where he had been when he was not in the chambers of the Sovereign.

Once the response arrived on the Orono it was handed to Marshal Salzat by the Communications Officer, Lieutenant Carif, a short, thin woman, who quickly returned to her station. Salzat examined the datapad and nodded, "Excellent," he whispered. Turning to his Second in Command, "Number One," he called out, "have they arrived yet?"

General Taran nodded his bald head, "Yes, Marshal," he replied softly, "Helios-2 made the transition about 20 seconds ago. They're currently shielded, directly over Felis Prime," he chuckled, "but we have a lock on their position."

"Well done," Marshal Salzat replied. "Lieutenant Carif," the Marshal called, summoning the Communications Officer, "I want you to send a greeting to Commander Dragar onboard Helios-2, stating the following, *'This is an EOG Priority One message; Eyes Only Guardians message, from Fleet Commander: Per your message, my sincerest condolences regarding the loss of our friend and the injury to the First Advisor; I am, however, expecting a speedy recovery. Marshal Salzat, EOG, out.'* I want you to make sure that is sent precisely like that, understood?"

Without batting an eye, Lieutenant Carif saluted and replied, "Of course, sir," she memorized the message, but it had also been recorded by her datapad for the ship's records. Without another word she turned on her heel to rush off and transmit the message. Marshal Salzat knew he could trust the Lieutenant with any message, but this was different and he wanted to be certain: the security of the Alliance was potentially at stake.

(* | *)

As soon as the troublesome Administrator had left his chambers First Counselor Regar heard the familiar sound of the door from his sleeping quarters sliding open as his wife emerged. It was difficult to contain his joy as his wife asked whether what the Administrator had said was true. Regar was pleased to see that she shared his enthusiasm over the demise of the Sovereign. Now, the only thing that had to be done was for him to somehow work out a way to manipulate the Board of Governors of the Stellar Mining Bureau into selecting him as her replacement. It was the only part of his plan that was out of his direct control, which annoyed him tremendously. Regar did not like leaving things to chance, but he felt restraint was the best course to take at this time, otherwise it might look unseemly. After all, he reasoned, he could not have too many questions being asked regarding the death of the Sovereign and his ascension to the most powerful position within the Alliance. Were that to happen there might be an investigation, and that could be … he shook his head at the thought.

As he spoke to Lareena he could smell her heady perfume while she wrapped her arms around his thin frame. Her full-lips rubbed against his ear as she whispered, "It's really true, isn't it, my darling," she exhaled, "that despicable shapeshifter is *finally* dead!" He felt the firmness of her breasts pressing against his back as he continued to gaze out the large window and felt himself growing aroused as her hands probed his bony ribs. "I can feel it," she said as her hands slipped beneath his robes, "you're going to be the next Sovereign. I can feel the power, flowing through you, my love."

It was true, Regar realized, power was the ultimate aphrodisiac. Some used to believe that wealth was a great attractor, but in the Alliance that was fairly irrelevant considering that everyone had everything they needed and personal wealth was no longer an issue. There were neither rich or poor anymore, which bothered some, but economic equality had proven to be one of the best things to happen to the trillions of Citizens living under the flag of the Alliance. Ending the pursuit of wealth had simultaneously ended many of the worst problems associated with society, including a majority of the crimes that occurred which were motivated by greed.

It had not, however, resolved the question as to what made some people more attractive than others, and power was definitely something that seemed to have been the thing, in Regar's mind, that had worked for him in regards to capturing the heart of Lareena. At least, that had always been what he had thought since their first meeting on Altus 9.

"Yes, my darling," he gasped as her hands continued their gentle ministrations, "I only hope the Board of Governors agrees with you …" he looked up through the dome of Felis Prime and, for the first time, noticed the large Battlecruiser in orbit over the northern pole of Felis Magoris. Regar immediately recognized the flagship and something inside him grappled with the incongruity of its presence over the home world. It may have been an uncommon sight, but it certainly was not an unheard of situation. Except … he thought to himself, his mind reeling as Lareena continued to massage him, making it virtually impossible for his mind to function. Her perfume having its usual effect on him, driving him deeper into a trance, making rational thought virtually impossible.

He kept wondering about what was so troubling about the flagship even as Lareena guided him toward their bed, asking him about any other messages he had received from the useless Administrator. Yes, he thought about the demise of the Sovereign and her precious Guardian, now gravely injured; he would definitely have the Administrator banished from Felis Prime. Surely he would be able to find some way of arranging that for the meddlesome creature. His mind was now swimming in the pleasures that only his wife could elicit when he finally made the connection he had desperately been searching for regarding the flagship. It was standard procedure that whenever the flagship returned to the home world the Commander, in this case Fleet Commander Marshal Salzat, would present himself to the Sovereign. Since the Sovereign was absent, something the Fleet Commander would have been informed of as a formality by the Guardians, the Marshal should have paid that courtesy to the First Counselor of the Cadre.

Such a breach of protocol should have upset the First Counselor, and under normal circumstances it would have enraged him, but he was far too intoxicated by Lareena's perfume for his mind to be disturbed by such a trivial matter during this glorious moment. Lareena's hands were doing all the things he loved, and his body was responding; this was a time to celebrate: his victory was imminent, he could practically taste the power that would be his once he ascended to the position of the Sovereign. It should all be a formality now … but first, his addled brain thought, they would celebrate, luxuriating in the pleasures of their flesh as their bodies were joined as one.

(*|*)

Onboard Helios-2 both Tanya and her Grandfather were of the same opinion when it came to Pan-dimensional travel: it was not something they had particularly enjoyed, though the Colonel had to grudgingly admit, it beat the transport planes he had been packed into during his stint in the Army. He had complained that some of those rides had felt as though he was getting a bit too close to the soldier seated next to him.

"Whenever we hit turbulence," he always said, to anyone who would listen, "it was as though we was more than members of the same platoon, if ya knows what I mean," he always poked the person in the ribs to add emphasis to his point. They knew. At least with Pan-dimensional travel it was over, quite literally, in the blink of an eye; the discomfort seemed to last for a few minutes after arriving, but the trip was over; they had reached their destination. As he and Tanya unbuckled themselves from their seats and moved to join the others in the forward cabin the old man looked out one of the portholes of the ship and gasped.

"What's the matter, Gramps?" Tanya asked, concerned he was in pain. "Are you alright?"

He just stared, pointing out at the crowded space around them and gestured for her to look, "Where'd that cat of yours bring us?" he managed to ask, causing her to laugh.

"Gramps," she replied with some poise, "remember, she isn't really a cat. She explained all of that," she was about to continue but he waved her off.

"I know," he said impatiently, "she's a *Sovereign* something, but ..." he gestured out the porthole again, "look out *there*," he was pointing to Felis Prime, "ain't never seen nothin' like that, has you?"

"Gramps, I doubt we're going to be seeing a lot of anything familiar ... for a long time," Tanya replied, looking at some of the sleek vessels flying past their position. Felis Prime was indeed unlike anything she had ever seen, looking more like some conceptual drawing from one of those Science-Fiction magazines, the type that predicted the colonies that humans would be living on in orbit over the moon in several centuries. Well, she thought to herself, they were only wrong about the time, and the location.

"What do you say about us going to see what's going on up front?" she asked, trying to divert her grandfather's attention from the porthole, although she had to admit, everywhere she looked there was something amazing to behold. She had never imagined seeing anything so bizarre in her life, anything so unreal, and yet, here she was, on a spaceship near an orbiting city. As she looked at Felis Prime she realized that it was not just an orbiting city, it was an orbiting fortress, designed to withstand an assault from space. She could see that the domes were constructed from something that looked like a honeycomb configuration of cells, each of which contained a pane of some clear material. She made a mental note to find out more about the engineering behind this technological marvel.

Then there were the other ships. Even the smallest ones seemed outrageous by Earth standards. Some were sleek, others more utilitarian in design, and then, there were the ones that seemed to just blink out of existence, disappearing from view without having moved an inch. Others appeared in the same manner, like the ones that were congregating over the planet.

"Holy Mary, Mother of ..."

"What now?" she asked, suddenly concerned at his tone.

"Take a look at tha' ship, over the planet," he was pointing at the Orono, which she had just been looking at as well. "That's the biggest damn thing I ever seen! Can you imagine if we had *that* when we went to war against the Nazis and the Japanese? That would have been a different war," he was chuckling to himself, "criminy, that monster makes the Iowa look like a dinghy ..." he turned to Tanya. "Pumpkin," he said, lowering his voice to a whisper, "we may be in too deep," he had an extremely serious look on his face, which made Tanya laugh.

"You mean to say," she replied, wiping tears from her eyes, "watching our house get vaporized by a ship from space, a different alien ship I remind you, meeting an alien capable of changing her shape from a cat into a human who happens to be over one hundred thousand years old, and being onboard a ship that can travel halfway across the universe in a few seconds didn't bother you, but that," she pointed to the Orono, "that makes you think we're in too deep?" she laughed so hard she had to sit down.

He looked at her, shaking his head, "Kids," he said, "youse don't appreciate the experience of yer elders," he returned his attentions to the porthole, staring in awe at the massive ship as a few more ships blinked into orbit nearby.

This only made Tanya laugh harder, "I'm sorry, Gramps," she managed between spasms of laughter, "you know I love and respect you," she finally said, taking his hand.

"Humpf," was all he said, keeping a watchful eye on the massive Battlecruiser as it maintained a stationary orbit over the northern pole of Felis Magoris. Somehow its presence did not comfort him, though he had no idea why. "Remind me to ask tha' Commander Drago guy about tha' ship, 'kay dear?" he said, squeezing her hand now that she had managed to stop laughing.

"It's Dragar, Gramps," she laughed again, and they started making their way forward, where the others were talking to something that looked like the cat Tanya had known for three years as Sayoose, but it had no legs and was a bit larger.

"Sayoose?" Tanya called out, "Is that you?" the others turned as the Terrans entered the bridge.

"Yes, Tanya," the Sovereign replied, telepathically, *"I have assumed the form of a creature popular as a companion animal in the Alliance; it is called a Torgon, I would have remained in the form of a cat, but they are not indigenous to our home world, and I must remain in disguise for a little while longer. Torgons communicate using telepathy; they do not have vocal chords, which was why I was able to speak while in the form of the cat,"* she launched herself from the lap of Brem, flying the short distance into the waiting arms of Tanya who caught her with ease, cradling her while she affectionately stroked her fur, just as she had when she was in the form of the cat.

"Your fur is as soft as when you were a cat, maybe softer," she announced, stroking the silky fur of the Sovereign's back, eliciting a grunt from Brem and a giggle from Pertu, who was trying to contain herself, knowing she was in danger of triggering another coughing fit if she began laughing again. Dragar remained silent, frowning at the antics of the Sovereign. He still had difficulty viewing her in this manner, but, she was the Sovereign; who was he to deny her the simplest pleasures?

"If I may, my Sovereign," Dragar interrupted, "I believe everything is ready," he looked around at the others, each of whom nodded in agreement, "if you are, that is; we really shouldn't wait much longer. We don't want him to have an opportunity to escape, not that I think he'll try, given his intense sense of pride."

"You are quite correct, First Advisor. It is time to return to Felis Prime. I am certain the Cadre would be quite interested in receiving a visit, particularly First Counselor Regar. I expect they would be convening their Special Session by now, do you agree?" this time the Sovereign had directed her thoughts toward Commander Dragar, who nodded discreetly at the Sovereign.

Dragar nodded in agreement, "Indeed," he replied, quietly. He asked, his voice soft, "Have you given any thought to the reorganization of the Cadre, once everything has been ..." he paused, choosing his words carefully, "settled?" Even though Tactical Sergeant Brem had not heard the first part of the exchange he grunted at the question. He had his own opinions regarding the Cadre, but knew enough to keep his opinions to himself. He was a Guardian, not a bureaucrat, which suited him just fine; he had no aspirations of getting involved with politics and was quite certain everyone around him, especially the Sovereign, was well aware of his views.

Dragar shot the stocky man a glare, but smiled despite himself; he knew it could not have been easy to have first encountered the missing Sovereign in the form of a cat and now as a Torgon. Before he could say anything the voice of the Sovereign filled their minds, *"I understand your reticence, Tactical Sergeant, and it is well founded. The Cadre has acted highly suspiciously, but,"* she paused, looking directly at Brem, *"I have reason to believe that the other members of the Cadre were completely unaware of the machinations of the First Counselor. There has been no evidence, based on what we have heard, that the Cadre has even been called into session during the time since you departed to find me on Terra, which places all responsibility for the betrayal on First Counselor Regar,"* she twisted in the arms of Tanya, allowing the woman to have access to what she presumed was her stomach. *"Since the Cadre has not been involved,"* she continued, sighing at the ministrations of the human, *"he shall be the one brought before the First Tribunal, where he shall face a fair trial for his betrayal of the Alliance."*

Brem grunted at the mention of the First Tribunal. In his mind the First Counselor did not deserve a trial: he deserved to be executed for trying to have the Sovereign assassinated. "By Caiphus," he declared, finally losing his temper, "we have one of the members of the Fire Team that was sent to assassinate you, my Sovereign," his face had turned a deep crimson, "how much more evidence of his betrayal is required?"

Captain Pertu moved next to the thick-set man and placed her small hand on his shoulder in an effort to calm him, but he shrugged it off, "I'm fine," he said, glaring at the third Guardian. "Besides, I don't want to be calm right now. When I face that Tarvok I want to feel like this, I ..." he was about to continue but the Sovereign cut him off.

"I understand, Brem," she rarely addressed him simply by his name, *"and I appreciate your faithfulness and passion: you are one of my most trusted friends,"* she looked at the three Guardians, twisting around so she was facing the right side up again, if there really was such a thing for a Torgon. Tanya understood it was time to simply hold her, *"However, before we do anything else, I must apologize to the three of you,"* the voice in their minds was filled with contrition and sadness,

"when I left Felis Prime it was not my intention to cause the three of you any distress. Really, that was the last thing that I wanted to happen. For many years I had suspected that the First Counselor was involved in something nefarious, but I had no specific evidence with which to confront him: the only way to prove my suspicions was by leaving and putting him in a position of increased power, thus allowing him to reveal himself to be the traitor he seems to have been all along." She looked at the floor of the cabin, *"Please, believe me when I tell you my intention was never to cause you to worry. His treachery confused me as to who I could trust, though I assure you,"* she quickly added, *"I never once considered any of you to be part of the conspiracy, nor would I have ever doubted your faithfulness to your positions as my Guardians,"* she paused for the briefest moment, *"or as my friends."*

As she finished Pertu had a tear in her eye, which she wiped away on the sleeve of her uniform, and Brem bowed, almost whispering, "You have nothing to apologize for, my Sovereign. If anything, we should be apologizing to you for putting our own feelings before your needs and the security of the Alliance," he looked up, making eye contact with the orange eyes of the Sovereign. Even in the form of a Torgon, her eyes were mesmerizing, unlike anything he had ever seen.

Dragar was nodding his agreement, and simply added, "I couldn't agree more with Bren, my Sovereign," and was pleased to see that Pertu was also nodding in agreement.

"What in tarnation is goin' on here?" came the voice of the Colonel, who had moved up from behind Tanya. Her final thoughts had been directed at the three Guardians, so the others had no idea what had been said, save for the responses, which sounded quite odd to the military veteran.

Dragar smiled at him, "Nothing to worry about, Colonel," his voice more commanding now, "we're about to take a trip over there," he pointed at the view screen above the helm which showed the immense orbiting city. "That's Felis Prime, it's the capital of the Felis Alliance, and that," Pertu adjusted the angle of the image, "is Felis Magoris," Dragar was pleased to see that the Orono had been joined by a fleet of about fifty other ships, including at least a dozen Carriers and several Battle Transports, many of which were marked with a yellow lightning bolt striking a Red Giant star, the distinctive markings of the ASCAR.

He turned to the Sovereign, smiling broadly, "It looks like the reception party has arrived, my Sovereign," he said, barely containing his joy. "I'm guessing at least two Sector Battle Groups, if not more, and if I know the Marshal, there's more on the way."

A sound of a throat clearing behind him caused Dragar to turn, his eyebrows raised in question, "Party?" the old man asked, "I know youse folks brought us halfway across the universe, or further, but would somebody please explain t'me what in tarnation is going on? Especially before I step back onto the thing tha' zaps me across space into tha' floatin' abomination yer calling a city!"

Surprised by the outburst from the old man the three Guardians looked at each other, and then, as though the ridiculousness of the situation had finally struck them, they began to laugh. Even Sergeant Candille was joining in as the two Terran's watched, their mouths open, thinking they were on a ship full of psychotic aliens.

Dragar finally raised his hand to silence the others, "Alright," he said, regaining his composure, "you deserve that much," he looked to the Sovereign, who seemed to nod her small head. "Before we transport to Felis Prime I'll briefly explain what has been going on," he first gestured to the gathering mass of ships in orbit over Felis Magoris, "What you should know, first of all, is that those ships are with us," he pointed toward the gathering fleet of ships over Felis Magoris and chuckled, "they're here to ensure we have all the support we need."

Colonel Little groaned, "Oh, for the love of all that is sacred and Holy! Youse gone and brought us into the middle of a dang civil war!" He stamped his foot in growing frustration, causing Tanya to place her hand on his shoulder in an attempt to calm him. She was genuinely concerned that he was about to have another heart attack.

Bob just shrugged off her touch and continued his tirade, though he was a bit less vehement, "Look, Commander, if it's all the same with you, I already been in three wars where I came from ... I got the scars to prove it. They even gave me a bunch of medals, but ..." he paused, looking down, "I guess they was vaporized by that other alien ship, along with my house," he sounded angrier no, recalling the destruction of decades of irreplaceable memories. "Why don't you just take us back there and we'll sit this one out, okay?" His cheeks were bright red and Tanya was still trying to calm him, concerned for his health.

Dragar looked dumbfounded by the man's sudden outburst, then shook his head, "Colonel Bob, let me assure you, the last thing we're about to have is a war. That's why those ships are here: they represent the fleet of the Alliance, and they're on our side. Really," he sounded reassuring, "the person we've come to stop doesn't have a fleet of his own."

He then spent the next several minutes explaining what had been transpiring over the past few years, with the Sovereign adding a few details as well, until both Tanya and the Colonel had been fully briefed on the matter. When he had finished he looked at the two Terrans, "Does that satisfy your curiosity?"

Without missing a beat, the old man replied, "Always knew somethin' was wrong with tha' cat," he said. "Didn' I tell ya?" he asked, turning toward Tanya, who had remained silent. She seemed overwhelmed by the entire situation. "Tha' ain't no normal cat, I said, but no ... youse never listens to yer elders."

He was now fully convinced that he had truly gone mad. Civil war or not, Bob was certain he was about to die, or perhaps just lose his mind, which might actually be worse. He was not really sure, but he remembered that the doctors at the Veteran's Administration had warned him of this; even Doc Samford had said he was at that age where things might start to seem unreal. His imagination was beginning to run wild, the doctor had told him, which was why he had quickly dismissed the thought that the cat had been reading his newspapers and turning on the radio; it was all simply his imagination run amuck.

Of course, none of that that would explain the fact that their house had been vaporized, or that he was in a spaceship, purportedly on the other side of the universe. It had to be a psychotic break. Some grand delusion, or worse.

"Damn kids these days," he finally muttered, "talkin' cats and aliens ... what you get yerself into, Bob?" He looked back up at the Commander and smiled, "Yeah," he said, "I'm satisfied ..." he chuckled, "if that's what you want me to believe, why the hell shouldn' I?" It sounding more like a challenge, but Dragar decided to let it go; it was time for them to pay First Counselor Regar a visit.

While Captain Pertu and the others proceeded to the Long Distance Matter Transporter to prepare for their departure Commander Dragar pulled Tactical Sergeant Brem aside for a moment, "Before we leave there's one more message for you to send."

A few moments later the entire group was assembled on the LDMT pads, ready to be transported to the corridor just outside the Chambers of the Cadre on Felis Prime. As soon as the timer that Captain Pertu had set reached zero the device was automatically activated and the group disappeared. They reappeared a breath later in front of the Chambers where they could hear the sound of an Octavo being played.

"Excellent, we're just in time," Dragar whispered as he used his palm print to unseal the locked doors of the Chambers of the Cadre, allowing the group to enter into the rear of the Chambers in silence.

(*|*)

Once the delivery of the false message from Helios-2 had arrived the first order of business would be for First Counselor Regar to convene a Special Session of the Cadre to address how they would proceed. Losing a Sovereign to an unexpected death was something that had not occurred in the lifetime of any Citizen of the Alliance, so the news of the death of Sovereign Sayoose would be a great shock to her Cadre, leaving the group in turmoil. Since a new Sovereign would have to be selected First Counselor Regar knew that he would have to send a notice to Chancellor Valox, the Alliance's representative of the Stellar Mining Bureau on Felis Magoris, asking him to attend the Special Session. It would be up to Chancellor Valox to then convene the Board of Governors of the Stellar Mining Bureau, beginning the process of choosing the new Sovereign.

While the Cadre was empowered to act in the absence of the Sovereign, they could not select a replacement in the event of her death. Only the Board of Governors of the Stellar Mining Bureau, led by the stern, unyielding Chancellor Valox, who reported directly to the Premier of the SMB, the Paragon, were empowered to make that decision. Ultimately, it was the Paragon who would give the final approve to the recommendations made by the Board of Governors, which would have received the endorsement by Chancellor Valox. It was a process that had been codified as part of the *Felis Alliance Rules of Governance*, which served to guide the most massive bureaucracy in the universe, and had served the Alliance well for several hundred thousand years. Valox ran the Mining Bureau with an iron fist, adhering to its rules and regulations as though they were written in blood, which was something he also expected from his counterpart in the Ursus Consortium Branch of the Bureau, Chancellor Zarkun.

It was not supposed to matter to either Chancellor that they worked for potential enemies; their first duty was to the Bureau, and the Bureau existed for the singular purpose of making a profit. Their

sole interest was the portion of profits they received from the mining operations paid to the Bureau from both the Alliance and the Consortium in order to maintain their mining rights, something each Chancellor reminded the leaders about at every opportunity. What either company did with its considerable wealth was of little concern to the Bureau, so long as they paid the SMB their allotted portion of profits, as per their contractual obligations.

Given the financial benefits of the arrangements the Mining Bureau had bestowed upon the Alliance it had been decided over time to grant the Board of Governors the responsibility of appointing a new Sovereign in the event of their death during their term of office. If a Sovereign served their full term, a period of fifteen thousand years, they were afforded the option of being reappointed if they were interested in continuing to serve, and there were no limits to the number of terms that could be served, though there had only been a few cases in which a Sovereign had asked to serve for more than two terms. After all, thirty thousand years was a long time to serve in the highest office in the universe.

Things worked differently in the Consortium where the Factotum was selected by a secretive group known as the Seventeen, a group comprised of the most elite, exclusive individuals living on Ursus Minor, the home world of the Consortium. Without exception, members of the Seventeen were the richest members of society, living in the First Quarter of Hydra, the capital city of Ursus Minor. While the Factotum was the Supreme Leader of the Ursus Consortium he was acutely aware that anytime the company began to lag in its performance it was within the purview of the Seventeen to have him replaced, which was one of the main reasons Factotum Ebla Mar was maniacally single-minded in his pursuit of success when it came to outperforming the Felis Alliance. It made little difference to him that the Consortium was much smaller than the Alliance, he just wanted to see them destroyed.

Tactical Sergeant Brem sent his message directly to Chancellor Valox, who was still in his Office at the Stellar Mining Bureau's Felis Alliance Branch. It was a short message that immediately caught his attention, informing the Chancellor of the distinct possibility of a coup attempt by one of the members of the Cadre. It also surprised him by making it quite clear that Sovereign Sayoose was alive and well and had no intention of relinquishing control over the Felis Alliance. This was a surprise to the Chancellor since he had heard nothing regarding the

Sovereign being missing, let alone having died.

While the Board of Governors was empowered to select a new Sovereign in the event of their death they had no authority to replace a sitting leader, unless they were found to be in violation of one of the treaties pertaining to the mining of a stellar body. Infractions of mining treaties were taken extremely seriously by the Bureau; such an infraction would lead to a mandatory investigation, and somebody would be brought to justice. Valox shook his head in disbelief as he opened up the remaining portion of the message that the Tactical Sergeant had appended to the initial message.

He saw that appended portion contained visual logs from Helios-2 displaying the Consortium mining vessels and Battlecruisers in orbit over the star in the Terran system which clearly displayed them sending their probes into the young star as they prepared to commence their mining operations, only a few seconds before they were destroyed by the plasma torpedoes fired by Helios-2. A short message flashed under the portion of the visual record displaying the mining vessels: *"Callisto Treaty violation? Mining operations in Sector 0107, in the Terran System – an inhabited system – perpetrated by the Ursus Consortium."*

Valox watched in horrified fascination as each of the Battlecruisers was destroyed, followed by the mining vessels. He had seen Helios-2 firsthand and knew that the Battlecruisers outgunned the Sovereign's ship many times over, but they lacked one thing that Helios-2 had, something the Consortium would never be able to duplicate: the skills of a pilot like Captain Pertu. When combined with the technology that she was equipped with onboard Helios-2 it hardly surprised the Chancellor to see the much larger Consortium vessels destroyed as though they were drones. He knew the Guardian would have been pained at the loss of life, but the Consortium had sent those ships in a blatant violation of the Callisto Treaty. Factotum Ebla Mar had been well aware of what he was doing when he issued the orders for them to go to that system, and it had cost those people their lives.

At the end of the brief message Chancellor Valox was directed to tune his view screen to one of the Alliance's security channels. As he did so he was provided with an image of the flagship of the Alliance and the gathering fleet in orbit over the planet. It was an obvious demonstration of the support being shown for the Sovereign by Fleet Commander Marshal Salzat and other members of the Unified Armed Services. As the Chancellor was looking at the display he could see more ships joining every few seconds. It was a truly impressive sight.

He was about to turn away from his view screen when an urgent message from the First Counselor of the Cadre arrived. It was an official invitation to attend a Special Session in the Chambers of the Cadre, scheduled to convene the moment he arrived on Felis Prime. As he studied the brief message it occurred to him that the one thing missing from it was any mention of the death of the Sovereign. A Special Session of the Cadre was an extraordinary event in and of itself. A Special Session that required the attendance of the Chancellor of the Stellar Mining Bureau's Felis Alliance representative had to mean that they were convening in order to ask the Board of Governors to begin the process of selecting a new Sovereign. Otherwise, there was absolutely no reason for Valox to attend a Special Session.

As Chancellor Valox sent a brief reply to the First Counselor he muttered, "Well, here I thought today was going to be just another routine day at the office," and then he sighed.

Before leaving he considered reporting the situation to Governor Charkan, the head of the Board of Governors, but decided against it; there would be no reason to involve the Governor unless his signature was required on a decision of the Board. Since there was no need to select a new Sovereign based on the message he had received from Tactical Sergeant Brem, the Board of Governors would not become involved in this situation. Besides, Valox thought to himself as he selected a datapad from his desk, Governor Charkan was a relatively useless man. He walked over to the Long Distance Matter Transporter in the corner of his office, slipping the datapad into a deep pocket in his jacket.

Valox knew that Governor Charkan was only in his current position because he was a close friend of the Paragon and was well aware that the Paragon was hoping that he would soon retire so he could elevate his friend to the role of Chancellor. He smiled to himself; not anytime soon if that was who you want as my replacement. Fortunately, he thought, there were no limits to how long he could serve as Chancellor and had no intention of leaving his position, at least, not while he still enjoyed the job and was still capable of doing the other things he loved.

After entering the coordinates for the Reception Hall on Felis Prime and setting an activation-delay he stepped on the pad and prepared himself to arrive on the orbiting city, half convinced that his molecules would be scattered halfway through space and the orbiting city rather than arriving at the chosen destination. He had never been fond of this form of transportation, but using a shuttle would only add extra time to his journey, and cause him to interact with more people than necessary.

Once he had arrived he was greeted by the First Counselor and his wife, both of whom were smiling as though they were greeting a long-lost friend.

"Welcome back to Felis Prime, Chancellor Valox," Lareena gushed, slipping her arm through his; his stomach churned as he began to sense the lingering odor of her perfume, even though she had not applied any in several hours. Going through the LDMT disagreed with his stomach and the perfume did nothing to help matters.

He extricated his arm from hers and turned to the couple, "I believe there are some business matters to which we must attend?" he asked, his manner brusque and formal.

First Counselor Regar nodded, "Of course, Chancellor," he bowed in deference to the man's authority, "the Cadre has assembled and is awaiting your arrival."

Chancellor Valox let out what could only be described as something between a sneer and a laugh as they walked toward the Chambers of the Cadre, "Yes," he said, "I'm sure," causing Lareena to look at him quizzically, then at her husband, who only shrugged. Valox was not supposed to know anything, so they proceeded toward the entrance to the Chambers in silence.

CHAPTER XII ~ BETRAYAL

"Operating as a wholly independent body, the Stellar Mining Bureau is autonomous from both the Felis Alliance and the Ursus Consortium. Its entire mission being both the development and protection of stellar mining claims, and their administration, throughout the known universe. Mining claims are based on a system designed to give each company an opportunity at earning profits through the mining of stellar bodies as they become available in any of the 1,024 Sectors of the known universe currently mapped by the Universal Survey Team, a subsidiary of the Stellar Mining Bureau."

[...]

Excerpted from the *Operational Handbook of the SMB: a Primer for Schoolchildren,* by Laxapro, the Paragon, Premier of the Stellar Mining Bureau; for both the Felis Alliance and the Ursus Consortium

(*|*)

As the doors to the Chambers of the Cadre slid open, Chancellor Valox scanned his surroundings, taking in all those assembled for the Special Session. He had met each member of the Cadre on numerous occasions, though not over the last three years. Most of the interactions had been through the infrequent social event, things he abhorred, but attended as part of his duties as the Stellar Mining Bureau's Chancellor for the Felis Alliance.

In the Chancellor's mind social events had to be the most tediously vile thing he could do with his time; he invariably ended up being cornered by some ambitious young bureaucrat, their mind filled with inane ideas regarding how they believed the Bureau could function more efficiently. Oh yes, Valox thought to himself, he had heard all of the ideas before, but listened patiently while sipping at his tri-colored *Nebula Swirl,* an orange, green, and blue cocktail he preferred as it was served in a tall, wide glass, accompanied by a skewer of exotic fruits. He effectively used the glass to conceal the scowl creasing his face while he endured the unceasing litany of advice from whoever managed to corner him, something that was more difficult to accomplish with a simple glass of wine. As these were usually official functions he felt obliged to attend, but as soon as was reasonable, usually after his Assistant had contacted him, feigning some urgent Bureau business back in the office, Valox would excuse himself after making appropriate apologies to the host of the function for his early departure.

In truth, Valox knew that nobody would miss him at such events; he was not known as a great conversationalist and had little interest in socializing. This meeting with the Cadre, on the other hand, was something else entirely: he would not be leaving until every last word had been spoken. After receiving the message from Helios-2 his curiosity was piqued to the point that he was honestly looking forward to being amongst these people, something quite unusual for the Chancellor who preferred to keep his own company.

Although he had been married for over five hundred years, and he loved his wife dearly, the two spent much of their time apart. She respected his need for solitude, and understood that his work for the Bureau was often tremendously taxing, leaving him with a need for the solitude of his artistic pursuits, which consumed his time away from the office. His first love had always been music; he had pursued several advanced degrees in Musical Composition, Analysis, and Theory, before deciding to seek the administrative training that ultimately led him to his career with the Stellar Mining Bureau. That career, however, came after he had already established himself as an extremely successful composer.

Valox had been able to use his career as Chancellor to help his music spread across the universe. Thanks to his connections within the Bureau his music had been performed on virtually every planet within the Consortium, his music had also been performed throughout the Alliance, providing him with unusual access to the artistic community throughout the universe. Even so, considering his renown as a composer, and the numerous requests he received to create new works, Valox genuinely loved his position as Chancellor and had no intentions of resigning. Certainly not with the threat of Governor Charkan taking over his position. Until there was someone genuinely capable of filling his shoes, he had no intention of retiring. Based on everything he had seen, surveying the junior and senior bureaucrats working within the Administrative Departments of the Bureau, the people who represented his possible replacements if Charkan were out of the picture, the chances of him retiring anytime within the next several thousand years appeared tremendously slim.

That did not stop the Paragon from trying to pressure him, though it had been good natured. After the last time he had met with the Premier of the Stellar Mining Bureau, while visiting Ursus Minor for a series of concerts of his music in the capital city of Hydra, they had discussed whether Valox was interested in devoting his life to a full-time career as a composer. Valox had replied that a Synthetic Living Intelligent Systems device was more qualified to replace him than anyone the Paragon currently had in mind for the position.

Valox continued by saying that, "At least SILS managed to maintain a cool head under stress, if only because they had no hearts and were incapable of feeling anything within their synthetic brains, which was something he could not always say about a certain Governor back on Felis Magoris," who he well-knew was a friend of the Paragon. That comment, he reminded himself, was also a form of prejudice which he found distasteful and struggled to suppress, even if SILS made him uncomfortable whenever they were nearby.

"No," Valox had told the Paragon in no uncertain terms, "retirement was definitely not an option."

To his credit, Laxapro had laughed at the Chancellor's insult to his friend, and had not been at all offended by the candor of the man. Despite wanting to elevate his friend, which he did want to do, he genuinely liked and respected Valox as well. He could not fault a man who was unafraid to speak his mind and was not intimidated by ostentatious displays of wealth and power. After all, the concert had taken place in a property owned by the Paragon, which Valox was well aware of, and he was staying as a guest at the Paragon's personal residence while in Hydra.

For his part, Valox also respected the Paragon and knew that his position as Chancellor was safe for the simple reason that he did his job exceedingly well, and that was more important to the Premier than anything, including his friendship with Charkan. Valox knew that if Charkan did one day become Chancellor and was unable to fulfill the duties of the position his friend would have no qualms about replacing him with someone who could, before the organization suffered. When it came to business the Paragon was first and foremost the Premier of the Stellar Mining Bureau, and he did tolerate incompetence in the organization.

Chancellor Valox returned his attention to the room: unlike many of the social gatherings he had to attend, this Special Session of the Cadre seemed to have the promise of being an entertaining diversion. Perhaps, if things turned out the way he expected, it could be transformed into the topic for his next Opera, Valox thought to himself, trying to conceal the smile crawling across his thick lips. His last Opera, which had been entitled *Chronicles of a Blue Dwarf*, had been a resounding success even though it was over four hours in length. Audiences had found the tale of the Blue Dwarf, a stalwart character based on the life-cycle of the Blue Dwarf sun in the Marnse system, something that resonated in ways that Valox had difficulty understanding, even though he had written both the text and the music. He was, after all, just a composer; he often had no idea what people wanted to hear, though he was tremendously pleased when audiences enjoyed his work, which usually happened.

Since the success of that opera he had been receiving many calls to write another, and had begun preliminary sketches on the musical materials, but he had yet to find a suitable text to match to the dramatic music that he had been composing, and that was something that was troubling him artistically. Once he was inspired, he knew, it would only be a matter of a few days before he was able to assemble the entire text thanks to the use of the Neural Interface that would allow him to, quite literally, write the text in his mind and have the completed text entered into his composing datapad as a completed work. All it would require after that would be some minor changes as the work took shape, but that was merely the polishing process. As he composed the opera it would all come together.

As he considered the message that he had received from Tactical Sergeant Brem he could already imagine several different scenes that might be extremely successful if translated into a musical drama. Yes, he thought to himself, the *Sovereign's Betrayal* might be the next work to come from Valox the Composer. The more he considered the idea the more he liked it; that subject would have a broad appeal in the Consortium as well, though he would definitely have to follow the results of whatever happened after this Special Session.

His brief reverie was broken by the familiar voice of Counselor Trema who had walked over to greet him, "Welcome, Chancellor Valox," he looked up at the senior member of the Cadre after First Counselor Regar.

Valox gave the woman a genuine smile; she was the one member of the Cadre that he truly enjoyed being around. Trema was soft-spoken and brilliant; more importantly, she was the one member who intimidated First Counselor Regar. It was entirely unintentional, and not anything she desired. It all came as a result of First Counselor Regar's belief that the small woman posed a direct threat to his position and authority as First Counselor. In truth, she did: she was far more qualified in every way, and she was intensely loyal to both the Sovereign and the Alliance, which was why the First Counselor had been extremely careful about keeping her in the dark regarding the status of the Sovereign, as well as everything else that had transpired since the departure of the Guardians for Terra.

"It's good to see you again, Counselor Trema," Chancellor Valox replied, taking her small hand in his and kissing it gently.

She blushed at the gesture, but made no attempt to withdraw; she enjoyed speaking with the Chancellor and had frequently discussed his passion for music. Trema had down-lined several of his recordings and enjoyed relaxing while listening to his works. Music was a passion they shared as she had also pursued it actively before becoming a member of the Cadre. While Trema had dabbled in composition, having composed several pieces for her own enjoyment, she preferred performance, finding that playing music was the best way to relax and express herself when she was not working. Trema had become extremely proficient on the Octavo, a keyboard instrument not unlike the piano on Terra. It was an instrument that had been developed on Ionia, having a range of eight octaves, with 97 keys.

When First Counselor Regar had announced the calling of the Special Session of the Cadre and informed Counselor Trema that Chancellor Valox would be present she had requested that an Octavo be brought into the Chambers, explaining her reason to the First Counselor. Considering their relationship, Trema had fully expected that the request would be denied, but the unusually relaxed Regar had consented, agreeing that her idea was quite appropriate and would help lift the mood of the somber proceedings. Trema was confused as to what the First Counselor meant when he referred to the somber proceedings, but she had been preparing a short recital of works by Chancellor Valox and having an opportunity to perform them at the Special Session would be ideal considering that the composer would be present. It was an honor that any performer would surely take advantage of given the opportunity.

Leaning toward the Chancellor, "I have a surprise for you," Trema said, then she guided him toward the seat that had been reserved near the front of the room. It was just to the left of the massive instrument, providing him a clear view of her hands. She would be performing his three *Nebula Sketches*, which had been premiered, to critical acclaim, only a few months earlier.

"I'm quite impressed," the Chancellor said, as he looked at the striking instrument. "I had no idea you would have been able to prepare such a difficult program given your demanding schedule," he smiled at the Counselor, who had produced a small printed page with the names of the pieces she would be playing.

"In truth, Chancellor," she whispered, "the Cadre has had precious little to do for a while. First Counselor Regar has taken it upon himself to make most of the decisions, choosing to brief us afterwards, in case we might have any objections. My colleagues and I," she bent closer to his left ear, "met without him during the Sovereign's absence … you *were* aware she had taken a vacation, weren't you?" Valox gave a nearly imperceptible nod. He had not been, but though that playing along would be best. "We decided that unless something critical arose, it didn't seem to be of tremendous importance," she stopped as First Counselor Regar and Lareena took their seats at the far end of the front row, away from the Chancellor.

Counselor Trema smiled as she straightened up, "I hope you enjoy my short recital, Chancellor," she bowed toward him and went over to the Octavo, turning toward the small audience, which included the rest of the Cadre, First Counselor Regar's wife, and five members of the Sovereign's Guard, the ASCAR platoon assigned to protect the Sovereign, including their commander, Lieutenant Kar, all of whom had taken seats at the back of the chamber. As protectors of the Sovereign they were always considered to be on duty, and were always fully armed; their weapons at the ready in case they were required for any unforeseen circumstance.

First Counselor Regar stood nearby the Octavo and faced the assembled group, ignoring Counselor Trema who had sat down at the bench by the keyboard. "Welcome fellow members of the Cadre," First Counselor Regar began, his voice stronger than he had expected. "We are gathered here for a Special Session of the Cadre of the Felis Alliance, for which we are honored to have Chancellor Valox of the Stellar Mining Bureau present amongst us," he gestured toward the Chancellor, sitting at the front, and the big man bowed his head, waiting for what the First

Counselor would say next. He wanted to see how the rest of the Cadre would react knowing that it would speak volumes regarding the plot to his opera.

"Unfortunately," First Counselor Regar continued, looking at the face of his wife who was smiling at him, "I must begin this Special Session by informing you all about a message that was received only a short time ago from Helios-2," he paused long enough to take a deep breath and look down, as though he were struggling with the gravity of the situation. "It is my sad duty to inform you that Sovereign Sayoose … that the Sovereign … that she was killed in an attack by a Consortium Battlecruiser …" the room erupted in groans and shouts of dismay and grief.

Every member of the Cadre was in tears, and even the members of the Sovereign's Guard were protesting the news. Lieutenant Kar looked stunned at what she had heard and silenced the other guards. Regardless of what may have happened, they still had a duty to perform. They were still soldiers. Grieving would come later.

"I know," Regar continued, his voice softer, "this is difficult to accept. Prime Guardian Dragar was seriously injured in the attack and is not expected to survive," he looked toward the back of the room at Lieutenant Kar, but she refused to reveal her feelings. Turning away, however, she wiped away a single tear as she struggled to maintain her composure.

"In honor of our departed Sovereign, and to celebrate the talent of our esteemed guest," Regar once again gestured toward the Chancellor, "Counselor Trema has prepared a short recital of works by Chancellor Valox." With that, he walked away and sat down next to Lareena, who took his hand and leaned against him as though they were alone at home. Valox watched the two and just nodded to himself. His opera would be spellbinding, he thought to himself.

Trying to regain her composure, Counselor Trema stood up to introduce what she was going to play, but found it difficult to speak through the tears that were still flowing down her cheeks. After several uncomfortable seconds of silence where she knew the First Counselor and his wife were glaring at her she finally managed to begin, "In honor of the presence of the Chancellor I shall now perform a short program of his three *Nebula Sketches* for your listening pleasure," she turned to sit, then quickly added, "and also to honor the life of Sovereign Sayoose, the greatest Sovereign the Alliance has ever known, one who shall not be easily replaced." She was surprised by the vehemence of the applause that followed her comment, though when she looked at the First Counselor and his wife she noticed that the two of them were frowning, their hands folded in their laps.

Chancellor Valox had intended his *Nebula Sketches* to be a showcase of virtuosity, exploring the diverse possibilities of the instrument, which had the greatest range of any single musical instrument. This was apparent from the first notes of the broody opening of the *Shadow Nebula* through to the thunderous finale of the *Nova Nebula*; Counselor Trema's performance of the music held the small audience's attention so well they did not notice when the doors at the back of the Chambers slid open and the contingent of three Guardians walked in, accompanied by four others, including a young woman carrying a black and white Torgon. With the three Guardians was Marshal Salzat, the Fleet Commander of the Alliance, his back ramrod straight as he stared at the back of the First Counselor of the Cadre, not even trying to conceal the animosity in his eyes.

As the music ended and the audience began to applaud Commander Dragar called out in a booming voice, "Wonderful performance, Counselor Trema, truly brilliant. Congratulations on another masterpiece, Chancellor Valox!" Dragar was applauding with the others, but his eyes were firmly set on the First Counselor, who had leapt to his feet like a frightened newborn kit of a Verkallian Tarvok, reacting to the sound of the voice of the Prime Guardian.

Dragar had been the last person he had expected to see, not to mention the Fleet Commander: he had received a message indicating that the Prime Guardian had been gravely injured in the attack that had killed the Sovereign and they were unsure if he would survive his injuries.

After bowing several times Counselor Trema moved away from the Octavo, joining the rest of the Cadre who had risen from their seats, separating themselves from the First Counselor who seemed to be acting quite erratically as Commander Dragar approached him in the center of the room. "You …" the tall man stammered, "you … you're …" he seemed to find it impossible to say what he wanted, which frustrated all the more, causing him to blush furiously at his sudden inability to express himself.

He finally cleared his throat and said, with some difficulty, "We were told that you had been seriously injured," he spat, almost accusingly. Turning to the Fleet Commander, "It is, as always, an honor to have you present on Felis Prime, Marshal Salzat. I noticed the Orono in orbit over Felis Magoris some time ago and was wondering when you would be paying your respects," his tone had changed to one of petulance, while he continued to attempt to calm his wavering voice, which failed miserably. His nerves were getting the better of him; the situation was not at all as he had anticipated.

Marshal Salzat glared at the thin man, glancing out of the corner of his eye to Commander Dragar before replying, "Yes, the Orono arrived some time ago," his voice icy, "I would have come sooner, First Counselor," he continued, controlling his anger, "but I was waiting for more of the fleet to arrive," he paused, glancing around the room at the others, including Chancellor Valox, at whom he nodded before continuing, "to demonstrate our support for the Sovereign."

Regar's mind was reeling; he was confused, but turned his attention back to Dragar, who was still glaring at him, "That doesn't explain what you're doing here," he practically shouted, finding it impossible to conceal his contempt for the First Advisor and Prime Guardian of the Sovereign.

Dragar nodded slowly, smiling, "Yes," he said, "I can understand your confusion, First Counselor," if the title could be used as an epithet, Dragar had just done so, "you see, the message you received may have been sent in error," he glanced over at Tactical Sergeant Brem, who stepped forward, nodding at Lieutenant Kar as he passed her and the other four members of the Sovereign's Guard. Lieutenant Kar was smiling broadly, as were the other members of the Sovereign's Guard. They had understood what was happening the moment the group had entered and were waiting to see things unfold. Their weapons were ready.

"It's all my fault," the Tactical Sergeant broke in, "if you really need to blame someone," adding a grunt to emphasize his seeming dismay at the situation. "You see, when the Consortium ship fired upon the position of First Advisor Dragar it was our assumption that he had been lost, along with Sovereign Sayoose and the two Terrans she had been living with at the time," he nodded his head toward the two Terrans who were now standing behind Commander Dragar, "imagine my surprise when we found out there had been survivors."

First Counselor Regar's mind was spinning out of control: everything was falling apart around him and he could not process what was happening. Survivors, he thought to himself, trying to piece everything together. Fleet Commander Salzat was here, along with a gathering fleet of Alliance ships in orbit over Felis Magoris, "... to demonstrate our support for the Sovereign" he had said, and now that Marshal Salzat had arrived he was with the Guardians of the Sovereign … it all meant something, but his mind could not process the meaning of the information, not while his wife was standing so close to him; he could still sense her intoxicating smell, even without the intense perfume she wore when they were alone.

Then, in an instant, the First Counselor felt his mind begin to completely fragment, as though he had lost all sense of reality and his sanity had fully abandoned him.

"What is the problem, First Counselor?" a voice spoke to him, in his mind and, for the first time, he noticed the black and white Torgon with the intense orange eyes looking directly at him, being held in the arms of the young woman. "Are you not pleased to have your Sovereign back on Felis Prime?" the creature asked.

It was all the man could take; his already fragile mind seemed to disintegrate as he came to the realization that he had been deceived by the group standing in front of him, but how? How had the deceiver been so easily deceived? Everything was now falling apart right in front of him. As impossible as it seemed, this black and white Torgon was the Sovereign. As he looked at the orange eyes of the creature he immediately recognized the intense intelligence dwelling behind them, realizing that this was no ordinary companion creature. Sovereign Sayoose had taken on the form of the creature to intentionally deceive him, and it had worked; cursed shapeshifting wretch of a woman.

Without having anything else to lose, Regar reached into one of the deep pockets of the black robes he always wore and withdrew the weapon he had stowed there for such an occasion. While he had never expected to have to use the device, he had always thought it prudent to be prepared, just in case it became necessary to take matters into his own hands. Those standing closest to him gasped at the site of the PPD-77 as the First Counselor raised the weapon at the Torgon and prepared to finish what should have been accomplished by the Consortium Fire Team, and then the Battlecruiser, but his finger never came close to touching the trigger.

"Hit the floor!" rang out as Sergeant Candille flew through the air toward Tanya, her arm extended so she pulled both Tanya and the Sovereign out of the First Counselor's line of fire.

At the same moment a flash of plasma engulfed the weapon and right hand of the First Counselor, leaving him with a perfectly cauterized stump where his hand had been. Regar began howling in pain, clutching his arm to his chest, but the only person showing him any sympathy was Lareena, who had remained placidly by his side throughout the entire episode. She had not appeared at all surprised when her husband produced a prohibited weapon, then proceeded to aim it at the creature being held by the woman who had entered with the Guardians. Lareena had not heard the creature speak so she was quite shocked when she looked up again to see that the Torgon had disappeared; in its place stood Sovereign Sayoose, staring at her with her intense orange eyes.

"Excellent shooting, Lieutenant Kar," the Sovereign said, offering her hand to help Tanya back to her feet as she acknowledged the platoon commander who had saved her life from her position at the back of the room. She looked at Sergeant Candille who had also saved her and Tanya, "Are you alright, my dear?" she asked, a note of genuine concern in her voice. Both women were nodding, dusting themselves off.

"Are *you* alright, my Sovereign?" Sergeant Candille replied, brushing aside the Sovereign's concern. She had been trained for that sort of roughhousing and had endured far worse in her career. She was not even bruised, particularly since the uniform Captain Pertu had provided had exceptional padding, providing more protection than her STAWS uniform. She turned to look at Tanya, who also seemed fine, but she was also more concerned with the Sovereign's condition, surprised to see that she had made her transformation so quickly.

Sensing the question, the Sovereign responded, "Please, do not be troubled, I am fine," turning to Tanya, "changing forms is quite easy for me, Tanya," she said, "it takes less than a few seconds." She then looked over at the howling form of the injured Regar, "It would seem that the First Counselor may require some medical assistance," she walked over to the man who was still whimpering in a heap on the floor, clutching his handless wrist against his chest as tears flowed from his eyes. "Please summon the Medics and have this," she looked down at the betrayer, frowning, "prisoner removed from the Chambers of the Cadre." She then turned to Lareena, "I know this must be difficult for you, Lareena," she began to say, but Sergeant Candille came up behind her and whispered something into her ear. Sovereign Sayoose turned in what looked to be surprise at what the former commando had to say and stepped back from the wife of the First Counselor.

"You're supposed to be dead!" Regar spat through his pain, causing Commander Dragar to step forward, his own PPD-77 in his hand. Dragar had his weapon pointed menacingly at the head of the injured Regar.

"One more word from you, *former* First Counselor," he said menacingly, "and *you* will be; is that understood?" His only reply was another whimper. A moment later two medics from the Medical Center arrived and, after eyeing the wound with suspicion and seeing the weapons in the hands of the guards and Guardians, they gingerly placed the former First Counselor on a stretcher, preparing to deliver him to the Medical Center in the core of the orbiting city.

Before they could leave Dragar stopped them, "This man is to be kept under strict guard. As soon as he's able, he'll be facing charges for crimes against the Alliance, including the attempted assassination of the Sovereign. Once his injuries have been dealt with he's to be transferred to the High Security section of the Detention Center, is that understood?" Both medics blanched at the words, but nodded; they understood that the Prime Guardian was not someone they could disobey in such matters.

"Yes, Prime Guardian," they replied in unison, and began to leave the Chambers. With a nod of his head to Lieutenant Kar she had the four members of the Sovereign's Guard follow along as well; Dragar did not want to take any chances of having Regar escaping after the trouble he had caused.

Sovereign Sayoose had finished her private discussion with Sergeant Candille and turned back to face Lareena, "I know the two of you have never met," she said, gesturing toward Sergeant Candille, who was smiling enigmatically at the wife of the First Counselor, "but apparently you have a great deal in common."

Lareena had a look of confusion and defiance on her face as she shook her head, too emphatically, "I believe you are mistaken, my Sovereign," she replied, her eyes looking everywhere but at the Sovereign. "I've never met this …" she looked Sergeant Candille over from head to toe, "woman, in my life," her eyes shifted to the left as she tried to turn away, but found her way blocked by Tactical Sergeant Brem, who was standing right behind her, blocking her path.

"Don't you know it's rude to turn your back on the Sovereign," he said, grunting, as he spun her around to face both the Sovereign and Sergeant Candille. She cried out at being touched by the stocky Guardian, but he had not hurt her; he merely twisted her shoulders so that she would be facing the two women.

"Oh no, we haven't actually met," Sergeant Candille continued, her voice calm, "but you and I do have a great deal in common."

"I find that difficult to believe," Lareena practically spat, growing increasingly agitated.

"Oh, we do," Sergeant Candille continued, undeterred, "you see, we were both born on the same planet," she said calmly, "in case you're wondering where that was," Candille smiled, "I was born on Ursus Minor … in Hydra, the home world of the Consortium," Lareena gasped, eliciting a grunt of satisfaction from the Tactical Sergeant behind her, but Sergeant Candille pressed on, undeterred, "but, that isn't the important part," her smile was beginning to drive Lareena into a state halfway between intense anger and psychosis; she wanted to reach out and scratch the eyes out of this impertinent woman with her long nails, but she knew that the Guardian behind her would easily restrain her if she tried. "No," Candille continued, "I learned about how you were sent by your second cousin, Factotum Ebla Mar, to the conference on Altus 9. I even know that you were known as Laranna, and that you were sent with a mission to seduce the First Counselor …," she would have continued but there was no need; Lareena had been overwhelmed by the encounter, and fainted. Fortunately for her, the quick reflexes of Tactical Sergeant Brem prevented her from hitting the floor and injuring herself; he caught her in his powerful arms and gently lowered her into a nearby chair.

Sovereign Sayoose turned to face Sergeant Candille, a smile on her face, "Well, I would say that went almost exactly as we had expected, thank you, Sergeant. I am indebted to you … again," Sergeant Candille nodded, and then the two women began to laugh as they left Brem standing there, guarding the unconscious woman.

"Excuse me," he called out gruffly, "what in Caiphus am I supposed to do about *this*?" he gestured at the unconscious Lareena, who was completely unconscious after her encounter with the Sovereign and Sergeant Candille.

Sovereign Sayoose smiled, "Find her a comfortable cell in the High Security section of the Detention Center," she replied, "but make sure that it is well away from where her husband will be: they are to neither see or speak to each other until their trial. Only their official Advocates shall be permitted to visit them, and they are not to have the same Advocate; is that clear?"

"Yes, my Sovereign," Brem replied, "it shall be as you wish." With the ease of someone carrying a sack of carrots, he scooped the unconscious form of Lareena up off of the chair and was about to leave when the Sovereign beckoned to him.

"One more thing, before you go," she said, her sweet voice carrying across the chamber effortlessly. Brem stood, waiting for what the Sovereign had to say, not sure of what to expect, "Thank you, Tactical Sergeant Brem," she finally said, her voice gentle. "This would not have been possible without your assistance."

Brem blushed at the compliment and bowed his head. He then carried Lareena out of the Chambers; he would not even break a sweat carrying her to the Detention Center, where she would be deposited in one of the High Security cells according to his instructions.

(* | *)

Once the medics had removed the injured Regar from the Chambers of the Cadre, and his unconscious wife had been taken to the Detention Center, the Sovereign was left facing the remainder of the Cadre, as well as Chancellor Valox, Marshal Salzat, and the rest of those who had returned with her from Terra. To her surprise, the old man, the Colonel, had not uttered a word throughout the entire series of events. He had a look of shocked confusion on his face, and the Sovereign felt deeply concerned for his emotional well-being.

Turning to Captain Pertu, she asked the Guardian to accompany both Terrans to the Medical Center so they could be assessed and then begin receiving treatments with the Genomic Therapy that she had promised before they left Terra. Captain Pertu smiled and nodded, guiding the two Terrans from the Chambers, both of whom seemed quite relieved to be leaving the bizarre situation behind. As they neared the sliding doors the Sovereign called out to them, "I shall see both of you later, after you have acclimatized yourself to your new home."

This earned her a doleful look from the old man, who seemed to be on the verge of a breakdown, but Tanya responded, "I look forward to that, my Sovereign," she then bowed, before following Captain Pertu out of the Chambers. Tanya put her arm through her grandfather's and whispered, "Don't worry, Gramps, this is all going to be great fun," to which the old man merely grunted.

He was now thoroughly convinced that he had completely lost his mind. Talking cats were one thing, but ray guns that completely took off someone's hand, that was simply too much. Not to mention that this Sovereign character had just transformed, right before his eyes, from that legless creature, into the form of a young woman in barely a breath. No, Bob was thoroughly convinced that he was beyond senile; he was sure of it, either that or this was all some bad dream. He followed his granddaughter down the hall, which was filled with a wide assortment of people of all shapes and sizes, only adding to his confusion and disorientation.

As they passed one corridor a tall man with blue hair and yellow eyes saluted the Captain, giving each of the Terrans a polite nod before continuing down the corridor. Pertu could tell that the old man was confused and tried to explain as well as she could, "Colonel, that was Corporal Derksis," she said, her raspy voice penetrating his befuddled mind, "he's from a planet called Telgar II, where many of the people are known for having highly colorful hair." She hoped the explanation would satisfy him, but he was just shaking his head.

"Thought he was a punk rocker," he muttered, shaking his head in disbelief, "reminded me of the seventies, back on Earth," he looked at Pertu with a puzzled gaze, "this *is* for real, ain't it?" Tanya looked at him, surprised at the question.

"Yes, sir," Pertu replied, smiling. "It's as real as it gets," they turned another corner and she pointed to a sign indicating they had arrived. "Believe me, Colonel, once you've had your treatments, and a few days to get settled, everything will be making far more sense to you," she took one of his arthritic hands in hers, "I promise. Now, the doctors in here are going to take wonderful care of both of you. Okay?" For the first time since watching his house get vaporized the old man began to visibly relax. He liked this young woman and found he trusted her, though he did not really know why; perhaps it was because she was military. That was a good enough reason for him.

"Whate'r you say, Captain," he said, holding his head up high. He took Tanya's arm in his and walked into the Medical Center.

(* | *)

Sovereign Sayoose faced the remaining members of the Cadre who were standing at the end of the Octavo, which now seemed totally out of place after everything that had transpired. Counselor Trema's performance was all but forgotten. She was standing closest to the instrument, and discovered, much to her dismay, that a few particles of the First Counselor's hand had been splattered across the strings of the majestic instrument. She knew that it would be quite a chore to have the fine instrument cleaned, but if that was what it took to rid themselves of Regar, it would be well worth the effort, she thought to herself as she turned to look at the Sovereign, who was studying the Cadre with what seemed to be a look of concern on her face.

Counselor Trema was the first of the remaining members of the Cadre to step forward from the group to address the Sovereign, a broad smile on her attractive face, "I believe I speak for the entire Cadre," she began, gesturing to the others, "well, what's left of it," she paused awkwardly as she looked at the three other members, "when I say how wonderful it is to see you, my Sovereign." She bowed deeply at the woman who had just survived her third assassination attempt. Each of the other members of the Cadre were nodding enthusiastically in agreement, grinning broadly and bowing toward their leader.

"It is good to be back," Sovereign Sayoose began, looking over their faces, searching for any signs of deception but not detecting any. She had never felt any indication of disloyalty from these members, and liked to believe that she could consider them friends; but then she reminded herself that she had thought the same of former First Counselor Regar, until things had started to seem odd, about fifty years ago. That was when she had begun to suspect that Regar was not what he said, but she had not been able to prove anything and had not been able to reveal any concrete evidence to confirm his betrayal against the Alliance. After several years of trying to lure him out with false messages and decoys she finally decided that the only way to prove her suspicions was to appeal to his obvious lust for power, which was when she began formulating her plan to take her trip to Terra.

Her plan of action had further crystalized after receiving a report from the Communications Administrator. Administrator Marta had informed her that after an audit of the transmission logs from the Communications Array she had detected a series of unauthorized messages had been sent from within Felis Prime. They had originated from an unregistered communications console, which meant she had not been able to determine where the console was located, but that had not prevented her from discovering that the transmissions had taken place. Even though the console was unregistered it was still necessary for the device to connect, even remotely, to the Communications Array before it was capable of successfully transmitting its messages. By connecting to the Array an electronic trace of having been active was left, which was enough for the Administrator to track its existence. Marta may not have been able to find the physical source of the messages from within Felis Prime, but she had been able to determine their destination: they had been directed to the Subspace Communications Web within the Ursus Consortium. A wide array of messages and information was being sent to the Web, including messages regarding movements of Alliance cargo vessels and various orders pertaining to the movement of the fleet of the Unified Armed Services. There had also been a series of messages that related to the internal security of the Alliance.

Once this information had been conveyed to the Sovereign she was certain that it could only have come from the First Counselor; he would have been the only one who had access to the specific material being transmitted, but she could not understand his motives. When she received the information from the survey vessels regarding Terra she realized that the planet, and the young star of its solar system, was something she could use as bait, something that would provide her with all of the evidence she required to catch the betrayer, if he was acting treacherously.

From the surveys she had seen that the planet was in a system with a young star, something she knew the Consortium would be willing to go after if the prize was worth the risk. It was something that the Consortium had done before, she knew, but that had been in systems where there had not been any Green Zone planets in question. This time she would be providing the First Counselor with an irresistible temptation: an opportunity to seize control of the Cadre while also eliminating one of the things standing in his way of becoming the Sovereign by making herself an irresistible target. She knew it was a calculated risk, but she was not counting on the First Counselor to be thinking with the greatest of logic once an opportunity to have more power presented itself.

She knew that there was no guarantee that the Board of Governors would have chosen the First Counselor as Sovereign, but she had also expected that Regar's ego would not have allowed for any other scenario to exist. He had acted as he believed, that he was the only logical choice for the Board of Governors: his ruination came from his pride. She knew that she had been putting herself in danger, not to mention the lives of every Terran who might have been killed had the Consortium successfully commenced their mining operations, irreversibly damaging the system's star, but there was no other way; at least, none that she had considered at the time.

In retrospect, she realized that she should have never doubted the fidelity of her Guardians, but the potential betrayal of the First Counselor had aroused within her a certain level of paranoia, even for those with whom her safety had been entrusted. Now, as she considered the revelation that only the First Counselor, with the participation of his wife, had been involved with the betrayal of both her and the Alliance, the Sovereign once again felt a pang of guilt for having put her friends through such an ordeal. She knew that they had been genuinely thrilled with her safe return, and were not upset with her actions. There was no question in her mind that she would definitely have to do something to make things up to her faithful friends.

Each of the four Cadre members were facing the Sovereign, looking as though they had something to say but did not know where to begin. Counselor Mintu, the only other male member of the Cadre, finally broke his silence, speaking in a soft voice that seemed incongruous considering his stocky, muscular build. He was from Ionia, the same planet as Tactical Sergeant Brem, and shared many of the physical characteristics of the heavyset Guardian. "My Sovereign," he began quietly, "it's so good to see you again; First Counselor Regar," he paused, blushing at having used the title, "excuse me, Regar," he continued, frowning at having said the name, "was adamant about not informing us about the situation concerning your prolonged absence. We only convened for two sessions in that time, during which we discussed trivial matters," the other three were nodding, murmuring their agreement.

Counselor Vas, the most gregarious member of the Cadre, was finding it difficult to contain her enthusiasm at the return of the Sovereign, and finally blurted out, "My Sovereign! It's a joy to see you again, I was … we were, so worried about you," she stepped forward and, breaking protocol, grasped the hands of the Sovereign in her own, falling to her knees in the process. This finally lightened the heaviness of the moment and everyone found themselves laughing.

Sovereign Sayoose held the hands of Counselor Vas for a moment, squeezing them before releasing them, allowing the Counselor to return to his feet. "Thank you," she said softly, nodding in acknowledgment of what had been said by the two counselors. "We do have some business to discuss," she continued, looking at the group as they watched her every movement, "however," she turned toward Chancellor Valox and Marshal Salzat, "I would first like to thank the two of you for taking the time to come to this impromptu gathering," she nodded at the two men who were now standing next to each other.

Chancellor Valox smiled broadly, "Sovereign Sayoose, it was not only a distinct pleasure," he chuckled, "it was an honor to have heard my work performed so beautifully, by such an accomplished performer," he nodded his large head toward Counselor Trema, who bowed in response to the compliment, blushing deeply as the rest of the Cadre applauded their colleague. "Quite frankly," he continued, "I wouldn't have missed this little display for the Alliance's share of profits for the next thousand years," he paused for a second, "but, don't quote me on that, I believe the Paragon might have something to say should I make such attempt to make such an arrangement," he chuckled.

"Besides, this will become the basis of my next opera," he paused, "assuming I have your permission of course, my Sovereign?" She nodded, smiling at the idea of this drama being set to the music of Chancellor Valox. As much as she had grown to love the music of the Terran composers, Valox was definitely one of her favorite composers and she never failed to down-line his latest work when it became available.

He continued, "I shall, of course, be at your disposal should you require my testimony at the trial of the ... Betrayer," he refused to utter the name of the former First Counselor, "as well as that wife of his, though, I must confess, I do not know much about her." He hesitated before bowing, causing the Sovereign to nod for him to continue, "I apologize, my Sovereign," he sounded genuinely contrite, "but, as I've decided to memorialize this in an opera, it would be immensely helpful if ... I mean, I know that you are an extremely busy person, but, if I might have a short meeting with you, to discuss the rest of the story, it would help me beyond anything I could ever express," he smiled, looking down at the floor of the chambers.

"Of course, Chancellor Valox," Sovereign Sayoose replied, surprising the man, "it would be my pleasure to meet with you. Of course, it will take a few days for me to clear things up since I have been absent for so long, but ..." she laughed, a sound he found surprisingly attractive, "I am quite certain that we will be able to arrange a suitable time to meet."

"Thank you, my Sovereign," he replied, and bowed, taking his leave of the group.

Marshal Salzat remained standing at attention, as though under inspection, and spoke once the Chancellor had left the Chambers, "As always, my Sovereign, it is an honor to serve," looking at the members of the Cadre, he nodded curtly, "and you as well. Our ships shall remain in orbit for as long as you feel necessary."

"Thank you," the Sovereign said, almost under her breath, but loudly enough for the Fleet Commander to hear. He gave a crisp salute and was about to leave, but paused expectantly.

"Marshal Salzat," the Sovereign continued, "I realize that this order has been issued in my absence, though it may not have reached the fleet; for that reason, I am issuing it again, for the record: please ensure that every Alliance member and Protectorate planet has sufficient protection, as per my previous orders, especially planets in Sector 0107, where Terra is located. I do not want the Ursus Consortium, or Factotum Mar, to get any ideas about the Alliance being incapable of defending our interests, is that clear?" she spoke with such vehemence that there was no doubt as to whether the Sovereign was ready to resume command of the Felis Alliance; she was in total control.

Marshal Salzat saluted again, "As you command, my Sovereign, it shall be done; the order has already been given. My Battle Group remained on station in the Terran system when we returned," he replied, nodding his head and smiling.

"Excellent," she said, "please convey my compliments to the entire fleet and her commanders, Fleet Commander; you are dismissed." This time he saluted, bowed, and marched out of the Chambers of the Cadre as though he were still a cadet being inspected by the Sovereign rather than the Fleet Commander on his way to return to the flagship of the Alliance. There was a great deal for him to do, but it was the type of work he lived for, and the smile on his face was broad and genuine.

Now that Regar had been arrested his private quarters would be carefully searched, and the Sovereign was certain they would uncover all of the evidence they needed to connect the former First Counselor to the unauthorized communications that Administrator Marta had detected. Sovereign Sayoose suspected that by the time the trial began before the First Tribunal there would be more than sufficient evidence to convict both the former First Counselor and his wife for high treason against the Alliance, as well as the attempted assassination of the Sovereign herself, for which there were an abundant number of witnesses.

Sayoose turned and faced the Cadre again, smiling at their enthusiastic faces, "Well," she began, "the first order of business, I believe, is the selection of a new Counselor. It has been a long time since we have had to replace a member, but," she paused, "from time to time, it is necessary to inject some new blood into every organization." She turned to Lieutenant Kar, who was standing next to Commander Dragar and asked for her to come over to the group.

"Yes, my Sovereign, how may I help?" the Lieutenant asked, standing at attention. Sovereign Sayoose whispered into the Lieutenant's ear for a moment and the young woman nodded, then immediately ran out of the Chamber.

She then looked over at Commander Dragar and nodded her head toward Sergeant Candille, indicating that he should take her to the Alliance Security & Intelligence Services offices, where she could have her memory down-lined in order to confirm what she had told Tactical Sergeant Brem and Captain Pertu on Helios-2. She had little doubt regarding the former Consortium commando given that the woman had put her life at risk during the assassination attempt by the former First Counselor, but she had agreed to the procedure. Besides, the process was painless and would only take a few seconds. ASIS had developed the down-lining process to such a degree that a person's memories could, quite literally, be fed into a data device faster than you could recall them consciously.

It was a process that worked in the same way that the Neural Interface allowed people to write or compose with the assistance of the automated devices. In the case of the memory down-lining procedure, however, an individual would have their entire memory down-lined rather than the specific ideas they were working on for a particular creative endeavor. Once that had been done, and the records were automatically compared to the interview records made on Helios-2, Sergeant Candille would be free to begin her new life as a member of the Alliance, which she seemed quite willing to do given her recent actions.

When Commander Dragar told her where they were going she replied, "Wonderful! I've been looking forward to that since we arrived," causing the large Guardian to smile in return. Despite his initial misgivings, he could not help but like this woman, and had to admit that he also found her quite attractive.

By Caiphus, Dragar thought to himself, he found her tremendously attractive. She was not only athletic, she had a face he found he could look at all day, and he it was possible for him to easily get lost in her emerald-green eyes that seemed to sparkle under the lights of the Hab-Domes.

"Alright then," he said, placing his hand on her lower back, "let's get going," he gently guided her from the room, pleased that she did not resist his touch.

As they were leaving the Chambers Lieutenant Kar was just returning from her errand, with the short Communications Administrator in tow. A small trickle of sweat was trailing down the side of her face at having kept up with the quick pace set by the Lieutenant, who had obviously forced the woman to run all the way from the Array. Administrator Marta ran into the room with an almost crazed look in her eyes, but quickly began to laugh when she realized that the Sovereign was standing there and all of her worst fears had been assuaged.

"My Sovereign," she exclaimed, "I'm so relieved to see you," she said, almost stumbling as she ran into the first few chairs that had been set up for the brief recital before the commencement of the Special Session.

It was too comical a situation for the others not to respond to, and they joined in the laughter, causing the Administrator to blush, "My apologies, my Sovereign, it's just ..." she stammered, "well ..." she was at a genuine loss for words, a truly unusual situation for the Communications Administrator who was usually quite talkative.

Sovereign Sayoose just smiled at the woman. She had always liked the Communications Administrator; even more, she knew that her First Advisor, Commander Dragar, trusted her implicitly. They had been good friends for many years, and he had spoken extremely highly of her on a number of occasions. Marta had flaming red hair, and a personality to match; her ability to speak several of the languages spoken across the vast Alliance was uncanny, which had made her a natural choice for the position in Communications, but she had served the Alliance in that position for many years: it was now time for a change.

"Administrator Marta," the Sovereign began, stepping toward the woman who was still slightly out of breath, "I have a proposal for you. You have served the Felis Alliance faithfully for thousands of years, and I want you to know that this has not gone unnoticed. As you may have noticed," she gestured to the four members of the Cadre standing behind her, "the Cadre now has only four members, but it requires a fifth in order to fulfill its duties," she paused, looking directly into the eyes of the short Administrator. Both women were about the same height, with the Sovereign being only slightly shorter. "I would like to ask if you would become that fifth member," she continued looking into the eyes of the Administrator, who seemed to be finding the entire situation unbelievable.

"I ..." she tried to say, "I ... I don't understand," she finally managed to finish.

"I am asking you to join the Cadre; to be one of my Counselors. Will you serve your Sovereign?"

Marta looked into the orange eyes of the leader whom she had respected for so long, and found herself nodding. "Of course, my Sovereign," she finally said, "it would be an honor to serve you, and the Alliance, in any way that I can," to her surprise the Sovereign stepped forward and hugged her, welcoming her into the Cadre with a warm embrace.

"But ... what about the Communications Array?" Marta finally asked.

"Oh, I am sure your deputies will be able to manage, until we find a permanent replacement, do you not agree, Counselor Marta?" Marta was nodding, enjoying the sound of her new title. Of course, it was the truth. She had taken time off in the past and her deputies had done fine in her absence. They were well qualified, and she was sure they would be able to find someone more than capable of filling her position. Perhaps the Deputy Administrator, who had served in the role for over five hundred years, might be selected. Deputy Nir would be able to do the job quite well based on everything Marta had seen.

Nodding her head at the idea, "I believe Deputy Nir would be a perfect choice, my Sovereign; she understands the Array as well as I do and I'm quite certain that she would serve you, and the Alliance, without reservation."

Sovereign Sayoose nodded as she took Counselor Marta's hand and guided her to the rest of the Cadre, who welcomed her warmly to their group, "Consider your recommendation taken under advisement, Counselor Marta," she smiled again, knowing that she had made the right choice with Marta. "Now, however, there is also the small matter of filling the position of First Counselor," the group fell silent. "I have given this some serious thought and believe that while the four of you have served for many years, it goes without saying that there is one who has consistently demonstrated certain talents and abilities that have placed them in a position of distinction. On top of that," her smile widened, "I would note that this particular Counselor was the one with whom the former First Counselor was consistently at odds, which I find, in retrospect, is something to be lauded," the three original members were each looking at Counselor Trema, knowing that the Sovereign was referring to her, and they were nodding in agreement. "So, I ask if you will approve my recommendation of Counselor Trema to be the new First Counselor of the Cadre?"

"Tabled!" came the loud voice of Counselor Vas, slapping his hand in lieu of a gavel.

"Seconded!" Counselor Mintu quickly added, almost on top of Counselor Vas.

"I move that the motion be carried, unanimously," Counselor Lezra said, glancing at the newly appointed Counselor Marta, who was nodding enthusiastically. She knew Counselor Trema and thought she was a wonderful woman; she would be a brilliant First Counselor of the Cadre and an excellent Counselor to the Sovereign.

"Excellent," the Sovereign replied, turning to Trema, "congratulations, First Counselor Trema," she said, "I look forward to many productive sessions with you," she looked at the rest of the group, "and with all of you. Now, I believe there is a trial for us to prepare for, as well as a great deal of other work that has been set aside for far too long in my absence, am I correct?" the group nodded, then clasped the new First Counselor on her back in congratulations.

For her part, First Counselor Trema found that she could not stop herself from grinning. She had started by breaking down at the news of the death of the Sovereign, before playing the Octavo for the Chancellor. Throughout the entire performance she had been wondering whether the former First Counselor was going to manage to do something that would lead to him becoming the Sovereign. After all of that, as difficult as it had been to believe, here she was, the new First Counselor.

She knew that her family would think she was intoxicated when she told them the news of her appointment when she returned to her chambers after this meeting, but they would have no choice but to believe her when she showed them her new Medallion. She was sure that she would receive it before the end of the day. Each member of the Cadre wore a Medallion indicating that they were members of the Cadre of the Sovereign, but the Medallion of the First Counsellor was distinct from the others and was easily recognized by anyone who knew anything about the Alliance and its power structure. Each of the Cadre Medallions was unique, displaying the name of the Counsellor, or the First Counselor, as well as the date of their appointment to the position, and they were all struck in a foundry on Felis Magoris. Both Trema and

Marta would receive their new Medallions before the end of the day, even though the Sovereign would have only requested them at the conclusion of the Special Session.

CHAPTER XIII ~ EVIDENCE

"Advocates within the Felis Alliance Justice System guarantee the rights of Defendants throughout the legal process. They are permitted to visit their clients during their incarceration in Detention Centers, understanding that any and all communications shall be recorded and, if found to be probative, used against the Defendant in the course of their trial.

"It is the responsibility of the Advocate to aid the Defendant in the preparation and presentation of a cogent defense for their client. No trial shall be undertaken without a clear burden of proof having been established by the Prosecution to the satisfaction of the Tribunal overseeing the procedure. An expectation of conviction, beyond all reasonable doubt, must exist before any trial may proceed in any case where the Ultimate punishment is being considered as a possible penalty. At the conclusion of the trial the final decision regarding the Defendant's innocence or guilt shall fall to the three members of the Tribunal."

[...]

"Within the Justice System of the Felis Alliance the severest sentence for any crime is banishment to the Dark Zone in which convicted individuals experience perpetual torment while remaining in a state of semi-consciousness, from which there is no escape. It is known as the Ultimate punishment. For lesser egregious offenses the penalty of Death may be invoked, though this is far less preferable. Another option is internment in a Cryo-Freeze facility in which a convicted Defendant is placed in a state of suspended animation for a predetermined period, not to exceed twenty-five thousand years.

"It has been argued, in lower Tribunals, that the use of the Dark Zone as the Ultimate punishment was excessive and cruel as a form of punishment. After an

*appeal before the First Tribunal it was declared to be
within the strictures established by the Pan-Universal
Alliance Charter of Rights and Freedoms as being a form
of punishment commensurate to the crimes for which
Defendant had been convicted. Subsequently, usage of
the Ultimate punishment has been restricted to cases of
High Treason, Espionage, and Crimes Against the Felis
Alliance or against the Sovereign."*

[...]

Excerpted from *Justice in the Felis Alliance*,
by Justice Renata, Prime Justice of the First Tribunal

(* | *)

Deep within the core of Felis Prime, far from the natural light that filtered in through the Domes, lay the Detention Center. It was located in the most secure portion of the orbiting city, surrounded by shields and, when occupied, under constant guard. Since crime was relatively uncommon there were only two dozen cells, which were empty most of the time. This made following the directions of Sovereign Sayoose to keep the newest prisoners far apart from each other quite easy, preventing them from either seeing or speaking with each other during their pretrial confinement. It had been most difficult for Lareena. She had grown accustomed to the luxuries of the chambers she shared with her husband and found the scantily-furnished cell made her feel more than a little claustrophobic. At the same time, Regar was transferred to the Detention Center after only a few hours in the Medical Center since his hand had been surgically removed by the plasma weapon when he had attempted to kill the Sovereign. They had given him something to deaden the pain, which he still claimed to feel, but he had been told that this vestigial pain was purely psychological.

He was experiencing a phenomenon called *Phantom pain*, which was often experienced by individuals who had lost a limb, especially by soldiers in combat situations. Even with the limb gone, there were reports of sensations being felt when it was physically impossible to feel anything. Some people felt subtle tingling sensations while others experienced pain. Sometimes it passed, after the person became reconciled to the loss of the limb, but sometimes it persisted for many years.

It was yet another blow to the former First Counselor as he struggled to cope with the loss of everything he had ever cared for and watched his dreams float away. Sitting in the cell he found that he missed his wife more than his personal chambers, but the sparse furnishings of the cell were also quite frustrating. Each cell was furnished with a simple metal bed that was firmly attached to the molded wall, with a thin mattress and pillow. There was also a small table and chair, both of which were attached to the floor. Defendants could sit at the table to read or work on the preparation of their defense, but there was little else to divert their minds. This was decidedly not a place with luxuries.

Each cell was also equipped with a toilet, which could not be flushed more than once every two hours, to prevent the prisoner from attempting to clog the unit, and a small sink which would dispense a measured amount of water every hour, also to prevent attempts at flooding the cell. Recreation was limited to pacing the small cell, which Regar had found to be meditative, but Lareena quickly abandoned as a useless pursuit, choosing instead to lie on her bed with her eyes closed, trying to summon images of more pleasant times.

Each prisoner was provided with a single datapad, upon which they could record their thoughts and ideas. It had one library installed, providing the Standard Legal Library of the Alliance to assist in the preparation of a defense. Prisoners also had access to recreational reading materials published from across the Alliance, which the devices would be able to down-line through the directories provided by the publishers, but it was impossible to use the devices to send or receive any communications.

Both Defendants were also advised that anything they wrote had to be presented to their Advocate whenever they visited, at which time the material would be downloaded by the Advocate to ensure that anything the Defendant had developed could be shared with the Prosecutor, as required by Alliance law. At the time the download took place the memory of the device would be timestamped, allowing both the Advocate for the Defendant, and the Prosecution, to trace any changes in the thinking process of the Defendant in the event they attempted to change their testimony.

Since Regar still had several contacts within the Alliance he had managed to arrange for two of the finest Advocates on Felis Magoris to agree to represent himself and Lareena, though he was unsure whether it would make any difference considering the charges they were facing.

When he had his first meeting with his Advocate, a severe looking man named Xylix, he realized that the man was from the same planet as Commander Dragar, which was more than a little unsettling considering the history between the two men. At the same time, the Ventian Advocate with the penetrating black eyes that seemed to glare directly through him was renowned for his acumen before the Tribunals, and had successfully argued several cases before the First Tribunal. Advocate Xylix possessed a reputation for being one of the most brilliant legal minds in the Sector, let alone the Alliance; even more importantly, Regar reflected, he had agreed to represent the disgraced former First Counselor, which was more than many Advocates had done given the reputation he had earned.

Regar was facing the most severe charges that could be levied against any individual: Crimes Against the Felis Alliance, Espionage, specifically spying for the Ursus Consortium, and crimes against the Sovereign; perhaps the most serious of the offences for which he was being charged was having personally tried to assassinate the Sovereign. Each of the charges carried the potentiality of the Ultimate punishment, of eternal banishment to the Dark Zone, the most severe punishment the First Tribunal could render.

Worse than that, if there could be a worse than that, Regar knew that the Prosecutor appointed to the case was Prosecutor Marhlor. She had the most impressive winning record in the justice system, and the first thing she had done after the charges had been announced was to declare that she intended to seek the Ultimate punishment.

"Anything less," she had said, "would be a miscarriage of justice; it would send a terrible message to those who might think that treachery against the Felis Alliance is something from which someone might profit. It is not: I'm here to tell you that these are heinous crimes; the punishment shall fit the crime."

For many Defendants the penalty of death was preferred to the Ultimate punishment, and was something they begged for rather than facing an eternity in the Dark Zone, but death was considered too lenient when considering the seriousness of the crimes to which the former First Counselor had been accused; these crimes required a punishment that could only be meted out over an eternity of suffering, and that could only mean the Dark Zone. Many believed that the Dark Zone was a form of torture, that it was a barbaric for of punishment, but that was too simplistic a way of viewing what it meant to face the

Ultimate punishment. When sentenced to the Ultimate punishment the convicted prisoner was sent to a special vault, deep beneath the Stadium of Justice, in which a micro-singularity was contained, held in place by specially designed force-shields.

The guilty party would spend as much time as necessary exposed to the micro-singularity while remaining in a form of semi-consciousness, where they would be aware of their body being dismantled, molecule by molecule. After several millennia the only thing remaining of the individual would be their consciousness, which would ultimately be consumed, and obliterated, crushed out of existence.

In every sense of the word, it was a death sentence, just one that would take an excruciatingly long time before the final blow was struck. Most importantly, the Ultimate punishment acted as an effective deterrent. Since it had become available as an option as a form of punishment for heinous crimes the incidence of those crimes had been reduced drastically.

Even the thought of facing this form of punishment for his actions made Regar's blood run cold; he had hardly been able to sleep during the three weeks since he had arrived in the small cell and he was wondering why things were taking so long. Surely, he had thought to himself a number of times, the prosecution had to have assembled everything they needed to begin the trial. Advocate Xylix had, after all, revealed to him that the Alliance Security & Intelligence Services Investigators had quickly, and easily, discovered the unauthorized communications console he had so casually hidden in his quarters. Their tests had revealed that he had personally used it to send thousands of messages to the Consortium's Subspace Communications Web over the past century. He simply could not imagine what more they could be looking for, as he tried to make himself comfortable on the thin mattress, while massaging the stump where his right hand had been.

Lareena was being defended by an equally talented Advocate named Tryliss, an Ionian woman who had only been on Felis Magoris for a few years. She was not as well known as Regar's Advocate but still had a reputation for defending her clients well, which gave Regar as much comfort as he could have given the bleak nature of the situation. Unfortunately, Regar thought to himself, Lareena seemed to be facing guilt by association, otherwise she would still be enjoying her freedom, though without any of the perks of being married to the First Counselor of the Cadre.

Regar was unaware of the revelations made by Sergeant

Candille, and his own Advocate was not privy to that information; as far as he was concerned the only reason the former First Counselor's wife was being prosecuted was because of their marriage. One of the few things that kept Regar going was the faint hope that he might be able to make a plea to the First Tribunal for mercy on behalf of his wife, to somehow beg for her freedom. He believed that his own life was over, but there was no reason for his innocent flower, for his precious wife, to suffer the fate he had assured for himself. Regar had just started to doze, a dream of his last encounter with Lareena dancing through his mind, when the guard arrived and announced that his Advocate was there to see him.

After being taken to the small interview room Regar handed Advocate Xylix his datapad, which he dutifully downloaded, timestamping the memory in the process, before handing it back to his client. He looked at his client with his piercing black eyes and made a clucking sound with his tongue, "By Caiphus, Regar," he pronounced, "you look terrible."

"Thank you, Advocate Xylix," Regar replied dryly, not in the mood for any of the man's sarcasm, "why don't *you* try and sleep on that thin mattress, alone, facing banishment to the Dark Zone, and see how you look after three weeks." Regar looked away; Xylix looked far too much like Commander Dragar for his liking, though what Xylix wore was not nearly as intimidating as the Guardian's uniform worn by Dragar. Seeing the *Ghost Corps* patch on the man's uniform, accompanied by the ribbons representing his numerous awards and citations only served to make the Commander an even more imposing figure, if such a thing was possible.

"Now, now," the Advocate said softly, almost sounding paternal, "I'm just concerned," he patted his client on his right arm, making him flinch. "Oh," he withdrew his hand, "... sorry. Look," he continued, "the reason I'm here is to tell you that you're being transferred to the HSDC on Felis Magoris tomorrow morning," the news caught the former First Counselor off guard. The Detention Center on Felis Prime was extremely secure. Why would they be transferring him to the High Security Detention Center on Felis Magoris?

"I ... I don't understand," he finally said, looking down at the stump where his hand had been, seemingly lost in the moment. He was once again experiencing the strange sensation that his hand was still there, which was even stranger since he was looking right at the stump and knew, in his mind, that this was impossible. As he tried to flex the non-existent fingers he felt a wave of nausea wash over him as the pain he had experienced the moment Lieutenant Kar's pulse of plasma had removed his hand course through his arm as though it had just happened.

Advocate Xylix clucked his tongue again and looked Regar squarely in the eye, "It's simple; the First Tribunal has published the date for the trial," he announced. "We appear before them in three days, and Regar," his voice lowered to the level of a whisper, though he was well aware that the microphones in the interview room were more than powerful enough to hear every word, "they rejected my motion to sever the cases: you will both be tried together."

Regar's head fell into his arms and he began to weep. It was the worst possible news; although he had expected the motion to fail, it had still been worth trying. He still could not believe they were prosecuting his wife for something he had done. How barbaric was the Sovereign?

"If only that useless shapeshifter had been *killed*," he hissed, barely under his breath, "if only that Fire Team had not been as useless as a bunch of Torgons. By Caiphus, I can't understand how five commandos could have failed against one Guardian," he continued, until Advocate Xylix slapped the table with his massive hand, startling the former First Counselor so much he practically jumped out of his seat.

"*Regar*," he snapped, barely containing his anger, "stop flapping your lips or, by Caiphus, I'll stop them for you, is that understood?"

Regar was suddenly aware of where he was, and what he had said, and blanched visibly, nodding his head slowly. This had not been his first lapse: in his second meeting with Advocate Xylix he had found himself muttering repeatedly that he, "Had missed his chance," which had resulted in Advocate Xylix slapping him in order to silence him. Shortly afterwards the Advocate submitted a motion seeking an extensive panel of psychological assessments for his client, fearing that he might be experiencing a mental breakdown, but the medical team had disagreed. After the examination it was determined that, at best, the former First Counselor was depressed; he was offered an appropriate treatment, which he had rejected, claiming that the doctors, who were under the control of the Sovereign, only wanted to poison him.

Advocate Xylix argued that this supported the argument that his client was experiencing a mental breakdown considering that paranoia was one of the hallmarks of several advanced mental illnesses, but the

Court disagreed. They argued that the Defendant was attempting to manipulate the system, and it was an impossible claim to argue against given the knowledge the former First Counsellor possessed regarding the Alliance. Regar was offered treatments for both the depression and the paranoia, but rejected them both as well. Since he had been contributing to the preparation of his own defense and had not made any attempts to harm himself the First Tribunal had ruled that he was not in a state that sufficiently warranted any special treatment. Regar had been declared competent to stand trial; in the eyes of the Court the matter was settled.

Several other motions had been made by Advocate Xylix on behalf of his client, including one to recuse the First Tribunal on the grounds that as the Defendant was the former First Counselor of the Cadre and, as such, they would be predisposed to rule in favor of the Sovereign, but each motion had been rejected, as Advocate Xylix had expected. It had all been a delaying tactic, but he still had to try. As an Advocate it was his responsibility to zealously defend his client, regardless of what he may have felt regarding their innocence or guilt. Now, as he looked at the man he saw an obviously distraught individual. Regar was broken and mentally drained of his will to continue and Xylix felt genuine compassion for him, even if he had developed a fairly intense distaste for the case after reviewing the evidence the Prosecutor had assembled against his client.

To say that the Prosecutor's case was strong would be an understatement: it was stellar, and his client was only making it stronger with his ludicrous mutterings, even if they could be used to support the argument that the Defendant was mentally unstable, but Advocate Xylix had already gone down that path, and the motion had been denied. Regardless of his mental state, he was going to stand trial, it was as simple as that; he would face the First Tribunal, the Prosecutor, and Advocate Xylix was fairly certain that he would not be able to do much to help defend him against the charges he was facing.

"My apologies, Advocate," Regar muttered, ashamed by how he had acted. "Thank you for your visit," he was once again averting the intense gaze of the Advocate, not wanting to meet his black eyes. "I shall do my best to prepare appropriate opening remarks before the trial begins," he took the datapad from the table and tucked it under his arm, then awkwardly shook the Advocate's hand before he left the room. It fell to the Defendant to make their own opening remarks, though their Advocate would be able to guide them should they find it necessary.

Advocate Xylix could only imagine what the disturbed mind of the former First Counselor might come up with over the next three days as he prepared to address the highest judicial body in the Felis Alliance. As Regar was led back to his cell he found he could not believe that he had once again allowed himself to be so stupid.

"Why don't you just hand them your head on a platter," he muttered to himself, once the guard had locked the door to his cell and reactivated the force-shield, making escape impossible.

(*|*)

At the same time Regar was meeting with Advocate Xylix, Advocate Tryliss was meeting with Lareena in an identical meeting room on the opposite side of the Detention Center. When she was told about the plans to move her to the High Security Detention Center she seemed neither upset or surprised by the news. Lareena simply stared at her Advocate as she handed her the datapad she had been working on in her cell.

"Will you have an opportunity to see my husband's Advocate?" she asked, surprising Advocate Tryliss. In their meetings she had not once mentioned the former First Counselor, save to deny having had anything to do with the espionage for which she had been charged.

Advocate Tryliss nodded in response as she watched while the information from Lareena's datapad was copied onto her own, timestamping the material before she returned it to Lareena. While the two Advocates had not been allowed to meet during the pretrial period, once a date for the trial was set they would have an opportunity to meet in order to strategize, but they would not see clients again until just before the beginning of the trial, at which point they would only review the opening remarks they had written to offer any final words of advice.

"Good," Lareena replied, sadly. "Please tell him that regardless what anyone else may say, I truly did love him," as she finished speaking she bit down hard, a tear coursing down her cheek; Advocate Tryliss heard a cracking sound, but nothing else that indicated that anything was amiss. Advocate Tryliss nodded again, looking at her datapad to see what had been copied. When she looked up it was already too late; Lareena had begun to turn a strange shade of blue, and had fallen off of her chair, slumping to the floor with an agonal exhalation of breath.

Tryliss ran around the table, shouting for the guards to enter, desperately hoping she could help, yet knowing that Lareena was beyond anyone's assistance. Lareena had somehow ingested some form of poison, but why? Barely seconds after calling for them two guards rushed in and immediately began attending to the unconscious prisoner, but it was obvious to everyone that she was already dead. Several attempts at resuscitation were made, and the efforts continued after two medics from the Medical Center had arrived, but they ultimately surrendered to the futility of the situation; which was when one of the medics announced their discovery.

"It was one of her molars," he announced solemnly, removing a few fragments of a broken tooth from her mouth, careful not to let any of the fragments make contact with his skin. Advocate Tryliss could see even from where she stood that the fragments were heavily discolored, as though there had been a caustic substance inside the hollowed-out tooth. "This must have been implanted many years ago," he continued, "it was a false tooth, hollowed out and filled with a fast-acting neurotoxin and central nervous system paralytic; as far as I can tell from what we gave her, there is no known antidote, at least, nothing we possess. It's something the Consortium has utilized before ... we've been briefed on it, but this is the first time I've ever personally encountered one. Of course," he mused, "we'll know more after the toxicological panels return and her dental work has been fully examined, but," he looked into her mouth again, "I'd guess that this was prepared before she was even married to the former First Counselor."

Advocate Tryliss shook her head, wondering why her client would act so desperately. Most of the evidence Tryliss had seen had pointed at her husband. It looked as though Lareena would only receive a short sentence in a Cryo-Freeze facility, which was the least severe punishment considering the severity of the charges she was facing, unless there was more to her case than she had been informed about by the Prosecutor. Her mind was trying to comprehend her client's motives when her eyes fell to what Lareena had written, at which point her heart caught in her throat.

"If you don't need me for anything else here," she asked the medics and guards, who were still examining the body, "I must get back to my office," she was trying to control her racing pulse. "I ... there's another matter I have to attend to and I completely lost track of the time." Without waiting to see if any of them wanted her to remain she gathered her things and rushed out of the room, but they were completely focused on the body of the prisoner, not the odd behavior of the Advocate as she slipped out of the interview room.

(*|*)

By the time Advocate Tryliss returned to the main level of Felis Prime's Hab-Dome she was still unsure as to how she would proceed with the information given to her by her client, her now deceased client. As an Officer of the Court she recognized that her first duty, of course, was to turn it over to the Prosecutor, but she wondered to herself whether that was really necessary now that her client was dead and would no longer be facing a trial. She shook her head, frustrated with herself; of course it was necessary: that was the type of legal question used to trip-up junior Advocates who had an imperfect understanding of their responsibilities to the Law and how they were supposed to deal with any evidence that happened to end up in their possession. No, as Tryliss reviewed the information on the datapad she knew that her first stop would have to be the office of Prosecutor Marhlor. After that, however, she would be free to pay a visit to Advocate Xylix. She was quite certain he would be interested in what the wife of his client had revealed moments before taking her life.

When Tryliss arrived at the Long Distance Matter Transporter, which would send her back to the surface of Felis Magoris, she was surprised to see Advocate Xylix also standing in line, waiting to be transported down to the surface. He was only a few feet in front of her so he had not seen her approach. Tryliss had no way to signal him of her presence, without making others aware of her desire to speak to him, which, she thought, might raise suspicions. It seemed as though that everyone on Felis Prime was aware that the two Advocates were representing the Betrayer, as Regar was now known, and his wife in the upcoming trial. If they were seen speaking together this close to the trial it would definitely be reported, which could easily lead to a Misconduct Hearing. Tryliss bit her tongue and studied the datapad, committing Lareena's text to memory as quickly as she was able to read the words on the small screen of the device. Fortunately for the Advocate she had an eidetic memory and was able to perfectly recall anything she read, even after only seeing it once, which served her extremely well as an Advocate.

At a time like this it was an even more important gift. As she reached the end of the long file on the datapad it was finally her turn to step onto the pad of the LDMT and she gave the operating technician the address for the Office of the Prosecuting Attorney on Felis Magoris. While Tryliss prepared herself to be transported down to the surface a SILS device wearing a smartly pressed uniform that looked somewhat like those worn by members of the Unified Armed Services entered the coordinates into the LDMT console and activated the device, sending her back down to the planet. Tryliss had no doubt she was doing the right thing, even though she was going about it in an unorthodox fashion. A few seconds later she was standing before the large metal door of the Prosecutor, waiting to see the person who would be guiding the case against the former First Counselor of the Cadre.

"Enter please," a soft voice called out, after she had knocked on the heavy looking door. She pushed on the door and was surprised at how easily it slid open, revealing a small, sparsely furnished office. As the Head Prosecutor of the Main Judicial Office in the Sector this was not what Advocate Tryliss had expected of one of the most feared women within the Alliance Judicial System. She had been sure that the woman would be sitting in a large, opulent suite, filled with the trappings power; instead she was sitting at a simple desk, adorned only with a large view screen, keyboard, her datapad, and a small picture frame, displaying a rotating series of images, which the Advocate presumed were of her family.

Tryliss should have known better, she reminded herself as she looked around the office of Prosecutor Marhlor. She was well aware of the fact that personal wealth was not something that people were too concerned with within the Alliance. While it was possible for someone to amass a collection of many possessions, should they desire to do so, and there were no prohibitions against private ownership, it was considered unnecessary when it was possible for people to have easy access to any of the necessities they may need in life, without having to be concerned about the cost of things. Even so, there were always some people who wanted to surround themselves with possessions of some sort, sometimes just souvenirs of their travels, which was something that Alliance Citizens could do quite easily thanks to its tremendous wealth.

Bringing cultural samples home from across the universe was a common practice amongst many Alliance Citizens who took advantage of the numerous opportunities to travel to the different member planets. It was, Tryliss supposed, a collection of souvenirs or other reminders of her life that she had been expecting to see in the Prosecutor's office rather than such a utilitarian space. But that was not the case; Prosecutor Marhlor preferred an uncluttered office rather than being surrounded by too many things; she found it was too easy to become distracted and when she was in her office she was there to work, preparing her cases for prosecution, and studying the law as it related to each case.

Her workload was as heavy as any senior Prosecutor, perhaps even more than the average, for she was not only the most experienced, she had the best record of any Prosecutor on Felis Magoris. Marhlor had not lost a case in over two hundred and seventy-six years. Her last loss had come as the result of a technicality: The Defendant's Advocate had discovered an unfortunate and inadvertent breach in the chain of custody of the evidence which was being used against the Defendant which resulted in some of the most important evidence being ruled inadmissible by the Tribunal. As a result of this the Prosecution's case ultimately fell apart. Marhlor had never allowed that mistake to be repeated, especially in the preparation of a case which was going to be presented in front of the First Tribunal.

When it came to the case against the former First Counselor, the Betrayer, Prosecutor Marhlor had personally overseen the gathering of the evidence. She had even been present in his chambers when the communications console had been discovered by the Investigators from the Alliance Security & Intelligence Services. Unwilling to risk any errors, she supervised the ASIS Investigators as they took the device to their Forensics Lab and her Personal Assistant had overseen the testing of the device for evidence as to who had used it, ensuring that nothing untoward took place during that process. Marhlor had been certain that everything had been done according to regulations: there was absolutely no way that she was going to see this case slip through her fingers, not with so much at stake. Her case against his wife was similarly well prepared, and now that a date had been set by the First Tribunal, Prosecutor Marhlor felt unusually confident about her chances of having two dangerous offenders banished to the Dark Zone for a well-deserved punishment.

As Prosecutor Marhlor looked up at the visitor who had entered her small office her heart skipped a beat: the look on the face of Advocate Tryliss told her that something terrible had happened. If there was one thing that Marhlor was not in the mood for it was surprises, not when things had been going so well in her preparations for the opening of the case.

She gestured toward one of the two chairs in front of her desk, "Please, Advocate Tryliss," she said, her voice calmer than she felt, "have a seat. May I offer you something to drink?"

Advocate Tryliss sat in the offered chair, but shook her head, rejecting the offer. "I'm afraid I have some bad news," Advocate Tryliss said, as a loud chime rang from an unseen speaker beneath the Prosecutor's desk, announcing an urgent incoming message.

"Excuse me," she said, "I must attend to this." She looked at the view screen and her face went pale as she read the brief message.

"I assume you're here to tell me about the death of your client?" she asked when she turned her attention back to her visitor.

Advocate Tryliss nodded, looking down at the floor.

"A tragedy," Prosecutor Marhlor said, her voice controlled, "but I sense there's something else you have to say about the matter," it was a statement, not a question.

Tryliss looked up at the Prosecutor and nodded, withdrawing the datapad from the small pouch on her lap. "This," she said, "was given to me just before … well, before she … killed herself. You should read what she wrote. It may change your views on the case you have against the former First Counselor." Prosecutor Marhlor reached across the desk and accepted the datapad, downloading the information onto her own device the moment they came into contact. As she scanned the screens of data her eyes widened in surprise.

"Have you read this?" she asked the Advocate, shaking her head at the same time, "Of course you have … and you've already committed it to memory, haven't you?" she chuckled softly. "Well, I'm not sure this changes anything," she announced, in a matter-of-fact tone, "you see, there is far more against the former First Counselor, and against her, than either of them realized." She looked directly at the Advocate, "She has been identified as a spy, a relative of Factotum Ebla Mar; had she mentioned that to you?"

Lareena had not mentioned that; she had been charged with espionage, but the charge did not specify that she was a relative of the Supreme Leader of the Ursus Consortium. "We had also discovered that she had been directly manipulating the former First Counselor by using a perfume designed with genetically engineered pheromones, with specific genomic markers aimed directly at the former First Counselor. This information was going to be forwarded to your office with the final packet of Pre-Trial Disclosure Evidence that I was sending over this afternoon. This will confirm what I've told you," she picked up a datapad marked with the sign of the Office of the Prosecutor from the corner of her desk and handed it to the Advocate.

"However," she continued, watching as Advocate Tryliss quickly scanned the evidence she had been handed, "the former First Counselor was the one responsible for initiating and carrying out the transmissions to the Consortium. We also have evidence that he was the one who, on his own initiative, refused to carry out the binding orders of the Sovereign, to send Alliance forces to guard Alliance planets and Protectorates. That left them vulnerable to attack from the Consortium. No," she shook her head, "there was more than ample evidence to convict them both."

Having already memorized the contents of the datapad she returned it to the Prosecutor's desk. "What about the end of what she wrote?" Tryliss asked, hoping there was some way of helping the former First Counselor, even though he was not her client. "She specifically said, and I quote, *'Everything my husband did was a result of my manipulations; he would have remained completely faithful to the Alliance, and the Sovereign, were it not for my actions. It was only as a result of my treachery that he entered upon the course of action that resulted in his acts of treason.'* End Quote. Don't you think that gives you even the slightest doubt as to the level of guilt of the former First Counselor? Or," she looked directly into the eyes of the prosecutor, "perhaps make you change your views as to whether he deserves the Ultimate punishment?"

Prosecutor Marhlor closed her eyes, thinking for a moment before replying; she was nothing if not fair minded, and liked to believe she had never sought to send someone to the torment of the Ultimate punishment unless they deserved it, but this testimony was problematic, and both she and Tryliss knew it: for one thing, how could it be cross examined? Death-bed testimony had always been given a certain amount of credence by Alliance Tribunals, for the simple reason that it was believed that someone who was about to die was less likely to intentionally be misleading in the presentation of a statement. At the same time, it presented a dilemma with the person making the declaration being unavailable for cross examination.

Marhlor thought to herself that it was quite convenient to have testimony exonerating the husband while making it impossible to cross examine its source. Even more troubling to Marhlor was that Lareena had also been facing the possibility of the Ultimate punishment, making this testimony even less credible the more she considered it, but she would certainly not make the mistake of not sharing it with the Defendant's Advocate. There was no way that the Betrayer was going win his case on a technicality, not while she was prosecuting the case.

Shaking her head Prosecutor Marhlor finally replied, "No ... I don't believe that changes anything," she placed her datapad on the desk, "I shall, of course, share this with Advocate Xylix, though he will be advised that it is the view of the Prosecution that, since the witness cannot be cross examined, and due to the overwhelming evidence we have against his client," she looked across the desk directly at the Advocate, "nothing will change; the Ultimate punishment shall remain on the table when the trial commences."

Prosecutor Marhlor seemed to consider the situation for a moment, while studying the face of Advocate Tryliss, then turned to the console on her desk and quickly typed in a short message before turning back to her visitor. "I've sent Advocate Xylix the data," she said, "as well as my opinion regarding its value to the case, but there's something else I want you to consider, given these recent events," she looked over at the picture frame on the corner of her desk for a few seconds, before continuing.

"Since you no longer have a client in this matter, would you consider joining Advocate Xylix in defending the former First Counselor?" the question caught Advocate Tryliss off-guard. It was unusual for Defendants to have more than one Advocate at a trial, but this would be an unusual trial. Advocate Tryliss also had the advantage of having known the case against the former First Counselor's wife, which could be used to assist in the defense of the Betrayer. She was not sure why the Prosecutor was asking if she wanted to assist, but Tryliss wanted to be part of this trial, even if she would not be representing the client she had started with, though she found herself feeling some misgivings at the Prosecutor's sudden change of attitude. Something seemed odd about her request, she just could not understand why she felt so conflicted.

Without realizing she was doing so, Tryliss nodded her head, finally saying, "Yes, Prosecutor, I would appreciate the opportunity to join in the defense of the former First Counselor with Advocate Xylix."

"Well then," Prosecutor Marhlor said, rising from her seat, "perhaps you should meet with him," she smiled, extending her hand to thank her for coming. "Please convey my regards to Advocate Xylix, and remember," she cautioned, "without the ability to cross examine the former First Counselor's wife, her statement is of little probative value," she smiled enigmatically, gesturing at the datapad, "I consider this a mere tactical ploy, designed to divert our attention away from her husband in the hopes that he might continue his treachery, or perhaps simply escape the Ultimate punishment."

Advocate Tryliss nodded as she walked to the door of the small office, "As you say, Prosecutor," she replied, "yet," she paused, "I have to wonder, had she lived, would you have taken her words more seriously?" Even as she asked the question, she was fairly certain she knew the answer.

Prosecutor Marhlor stood, staring at the Advocate, and then smiled, shaking her head, "In truth, no. Not with the evidence we have against them," she smiled again, "you've seen it, haven't you? Don't you think the case is quite strong?"

Advocate Tryliss could only nod in agreement. Calling what she had read strong was an understatement; the case that the Prosecutor had was overwhelming. She was quite certain that the former First Counselor could have had twenty Advocates defending him and the outcome would have still been the same: he was going to face the Prosecutor and she was going to win. His guilt was undeniable.

Prosecutor Marhlor smiled, "I look forward to seeing you in Court." After the Advocate left she returned to her desk and sent a short message to Advocate Xylix informing him that Advocate Tryliss would be joining him in defending his client.

She looked at the picture frame on her desk and winked at it as an image of her husband holding their Torgon flashed by, his piercing black eyes staring back at her from the picture. Hopefully, she thought to herself, their busy schedules might allow them to share an evening meal together before the trial began, though she doubted that would happen after the recent developments. They were both successful professionals who loved their jobs, and each other; they also respected each other enough to know that their careers were a priority, which meant setting aside personal things for later. Sometimes dinner together would have to wait until trials had ended; then they could celebrate, or console one another, depending on the circumstances.

Unlike the sparsely decorated office of Prosecutor Marhlor the office of Advocate Xylix was a reflection of his success as an Advocate for his clients. He had filled his office with small pieces of art from across the Alliance, most of which had been gifts from grateful clients whom he had represented in various cases throughout his successful career. Much of his success as an Advocate hinged upon the fact that he rarely encountered Prosecutor Marhlor in his cases; he was acutely aware of the record of the Prosecutor, and had an uneasy feeling that his defense of former First Counselor Regar was not going to go as well as the majority of his other cases.

When he received the two messages from Prosecutor Marhlor he was at first elated, and then confused. Lareena's message had at first seemed to exonerate his client, but without even having read the message the Prosecutor had added he recognized the troubling issues the testimony presented: *'Cannot cross examine or confirm. More than sufficient evidence remains to convict. Ultimate punishment remains on table.'* One thing was for certain, Prosecutor Marhlor was not one to mince words.

Then her second message arrived, causing his confusion to grow deeper. It had stated that Advocate Tryliss would be joining him in defending his client. While there were no specific rules regarding the number of Advocates a client could have, they rarely appeared in Court with more than one. Why would the Prosecutor be so interested in sending him assistance, particularly the Advocate who had worked with the wife of his client? It troubled and confused him, feelings that Xylix did not like having, especially just before a trial was set to begin.

As he looked at the picture frame on his own desk, which was nearly identical to the one on the desk of Prosecutor Marhlor, it suddenly occurred to Xylix that he understood the motives of the enigmatic Prosecutor: she had made the decision in order to prevent any appearances of impropriety given the fact that they were married. While there were no laws preventing a Prosecutor from appearing in Court against an Advocate to whom they were married, in a case with as high a profile as this one he realized that his wife only wanted to ensure that the former First Counselor had no grounds to appeal based on the quality of his legal representation. There could certainly be no appearance of impropriety in the defense when there were two Advocates, particularly when the second had been representing the co-Defendant in the same case.

Taking into consideration the fact that the co-Defendant of the

Betrayer was now dead was, quite frankly, irrelevant. Advocate Xylix shook his head and smiled at the cleverness of his wife: once again she had managed to surprise him with her legal mind, and it only reminded him as to how much he admired and loved her. He would definitely want to bring this up the next time they managed to share a meal together. He looked at the picture frame and smiled as an image of the two of them with their Torgon appeared: it reminded him of the calm, quiet times they shared between cases. It would be nice when this case was over and they could take some much-deserved time off; perhaps they would go to their cottage in the outskirts of Partnash, a quiet village outside of the metropolitan area of Beryl, just to get away from the hustle and bustle of the Stadium of Justice.

A knock on his office door announced the arrival of Advocate Tryliss and, with the press of a button on a panel of his desk, Xylix allowed his guest to enter. He rose from his seat, gesturing for the Advocate to join him by his desk, "Welcome to my office, Advocate Tryliss," he said, smiling warmly, "may I offer you something to drink?"

"Please, just call my Tryliss," she replied, sitting in one of the comfortable chairs in front of the large desk, which was cluttered but well organized, "I'd love something cold, if you have anything," she was looking around the office, admiring the many decorations when her eyes noticed the picture frame on the corner of the desk, just as an image of Prosecutor Marhlor appeared, smiling enigmatically from the image.

Xylix noticed her look of confusion and laughed as he handed her a tall glass of cold Larksa juice, an exotic fruit imported from a planet on the rim of the Cara Nebula, near Tarlos II, the home world of the shapeshifters. "I see you've noticed the picture of my wife," he said casually, as he took a sip of his own Larksa juice, savoring the rich, creamy nectar. It had the unique property of remaining cold far longer than water once it had been poured, and despite its creamy texture, it was extremely refreshing. Xylix often had the precious nectar as a meal, though it was sometimes difficult to procure given its short growing season. He looked at Tryliss and could see she was shocked at learning that he was married to Prosecutor Marhlor, which only made him laugh.

"I'm sorry, Tryliss," he began, "I'd assumed you knew. We don't try to keep it a secret, you know," he took another sip of the nectar before setting the glass on his desk and returning to his chair. "We've been married for three-hundred and seventy-two years; when we were first married I was still with the Office of the Prosecutor, but left when I decided I wanted to be on the other side of the system, as often happens," he winked, which earned him a giggle.

"Anyway," he continued, eyeing the Larksa juice, "we've only appeared against each other a few times," his voice lowered, "I'm sorry to say that my record against my wife is not nearly as good as my record against other Alliance Advocates, or other Prosecutors," he laughed, mostly to himself. Tryliss was listening, but still having difficulty processing what she was hearing.

"I'm sorry, she said," looking at the frame again, "I've only been on Felis Magoris for a short time, I've never faced Prosecutor Marhlor before," she replied.

"Oh, that's right," Xylix responded, "you transferred here from the Ionian Stadium, didn't you? Well, it doesn't really matter," he said casually, "what does matter is that we are going to have an uphill battle ahead of us. My wife is not going to sit back and let either of us allow the former First Counselor of the Cadre escape the Ultimate punishment without the fight of our lives."

Tryliss still looked confused, but was not about to argue with Advocate Xylix. She knew when it was time to get to work, and that was why she was there: the trial was to begin in three days, and based on what she knew about the evidence, the former First Counselor was going to need all of the help they could provide.

"Where do you suggest we begin," she asked, her voice soft, feeling quite relaxed thanks to the calming effects of the Larksa juice, which she took another sip of, "by the way, this is truly wonderful, thank you so much; it's exactly what I needed after walking over here from," she paused for a moment, "your wife's office." They both laughed, then began discussing the case against their client.

(* | *)

As much as Sovereign Sayoose had enjoyed her vacation on Terra, she had to admit it was good to be home, even if things were more hectic than normal. She quickly discovered how poorly her former First Counselor had been performing his duties when she returned to her private office and began examining the number of Requests for Action – RFAs – waiting to be dealt with on her computer. Many of them should have been dealt with as simple routine work by the Cadre, but she could see that Regar had not even bothered looking at most of the requests. He had instead decided to deal with the oddest assortment of things, none of which required the consultation of the entire Cadre. As the First Counselor, the de facto leader of the group, Regar had limited executive authority enabling him to make certain decisions without having to consult the Cadre, but the Sovereign was still confused as she looked through the piles of RFAs, trying to find some common denominator: she kept asking herself what he had been doing as she searched through the hundreds of records.

Somewhere embedded within the data there seemed to be a pattern, but at first glance it did not make any sense. Many of the decisions that Regar had made had to do with sending orders approving the changing of routes taken by transport vessels; this was not, in and of itself, an uncommon practice, but there was something that seemed strange. Whenever the Sovereign was absent from Felis Prime, regardless the duration, the standard procedure was for the First Counselor to receive briefings regarding any risks to Alliance transport routes, which would then be passed along to Sector Dispatchers, who would warn the Captains of the transport vessels.

This was especially important given the rising risks from Consortium marauders, but the orders from the former First Counselor seemed particularly odd: as the Sovereign checked she found that they did not correlate with any corresponding data from the Alliance Security & Intelligence Service warning of specific Consortium threats appearing in Threat Assessment files. In fact, the more Sayoose examined the data, the more she wondered why they even appeared as RFAs: it made no sense, and that was troubling. After highlighting one of them the answer was revealed instantly: the cargo was the precious Beryllium 8, from one of the Red Dwarf sites in Sector 0109, in the Varkuut system, bound for processing in the Element Refineries Plant on Ventia.

Sovereign Sayoose examined the RFA Outcome to determine the fate of the shipment, fearing she knew the answer. As she read the Outcome her fears were confirmed: the vessel had never reached its destination; it had been reported missing shortly after the orders from the former First Counselor had been transmitted to the commander of the vessel. Her blood ran cold as she reviewed several other RFAs that Regar had approved, each one rerouting Beryllium 8 shipments, none of which arrived at their final destinations. As she reviewed all of the RFAs in question she made an even more astonishing discovery: the orders sent by the former First Counselor had originated from an official communications console, providing each message with proper security encoding, but the same could not be said for the RFAs themselves. Each of the messages from the ships requested information as to whether or not their current course was safe, but the Sovereign was able to see that the messages purportedly originating from the vessels had originated from within Felis Prime itself. Sayoose could see that they had the same forged identity as the other messages sent from the unregistered communications console that had been used by her former First Counselor.

Once the Sovereign had confirmed all of her suspicions regarding the RFAs she copied them into a file and forwarded it to Prosecutor Marhlor with an accompanying explanatory note. She received a reply within a few moments, asking if the Prosecutor could visit her as soon as possible. Sovereign Sayoose smiled to herself as she replied in the affirmative. It would be lovely having the Prosecutor as a guest, although she had already been deposed, at great length, in preparation for the upcoming trial.

Prosecutor Marhlor arrived only a few minutes later, clearly out of breath from having rushed to the Long Distance Matter Transporter Station located near her office. "Thank you for seeing me so soon," she said after Commander Dragar confirmed she could enter the Sovereign's office; she nodded to the large Guardian who was sitting in the outer area, a bemused smile on his face at the unexpected arrival of the Prosecutor. In his mind anyone who might be sending the Betrayer to the Ultimate punishment was always welcome.

"Is there anything either of you would like, My Sovereign ... Prosecutor?" Commander Dragar asked, trying to be cordial, though it was not his duty to act as a valet. He liked the Prosecutor, and wanted to do anything to help in the prosecution of the Betrayer, for whom he made no secret regarding the contempt he felt.

"Thank you, Commander, no," the Sovereign replied, looking at her guest, "is something you would like?" Prosecutor Marhlor shook her head, anxious to begin her interview without delay. "No, Commander Dragar, we are fine. Thank you." Dragar slipped the door shut so the two could meet in private and returned to his datapad: he was studying the music that Tanya had brought with her from Terra as he had developed a fondness for it while guarding the Sovereign. He was particularly attracted to the music of Ludwig van Beethoven and Robert Schumann. As odd as it seemed, he had learned, Beethoven had been almost completely deaf when he had composed his greatest masterpieces while Schumann had battled an intense mental disorder, which had ultimately led to his premature death. It all seemed so tragic, Dragar thought to himself, wondering how the two masters might have benefited from the medical technology of the Alliance.

Once Prosecutor Marhlor was seated across from Sovereign Sayoose she took out her datapad and said, "You do realize, my Sovereign, this changes everything, don't you?"

Sovereign Sayoose nodded. As the leader of the Felis Alliance the Sovereign had been well trained in the niceties of law, and understood that what her former First Counselor had done had directly resulted in the loss of no less than sixteen shipments of Beryllium 8, the vessels transporting it, and their crews. Each ship had a crew of ten, which meant that no less than one hundred and sixty people had been killed as a result of his actions. Even if the crew members had only been captured and were now prisoners of the Ursus Consortium, they were being denied their freedoms as provided for by the Pan-Universal Alliance Charter of Rights and Freedoms, something guaranteed to all Alliance Citizens, which was still a gross violation of Alliance law, punishable by the Ultimate penalty.

Prosecutor Marhlor looked intently at Sovereign Sayoose, "How certain are you about this information?" she gestured to the datapad, "I mean, please," she stammered, "I don't want to sound as though I'm doubting you, my Sovereign," she blushed, "I just …" she paused, looking down, self-consciously.

"Do not worry, my dear," Sovereign Sayoose said, her voice soothing, "I would be concerned as well were I in your position. I have gone over the data several times. You will find that the incoming Requests for Action, or RFAs, all possess the same originating data stream from within Felis Prime as the other messages sent from the unregistered console found to be in possession of the former First Counselor. A device that has been demonstrated, I believe under the direct supervision of Latinnar, your Personal Assistant, and that the forensics evidence conclusively demonstrated that it was only used by one individual," Prosecutor Marhlor was nodding enthusiastically as the Sovereign spoke. "If that is not sufficient, I do not know what would be, do you?" Sayoose crossed her arms across her chest and looked directly into the eyes of the Prosecutor, which made the other woman slightly nervous.

Shaking her head to break the spell of the Sovereign's gaze, "No, my Sovereign, I don't imagine that anything else would be needed. In fact," she looked at her timepiece, "you're going to make this evening's dinner quite interesting," she laughed as she thought about how Advocate Xylix would react when he received the news regarding the new evidence against his client. Marhlor would amend the charges against the former First Counselor to include one hundred and sixty charges of murder, as well as the misdirection of the Beryllium 8 cargo, amongst other things, although much of that could still be included in the general charge of Crimes Against the Alliance. Even so, Marhlor preferred to be as concise as possible when it came to seeking a conviction against someone who had turned out to be a mass-murderer, not to mention a pirate, and spy.

"I don't know how I can thank you, my Sovereign," she said, rising from her seat as she prepared to leave the office.

"Well," the Sovereign replied, "I can think of one way," she mused, "you could invite me to dinner," and the two women laughed. "Of course, you would have to endure the company of my Guardians as well," she added, lowering her voice to a whisper, "I have not been able to go anywhere without them since my return from Terra," she glanced toward the door, "I believe they are afraid I will transform into a Torgon, or something else, and disappear for another three years," they both laughed.

"You're more than welcome to join us," Prosecutor Marhlor said, "but, I'm afraid it would seem inappropriate before the end of the trial, given that both you, and your Guardians, are witnesses, and my husband is the Advocate for the Defendant," she looked down, not wanting to offend the Sovereign, "but once it's over," she quickly added, "I promise to make you my specialty, which I'm sure you'll love! My husband gets a wonderful supply of Larksa juice, which I use as a marinade for fish. It would make the monks on Caiphus sing with delight!"

"Larksa juice," Sovereign Sayoose said, wistfully, "I have not had that in several years. I shall have to have a talk with your husband about his connections," she winked at Marhlor as she accompanied her to the door, walking her out. She smiled as the Prosecutor rushed out of the outer office toward the LDMT so she could return to Felis Magoris and continue working on her case against the former First Counselor.

"Problems, my Sovereign?" Prime Guardian Dragar asked as he listened to Schumann's *First String Quartet*, which the Sovereign recognized from her time on Terra. She had grown particularly fond of the piece, particularly the lyrical slow movement, which was coming up shortly.

"Not at all, my friend," she replied, a smile on her face, "In fact, things could not be any better. Unless your name happens to be Regar," she let out a small laugh as she walked back into her office, leaving the door open so she could enjoy the music as it continued to play. It was just what she needed right now, a reminder of her vacation.

CHAPTER XIV ~ STONE OF JUDGMENT

"At the conclusion of a trial no doubt may remain regarding the guilt or innocence of the Defendant. In earlier times, miscarriages of justice were often witnessed when individuals were accused and convicted of crimes based on faulty evidence, much of which should not have been admitted into the proceedings. For this reason, the Court now insists that Defendants be fully protected throughout the judicial process. All evidence must be shared with the Advocate representing the Defendant, and no Defendant shall face a Tribunal without the benefit of a fully prepared defense against the charges laid against them before the commencement of the trial."

[...]

"Defendants are entitled to have all evidence against them examined by their own experts, so long as that examination does not result in the destruction of the evidence."

[...]

"No Defendant may receive the sentence of the Ultimate punishment, or Death, solely on the grounds of an eyewitness to a criminal act due to the unreliable nature of such testimony. Only when substantial corroborative evidence exists linking a Defendant to the crimes to which they have been accused may the severest sentences be invoked; otherwise, they must be removed as a possible penalty. In cases where corroborating evidence is lacking and the possibility exists that the Prosecutor will not meet their threshold of overcoming the burden of proof, it may be necessary to withdraw the charges against the Defendant, until such time as sufficient evidence may be presented in Court."

[...]

Excerpted from *Justice in the Felis Alliance*, by

Justice Renata, Prime Justice of the First Tribunal

(*|*)

As Clerk of the First Tribunal it fell upon Clerk Sistu to make any announcements to those who had business before the Tribunal. She was also tasked with recording every word spoken during a trial. As an Ionian, Clerk Sistu was ideally suited to the job as she tended to take things extremely seriously. She preferred to keep her brown hair in a short, easy to manage style, but her most dramatic feature had to be her dazzling eyes, which would light up any room she entered. Whenever she began to speak it was impossible not to look directly into her crystal-clear blue eyes, making it easy for those attending the proceedings to sometimes forget they were supposed to be listening to her voice rather than watching her eyes while she spoke. That would be an issue on the first day of the trial of the former First Counselor of the Cadre: nobody would be missing a single word she uttered. People had been waiting for this trial to begin since the arrest of the Betrayer and the announcement that he was facing numerous charges, most of which qualified for the Ultimate penalty.

The main Stadium of Justice on Felis Magoris was a veritable temple to the law. It was one of the largest structures in the capital city of Beryl, and included both the Law Library and the courtrooms for the all of the lower Tribunals, which also dealt with lesser offences and the appeals of decisions of the other Tribunals. Each member planet within the Felis Alliance dealt with judicial matters on their own, with planets having as many Stadiums of Justice as they felt was necessary. Each Sector also had one Supreme Tribunal to hear all of the appeals from the lower Tribunals in the Sector. There was, however, only one First Tribunal, which served as the final word in judicial matters for the entire Alliance. Only cases that had passed through every level of the magisterial system on their individual planet, including having passed the Supreme Tribunal, could appeal to the First Tribunal on Felis Magoris. Otherwise, the vast majority of cases within the Felis Alliance were heard, and settled, within the System Circuits, on the planets upon which the cases had originated.

Matters pertaining to crime and punishment were settled within a Stadium of Justice, and for those who had committed the most egregious acts they were also where the most severe sentences were carried out. If someone found themselves sentenced to the Ultimate penalty, consigned to the Dark Zone, they would be sent to the Chamber of the micro-singularity, housed in a special high-security area deep beneath the Stadium. Those sentenced to lengthy terms within the Cryo-Freeze facility were also taken to locations deep within the bowels of the Stadium. It was not something anyone wanted to witness, but it was the rule of the Tribunal: once a ruling was made, justice was delivered. Appeals might take place, but the Defendant would have already begun serving their sentence.

There was only one exception, and that was the penalty of Death. Anyone sentenced to that penalty found themselves consigned to a short appeal process, followed by an execution if the process failed at the hands of a specialized Long Distance Matter Transporter, which would transport the convicted Defendant into deep space in a wide field, scattering their molecules to prevent them from regaining molecular cohesion. Death was instantaneous and painless, at least, that was the supposition. Only the First Tribunal heard cases in which the Defendant was charged with crimes against the Alliance.

Since the First Tribunal heard only those cases that had been heard by every level of the System Magistrates and were considered to be of merit, they met in the largest Court in the Stadium of Justice, which could seat over one thousand visitors. For the trial of the former First Counselor there would be many others watching in other parts of the Stadium, in any Court not in use during the proceedings. It had also been decided that due to the high profile of the case, and the heinous nature of the offences, the proceedings would be transmitted throughout the Alliance. Anyone interested in watching the proceedings would be able to downline the daily recordings onto their datapad. Prosecutor Marhlor had at first been reluctant to agree to this, not wanting to make a spectacle of the case, but she came to the realization that if the case was tried in secret it might appear as though they were trying to hide something, which was definitely not the position the Prosecutor wanted to take. To her surprise, the Defendant's Advocate also agreed, and the Prime Justice of the First Tribunal subsequently approved the broadcast.

Once Prosecutor Marhlor entered the court and seated herself behind her table the Defendant was brought in by two guards and was seated with his Advocates. Once everyone was in place they awaited the emergence of the First Tribunal from their chambers which would only happen after Clerk Sistu made her opening declaration.

When Sistu was satisfied that everyone was in their places she announced in her clear, melodic voice, "All those having business before the First Tribunal, stand and be heard. The First Tribunal shall hear the case of the Felis Alliance against Regar, former First Counselor of the Cadre of the Sovereign of the Felis Alliance." A loud murmuring went through the room as people expected the announcement of the case against Lareena.

Regar was trying to look around and appeared confused, but he was unable to move because of the force-shields that only permitted his head to move slightly from side to side. Advocate Xylix rested his hand on the man's shoulder to quiet him and whispered something in his ear. It was obvious he had not been told of the death of his wife and had been expecting her to be present at the trial.

Clerk Sistu was undeterred by the murmurs from the crowd, "Silence in the Court!" she called, her voice carrying easily in the large room. She then continued, as though there had been no interruption, "All rise for the First Tribunal: Prime Justice Renata, Justice Kagar, and Justice Mentar," she paused as the three Justices took their seats behind the large podium, then turned back to the Court, "you may be seated," she said, turning back to the First Tribunal.

"Thank you, Clerk Sistu," Prime Justice Renata said, in a soft voice, her brown eyes scanning the entire room, seeing everything in an instant. "Please announce the charges against the Defendant."

"Yes, Prime Justice," Clerk Sistu replied, lifting her datapad from the table. She looked at the former First Counselor and was about to begin her reading of the charges when she realized that the man was sitting, "The Defendant will rise." It was not a request, and Regar was lifted to his feet by his two Advocates, who stood on either side of him. As Clerk Sistu spoke her hand made a quick adjustment to the control device on her table, allowing Regar's legs to straighten. Satisfied that the Defendant was in the proper position, Clerk Sistu took a quick look at the datapad, then took a deep breath before starting.

"Former First Counselor Regar," she began, looking directly at the man, "you are charged with the following: Crimes against the Alliance, to wit, the systematic redirection of no less than sixteen shipments of Beryllium 8 and other substances from authorized transport routes using an unregistered communications console; further, you are charged with the deaths of the crews of those sixteen vessels, or the deprivation of their rights under the Pan-Universal Alliance Charter of Rights and Freedoms, to wit, one hundred and sixty individual counts," this announcement brought a gasp of disbelief from those in the Court, followed by a glare from Clerk Sistu. "Furthermore," she continued, "you are charged with conspiracy to overthrow the Cadre of the Alliance, by failing to follow lawful commands delivered by your Superior, to wit, the orders sent to support Protectorates and member planets. You are also charged with spying for the Ursus Consortium through the use of the aforementioned unregistered communications console, from which you systematically transmitted multiple messages compromising the security of Felis Alliance personnel throughout several Sectors of the universe. Furthermore," Clerk Sistu cleared her throat, "you are charged with conspiring to incite a war with an enemy, to wit, the Ursus Consortium, through direct actions and inactions through your gross negligence in regards to your deliberate mismanagement of the Cadre in the absence of the Sovereign. You are further charged with attempted genocide by aiding and abetting the Ursus Consortium in their mining operation of the Terran star, which would have resulted in the deaths of several billion sentient lives on Terra, in direct contravention of the Callisto Treaty, as well as directly organizing the attempted assassination of the Sovereign of the Felis Alliance, for which there are two separate counts, as well as one count of personally attempting to assassinate the Sovereign, including an additional charge of attempting to overthrow the Sovereign of the Felis Alliance. Finally," her eyes seemed to bore directly into him, "you are charged with possessing a Class-t weapon, to wit, a PPD-77 hand-held plasma pulse-weapon, in a Blue Zone." She paused for a brief breath then continued, "How do you plead to these charges?"

Regar tried to look down at the table, but his head could barely move; his eyes stared, seeing nothing. All he wanted to know was where Lareena was; why had the Clerk not mentioned any of the charges against her? Had Lareena decided to testify against him? No, he pushed the thought from his mind, that was inconceivable, the one thing he knew was that theirs was a love unlike any other. Still, he could not understand why she was not appearing before the First Tribunal, nor could he comprehend who the second Advocate appearing with Xylix was and why she was there.

He had met with Advocate Xylix just before the commencement of the trial, but that had been a short, perfunctory meeting, at which time Xylix had quickly reviewed what he had prepared as his opening statement. He had not mentioned anything about another Advocate joining his defense, at least, Regar could not remember him having mentioned anything. His memory of the last three days was, he had to admit, more like a bad dream than anything specific. He could hardly remember what he had eaten, if he had eaten, let alone what he had been told by his Advocate. Regar did recall, however, that he had received a notice about the new charges against him after he had arrived at the High Security Detention Center on Felis Magoris, before the beginning of the trial. They had not been a surprise.

"Defendant!" Clerk Sistu's voice penetrated his reverie, snapping him back to reality: he was still standing, facing the Clerk of the First Tribunal, but what did she want from him? "How do you plead to these charges?" she repeated, an edge of irritation entering her voice. Advocate Xylix leaned over and whispered into his ear and he felt himself trying to nod, but the force-shields frustrated his attempt.

"May it please the First Tribunal," Regar began, his voice quivering.

"You will have to speak louder, former First Counselor," Clerk Sistu interrupted, and one of the guards walked around the table and moved the microphone closer to him so that he would be heard more clearly.

Regar blinked a few times before continuing, "May it please the First Tribunal," he began again, his voice a bit stronger now, "it is my intention to throw myself on the mercy of the Tribunal … I have no defense against these charges, nor excuses to mitigate my actions. I freely admit to having done everything to which I have been charged," he paused for a brief instant before adding, "and more." His words elicited a series of surprised gasps and several barely concealed murmurs as the Court erupted in chaos, earning a severe glare from Clerk Sistu. "I only ask," he continued, as he tried to look down again, forgetting that the restraining power of the force-shields prevented him from moving, "that you might consider showing some small amount of mercy on my wife … in consideration for my cooperation," his voice was now barely in control and he was visibly trembling, despite the restraining power of the force-shields.

Clerk Sistu glanced at Prime Justice Renata, appearing genuinely confused by his request and unsure of how to proceed. Prime Justice Renata shook her head, which Sistu took to mean that there was no other case before the First Tribunal, which was, as far as she knew, the truth.

"Defendant Regar," Clerk Sistu turned back to the former First Counselor, trying to sound as sympathetic as she could to the man, "you are the *only* Defendant appearing before this Tribunal. Your wife is not facing any charges before the First Tribunal," as far as Clerk Sistu knew, it was the truth. She knew nothing regarding Regar's wife.

For the first time since this ordeal had begun, Regar allowed himself to believe there was hope for his Lareena, that she might actually escape the horrors of prosecution for the crimes he had committed. He did not care what happened to his own life, so long as he knew she would live, that would sustain him even through the Ultimate punishment.

Advocate Xylix glanced at Advocate Tryliss, but she refused to meet his gaze. During their meeting with Prosecutor Marhlor she had made it clear that they were not to inform their client of what had befallen his wife. Not, at least, until the end of the trial, when the First Tribunal had completed their deliberations and the verdict had been delivered. It was then that it had been decided that only Xylix would meet with Regar in their pre-trial meeting. Xylix had been concerned that the man might ask too many questions if Tryliss arrived, questions they would not be able to answer. He had also been concerned that Regar's mental state was too precarious to withstand more than one meeting.

Under ordinary circumstances, with a trial of two Defendants, the two Advocates would have only had one strategy session before the beginning of the trial. Now that they were working together, for just the one client, Xylix and Tryliss could spend as much time together as they desired in order to prepare for the trial. Prosecutor Marhlor was not particularly pleased with this development given that it resulted in her husband spending even less time at home than he had before, particularly during the busy days during his preparation for the trial, but he was quick to remind her that asking Tryliss to join him on the case had been her idea.

"Don't remind me," she had replied grumpily, smiling to herself as she went off to spend time with their Torgon.

As much as Advocate Tryliss had wanted to inform Regar of what had happened to his wife, she had more respect for the rule of Law. Knowing that the system had been designed to protect the Citizens of the Alliance, the people their client had been accused of threatening through his actions. When Advocate Xylix had his final meeting with him, shortly before the beginning of the trial it had been his idea for Regar to throw himself on the mercy of the Tribunal, though he had not mentioned anything about using that as a ploy to bargain for leniency for Lareena; that had been something the former First Counselor had devised within his own mind.

Prosecutor Marhlor rose from her seat to address the First Tribunal, "Prime Justice," she began, "it is my understanding that former First Counselor Regar has prepared a statement. Since he has decided to post no defense to the charges against him, I would ask that he be allowed to present that statement at this time," she sat, glancing over at the two Advocates, who were now sitting, along with their client, thanks to the adjustment Clerk Sistu had made to the device.

Prime Justice Renata looked directly at the Defendant and frowned, as though doing so left a bad taste in her mouth. This was not going as she had expected, but that was something she had grown accustomed to after many years as the Prime Justice of the First Tribunal.

She turned to face Prosecutor Marhlor, "As you wish," she began," then turned to face the Defendant, "the Defendant shall rise and be heard by the First Tribunal." Regar rose like a puppet and Advocate Xylix held the datapad so he could read his statement.

"You may begin," Prime Justice Renata said, "when you are ready."

Regar had never felt more exposed in his life. He knew there were more people watching the trial than he could imagine, both on Felis Magoris and countless planets across the Felis Alliance. He harbored no doubt that he was the most hated individual alive, after Factotum Mar. But it made no difference; knowing that Lareena had managed to escape a trial made his heart sing with joy, and that gave him the strength to continue, which he desperately needed. He needed that strength to read the statement that he had spent so much time writing over the last three days. Much of it had to be changed after being informed of the additional charges, but he had been expecting them; it was not as though Sovereign Sayoose would not sift through the Request for Action logs once she returned to her office. If nothing else, the woman was predictable: she was predictably efficient, and brilliantly so, and he hated her for it because he knew his mind was nothing compared to what she possessed. His arrogance had prevented him from deleting the RFAs, assuming the Sovereign would be dead, never to return to her office, but things had not turned out as planned.

He took a deep breath and looked at the datapad. How ironic, he thought to himself, thinking of the Prime Justice: she came from Vestus II, his home-planet. Well, that would certainly not be helping him now. "Prime Justice Renata, Justice Kagar," he tried to nod to the left, but failed, "Justice Mentar, there is no easy way of saying this, so let me start with this: everything that I have been charged with, everything you have heard declared by the Clerk of the Court, is the truth," a murmur emanated from the Court, but was silenced by a stern look from Clerk Sistu. "I was entrusted with the running of the Cadre," he continued, "and I violated that trust out of blind ambition. It is true, I received direct orders to send vessels of the Unified Armed Services to support our Protectorates and member planets, and I disobeyed those orders. Worse than that, I used an unregistered communications device in my quarters to transmit messages to the Ursus Consortium, ultimately leading to the capture or killing of no less than one hundred and sixty crew members of the vessels transporting Beryllium 8 and other materials, transport vessels I had intentionally redirected for the purpose of sending into the hands of the Consortium," he paused for a breath, and to allow the growing noise in the Court to die down.

His voice was no longer as strong, but the microphone still allowed him to be heard, "It is also true," he continued, now sounding tired, "that I conspired, with elements within the Ursus Consortium, to overthrow Sovereign Sayoose, and was directly associated with the two attempts to assassinate her while she was on Terra. I also personally attempted to assassinate her upon her return to Felis Prime. Furthermore," he tried to continue, but the noise in the Court had risen to such a level that Clerk Sistu had to rise to her feet.

"Silence!" she shouted, her voice thundering through the amplification system that filled the large room. One word was more than adequate and the room fell silent. "One more outburst and this will continue as a closed-session, is that clear?" Clerk Sistu looked over at the Prime Justice for confirmation, and was pleased to see her nod in agreement. "You may continue," she said, taking her seat again now that order had been restored.

Regar had been shaken by the outbursts, but had expected that his statement would upset those gathered to hear the proceedings. He was certain that many family members and friends of the crews of the transport vessels he had sent into Consortium territory, most of whom would want to see him receive the Ultimate penalty, or something worse, if that could be imagined, would be at the trial.

"Furthermore," he finally managed to continue, "my actions led to the Consortium's attempt to mine the star in the Terran system, which would have led to the genocide of several billion sentient beings, in direct contravention of the Callisto Treaty, which could have led to a war between the Ursus Consortium and the Felis Alliance. Every charge levied against me is true: I am a despicable man who deserves no sympathy from any member of the First Tribunal. My actions were calculated, but," his voice increased in volume, "I acted on my own, without the assistance of anyone else, and I alone should be punished for my actions." His eyes shifted over to Clerk Sistu and she pressed the button on her panel, allowing him to sit down.

As soon as he was seated Prosecutor Marhlor stood to address the First Tribunal, "If it may please the First Tribunal," she nodded toward Prime Justice Renata, "given the remarks of the Defendant, I believe it is in the interest of the Court to make some inquiries regarding some of the motives behind his actions, before the First Tribunal adjourns to consider its verdict."

Since Regar had, for all intents and purposes, admitted his guilt and offered no defense against the charges, the First Tribunal could have immediately adjourned the proceedings at the conclusion of his remarks, but Prime Justice Renata nodded her head at the Prosecutor's request. She was as curious as anyone as to why the former First Counselor had betrayed the Alliance and the Sovereign. Why would such a man turn against his people? It was troubling, and the answers might be revealing. She glanced to either side and was gratified to see that both of her colleagues were also nodding: they were as curious regarding the motives of the betrayer of the Cadre as the Prosecutor.

"Proceed, Prosecutor Marhlor," Prime Justice Renata said, her voice soft, but strong, "You may inquire of the Defendant, but remember," she paused, "this is no longer an ordinary trial; we are in an unusual situation and you are not to cross examine the Defendant." Prosecutor Marhlor nodded; she had not expected that, but it was unimportant. Her questions would not be that difficult to answer, so long as he was honest.

"Thank you, Prime Justice," she said, nodding to the First Tribunal. She moved to the podium reserved for addressing Defendants during the trial, which allowed her to face him directly, as well as his two Advocates. Regar was sitting stiffly, staring straight at her, unable to move thanks to the force-shields, but she suspected that he would not have been moving regardless: he had always maintained a rather stiff and formal attitude.

"I shall keep this short," she began, her voice amplified by the microphone on the podium so that everyone could hear her clearly.

"Could you please explain why you decided to take the course of actions which led you to betray the Felis Alliance in such a dramatic fashion, ultimately leading to the murder of one hundred and sixty Alliance Citizens, or the deprivation of their rights under the Pan-Universal Alliance Charter of Rights and Freedoms, not to mention what led you to attempt an act of direct murder by endeavoring to assassinate the Sovereign by your own hand. Please, explain your actions to the Court; I'm certain the families of the crews of the transport vessels you diverted into Consortium space …"

"Prosecutor," the voice of the Prime Justice interrupted her, "I remind you, the Defendant has already admitted his culpability. Are you asking him a question or summarizing the acts for which he has taken responsibility?" the Prime Justice sounded mildly annoyed, but there was a trace of a smile on her face.

"My apologies, Prime Justice," Prosecutor Marhlor said in a low voice, blushing at the rebuke. Turning back to the Defendant, "As I was saying, *former* First Counselor, please, what were the motives behind your actions?" she crossed her arms, stepping back from the podium.

Regar blinked a few times, wondering what he might say to satisfy the Prosecutor, or the First Tribunal, for that matter. He knew that no answer could ever be enough. At the same time, his mind could not help but think about his wife, and why she was not present in the Court, and he could only hope that anything he might say, anything he revealed, might be taken into consideration in regards to the case they were pursuing against her. Regar tried to take a deep breath but was frustrated by the restraint of the force-shields, nevertheless, he managed to get enough air into his lungs to prevent his voice from wavering too much.

"Prosecutor," he began, almost tentatively, "nothing I say will restore the lives I have ruined, nor will it ever fully explain the treachery I have committed," if he had wanted to sound more pathetic, it would not have been possible, "I can only say that my motives were guided by the oldest of human emotions: greed and lust. Two things for which I was powerless to control."

A murmur went through the Court, but Clerk Sistu quieted them quickly enough, and Regar continued, "Long before I became First Counselor of the Cadre I felt a lust for power that could only be satisfied by seeking out positions of greater authority, which was ultimately satisfied by my appointment to the position as a member of the Sovereign's Cadre, but it wasn't enough." As he spoke his eyes had taken on an almost crazed look as he described his desire for power, "Even as I became one of the most powerful men, one of the most influential men in the Alliance, perhaps in the entire universe, I knew that I wanted more … I needed more power. Being a member of the Cadre was never enough. The Cadre only did what the Sovereign did not want to do, she would throw us small bones of bureaucratic nonsense to contend with, things I could deal with while my eyes were closed. I knew, deep in my heart, that I could do whatever she was doing, and more," his voice had risen in volume to an extent that Advocate Xylix placed his hand on the shoulder of his client remind him that he was addressing the First Tribunal.

Regar pressed on, "Why should she be in such an elevated position, her … a filthy *shapeshifter*," the word came out as an epithet, "when I had worked so long to rise through the ranks of the Alliance's bureaucracy, becoming the senior member of the Cadre. What did she have that I lacked?" It was, of course, a rhetorical question, but it provided the Prosecutor an opportunity to interject, which she jumped at without hesitation.

"The respect and admiration of her peers?" she offered, her voice quiet.

"Yes," Regar responded. "She does have that … and much more. No matter what I did, or how well I did it, I could never manage to rise above a certain level. After being appointed to the Cadre, and serving for many years, years in which I worked hard to prove myself, I was elevated to the position of First Counselor," he tried to laugh, but the force-shields transformed the sound into a grotesque cackle. He then quickly added, as though it needed to be said, "But I *deserved* that appointment," he hissed, "she *had* to make me First Counselor. Who else would she have chosen? Well," he pressed on, oblivious to the fact that his raving was made him sound unhinged, "by then I'd come to the realization that I had reached the limit of my success within the Alliance, unless …" he paused, licking his lips, "unless," his voice lowered, "*she* was gone. I knew I had to eliminate the Sovereign. Then … only then, would I ascend to the position that should rightfully be mine." Advocate Xylix leaned over and tried to whisper something in his ear, but the former First Counselor was beyond receiving advice at this point and ignored the man.

"When I went to Altus 9, for a conference, I met the one piece of perfection in my life, my wife Lareena; we were married and she is the only thing that I have ever truly cared about, aside from ending the life of that filthy shapeshifter." Advocate Xylix leaned back in his chair and groaned, earning him a stern glare from Clerk Sistu, but she was sympathetic as well; she had rarely seen a Defendant act in such a self-destructive manner before the First Tribunal. Xylix nodded in apology, realizing his breach of etiquette.

Regar pressed on, oblivious to what was happening around him, "When we returned to Altus 9 several years later, to celebrate our anniversary, I acquired an unregistered communications device, which I installed in my private quarters. It was with this device that I began to communicate with the Ursus Consortium and send them decoded messages regarding troop movements, coordinates of Protectorates that would not have full the protection of the Alliance, and many other things. This is why I can assure you, there have been many more than one hundred and sixty Alliance Citizens deprived of their rights under your pathetic Pan-Universal Alliance Charter of Rights and Freedoms," he said it as though doing so left a vile taste in his mouth, but he continued, unmindful of the more than a thousand pair of eyes boring into him from the Court, and the equally distasteful glares from his own Advocates, and the First Tribunal.

"My first dealings were with high-level officials in the Consortium; my information would be passed onto the Factotum if it was of enough importance. Eventually, however," he tried to clear his throat, knowing the next thing he said would cause an uproar, "I was placed in direct contact with the Supreme Leader of the Consortium, Factotum Ebla Mar himself." Prosecutor Marhlor nearly fell over from the shock of the disclosure. This had not been revealed by the communication logs. They had not been able to trace the recipients of the messages, only that they had been transmitted to the Ursus Subspace Communications Web, which had allowed Regar to communicate with the Consortium without being noticed. As he had predicted, the Court erupted, but was quickly brought under control by Clerk Sistu, and an admonishing look from the Prime Justice, who used the black Stone of judgment to strike a terrifyingly loud clanging noise which was normally only heard at the time a verdict was rendered. It had the desired effect; the Court was instantly rendered silent.

Before he could continue, however, the Prime Justice addressed the Court, "I remind this Court that you are here at our indulgence," she glared at the many faces looking back at the raised dais upon which the First Tribunal sat, "if I have to interrupt these proceedings to silence you once more, we shall continue without you, is that understood?" It was a question requiring no answer, and none was expected. "Proceed, Defendant Regar," she declared tersely, obviously displeased with the way things were progressing, but unwilling to end the proceeding. She wanted to hear the rest of his statement as much as anyone.

Regar blinked a few times to gather his thoughts, "Once I was placed in contact with Factotum Mar," he continued, his voice stronger, as though he was enjoying recounting his story, "I realized I was closer than ever to true power. Slim as it may have seemed, I tasted the possibility that someday I might ascend to my rightful position as Sovereign, and I began formulating my plan," his eyes shifted to the left and right, as though he were looking for a way to escape.

"Another idea had occurred to me: I considered defecting to the Consortium, where I knew I'd be handsomely compensated for what I'd given them over my years of service. But, despite my betrayal, I enjoyed the life I'd established on Felis Prime and did not relish living under Factotum Mar; so I decided to change the fate of the world in which I lived by removing the impediment to my future. That was when I knew I had to eliminate the Sovereign," he took a few shallow breaths and cleared his throat, shifting his eyes toward the Prosecutor, who nodded, silently encouraging him to continue.

"By this time, I was actively subverting the authority of Sovereign Sayoose at every opportunity, though not in any way she might notice: I guided the Cadre to move certain agenda items in order for them to be acted upon quickly enough. When called to Counsel the Sovereign, I provided intentionally misleading advice based on what I knew from my communications with Factotum Mar," he swallowed hard. "This put Alliance forces at a distinct disadvantage in certain situations, and resulted in the loss of more lives, but it was all in the service of my supreme goal, to destabilize the Alliance and discredit Sovereign Sayoose. Unfortunately, I suspect that the Sovereign surmised my duplicity. She created the position of First Advisor fifty years ago, a position that had never before existed, and would certainly not have been filled by a Guardian of all people. Instead of relying on a member of her Cadre she chose to trust the counsel of her Prime Guardian … she chose *him* over me, her First Counselor!" He seemed outraged by the slight, "But," he managed to calm himself, "in truth, I couldn't blame her; Prime Guardian Dragar has turned out to be a far better man than I have ever been, and far more trustworthy. Certainly more worthy of the Sovereign's trust than I ever was," he mused, seemingly lost in his own thoughts for a moment.

In the Court, a few rows behind where the Prosecutor sat, Sovereign Sayoose smiled to herself. She had, in fact, created the role of the First Advisor only partly as a result of her suspicions regarding the First Counselor, although she had been ignoring much of his advice. What the former First Counselor had not taken into consideration when he began feeding the Sovereign disinformation was that he was not the sole source of her information. In the Alliance the Sovereign received regular briefings from the First Counselor of the Cadre, as a representative of the entire Cadre, but also from the Administrator of the Alliance Security & Intelligence Services, as well as from Command Officers of the Unified Armed Services, who reported to the Sovereign's office regularly. It was the ASIS Administrator, however, who had easily recognized that the information the First Counselor was providing was not necessarily in the best interest of the Alliance. Both the Sovereign and the ASIS Administrator had suspected that Regar was intentionally trying to lead the Sovereign astray with his poor advice, but they had not been able to find any proof to prove he was acting maliciously.

It had still been more than enough for Sayoose and it had prompted her to create the role of the First Advisor. In truth, she had chosen Commander Dragar for the position not only because she distrusted the advice coming from her First Counselor, but because she had come to trust Dragar's advice. She also enjoyed the company of her Prime Guardian. Given her background in the military she believed that Commander Dragar had more to offer than his abilities as a trained commando. Her instincts, as usual, had been correct. Dragar had served brilliantly since being appointed. She was only surprised that Regar's betrayal had been going on for so much longer than she had first suspected.

Regar resumed, "I continued my treacheries against both the Alliance and the Sovereign. Even after she created the First Advisor position, I never once considered that I was under suspicion. Pride has an odd way of shielding people, I suppose, but then, I thought my dreams were on the verge of being fulfilled. Then, as though Caiphus himself had answered my prayers, I awoke one day and the Sovereign had simply disappeared, without a trace. Of course, I now know that it was all part of her trap to capture me in my deceit, but ... at that moment, for the tantalizing span of three years, I truly believed that I was on my way to becoming the next Sovereign of the Alliance. I would have as well, had it not been for the cursed Guardians and their persistence, may Caiphus ..." he paused, "they *had* to find her, and she dangled that Terran star in front of me, something Factotum Mar couldn't resist, in the hopes that mining it would eliminate the Sovereign, along with the planet. Yes," he added hastily, "I admit, I recommended to Factotum Mar that he send a Fire Team to ... to deal with *her* while she was on Terra," he tried to laugh, and it again emerged as a grotesque cackle, making him sound even more deranged.

"I suppose part of me knew they would fail," he blinked a few times, "I knew that Prime Guardian Dragar would have remained with the Sovereign once she had been located, but by that point I really didn't care. How could I?" He cackled again, this time for several long seconds before continuing, "I admit it, I was desperate, but I don't care ... and what does it really matter at this point? So, I sent another five people to their deaths, but these five were from the Consortium. But no, that's not really true, part of me honestly believed that the Fire Team would be able to overwhelm him ... that one man. After all, there were five of them and only one Guardian, how could Dragar hope to stop *five STAWS commandos*?" He sounded genuinely awed by the feat committed by the Prime Guardian, perhaps forgetting that the Commander was one of the most decorated Alliance Special Combat Armed Response Corps commandos in the history of the Felis Alliance.

"I knew they would not have allowed her to remain unguarded once she had been located," he sounded deflated, "and when I saw the reports about the star in the Terran system, I knew I had to tell Factotum Mar about it," there was not even a trace of contrition in his voice, though the Prosecutor was wondering if the man even understood the ramifications of what he was saying. He was confessing that he had coldly planned and plotted the genocide of an entire planet, simply to expedite the assassination of the Sovereign, all in the misguided hope that he *might* be appointed the next Sovereign by the Board of Governors of the Stellar Mining Bureau. Prosecutor Marhlor was not sure as to how much more of this she could take, but the former First Counselor seemed to be near the end of his response. With some reluctance she nodded for him to continue.

"Even though it was a clear violation of the Callisto Treaty, Factotum Mar couldn't resist the idea of attempting to mine that stellar body," Regar continued, "especially after he had received the information about the elemental outgassing levels. It was as though I had sent him a thousand freighters of Beryllium 8: he was ecstatic, and dispatched the mining vessels, along with the Battlecruisers to accompany them into the Terran system. I had warned them of the presence of Helios-2, but I'm fairly certain the pride of the Factotum failed to believe that such a small ship would be able to do anything against his Battlecruisers, but what else could I do?" he sounded genuinely pained that this time his advice had not been followed, and he was: his plan had failed.

"When it was reported that the Battlecruiser had successfully fired upon Terra I honestly believed my plan was going to work, that it had worked, even if the Terran star had been saved and Factotum Mar was disappointed about losing its treasures," he paused, then added quietly, "not to mention being caught blatantly violating the Callisto Treaty … but, that would be his burden to bear, not mine. He knew what he was doing, just as I did," once again, he tried to look down, but the force-shields frustrated his effort.

Staring straight ahead at the First Tribunal, he continued, "When I was informed about the death of the Sovereign I convened the Special Session of Cadre, which was when my betrayal was ultimately exposed … and when I performed my final act of treachery. It was then that I personally attempted to assassinate the Sovereign, while she was in the form of that infernal Torgon … detestable creatures. Which brings me to the present, and my appeal to you, and my request, once again, that you view these actions as mine alone. I acted alone, without the influence of anyone else. My wife had nothing to do with my actions; there is no need for her to face a trial of any sort," he paused for a moment, trying to take a deep breath which proved to be impossible. He then added, "My apologies, Prime Justice … Justices. It's just that my wife, my Lareena, is the only bright light to have entered my life. I know that I can endure the Ultimate punishment knowing that she has escaped that fate. Thank you for allowing me to address the Court." Clerk Sistu adjusted the force-shields to permit him to sit and his body lowered into his chair, like a marionette dangling on its strings.

Prosecutor Marhlor looked pale and stunned after listening, but she was not sure what she had expected. She had simply wanted something for the record, so that the betrayer of the Cadre would have told something of his story before being sentenced, though it was likely a foregone conclusion as to what that sentence would be now: he was certainly not going to receive the lesser punishment for his crimes. After turning to the Prime Tribunal, Prosecutor Marhlor said, "I have nothing further to inquire of the Defendant, Prime Justice, thank you for this opportunity to address the Court."

"You may be seated," the Prime Justice replied, and turned to her two colleagues.

After whispering amongst themselves for a few moments, Prime Justice Renata turned toward the table where the two Advocates were sitting, and addressed the former First Counselor, "Defendant Regar," she began, her voice clear and controlled, "ordinarily my colleagues and I would adjourn at this time to consider our verdict, but you have made that unnecessary by virtue of the fact that you have admitted your guilt and, as you stated, thrown yourself on the mercy of the Tribunal. What we have heard here today has, quite frankly, turned my stomach, and I am not sure there is a punishment suitable for one such as you within our Justice System," she glared at him, making him whither inside. "You have not only betrayed the entire Alliance, putting the lives of trillions at risk, and I am not exaggerating, you directly plotted to destroy over seven billion lives, on one planet alone," she could not hide the contempt she felt, but continued speaking, managing to control her voice. "By the grace of Caiphus, your plan failed, but only thanks to the heroics of the three Guardians of the Sovereign: I speak specifically of Commander Dragar, perhaps the greatest hero to ever don a uniform in any branch of the Unified Armed Services; Captain Pertu who happens to be amongst the most exceptional pilots in the Alliance; and Tactical Sergeant Brem, one of the finest soldiers in all of the Unified Armed Services. We shall be indebted and eternally grateful to these three Guardians for an eternity," she nodded toward the Guardians, who were sitting on either side of the Sovereign with the hulking Commander Dragar sitting behind her, next to Sergeant Candille, their new citations clearly displayed on their uniforms. Each of them had been awarded the coveted Beryllium Cluster for their actions in saving both the Sovereign and the Terran system, not to mention the entire Alliance.

"Your blatant acts of mass murder, in the furtherance of your personal relationship with Factotum Mar is, in a word, sickening. I cannot think of anything more despicable than someone who would deprive others of their rights and freedoms for their own personal gain; it goes against the underpinning of everything that the Felis Alliance has stood for since the passing of the Pan-Universal Alliance Charter of Rights and Freedoms, the abiding foundation of our society. If you were so dissatisfied with our lifestyle you should have chosen to defect rather than betraying the lives of those who worked so hard to provide you with that lifestyle you claimed to enjoy so much," she paused to refer to the datapad on her desk, then looked back at the Defendant.

She nodded toward Clerk Sistu, who made an adjustment to the force-shields restraining the Defendant, "I shall now reveal why your wife is not facing the charges that were brought against her, which included spying for the Ursus Consortium, the manipulation of an Alliance Bureaucrat, to wit, the First Counselor of the Cadre, and Bearing a False Identity as a Consortium citizen while living within the Alliance, among other things, which need not be mentioned as they are no longer germane to this Tribunal," the look of confusion on Regar's face was soon replaced by horror. "Your wife, Defendant Regar, is dead. She committed suicide before her transfer from the Detention Center on Felis Prime, while meeting with her Advocate."

It was all too much for Regar's already fractured mind to process. His only hope had been that his wife, his precious Lareena, would continue while he paid for the crimes that had been committed, even if she had played a role in them ... but that could not have been the case ... how could she have played a part in this horror? His head was spinning out of control as he tried to summon the final images of their time together, but the memories were blurring together as the weight of the words of the Prime Justice pressed against his consciousness like a hammer on stone. It was too much to accept. How could she have died without him, he wondered, and then he remembered: she had whispered ... late one evening, so many years ago.

It had all been the perfume, of course, but that had opened his senses to his love for her, right from the beginning; when he inhaled that exotic scent he was overcome with the most wonderful feelings. Feelings that carried him away beyond space and time, into another dimension. But another memory was emerging, something Lareena had said about dental work that had been performed sometime around when they were married. She had taken him to the same Dentist, a few days later, after he suddenly developed a violent toothache in a rear molar. It had taken place on their return visit to Altus 9, where they had met. He remembered that the Dentist had replaced the tooth with a crown that looked as good as the real thing. At least, that was what he had been told by the Dentist.

Lareena told him the truth after one of their lovemaking sessions, when he was so intoxicated by the touch of her flesh, and the perfume, she could have told him she was a genomorph and he would not have cared. He detested everyone from Tarlos II, especially those who hailed from the southern continent of Waylacor, the home of the shapeshifting genomorphs, but that was not what she had revealed. It was something far more sinister, far more intriguing. Lareena had revealed that the crown was an artificial tooth and it was quite special, only to be used as a last resort: it contained an irreversible neurotoxin for which there was no known antidote. It would be fatal within a few seconds. All he had to do to crush the tooth was bite down hard on the molar, which would fracture it, releasing the poison. She whispered that she also had one, and would use it to escape being sent to trial for what she had done for the Consortium. Given the intoxicated state he was in, the news barely registered, but it was all coming back to him now, as were the ramifications of what it all meant: his precious Lareena really was dead.

No! His mind reeled, as the word repeated itself, she could not be dead. He could not be alone in this pathetic world, not while facing the Ultimate punishment. Just as he came to the realization that he could escape it all, that Lareena had provided him an opportunity to join her by choosing death rather than an eternity of suffering. Regar attempted to bite down on the molar, but as much as he tried, nothing happened. His muscles were frozen, as stiff as stone; he could not move a hairs-breadth. Desperately, he tried to look over at Clerk Sistu, but could not even move his eyes; he was only able to breath and blink, every other muscle movement had been frozen by the force-shields which had been adjusted to their full intensity.

Prime Justice Renata looked at the Defendant and raised the Stone of judgment in her hand so that everyone in the Court could see the large black orb. She struck the tablet it sat on, making a much louder sound than the previous time it had been used: this time she was using it to announce the decision of the First Tribunal: justice was being rendered. "We have arrived at our verdict," she announced, glancing over at Clerk Sistu, who caused the Defendant to rise from his seat, without moving any other muscles in his body. "It is our verdict," Prime Justice Renata continued, her voice loud, clear, and solemn, "that you are guilty of every charge which was brought against you." A ripple of approval went through the large room, but it was quickly silenced as the Prime Justice diverted her attention from the Defendant. She continued, "Having presented no defense against the charges, this Court sees no reason to show you either mercy, or leniency. You have betrayed the Alliance, deprived an unknown number of Alliance Citizens of their Charter Rights and Freedoms, attempted to commit a genocide against a Protectorate planet," she paused, taking a breath, "you have also participated in no less than three attempts to assassinate the Sovereign of the Alliance, and you have disgraced the office of the First Counselor of the Cadre. For these, and other crimes, you are being sentenced to the only punishment this Court has available to it, which most will feel is quite insufficient," a murmur of agreement passed through those in the Court, but Prime Justice Renata said nothing this time. "That said, I hereby sentence you to the Ultimate punishment: however," she paused, unexpectedly, "before you are taken to the Chamber of the micro-singularity, you shall be taken, while still under full control of the force-shields, to the Medical Center, where you shall see the Dentist who shall be directed to extract the tooth which was implanted by the Consortium Dentist at the direction of your former wife," she looked directly at the former First Counselor, as though she had just deflated his favorite toy.

"You shall *then* be taken to the Chamber of the micro-singularity, where you shall spend the next several millennia, banished to the Dark Zone, where each molecule of your body shall be stripped away while your consciousness remains; I can only hope that you consider the lives of those you destroyed by your actions and duplicity during that time, for that alone is the purpose of this punishment; otherwise, it is of no use. The First Tribunal has now concluded the case against Defendant Regar," Justice Renata declared, "as no defense was offered, no appeals may be entered against this ruling; this case is now considered sealed and the judgement entered as inviolable," the sound of the Stone of Judgment echoed loudly off of the walls of the Courtroom, as though saying to the Defendant, *all hope is lost*, and it was: he had thrown himself on the mercy of the Tribunal and they had shown him exactly what he had deserved.

Regar could only blink in response, but a tear rolled down his cheek as he realized the futility of his actions. He had no chance of escape now that the tooth had been discovered. Once it was removed he would be taken directly to the Chamber of the micro-singularity and that would be the end, or the beginning, depending on your perspective. His heart fell as the three Guardians, accompanied by a detachment from the Sovereign's platoon, and the Sovereign herself, appeared next to the Defendant's table.

Commander Dragar looked into the eyes of the former First Counselor and spoke, "I thought it might be a nice gesture, Regar," the name sounded like a slur, "if Tactical Sergeant Brem and I personally escorted you to the Medical Center, and then to the Chamber of the micro-singularity, unless you have any objections?" he laughed. Brem had retrieved the control device for the force-shields from Clerk Sistu, and was manipulating them to make him move toward the exit while a detachment from Lieutenant Kar's platoon formed a protective phalanx around him. They may have detested him, but they were not about to let anything happen before he began his sentence.

(*|*)

By the time they left the Medical Center and arrived in the bowels of the Stadium of Justice and were approaching the Chamber of the micro-singularity it appeared that the former First Counselor had resigned himself to his fate, which only made the Prime Guardian more concerned about the situation. It was unlike Regar to surrender, even in the face of superior forces. He was sure the man had no moral center, but Dragar was also quite certain that Regar never entered into a situation without an exit strategy, and this entire situation seemed to be going off too easily to the former ASCAR commando. All of his battle-hardened senses were on high-alert, and he was prepared for the worst. At his insistence Sovereign Sayoose had remained in the main portion of the Stadium with Captain Pertu, Lieutenant Kar, and the remaining members of the platoon that had accompanied them to the trial. Even though Pertu was primarily trained as a pilot, she was one of the Sovereign's Guardians. As such, she had received all of the rigorous training that any ASCAR commando went through once she had joined the Guardians. Dragar had personally tested her before she was entrusted with protecting the Sovereign, and he knew that she was more than to protect the Sovereign. He had no doubts that the Sovereign was perfectly safe while he and Brem accompanied the convicted Betrayer to his punishment. At the moment his main concern was that something might happen to Regar, not the Sovereign.

Dragar was expecting trouble and the last thing he wanted was to have the Sovereign anywhere nearby if his suspicions were correct: he would never forgive himself if something happened to her after everything they had gone through to find her after her prolonged absence. Not now. Not after finally capturing the Betrayer and convicting him of his crimes. As they drew closer to the Chamber of the micro-singularity the sound of the hum issuing from the room grew increasingly louder, and they knew their task was almost complete.

Once Regar entered through the door of the Chamber the sentence would begin and there would be no escape, but first, they had to get him through that door. As soon as the outer door was opened he would step into an automated device that carried him into the section of the Chamber designated for him, and the device would position him in front of the micro-singularity, which would then begin stripping away individual molecules of his body. In order to prevent him from dying from thirst or hunger he would be fitted with special feeding tubes that would provide him with all of the nutrients his body required in order to endure the rigors of the punishment, which could easily last several thousand years before it had completed its grisly task of dismantling his physical structure. Since it was such a horrific form of punishment, nobody wanted to face the Ultimate punishment; that was why it served as such a great deterrent to the most heinous crimes in the Alliance. Regar should have known better.

As the group approached the Chamber the sound continued to grow with each step until it almost sounded like the screams of those who were already experiencing the Ultimate punishment, but that was not the case. It was actually the sound of the micro-singularity being contained within robust force-shields, powered by the most powerful plasma reactors used in the Alliance. Each of the two main reactors was strong enough to provide the energy to one thousand Trans-Light drives on Battlecruisers twice the size of the Orono. It was all designed to run constantly, otherwise the micro-singularity could lose containment and begin consuming the Stadium of Justice, and then Felis Magoris itself, until the planet was eventually torn apart by the gravimetric forces. As a precaution, in case of a catastrophic failure, there were six smaller, backup reactors, making the chance of a loss of containment less than negligible. To make things even safer, the main reactors, and the backups, were serviced on a regular basis, making the chance of a failure incalculably small. As long as you could hear that sound, which was impossible to miss unless you were deaf, everything was fine. Enough power was produced by the two main reactors that they also provided all of the energy requirements for the Stadium, as well the entire Campus, where most of the Advocates and Clerks employed within the Stadium lived.

When they were about thirty paces from the door to the chamber the lights in the passage flickered unexpectedly, causing the group to stop in their tracks. It was an unanticipated development, but the First Tribunal had rendered its judgment and their job was to deliver the Defendant to his punishment, which was what they were doing; flickering lights would not stop them.

"Guardian One, do you copy?" Commander Dragar heard over his implanted receiver.

"I copy you, LT, report," he replied to Lieutenant Kar, who sounded as though she was right next to him.

"Sir," she sounded breathless, "I was just informed by the Felis Prime Array about an unidentified, heavily shielded ship has entered low orbit over Felis Magoris, right over the Stadium of Justice. Sir, they're in the upper atmosphere. I've been told that they suspect it's a Consortium vessel," there was a pause, "watch your back, Commander."

Dragar cursed to himself. With much of the fleet deployed to protect the Protectorates and other member planets it had been a calculated risk to leave only a handful of Battlecruisers and other heavy vessels in orbit over Felis Magoris to protect the home world and Felis Prime. Unfortunately, these were deep space vessels and were not capable of flying into the atmosphere to pursue this ship. If it decided to fire upon the Stadium, they were completely exposed. Since it was directly over them, firing on it was out of the question as the debris would damage the Stadium. It was a lose-lose proposition. Either way, they had been out-flanked by the Consortium. This must have been the final piece of the puzzle that Regar had been counting on, which was why he had appeared so calm, Dragar thought to himself.

"Understood," he replied, sounding grim as he checked his PPD-77. He was annoyed that he did not have his plasma rifle with him, but nothing like this had been anticipated, and it was not really acceptable to walk around the Stadium of Justice wearing a Battle Pack, even if you were a Guardian of the Sovereign.

"On your toes, people," Dragar whispered, "we may have company," he nodded toward the former First Counselor, who seemed oblivious to what was happening around him. Tactical Sergeant Brem also checked his PPD-77, holding Regar's control panel easily with one hand.

After taking another few steps the lights flickered again, and then the passageway was plunged into complete darkness for a few seconds until the emergency lights came on, providing a soft glow in the passageway; at that same instant the sound of the hum coming from the Chamber of the micro-singularity stopped, which meant the main containment reactors had gone offline. Dragar aimed his gun at the prisoner, but he was standing perfectly still, restrained by the force-shields. "Try something … *anything* … and it will be the last thing you do," the Prime Guardian growled, but he was too late. Regar had not moved a muscle, because he could not, but Dragar watched helplessly as the former First Counselor of the Cadre, the Betrayer of the Alliance, simply disappeared as he was transported out of the passageway.

"LT, stop that ship!" Dragar shouted. "I don't care what it takes: *stop that ship*! They have the prisoner!" As he finished the hum from the Chamber of the micro-singularity resumed as the backup generators activated, along with the regular lights in the passageway, leaving the Guardians and members of the Sovereign's Guard standing there, looking around helplessly. Nothing could be done, unless one of the Alliance vessels in orbit managed to capture or destroy that ship, but they all knew that the chances of that were desperately slim.

Dragar looked around a moment, shaking his head in disbelief. He could not believe it had even happened, and yet, he had just witnessed Regar being transported right before his eyes. Why had he not just shot the man, he wondered for a brief instant, but quickly dismissed the thought: he had wanted to see the Betrayer of the Alliance pay for his crimes; death would have been too easy for him.

He shook his head again and called Lieutenant Kar, "Report, LT, what's the status?" he was expecting to hear that the ship had escaped and braced himself for the inevitable.

"Sorry, sir," came the reply, her voice filled with sadness, "they knew exactly where to go and made it past the few armed Alliance ships that were in orbit without even being noticed," he could hear her take a deep breath, "and sir," she continued, "the vessel was identified by the Array: it was the personal cruiser of Factotum Mar. We don't think he was on board, but there's no doubt that he was behind this now."

Dragar was fuming; of course it had been Mar's personal Cruiser, he thought to himself, and they had used a Long Distance Matter Transporter, technology which had been stolen from the transport ships that the Betrayer had diverted into Consortium territory. Dragar wondered what else the Consortium would have been able to steal from those transport vessels, but the answer came sooner than he had expected.

"Commander," Lieutenant Kar's voice penetrated his thoughts.
"Yes, LT?"
"Sir, the ship wasn't equipped with a T-L Drive, at least, I don't believe it was based on our sensor readings, but it seems to have had a propulsion system that we've never seen before. It might be a variation

of the recent Star Drive modifications, but if it is, it's something that has yet to come into service … I just don't know …" she trailed off, her frustration evident in her voice which conveyed her intense dismay at the situation; it seemed that the technological advantages held by the Alliance might be coming to an end, and that could only lead to more conflicts with the tenacious Factotum Mar.

"Alright, LT," Dragar replied, feeling equally deflated. "Don't worry about it for now; we're going to get him back; of that you can be assured. How's the Sovereign?"

A short pause made him begin to worry, then he heard a familiar voice, "I am fine, First Advisor. I believe the time has come for us to return to Felis Prime," there was a tinge of sadness in her voice, but he was relieved to know she was secure.

Commander Dragar and the others turned to retrace their path to the Court of the First Tribunal, "Yes, my Sovereign, we're on our way."

EPILOGUE

"Usage of the Advanced Genomic Manipulation Program allows for the substantial extension of life for those living within the Felis Alliance and the reparation of damage to those receiving treatment from the Program, which was ordinarily reserved to those born on non-Alliance planets when they joined the Alliance. Every organism ultimately succumbs to death; the purpose of the AGMP is aimed at preventing this from happening for as long as possible by treating age as a disease, thus preventing an organism from becoming overwhelmed by the processes of both disease and age until it becomes impossible to maintain a satisfactory quality of life. Identifying age as a disease enabled Alliance scientists to not only eliminate most diseases, but increase the quality of life of virtually every Citizen within the Alliance."

[...]

"While the AGMP has prolonged the lives of Alliance Citizens, for those entering the Alliance it has become an effective therapy for those who have not had access to advanced medical technologies. For those who had been in ideal physical condition in their youth the Genomic Therapy had the most dramatic effects on their bodies, with results that were difficult to believe possible. Variations in genomic expression found across multiple Sectors suggests that life originating on planets throughout Sector 0107, the Sector in which Terra is located, as well as other Sectors, should respond exceedingly well to the AGMP due to the similar conditions of their origins, resulting in radically extended life-spans."

[...]

Excerpted from *Report on Terran Exposure to the AGMP* by Doctor Rathbu, Chief Medical Technician and Research Associate, Felis Prime Medical Center

(*|*)

After being on Felis Prime for just over three months Tanya had begun referring to her grandfather as Bob, as he insisted everyone call him. He no longer looked the part of the grandfather she had grown up knowing, though he was still the same man, at least, for the most part. There could be no doubt that he had changed in ways she could barely describe since their arrival on this incredible orbiting city from their home world of Earth only a short time before. While he insisted that everyone he met call him Bob, most people also added his military rank out of respect, even though he had never served in the Unified Armed Services of the Felis Alliance. Both Colonel Bob and Tanya had become celebrities on the orbiting city, with almost everyone they met asking them to relate stories of their lives back on Earth, or Terra, as most people referred to the planet.

People seemed particularly fascinated by how the Colonel had risen through the ranks of the military, having seen active service in three different wars. They seemed intrigued by the fact that the wars had been fought between different nations on Terra, something that seemed quite alien to those living on Felis Prime. What was even more unusual about Colonel Bob's history as a warrior was the fact that the Alliance had not experienced an all-out war in the living memory of many of its Citizens. While it was true that there had been several isolated battles with the Ursus Consortium, many of which had been extremely vicious, the two organizations had managed to avoid a full-blown conflagration thanks to the numerous treaties that had been negotiated between the two organizations. Diplomacy had won out, preventing the two groups from being thrown together into an overt conflict, though it seemed questionable as to whether that was something the Consortium truly desired after recent events.

Colonel Bob and Tanya discovered that the people of the Alliance loved to hear new stories, and the two Terrans had more than their share to tell, especially the Colonel; after serving as long as he had in the Army, though he realized he was little more than a babe compared to the average Alliance Citizen. Tanya considered herself extremely fortunate that she had always enjoyed listening to the stories her grandfather had loved to tell her while she was growing up, and she had made many notes about them as well, all of which she had diligently entered into her precious laptop. She knew that she would be able to write many books based on his life back on Earth, and they would be unlike anything the people of the Alliance had ever seen. All she had to do now, she knew, was write them, and gramps was not a writer. He had already told her that she was welcome to any of his stories for her work. He had other things that he wanted to do with his time.

Thanks to the Genomic Therapy they had received Bob had more than enough energy to talk to all of the interesting people he had been meeting since arriving on this fantastic orbiting city. On top of that, for the first time in many years, he finally knew that his faculties were not abandoning him, as he had been so convinced they had been when they had arrived. He had been quite certain that he had been losing his mind, especially when he had that encounter with the talking cat. He had to admit it, the whole thing still rattled him when he allowed himself to think about it; but he was willing to let it go, so long as he did not have to deal with too many other talking critters. At the same time. he had to concede that the idea of those Torgons still sort of bothered him, but he had come to understand that the Alliance was filled with many intelligent life-forms quite unlike anything one might encounter on Earth.

One thing was for sure, Bob thought to himself, the people here did not discriminate the same way they did back home; people came in a variety of shapes, sizes, and colors, and it seemed to make no difference to anyone. This was something he truly appreciated as a man who had lived through the tumult of the Civil Rights movement. He had seen terrible ugliness, right in his own backyard, and knew that this was the right way for things to be; the truth of the matter was that the Torgons were really adorable: you just had to get past the fact that they could speak inside your heads, which could be a bit disconcerting, but they were truly harmless creatures. After he and Tanya had met with the Sovereign she had insisted there was nothing wrong with his mind, assuring him that the episodes he had witnessed while she was in the form of a cat were entirely as he had suspected. It provided him a small sense of comfort, but having all the symptoms disappear after going through the Genomic Therapy was even better; it was something for which he could not thank the Alliance enough, except by giving them the only thing he had to offer: his life and experience as a soldier.

In truth, the absurdity of the entire thing had to make the Colonel laugh, though he was certain that if he had been given an opportunity to tell any of his old doctors at the Veteran's Administration that he had suspected his granddaughter's cat had been reading his newspapers they would have locked him up, without asking any questions; those VA doctors were notorious for having no sense of humor. It went without saying that mentioning he had also suspected that the cat had been turning on the stereo was completely out of the question. But, he thought to himself, smiling wistfully, that was all behind him now. He had been lucky: things could have been quite different, and not for the better: Tanya had rescheduled his appointment with Doctor Samford for him at the VA, after the doctor had cancelled it, for the day after their house had been vaporized by the Consortium ship that had tried to kill them. So, it was probably just as well that things had worked out as they had. Missing that appointment turned out to be a blessing, he realized: being considered dead to people on Earth was preferable to being locked away for being considered insane. Thanks to the treatments he had received it was as though he had been reborn in both body and mind. So much had changed it seemed as though the universe had been completely transformed, right before his eyes. Doctors on Earth had warned him about the possible onset of dementia, or senility as one young doctor who could not have been more than thirty-five had called it, giving him a patronizing wink.

"It happens," the young whelp had said, as though that made it something he should willingly accept. It had not helped matters that he had encountered a talking cat, but he now knew she had simply been the leader of an alien Alliance, visiting the Earth on a vacation.

Now, his mind was sharper than ever, and he had the body to match.

Once the Genomic Therapy had begun it was as though Colonel Bob had stepped into a time machine: his mind had been restored, and his body began to quickly follow. While Tanya had not aged nearly to the same degree as her grandfather, or experienced any of the ravages of illness associated with age, the Genomic Therapy had still had a dramatic effect on her, making her feel as though she had more than triple the energy than before the beginning of the treatments. Her capacity to concentrate and focus her mind had improved dramatically, as had her creative abilities, increasing to such an extent that even before the treatments had ended she managed to complete the novel she had been writing after only a few days by using the down-lining technology that she had been introduced to rather than having to type the words out on her laptop. She still loved the machine, if only for the connection it provided her to home, which was how she still thought of the Earth. She knew that it would be a long time before she would ever see the planet on which she had been born, but she was willing to wait.

Bob not only felt like a young man again, he looked like one: he barely recognized the face looking at himself when he saw his reflection in the mirror. He still kept his hair short, but it was growing back, and quickly. For the first time in many years he had visited a barber to have it trimmed to the close-cropped military style that he had continued to wear even after leaving the Army. More importantly than his hair was the way the treatment had changed his skin and body: his wrinkles had disappeared as his muscle-tone returned, and the pains that had ravaged his body for the past several few decades due to the infernal arthritis his own doctors had been unable to do anything about, except prescribe the damn pills that had been eating his stomach, had completely disappeared. No, Bob thought to himself as he jogged around the track in the Recreation Center one more time, increasing his speed to feel the joy of pushing himself as he had not been able to do for longer than he could recall, all of that was clearly behind him now. He felt as though he was once again a young cadet in the Army.

He was now in much better shape now than he had been when he had finished at Boot Camp. Now that his memory had been restored he could clearly remember his days with the 32nd Infantry Division and their time training at Camp Beauregard, in Louisiana. That was before he had been sent off to fight the Nazis, after the United States had joined the Second World War, though there were some memories that were not as sweet as others. War was not something he wanted to remember all that well, though it had definitely played a large part in his life, but he remembered it as well as it was yesterday. He had served his nation, and the world, in defeating the scourge of fascism as Hitler and the Nazis tried to devour Europe and North Africa, not to mention what their allies had attempted to accomplish.

Now that the Genomic Therapy treatments had been completed, along with the Up-lining Treatments, which had allowed the two Terrans to learn the equivalent of several thousand years of schooling in a matter of weeks, he and Tanya were unlike any Earthers alive.

Up-lining was a system developed in conjunction with the AGMP and enabled Citizens of the Alliance to enhance their learning process by directly implanting knowledge into the brain through the use of synaptic injections. It made it possible for people to learn something in as little time as it took to receive an injection of the specially encoded genetic material containing the desired knowledge. When someone was interested in a particular topic, or course of study, they accessed the materials they wanted to learn through the vast Alliance Educational Library Database and the knowledge would then be encoded into an injectable serum. After being injected, it would be up-lined directly into their brains by using specially encoded segments of RNA that were allowed to pass through the blood-brain barrier, finding the appropriate places in which to implant themselves within the memory center in the brain. The procedure takes place almost as easily as you could have memories and ideas down-lined to a datapad.

Through the use of synaptic injections, it was now possible to learn what might have taken a student several years in a classroom in only a matter of seconds, the time it takes for the injection. Once the injection is done the material is accessible or useable within a few hours, after the encoded segments had an opportunity to become fully incorporate within the brain in a process referred to as *Memory Settling*. Most people allowed themselves a good night's sleep to provide their new knowledge an opportunity to become active, but in some cases where it was necessary to use the material for specific purposes, treatment could be performed in the morning and the knowledge could be accessible by the end of the day, even sooner if the individual allowed themselves some time to rest.

Synaptic injecting worked on the principle that memories were stored in one of the most advanced computers in existence, the human brain. Memories were stored using a series of chemical and bio-electrical markers, then encoded onto RNA sequences which Alliance researchers manipulated according to each specific injection, allowing new memories and knowledge to be up-lined as though new software were being installed onto a datapad. This provided people with the ability to learn at speeds that had not been thought possible.

People could now spend more time enjoying their new knowledge and abilities rather than spending years of time repeating the lessons that traditional learning through aural and visual reinforcement would require. Once this method of education had been introduced into the Alliance's Educational System the effectiveness of their training programs improved by several orders of magnitude. They never looked back from that point of success. Programs involving physical elements still took time as people had to practice the skills in order to perfect their coordination, but the mental elements could be mastered, quite literally, overnight rather than spending months or even years in classrooms.

People who would have never considered pursuing advanced degrees now routinely achieved several, while continuing to enjoy their careers, or changing them if they desired. After humans in the Alliance were freed from the drudgery of manual labor by Synthetic Intelligent Living Systems those who chose to work in a particular area did so out of a genuine desire to do the work rather than out of an obligation or a need to make money. Thanks to the proliferation of SILS nobody had any excuses to remain in a position they found unfulfilling when they could be retrained for virtually anything thanks to the new technology. If someone had a desire to learn how to play a musical instrument it was now possible for them to learn everything they needed to know about the technique required to master the instrument with a simple injection; the rest of their time could then be spent on the pleasurable part of learning how to play the repertoire rather than dealing with the technical elements involved in mastering the instrument, which many considered the most tedious part of any art. Ironically, this facility in learning actually led to more people seeking out teachers than ever as they sought advice on how to better interpret the music they could now play. People who were serious about learning the repertoire wanted to play it well, and the best way to do that was by working with someone who had been performing the music for many years.

When Bob and Tanya began their indoctrination into the ways of the Felis Alliance they started by up-lining the history of the company and everything any Citizen raised within the Alliance would have learned about the Stellar Mining Bureau. They also learned about the history of the Alliance and its massive bureaucracy, as well as the challenges involved in running the organization. After that, they were offered the opportunity to explore the vast catalogue of courses available to every Alliance Citizen from the Alliance Educational Library Database, and the two Earthers took full advantage of what was offered to them. Education, after all, was free to Citizens of the Alliance: who would turn down the opportunity to learn as much as they could when it took less time to complete an advanced degree than it took to receive an inoculation against the Verkallian Pox? Both Bob and Tanya had received inoculations against the Pox as a standard protocol, and there had been no pain. Injections were performed through a trans-dermal injector which required no needle, a much more pleasant way to receive a shot, in Bob's mind, than the menacing needles he had been subjected to when he had gone through his days back in basic training.

Having spent much of his life in the military it was not surprising that Colonel Bob decided to study Military History, Strategy Methods and Tactics, Political Science and Diplomacy, Military Technology, Advanced Weaponry Design, and several other things that brought his mind up to date with his body and his desire to serve the Alliance in a practical manner, which he believed was now as in shape as any other member of the Unified Armed Services. He also decided to take an advanced degree in Alliance Language Arts. Even though English was the main language of the Alliance, and was spoken on most planets, Bob felt it would not hurt for him to learn some of the most common languages spoken in the Alliance. Much to the surprise of Tanya, most traces of his accent disappeared, practically overnight.

At the end of his treatments he asked the doctor who had been administering the Genomic Therapies if he believed he would be able to pass the exams to serve in the UAS.

Looking at him the doctor smiled and said, "Colonel, if they *don't* let you serve, it will be the biggest scandal to hit the Alliance since the Betrayer escaped."

Hearing that led Colonel Bob to seek out the one man on Felis Prime he felt he could call on, though he was not particularly thrilled with the prospect of meeting the imposing Prime Guardian after the man had burst through his front door like a wild-man, even though it had been to save his life, under which he had not been under any obligation. Dragar had been there to save the Sovereign, not him, or his granddaughter, for that matter. Prime Guardian Dragar was definitely not someone that Colonel Bob wanted to mess around with, but after meeting so many people during his short time on Felis Prime, he really did not know who else he could turn to with his problem.

He was surprised that his request for a meeting with Commander Dragar was met with enthusiasm. Dragar seemed genuinely pleased at how successful the treatments had been at reversing the ravages of age.

"How are you feeling, Colonel?" the Guardian asked cordially, as they sat down to meet in the outer office of the Sovereign. He smiled warmly at the Colonel, now dressed in clothes more fitting a civilian than a member of the Unified Armed Services, which was precisely what he wanted to discuss with the Guardian. He had rather enjoyed the feel of the uniform he had been given to wear when he and Tanya had first transported onboard Helios-2, and the Sovereign offered to bring them back to Felis Prime.

"Well, Commander Dragar," he began tentatively, "I suppose that's what you're going to tell me, isn't it?" Dragar looked slightly confused for a moment, then smiled. The last time he had heard the Colonel speak he had sounded quite different; he now sounded much more like his granddaughter. The accent was still a bit foreign to the Commander's ears, but nothing like the drawl the Colonel had spoken with before.

"Alright," Dragar said, "what *exactly* would you like me to do for you?" he asked, looking appraisingly at the man sitting across from him. As he looked at him he was impressed to see that the Colonel looked as though he had been given an entirely new body. If he had not known that he had been coming to the office he would have never recognized him when he arrived.

"Well, Commander, it's like this," Bob began, gesturing to the clothes he was wearing, "this outfit just doesn't suit me," he was wearing a non-descript shirt and pair of pants that had a distinctly utilitarian look to them, "not when my body has been restored to fighting condition ... if you know what I mean." He stood up and flexed his arms, showing off his impressively formed biceps in the process.

Dragar stared at him for a moment and smiled. He understood quite well; he was acutely aware that the Colonel had served gallantly on Terra, and that seemed to be what he wanted to do for the Alliance. Everyone had been referring to him by his rank out of respect, but it seemed he wanted to use his experience and serve his new home. Dragar looked at him carefully before responding.

"I hear you've been doing some studying, as well as some advanced training since completing your treatments?" he asked, fully aware that the Colonel had become certified on each of the weapons used by UAS soldiers. Dragar had personally authorized the Colonel's access to the Training Facility used by the Guardians and the Sovereign's Guard, where he had been able to train under the close supervision of the facility's Weapon's Master. According to the reports Dragar had received, the Colonel was not only a quick study, he was a terrific shot with both the plasma-rifle and the PPD-77. He had also been training heavily every day for the last two months in the Recreation Center, and looked as though he could give most ASCAR commandos a healthy challenge in any situation.

The supervisor of the Center had been keeping the Prime

Guardian apprised of the Colonel's progress, and the reports had been more than impressive. He was putting in as much work as any active UAS member, if not more, and his daily times around the track and obstacle course had continued to improve once his treatments had concluded; his performance numbers were as good, if not better, than most members of the UAS. More impressively, Dragar had noted, considering his experience and the several advanced degrees he had now completed relating to the military, Bob was now more than qualified for a command position over any brigade, if not having earned the experience to be promoted to the rank of Brigadier General, or even higher.

Colonel Bob was nodding, "Yes, sir," he smiled, "I'm fully briefed on all UAS strategies and ops, as well as protocols for operations on every class of vessel in use in the fleet at this time," he lowered his voice, "in fact," he winked, "I've just completed an advanced degree in Weapons Design and could give you some ideas as to how you might upgrade the plasma torpedoes, to decrease the latency issues relating to their aiming you've been experiencing in the Carriers." He went on to explain how the Carriers could increase the accuracy of their weapon's tracking systems by upwards of 19% by integrating and coordinating their firing systems with those on the Interceptors, creating an expandable, flying, moving tracking system. Dragar just sat there, listening with his mouth hanging open. Everything the Colonel said was not only valid, it was technically and strategically brilliant, though Dragar had to admit, as far as a few of the technical elements went, some of them were over his head. He was, however, able to recognize that the man sitting before him possessed a brilliant tactical mind, one which they could not afford to squander.

After several more minutes Dragar raised his hands, ending the conversation, "Please, Colonel, I'm convinced," making the Terran grin from ear to ear. "I'm going to talk to Sovereign Sayoose," he was shaking his head, trying to process everything he had just heard. "I'm going to recommend you be granted a commission to the Unified Armed Services, and that you be given an assignment to the SPD," he saw the confused look on the face of the Colonel, and explained, "that's the Strategic Planning Division, which I doubt you've heard of because, even though it's one of the most vital parts of the Unified Armed Services, it's also one of the most secretive. The SPD is part of our Military Intelligence Department," he smiled, "some might say the most important part. I'm going to recommend that you be placed in the section responsible for Strategic Development of Weapons and Tactics. I'm quite certain that your experiences and knowledge will be of great service to the protection of the Alliance." He rose from the couch and gave the man a crisp salute, which the Colonel resisted returning knowing he was not in the military, at least not yet.

"Thank you, Commander, I don't know how to express my appreciation," he said, tears welling up in his eyes.

"Colonel," Dragar replied, a smile creeping across his face, "I have a feeling it's going to be the Alliance that will be showing its appreciation to you," he stepped forward, shaking the man's hand as he left the outer office, then turned to knock on the door to the Sovereign's office.

(* | *)

Sovereign Sayoose listened to her First Advisor while trying to keep her emotions from showing. She was pleased with his enthusiasm and desire to utilize the talents of the Terran, but after having lived in the same house with the man for three years she was not as convinced as he was of the Colonel's abilities to serve the Alliance. After a few minutes, however, her mind had changed, particularly after he had shared what the Colonel had described regarding improving the weapon's tracking systems on the Carriers, and the reports he had received from the Recreational Center and the Training Facility where the Colonel had been spending so much time. By every indication Colonel Bob was something of a military prodigy, which attested to the great talent and abilities he possessed before coming to Felis Prime. Now, thanks to the Genomic Therapy, and having taken advantage of the educational opportunities afforded him, the Colonel had transformed himself into something rarely seen within the Alliance, and they would be foolish to not take advantage of his talents if he was so willing to offer his services.

By the end of their meeting the Sovereign had transmitted the necessary messages to the Commandant of the Military Intelligence Department, assigning the newly minted officer to the Strategic Planning Division, along with her strong recommendation that he be assigned to the section for Strategic Development of Weapons and Tactics, as suggested by Commander Dragar. As Sovereign she declared Colonel Bob an active member of the Unified Armed Services, and promoted him to the rank of Brigadier General. She then asked her First Advisor to take a new uniform, replete with the appropriate insignia and the single gold star indicating his new rank to the apartment Bob shared with his granddaughter, with instructions to report to the SPD once he was appropriately attired. She also asked Dragar to convey a message to Tanya: she wanted to meet with her, as soon as it was convenient; there were a few things she wanted to discuss with the young Terran.

Tanya arrived at the Sovereign's office with Dragar; the smile on her face instantly told the leader of the Alliance that the young woman had been present when Dragar had spoken with her grandfather. "I don't know how I can ever thank you, my Sovereign," she said, her face aglow with the rejuvenation from the Genomic Therapy. Sovereign Sayoose smiled in return, nodding for her to take a seat as Commander Dragar quietly closed the door to give them some privacy.

"Thank you for coming, Tanya," the Sovereign said, her voice quiet, "you have nothing to thank me for," she continued, "your grandfather has a special gift for military tactics, and the Genomic Therapy was more effective than anyone could have imagined, more than likely due to the wonderful physical condition he was in as a young man, which may have been due to his service in the Army on Terra."

Tanya nodded, remembering the pictures of her grandfather in uniform when he was younger. She suddenly felt a bit nostalgic at the realization that all of those family photographs, including all of the photos of her grandmother, had been vaporized by the Consortium attack on their home. "Well, all the same," Tanya replied, "Col ... I mean, *General* Bob is truly thrilled at having the opportunity to serve again, and I'm certain you will not be disappointed with your decision. I've known him my whole life; he's one of the smartest men that I've ever met," she looked quizzically at the Sovereign, "but that's not why you wanted to see me, is it?" she cocked her head to the right, looking around the office, wondering why she was really there. She knew how busy the Sovereign was, and she would not be taking time out of her hectic schedule to discuss the future of her grandfather.

She was surprised when the Sovereign began to laugh, while still smiling at her, "You are quite correct, my dear, that was not why I asked to meet with you," she looked down at the datapad on her desk. "First of all, I wanted to congratulate you on your novel," Tanya looked surprised, she had only finished the book a few weeks ago and had sent it to a few publishers that she had heard about on Felis Magoris, but none of them had replied. She wondered how the Sovereign could have even heard about the book.

Seeing her confusion, the Sovereign continued, "You must understand, your situation has become quite well known on both Felis Prime and Felis Magoris, which means that most people know of our relationship," she looked carefully at the young woman. "You happened to send your novel to a publisher, the largest in the Alliance, that happens to have close ties with the Office of the Sovereign," she smiled, "they publish all of my writings, which happens to be quite considerable, as I am sure you are aware of by now," Tanya nodded. She had read several of the Sovereign's books, and was extremely impressed by the breadth of her work. "When they saw your manuscript they were quite intrigued. Since I know you so well, the publisher asked if I would act as an intermediary, and I agreed," she paused, "so long as you have no objections, of course?"

Her question caught Tanya off-guard, but she knew that writers, and other artists, were not paid in the traditional sense in the Alliance; they were provided with everything they required to live and produce their works, and would be provided the opportunity to travel anywhere within the Alliance to find inspiration or research a new work. In every sense of the word it was a creative utopia. "Of course, that's fine," Tanya heard herself reply, knowing she truly meant the words.

"Excellent," the Sovereign replied, smiling. "Imprints Magoris wants to publish your novel, and they want to sign you to an exclusive contract for anything else you produce, either prose or poetry, for the next 15,000 years, a preliminary contract with the option to extend, or cancel, should you so desire," Tanya was stunned as she listened. "Your books will be made available to every downlining service once the editing process has been completed, over which you will shall, of course, have final approval." Tanya could hardly believe what she had heard: having final approval over the editing of her books? A 15,000-year *preliminary* contract? What more could she ask for?

"I ... I don't know ... what can I say?" she finally asked, blushing with embarrassment. Her editor on Earth would have given her left arm ... and leg for terms as generous as these, although she would have been slightly freaked out about the fact that no money would be changing hands, but this was a different world in which money was not an issue. All of her needs would be taken care of, and she would be able to write, travel, and do whatever she wanted with her life, without anyone questioning her.

"You could start with a *yes*," the Sovereign prompted, smiling at her, "unless there is something wrong with the offer?"

"*No!*" Tanya almost shouted, "I mean ..." she blushed furiously at raising her voice to the Sovereign, "my apologies, my Sovereign, and no, there's nothing wrong, and *yes*, I do accept," she began to laugh, giddy with joy as tears coursed down her cheeks. "I don't know how to thank you, my Sovereign, you've made me the happiest woman in ..." she paused, "well, I suppose the universe!"

"Wonderful, I am so pleased, but," she paused, "there is one more thing," her tone had become more serious. "Our technicians were able to down-line the contents of your device before the power source was fully depleted," she began, smiling at the Terran, "I am pleased to tell you that they were able to adapt a plasma-cell that will keep it running for the next several thousand years, though I understand you have found our datapads far more convenient, and easier to use. I also want to thank you: you have contributed a tremendous amount to our cultural database. I had no idea how much music you possessed on that device; it is truly outstanding. The complete works of Beethoven, piano, chamber and orchestral works of Schumann, most of Mozart's works, and several others; not to mention all of the books you have on the device. It is a treasure which we shall richly enjoy for many thousands of years. However," her smile disappeared, "there was also some questionable material, and that is what I really wanted to speak to you about," the Sovereign looked genuinely troubled and uncomfortable with what she had to say.

"I don't understand," Tanya said, "what's the problem?" she had no idea what might have been on her laptop that could cause the Sovereign such consternation.

"Well," the Sovereign continued, almost reluctantly, "it has to do with a work by one of the writers on your device, and please believe me, I only ask about this because of what happened after the trial of the former First Counselor and his escape from the Stadium of Justice. This was brought to my attention by one of the ASIS agents who happened to be inspecting the contents of your device," she quickly added, "it was a routine procedure, you must understand." Tanya nodded. She had learned a great deal about the security systems of the Alliance and knew that ASIS took things extremely seriously. Her Dell would have been looked upon with great suspicion as an alien device, so it did not surprise her at all that an agent had reviewed its contents.

Sayoose continued, "It is about the writings of a man by the name of Shakespeare," she was surprised that Tanya had started to laugh.

"Don't tell me," Tanya said, wiping another tear from her eye as she managed to stop the laughter, "It's from *The Second part of King Henry the Sixth*, Act Four, Scene two: a character by the name of 'Dick the Butcher' who utters the line: *'The first thing we do, let's kill all the lawyers.'* Am I right?" She asked, and then began laughing, while the Sovereign looked at her in bemused silence. Without waiting for her to respond, "Just wait until I explain his play, *The Merchant of Venice*, and the characters Portia and Shylock," she began laughing again.

This time the Sovereign smiled and nodded, there was no threat here. She was reminded again about what she had seen in this young woman and why she had chosen to stay with her when she had visited Terra. She also knew that Tanya, like her grandfather, would be a great asset to the Felis Alliance. Sometime in the future, Sovereign Sayoose knew, they would all be returning to that beautiful blue planet; it might take several years, she thought to herself, but it would definitely be worth it; the Earth was worth the wait.

~ fin ~

Continue reading for an exclusive preview of *Time Changers*, Book Two of the *Felis Alliance Series*.

PROLOGUE ~ FROM "TIME CHANGERS"

"Anyone following the Path must know that the Way of Kairtu is simple. All that must be done is adhere to the Three Laws of Kairtu.

"The 1st Law of Kairtu states: Be kind, one to another; treat each other as you would desire to be treated. In so doing you shall receive the same rewards that you have heaped upon others.

"The 2nd Law of Kairtu states: In all that you do, practice Love and love shall be returned unto you. Do this and you shall know peace and harmony in your life. You may not possess everything, but you shall not lack for Love and it shall sustain you through your most difficult trials.

"Most importantly, the 3rd Law of Kairtu states: Remember, Kairtu is jealous and watches over you continuously, smiting transgressors of Her Law with Love and gentleness."

From the *Sacred Scrolls of Kairtu*, Scroll I, Paragraphs viii-xi

(*|*)

A small creature sat high in the branch of a Bimba tree, contentedly wagging her tail while watching a few farmers toiling in the distant fields under the heat of the afternoon sun. She was mostly black, with a small patch of white between her eyes. She had white on her belly and front paws, making it appear as though she was wearing a pair of gloves. Her most impressive feature were her eyes. They were astounding, penetratingly orange, and unlike any other. Just by looking into them it was possible to see the intense intelligence possessed by the creature.

Her work for the day was done, so she was indulging in the opportunity to relax in the comfort provided by the great Bimba tree, which produced a comfortable umbrella of shade from the beating sun.

It was a favorite place for her to rest after tending to the family's crop of casa beans. She despised the bulbous beans, but they provided both food and something to trade in the village market, both of which they desperately needed in these difficult times. She recognized that it was necessary for her to do her part to contribute to the family's meagre income. It was essential, even though she was conscious of things that her family could not begin to know or comprehend, even if she spent an eternity trying to explain everything to them.

She had discovered that she knew things that nobody else could understand. There were many times when she still found that she was having difficulties understanding some of what was being revealed to herself, but at the moment, she knew, that was unimportant. What was important was that here, at this moment, she had to remain in this form for as long as possible. For as long and as often as possible.

It was something she knew, perhaps by instinct, but there seemed to be something more to the knowledge; a deeper understanding to the meaning behind her ability to shapeshift that only those on the southern continent of Waylacor possessed. It was something that lay hidden deep in the recesses of her memory, memories she knew she should not possess, that she had no business possessing, and yet, *they were there* ... just as the other memories were there. Mingling with so many other things, things she should not no, could not possibly know, and yet ... It was something that she knew, deep in the core of her being, just as she knew many of the other things, as improbable as it all seemed.

There were the memories of people that she had somehow known, somehow sensed, though she also somehow knew they did not exist, or no longer existed, at least not at this time, in *this* continuum. Somehow she knew that something had happened, something terrible, something cataclysmic, and unsettling to the continuum that had resulted in her returning to the planet of her childhood rather than where she should be ... wherever that was supposed to be. She knew where it was, but could hardly bring herself to believe that she was supposed to be living on some fantastic city, orbiting above the surface of another planet. It was beyond difficult to believe, and yet, the memories of that place were beyond real: she could see the city so clearly in her mind, it was as though she had walked through the corridors a thousand times and spoken to its residents more times than she had spoken to her own parents. If she closed her eyes she could see the domed structures as clearly as she could see the fields stretched out before her, and she knew it was real. In fact, she knew the memories were somehow more real, as odd as that seemed, than the life she was presently living.

At the same time, there were some memories that were more difficult to recall, though she seemed to be regaining more and more of them with each passing day. It seemed as though only twenty-five years ago she could hardly recall anything specific about the nature of the mighty Felis Alliance, but now, things were different. Now, she could remember so many things about the Alliance that she was thoroughly convinced they were not the senseless daydreams of a troubled young woman, as her father had thought when she first brought the issue up to him, about twenty years ago. No, now she was thoroughly convinced that she was both out of place *and* time. She *knew* that something had happened, something terrible, and she had somehow been displaced.

She also knew that *she had to get back there*: but how? That was the question that nagged at her, day after day.

While she tended the crops of casa beans she allowed her mind to travel through the increasing number of memories she had managed to recover over the last twenty-five years, treasuring each and every one of them, tending them just as she tended the fields. Each memory was cultivated with tremendous care; she reviewed the names and faces she had managed to recall day by day, agonizing over the ones she had trouble with, knowing that they were buried somewhere deep inside her mind. Somehow she knew that somewhere deep within her mind lay the key to the mystery, waiting to be revealed. If only she knew what she was looking for, she thought to herself, as she wagged her tail lazily in the heat of the afternoon.

Every recovered memory was carefully recorded in a small collection of notebooks that she had managed to purchase over the past several years, then hidden away in her room so she could study them when she was not working. By doing this she had been able to stir even more memories, while helping to solidify the ones she had already recalled. Each of the small notebooks was a treasured possession, and they were jealously guarded by being hidden away in a small hole in the wall of their stone house that was behind her bed, keeping them well away from prying eyes. She was not overly concerned with anyone finding her notebooks, but it was a precaution that she had to be cognizant of, especially after her parents had threatened to take her to the *Healer* when they had become concerned about her, several years ago. Now she knew it was better to record her memories in the notebooks, and that she should not be discussing them with anyone, particularly her parents.

Like many of the small farms in the area, her parent's farm sat on the outskirts of the small village of Tankanal which was a small, close-knit community, that had managed to survive by growing its own food and pooling its meagre resources. Most Waylacorians were proud of the fact that nobody on the southern continent ever died of hunger. Nobody lived lives of luxury, to be sure, but anyone who lacked the essentials of life were taken in as brothers and sisters. That was the foundation of the first Law of Kairtu: *Treat each other as you would desire to be treated. In so doing you shall receive the same rewards that you have heaped upon others.* It seemed that whether they believed in Kairtu or not, the idea of letting someone go hungry was simply unacceptable to the Waylacorians. Even those that found they had little to offer found they were able to find an extra meal to offer a traveler that was passing through their town, or a place to sleep if one was needed.

There was a weekly market in which merchants and farmers traded their wares, held in the center of each village next to the Place of Meeting, the spiritual focal point of every community. At least, it had been the focal point of Tankanal until three weeks ago when their Holy Man had passed from this world and gone to the Wellspring. Now, Tankanal was awaiting their new Holy Man, who would be arriving directly from the Temple of Kairtu in the city of Kintakar, the capital of Waylacor.

Nobody knew who the new Holy Man would be, but their expectation was that he would remain in Tankanal for at least as long as his predecessor, and he had served for over two thousand years in the Place of Meeting. His name had been Irsfakaar and when he died he had been a wizened old man, having lived over five thousand seven hundred years. Even though he seemed quite old when he had died she somehow knew that Irsfakaar should have lived much longer. Somehow she knew that Waylacorians were dying much younger than they should have been. Yes, she thought as she wagged her tail in the heat of the afternoon, her people may have been living for thousands of years, a length of time which seemed incredibly long at first glance, but her memories had revealed that shapeshifters should be living to ages that made that length of time seem insignificant.

As odd as it seemed, she was also quite certain that she was supposed to be much older as well, far older than her seventy years. When not in this form she looked as though she had just passed into adulthood, but her memories and physical sensations told her otherwise. It was for this reason that she practiced shapeshifting as much as possible.

Shortly after she began remembering things about the other continuum and taking on the form of the cat her father had confronted her, asking why she had assumed such an odd form. He was curious regarding the origins of such an odd creature and could not understand why she was taking on its form rather than what most shapeshifters on Waylacor tended to assume.

She had been expecting the question and replied without hesitation, "It is a cat, papa," hesitating to volunteer anything further.

He looked at her dubiously from beneath the wide brim of the hat he always wore in the fields, "*Cat?* What in the name of Kairtu is a cat?" he was understandably perplexed, never having heard of such a creature. It was a Terran word that she had not translated into the language spoken by her people.

Knowing it was necessary to provide some further explanation, she made up a story, "I had a dream," she had said, "where I imagined many wonderful creatures. This one, which I decided to call a *cat*, was one of them; I wanted to take on its form, and I enjoy the way it feels," she giggled at her own fiction, which made her father grin, much to her relief, "especially the tail, which is really quite enjoyable to wag," her smile was infectious, and she knew her father was believing the fictional story, "it is also quite useful for chasing away the Taka flies in the heat of afternoon, which can be quite annoying," she laughed, as he nodded in agreement.

Even as her father had nodded he swiped at a few of the harmless Taka flies that were flying around his head. They were harmless, but definitely annoying; they had a tendency to fly extremely close to your eyes and would occasionally fly right up someone's nose, especially while they were working in the fields, which made them all the more troublesome. Their name derived from their distinctive sound. After the insects landed on something and their six wings were folded against their multi-colored carapace they began making a repetitive clacking sound as they called out to their perspective mate. That *ta-ka-ta-ka* sound would be heard across the fields of the southern continent, often drowning out all but the loudest conversations. Once they had landed their mating calls would be heard well into the night, but only during the warmest months of the seasons, when it was still quite humid. Once it transitioned into the dry season the Taka flies were rendered silent. When it grew slightly colder, the flies all but disappeared. It was a sound that could be quite annoying after some time, but unlike the Pintaca fly, which would take a small chunk out of someone if they were not quick enough to swat them off of wherever they had landed, Taka flies were completely benign, except for the noise they produced.

After patiently listening to her explanation regarding the cat her father had nodded the way an indulgent parent might look at a child who had confounded them with some fantastic creation of their imagination, or some other tall tale that made them inwardly groan; he then walked back to their small home on the opposite side of the fields, shaking his head, but smiling. More than anything, he loved his daughter, but he still worried about her a great deal. She had never shown any interest in getting married, as the other young women in the village did when they had reached her age, and she rarely attended the services at the Place of Meeting. This was not something that was of too much concern to him since the teachings of Kairtu were quite clear on the issue of personal choice. Kairtu had insisted that the only people that she wanted in her Temple were those who desired to be there of their own volition. Anyone forced to attend would come to resent the teachings and reject them; it was better to love them and show them the truth of Kairturism by the acts of the believers rather than by trying to force an unbeliever into believing.

His daughter's independence was something that another parent might be more concerned about, but he had decided that she deserved the benefit of the doubt, yet he still worried. Still, if his daughter wanted to spend her spare time in the form of this strange creature, he had no reason to stop her: she was certainly not harming anyone; she was, after all, a shapeshifter. It was what they did, even if the forms she was choosing were not things found in nature. As her father considered his daughter's habit of making things up he wondered whether anyone else was shifting into a form they had conjured up from their dreams. He was quite certain that his daughter was the only one, but surely there could be nothing wrong with that. Or was there?

When he spoke to his wife about the situation she simply smiled, "Oh, leave the girl alone," she cooed, and the matter was settled.

A wise woman was not to be opposed, her father had wisely decided, and his wife was definitely not one to tolerate unnecessary contradiction. He still remembered how furious she had been when he had announced that he had decided to take their daughter to the Healer for *the Treatment* as a result of her erratic behavior, particularly the odd memories she had related to him. No. That would not be happening, he was told. On Waylacor women were not just the masters of the house, they were the heads of the family and the main decision makers. His wife had simply stared at him, shook her head, and the matter was settled. Nobody was going to see the Healer. It was a memory that still stung, but he knew that her wrath had been short-lived, and they had long since put the episode behind them, vowing to discuss such matters before any important decisions concerning the wellbeing of their daughter were made.

Even so, he was her father, and cared deeply for his child.

She knew that one of the reasons that her father had been so confused when he saw her in the form of the cat was that no such creatures existed on Tarlos. That was also another thing that she knew: deep down inside, she knew that the planet should have such creatures. Not cats, of course, but other creatures. She knew that there should be a variety of small mammals on the planet that should have evolved along different genomic paths as the people who dwelled there, and some of the creatures on the southern continent could even change their shapes, just like the Waylacorians. Even that knowledge was something she knew she should not have possessed. Her studies as a schoolgirl had not included anything along the lines of biology or evolutionary sciences. Nobody on Tarlos had studied such things for that matter. Science was not taken all that seriously on the southern continent. Waylacorians were still extremely superstitious; they were a people of great faith and the idea that they had evolved from lesser creatures, from thigs like clumps of bacterium or protozoa was simply inconceivable, even when a growing body of evidence was being uncovered indicating the truths surrounding evolution.

Evolution: that was another word she should not know.

People had been discovering fossils for many years in the stratified rock formations deep in the caves and foothills of the southern continent, but those who had been studying them seemed incapable of making the connections between the creatures entombed within those special rocks and those creatures alive today. *This is not how things are supposed to be*, she thought to herself.

Some of the first memories she had recovered were of the way her planet should be, of how it had developed into a technologically advanced world and a member of a pan-universal organization with trillions of citizens. She could clearly see Tarlos in her mind, as though she had been observing it from space, from the perspective of a vessel in orbit around the planet. In her mind's eye she could easily see many massive industrial centers, scattered across the face of the planet, along with thousands of artificial satellites and fantastic orbiting cities encircling the planet, but none of those things existed at the moment.

Some of the things she knew about the planet astounded her, though the knowledge was of little use to her at the present time. She even knew the navigational coordinates of the planet, that it was located in Universal Sector 0001, not that those coordinates would do her any good given her present situation. She also knew that Tarlos, should really have been called Tarlos II. It was also currently based on an agrarian economy and it had virtually no industry of which to speak, which was something else that was completely wrong. Right now, at this moment, the planet was devoid of all technology when, she knew, her people should have already been reaching out to the stars, travelling well beyond their own system into the neighboring systems. Tarlos II had been one of the founding members of the Alliance, but that was never going to happen based on the present state of the technological development of the planet. How could they travel into space if they could not even build a plumbing system that allowed people to ... she shook her head at the thought, driving it from her mind. She had spent a great deal of time considering this line of thinking and it had become a source of tremendous frustration, but no good would come out of such ruminations. What she needed was a way to escape this continuum, not more things to complain about. Complaining would only make her age faster and lead her to a premature death, and that was the last thing that she needed.

Regardless of the technological state that the planet happened to be in, there was one thing that she did know, though she was not sure how, since this was an agrarian world it should have made the conditions ideal for the coexistence of the human population and the other lifeforms, but that had clearly not been the case based on what she had been able to observe. Something had shut down the possibility of humans living within the biosphere in harmony with smaller creatures, and the southern continent was no exception. Something had somehow altered the balance of life, and that was a decidedly bad thing: nothing good would come out of such an imbalance.

She knew she should also not know of the small ape-like creature, their distant genomic relative, that also had the ability to change its shape. It was something the creatures did in order to prevent itself from falling prey to predators, but it had somehow disappeared in this iteration of Tarlos. Both the ape-like creature, which she remembered was called the *Taramin*, and its various predators, had simply vanished, and with it a great portion of the genetic history of the planet. Without the Taramin, and the many other creatures that no longer existed on Tarlos, she somehow sensed there was a precarious imbalance to life on this world that could not be sustained.

Tarlos was in danger of becoming an extinct world before it had even had a chance of becoming fully developed, but she believed there might be a way out of this descent into catastrophe.

Even though her memories did not include ever having studied the subject, she somehow possessed a profound understanding of biology and genetics, among many other things, such as the fact that there were thousands of other planets in the universe that were inhabited with people. People, humans that had evolved over the same genomic path.

Those living on Tarlos, however, believed that they were alone in the universe, if they even considered the universe as a state of being, but this was not the case. Other planets had life, and they were much like the people living on Tarlos, with one major exception. Humans had evolved similarly across the universe, but shapeshifters existed on only one location. For some reason, the shapeshifters, as they usually called themselves, or genomorphs as they should have been referred to, were only found on Waylacor, the southern continent of Tarlos II.

Something had gone wrong on Tarlos. It would have developed a wide variety of mammalian life, as had the majority of the planets with sentient life, and nearly all the planets with human life, but when the dominant genome had asserted itself most of the other mammals seemed to have mysteriously disappeared. Those that had survived were mostly smaller specimens that ended up as sources of food for the larger raptors that filled the skies, and the skies of Tarlos teemed with birds.

For some reason the birds on Tarlos had not only managed to survive, they had thrived. There were a tremendous variety from one end of the planet to the other. It seemed sometimes that you could not look up without seeing a flock of some sort flying from one place to another, and their calls were sometimes so loud it was almost ear shattering. There were some birds that could easily deafen an individual with their cries, but they did not usually travel in large flocks, otherwise they would have been extremely dangerous to the people.

In one village there had been one instance where a troublesome flock of Engrals had been plaguing the farmers for quite some time. Since the Waylacorians did not believe in violence the idea of killing the creatures seemed exceedingly cruel, even though they had been destroying their crops, but they had to do something. After consulting their Holy Man, in their Place of Meeting, he provided a solution: several of the youngsters in the village kept a vigil and would not allow the Engrals to land on any of the crops or any nearby trees. Many of them transformed themselves into larger Purple-winged Cartans, which the Engrals were deathly afraid of, and after a few days the birds were driven from the village. It was the first time that the Waylacorians had managed to engineer their environment, but they had not gone any further.

This was also wrong, but at the same time she understood that the reason the birds had emerged so successfully, in this continuum, was as a result of the abundance of the insect life that existed. Engrals were only a symptom of a larger problem. They had been attracted to an insect that was eating one of the crops growing in that particular village. Once the Engrals had disappeared, the farmers had to find another way to deal with the insects. Unfortunately, the Engrals had also been eating the crops, not just the insects. With such a plentiful food supply, the birds reproduced prodigiously. It was wrong, but it was also quite beautiful; although the insects also made life for the farmers quite difficult at times, as there seemed to be a bug that was attracted to every crop grown. Some years were particularly bad, which was why the Waylacorians had come to keeping the birds nearby.

One of the advantages of the birds was that they assisted the farmers in protecting their crops. Depending on what crops were being grown the farmers would keep a supply of birds around that ate the bugs which were particularly attracted to that crop. Her father had found that the Purple-winged Cartan was best suited to protecting their crops of casa beans. Unlike the Engrals, the Purple-winged Cartan only ate the Casaworm while leaving the casa beans alone. It was a beautiful bird, which she enjoyed having around. It had a call she enjoyed mimicking on those occasions that she took their form, when she was not in the mood of being a cat. The call began with a long, high-pitched trill, followed by a series of short chirps that ended with an ascending warble, which made it sound as if the birds were calling to one another, telling one another where to find the best location to find the Casaworm, their favorite food.

It only took a handful of Casaworms to devastate an entire crop, but with a few Purple-winged Cartans, four or six at most, the precious beans were protected. When the birds were not filling themselves on the hated Casaworms they would eat the flesh and seeds of the Bimballa fruit that grew on the Bimba tree, a sweet, pulpy fruit of which there was always an abundance since the trees produced far more fruit than could be eaten by the small population of the village. One tree could easily provide enough fruit for over fifty people, and it was the most common tree growing around the village of Tankanal. Unlike some of the other fruit trees in the area, the Bimba tree was able to produce fruit throughout the year. There was more of the fruit during the warm months, and it was a larger variety, but during the cooler months the fruit had a different taste, almost as though it came from an entirely different tree altogether.

Fruit from the warmest months could be fermented into a fortified drink the elders called Bimbala, which was served at special occasions, such as weddings and other celebrations.

Even with the abundance of the fruit provided by the Bimba trees, the poverty in the area was devastating, but what was most disturbing to her was the fact that the people seemed so disinterested, so apathetic in regards to broadening their horizons beyond their current state. Even as things like fossils were being discovered, few people seemed remotely interested in asking any questions or exploring any ideas pertaining to their origins. Somehow the curious nature of the Waylacorians had disappeared, replaced instead by a dangerous complacency that would, she feared, lead to their demise.

What it came down to was that life on this planet was out of balance, and the ramifications of that went deeper than the variety of birds in the air or animals wandering in the fields; it even affected the lifespans of the people living on the planet. It was something that troubled her greatly, but she was powerless to do anything about it, at least, at the moment she was powerless.

A time was coming when all of that would change. Until then, however, she would have to bide her time and wait.

It was easy to understand why there was such apathy towards progress, or the discovery of new ideas. It was not that her people were opposed to science, it was the circumstances of their lives. Producing sufficient food to sustain their families was a priority for everyone, and it required the involvement of nearly every person in their household to aid in the generation of enough income to keep the family alive, either through farming or trading in the markets. As a result, the advancement of scientific study on Tarlos had been essentially stunted. Leisure time simply did not exist, let alone the time to allow people to indulge in study for the sake of pure research.

Allowing people to take the time required to contemplate the world around them was simply a luxury that the people of Tarlos could not afford to take at the moment, not when feeding themselves remained a priority.

When people did take some time to reflect, it was usually to spend their time in the pursuit of spiritual enlightenment, and that was something that could not compete with this new area of study known as science. Those few who were released from the labors of the field dedicated themselves to the religious orders of the planet, and they were hardly interested in pursuing anything that had to do with experimentation in the pursuit of empirical data.

Schools on the southern continent of Tarlos barely taught children to read and write. Children were taught enough to aid in keeping records for their family farms and to assist in the markets, and to read the Scrolls of Kairtu. After that the children were expected to assist their parents in earning enough to care for their households. It was a difficult way to live, but those who lived there did not know any other life, but she did; she knew that struggling to grow your own food was part of her planet's ancient history, a history that they had left behind them thousands of millennia ago, before entering into an age of enlightenment, and great technological development that had seen the planet blossom. This was not the life the people on Tarlos should be leading today.

Struggling to scratch out a living with her bare hands was definitely not something she had been born to do, of that she was certain, and it was not about grandiosity, she just knew that there was another purpose in her life that extended far beyond the fields of the farm. Her people also had a purpose, a destiny, that was being squandered as they struggled against the sun that beat down upon their backs while they toiled in the fields. This was not the way things were meant to be on Tarlos, and it even extended to the way her people used their abilities to shapeshift.

While most Waylacorians who chose to exercise their ability as shapeshifters chose to restrict their use of the power to perform small feats, such as to change their height or some such nonsense but she knew there were far more practical purposes to be accomplished with the abilities she possessed. There were things that were of much greater importance to accomplish by changing one's appearance, which was why she had assumed the unlikely form of the cat. By transforming into a creature that had a faster metabolism, something else she should not know about, she understood that she would live to be much older than the other Waylacorians. She somehow knew that the more time spent in the form of another creature, particularly one with a faster metabolism than her natural form, the longer she would live. Of course, this had also led to some awkward situations, but her mind was quick and she had been able to adapt to the adversities she found herself in as a result of the knowledge she knew should not possess. She had chosen the cat as an image that had been unlocked from her memories over twenty years before, and represented one of the first things that she had remembered about her life in the great Felis Alliance.

It was a creature that she recalled having spent three years of her life in the form of while visiting a planet called Terra. Yes, as astounding as it was to believe, she had been to another planet. Her great mistake had been in telling her father about this when she first had the memory. She had not told him about the cat, but she had told him about some of the other things that she had remembered, which had nearly resulted in him having her sent to the Healer to receive *the Treatment*, but she cried out that she had only been joking. All of it had been an elaborate joke! Fortunately, before her father could drag her off to see the Healer, her mother had intervened, and her father, albeit reluctantly, decided that believed her. He also decided that harmony under the roof of his house required abiding by the wishes of his wife, and that meant that he could not have his daughter subjected to the torments of *the Treatment*.

Medical care was virtually nonexistent on the southern continent and the Healers were looked at with great distrust by many people. Anyone who had ever had previous experience with a Healer was not likely to trust one again, particularly with their child. She knew that she was lucky in the sense that her mother's sister had been unfortunate enough to visit a Healer, and things had not gone well for her, which had made her mother more than a little leery about the idea of sending her own daughter to the village's Healer.

Her parents decided that her dreams, which she had told them about on a few occasions, were simply getting the better of her; it was agreed that she had an extremely vivid imagination. She was cautioned that she ought to be careful about who she spoke to about her jokes, lest she find herself in a situation where someone less understanding might not take her stories so graciously. It was a lesson she would not forget. She also decided to no longer share her memories with her parents, especially with her father. It was now evident that they her parents were not experiencing the same phenomenon that she was, and that sharing her recovered memories, if that was what they truly were, might only be making things worse for herself.

(* | *)

It had become apparent to her that she was the only one on Waylacor, perhaps on the entire planet for as far as she could tell, who was living the duality that she was currently experiencing. It was difficult to imagine that there might be someone else experiencing the same things, and yet, she was the only one who knew, with any certainty, that the continuum in which she existed had been irrevocably altered.

Perhaps for the thousandth time she repeated to herself that something had to be done about the situation, but *what*? Tarlos II was devoid of technology; it did not even have any steam or internal combustion engines, let alone the ability to travel through deep space. They certainly did not have the ability to contact any other planets. This meant that the spaceship she required, and she *knew* that she required a spaceship, was entirely out of the question. But how could she even know about such things? That was only one of the many questions she was careful *not* to ask anyone, especially those within her own family.

That was, of course, until he arrived. Every village in Waylacor had one, and Tankanal was no exception. Every village had a Place of Meeting that served as the gathering place for most of the community on the first day of the week. It was where they came to offer their thoughts and prayers to Kairtu, their Lord and Prophet. Lord Kairtu had lived over seventy-five thousand years ago, and had left a legacy of teachings upon which the spiritual life of the Waylacorians had founded their deep seated faith. It had developed, over time, into a profoundly simple faith, guided by the Three Laws which were recorded in the *Sacred Scrolls of Kairtu*.

Those who followed Kairtu adhered to her Three Laws as though they were inscribed upon their hearts, living by them without question. As a result of this adherence to the Laws, life amongst the Waylacorians was quite peaceful and, for the most part, devoid of strife. It was the

Third Law, however, that managed to keep most people from acting out any aggressive tendencies they might have felt toward one another, accompanied by the intense level of superstition felt by most Waylacorians.

Believing that Lord Kairtu was watching their every move was more than sufficient to keep the average person from stepping out of bounds, and that, in and of itself, helped to keep things extremely peaceful. Crime was so rare, so out of the ordinary, that most villages on the southern continent only had one Enforcement Controller who monitored the activities of the village, working in conjunction with the Elder of the community. Infractions of the Codes of Conduct were so rare, and serious crime so extraordinary, that the main language spoken on the southern continent had not even developed a word for *jail* or *detention center*. The closest the language had arrived at was a word that roughly meant *to confine*, for having lost one's freedom, but there were no facilities for the long-term internment of prisoners anywhere on the continent.

When a crime was committed and punishment was required, offenders were treated as someone who had lost their way, and they were accepted back into the community according to the Laws of Kairtu. There was an exception, of course, that being if the crime had been so heinous that such acceptance was impossible for the wellbeing of the community. In such a case there was no reason to detain the criminal; judgment was passed and the punishment was dispensed immediately, which was another reason why crime was such a rarity.

Executions, which were exceedingly rare, were performed in view of the entire village, serving as a warning to all who might violate the Laws of Kairtu. Stories of executions had circulated from village to village, and the threat of the punishment alone was enough to prevent the worst offenses from being committed. Few Waylacorians risked following in the footsteps of previous offenders for fear of receiving similar treatment. It was a simple message: you did not necessarily have to be a follower of Kairtu, but the Laws of Kairtu were the Laws by which the people of Waylacor lived.

Kairtu had spoken plainly about punishment for serious crimes, and the people knew them well: *If you left a scar, you received one in return; if you killed another, your life was forfeit.*

Each Place of Meeting was assigned a Holy Man who spent his time in prayer and reflection while the rest of the village worked to provide themselves with sustenance. Every week he would oversee the services for the community and perform any ceremonies that were required. Part of what the village produced would be given to support him, freeing him from having to provide for himself. Shortly after the untimely death of Irsfakaar, after a brief illness, a letter had been sent to the Temple of Kairtu at Kintakar. Considering it only had a population of slightly over twelve thousand, calling Kintakar a city seemed generous, but it was still the largest settlement on the southern continent, and one of the largest on the entire planet. That was another thing that she knew was also exceedingly wrong with this world, but there was nothing that she could do about that at the moment.

Kintakar also happened to be the location of the main Temple of Kairtu, traditionally believed to be where Kairtu Herself had resided when she walked amongst the people, shortly before being taken up into the World of the Spirits, or the Wellspring, on the great wings of the Barnsach bird, now considered to be the most sacred of all creatures by the shapeshifting Waylacorians. When Irsfakaar, the Holy Man of Tankanal had died, the Elder of Tankanal sent a request to Kintakar asking the High Sister of the Temple of Kairtu at Kintakar to assign a new Holy Man to the village.

After a few days an answer arrived in the guise of a Holy Man named Shisularan, who arrived in the form of a Barnsach bird. When Shisularan arrived in Tankanal, late one afternoon, she had been sitting on the branch of the Bimba tree, enjoying the warmth of the sun while she lazily swatted at the Taka flies that dared fly too close to her tail. She recognized him at once: while shapeshifters could change their physical form at will, taking on the characteristics of virtually any creature they took the form of, only a Holy Man or High Sister would dare assume the form of the sacred Barnsach bird. There was no official prohibition against this in the *Scrolls of Kairtu* or teachings that proscribed this practice, but it was still considered taboo amongst the people to take on the form of the bird.

She watched as the fabulous creature settled itself onto the path and took a moment to fold its multicolored wings and fan out its tail feathers after its long flight. It was no wonder that the legends surrounding Kairtu stated that She had chosen to take on the form of such a wondrous bird as her final act, if such a thing had truly happened, she thought to herself. As she watched the creature she saw it quickly transform into the tall man she knew had to be the new Holy Man assigned to their Place of Meeting.

Even though she had rarely attended the services at the Place of

Meeting, she followed the progress of the new Holy Man with interest as he walked along the path beside the land her parents farmed, noting that he wore the traditional garb worn by the Holy Men of the Temple of Kairtu. It consisted of a flowing robe with billowing sleeves, cinched at the waist by a simple twisted rope. His hair fell below his shoulders, like most Holy Men, and he was wearing it loose, allowing the afternoon breeze to blow it haphazardly around his head. He also had penetrating, orange eyes, a common trait to many born on the southern continent, though she could tell, even from a distance, that his eyes were not nearly as bright as her own. For some reasons she found that pleased her, although she knew it was of little consequence.

As he approached the Bimba tree he looked directly at her, surprising her when he smiled. "I find it curious to find a cat here in Tankanal," he said, his voice gentle as he looked directly into her orange eyes. "I would have thought that such a creature would not be found on this side of the universe."

She was so startled by his comment that she almost fell out of the tree. Looking directly at the Holy Man, she replied, "Where would you expect me ... I mean, a cat, to be?" she asked, her voice sounding quite high-pitched due to her altered form as she carefully began climbing down from the branch she had been sitting on. It was not an easy thing for a cat to do, even with her claws. She knew that cats preferred to jump and did not enjoy going down trees backwards, but climbing was more of a challenge, and she enjoyed challenges.

He watched as she lowered herself to the ground before replying and smiled again, "Where would I expect you, well," he smiled mischievously, "on Terra, of course."

She looked up at him in shock, then transformed into her natural state, a short, slim woman of about five-feet in height with skin the color of rich caramel. Her hair was long and shockingly black, with a streak of white down the center, which had matched the markings that she had maintained while in the form of the cat, but her most notable feature, without question, were still her eyes. Like the Holy Man, her eyes were bright orange in color, reflecting an intense intelligence that her parents had been able to observe even when she was quite young.

Those eyes were now trained on the Holy Man, "What do *you* know of Terra?" she asked, raising her eyebrows, her voice soft and intense as she looked around, ensuring that none of her family was within earshot.

"What do *you* know of it?" he countered, also looking around.

341

Suddenly feeling reckless, she began unburdening herself of everything she knew about the planet from her recovered memory, "Terra is a planet, located in Sector 0107, where cats are indigenous. They are small mammals, commonly kept as companion animals on the planet, but many also run free, living much shorter, difficult lives," she sounded genuinely sad at this fact. "These creatures are usually referred to as *feral* by the indigenous humans of Terra, which they call Earth. It is a lovely planet," she said wistfully, glancing up at the Holy Man for encouragement, which she received in the way of a barely imperceptible nod of his head.

"Two-thirds of the planet is covered in water," she continued, "in oceans and seas, and there are seven continents, though only six are physically visible from orbit, from space, Europe and Asia are geopolitical constructs ..." she trailed off, pausing for a moment as her face clouded over. "I really should not know any of this, should I?" she asked, a note of desperation entering her voice.

He smiled again, a warm gesture that made her feel warm all over and nodded as he spoke in a quiet, gentle voice, "There are a number of reasons why you might have this knowledge," he said, sounding perfectly calm and reasonable, "but only one is the truth. I could say that you are one of the *Kartush*, one who has previously inhabited the body of another ... an *old soul*, as some might say on your Earth," he grinned a toothy grin, "but you don't believe that, do you?"

She shook her head slowly, looking around again to make sure that nobody had noticed their conversation.

"Fear not, Sayoose," he whispered softly, surprising her by addressing her by name. He raised his left hand, pulling back some of the loose hair that had flown into his face while he had been walking, in the process he revealed part of the elaborate tattoo on his arm that was a trait of the Holy Men of the Temple of Kairtu. He saw her examining the intricate design, "Yes, I am the new Holy Man for your Place of Meeting," he said, "but you knew that the moment you saw me land in the guise of the Barnsach bird," she nodded, feeling somewhat silly for how she was acting. "My name is Shisularan. I assure you, nobody can hear us," he continued quietly. "You may say whatever you want to me. Please, accompany me to the Place of Meeting. There is much for us to discuss."

Sayoose did not hesitate to join him. Even though she knew it was impossible for her to have met him before there was something about this Holy Man that seemed extremely familiar and they began walking toward the center of the village toward the Place of Meeting.

"How …" she began to ask, but he raised his hand, silencing her.

"You could also know what you know because your mind has been possessed by that of another," he let out a mirthless laugh, "but no, that is also just ridiculous superstition, is it not?"

She again nodded, frowning; it was unlike a Holy Man to dismiss such things as superstition. Many Waylacorians believed that these were routine happenings. It had been one of the things that her father had earnestly discussed when he had talked about sending her to the Healer for *the Treatment*: removing the spirit of *The Other* that was possessing her mind. Unfortunately, *the Treatment* was rarely successful, often resulting in the death or permanent incapacitation of the person being treated. Fortunately, her mother had been adamantly against the idea.

"Well then, let me ask you a question, Sayoose," he said, quite calmly, "how old do you think you are?" he surprised her with the question.

She continued walking in silence for a moment before replying. "Well," she began tentatively, "I *know* that I was born only seventy years ago …" she paused, "but, I also *feel* that I am somehow much older than that, though that seems impossible."

Shisularan was nodding, "Physically, I feel …" he shook his head, "I believe, and my family tells me, that I was born three hundred and ten years ago," he began, "but," he stopped, looking directly at her again. "But, I *know* that in reality I am over ninety-five *thousand* years old. I have memories that span dozens of worlds, several Sectors of the universe, and something called the Felis Alliance," he was pleased to see that Sayoose was not at all shocked by this disclosure.

"I thought I was the only one," she whispered, her voice barely audible above the breeze.

"No," he replied. "You are not, and there are others as well. We are few, for we are loath to trust others with what we know for fear of being considered insane and subjected to *the Treatment* by one of the local Healers, a barbaric procedure, as I'm sure you understand …" Sayoose was again nodding, knowing how close she had come to that fate herself for her own indiscretions.

"I ask again," Shisularan pressed, "how *old* are you?" he was staring directly into her orange eyes, though he found doing so for any length of time was quite difficult. She had a gaze that was extraordinarily powerful, belying a tremendous intelligence and many other talents, most of which she had barely begun to be express.

She stared back without any evidence of discomfort, as though it was natural for her to be in a position of dominance, "It is odd that you should ask," she began, holding his gaze. "I have considered this question a number of times, but the only thing that makes sense to me, based on the memories I have been able to recover, is that I am at *least* one-hundred thousand years old, though I find that quite difficult to understand at times …" she looked down for a moment, then continued in a softer voice, "but I am quite certain that I am even older."

"My Sovereign," Shisularan whispered, smiling as he released a sigh of relief, "it is an honor to finally meet you." He bowed toward her, "It gives me no pleasure, however, to have to confirm that your fears are true: we are, you and I, and the entire universe for that matter, living in a time that is not our own. Somehow we were brought here, back to Tarlos, as a result of some accident, some terrible cataclysm, that took place. I say it was an accident only because, as you shall no doubt recall, in time, that I worked within the Alliance Temporal Directorate. Nothing that *we* did could have resulted in this," she was nodding in agreement. While she had not remembered him, she had been able to remember details regarding the Temporal Directorate, and she knew that their missions would not have resulted in such a cataclysmic event.

He continued, "Regardless of how it came about, it has happened, and I can only suspect that we are here because we are ancient in comparison to the others living within the Alliance. As a result, we were caught within the temporal disturbance, and that subsequently brought us back to this continuum, here on Tarlos," his face darkened, indicating that he had given the issue a great deal of thought but still had many unanswered questions that were bothering him. After pausing for a moment he beckoned for her to continue walking with him.

"Tell me something, Sayoose," his voice dropped to a whisper as he looked around furtively, "my apologies, but I dare refer to you as Sovereign while we are exposed. I hope you understand," he had a pained expression on his face which told her that the formality of the title meant a great deal to him.

She nodded, feeling somewhat overwhelmed at having discovered such a kindred spirit after beginning to think she might be losing her mind. There had been a number of occasions when she had begun believing, if only for a short period, that the memories she had been recovering were a sign of an encroaching madness, but she had completely abandoned that line of thinking many years ago. She had decided that too much of what she remembered was far too specific.

There were names, dates, places, and memories of things that had occurred while she was in control of a massive bureaucratic organization. It was all far too fantastic, far too specific to be the product of mere daydreams, or the ill-conceived notions of a young woman whose mind was playing tricks on her.

No: she had thoroughly convinced herself that these memories were quite real; they were not the constructs of an unwell mind or some delusional fantasy, and the Holy Man by her side was fresh confirmation of that truth. It had also occurred to her, on a number of occasions, that the denial of something being real did not necessarily make it the truth. That was the ultimate conundrum when it came to discerning between the truth and fiction. It was virtually impossible for a deluded individual to assess their own state of well-being when it came to seeing things that may or may not be there, but there could be no doubt that Shisularan was real, and he had just confirmed that what she was remembering was also real. For now, that would have to suffice.

He continued, as their path took them away from the grounds of her parent's fields, "Can you recall any of your childhood?" She was about to respond, but he quickly added, "I don't mean what you *think* you recall, can you remember a childhood from *this* life," he looked into her face, "from the time when you went to school, growing up, anything from before thirty-five years ago?"

Sayoose returned his gaze as she considered the question, then shook her head, "No, my memories of school are all memories from my old … my *real* life, as I have come to think of it; it seems that everything here starts, as you say, thirty-five years ago," her mouth hung open, her eyebrows raised in shock.

"Precisely," he nodded, "everyone that I've met so far shares that same experience," Shisularan confirmed. "In this life I may be three hundred and ten years old, but I also know that my life, as it is right now, only originated on this planet thirty-five years ago. All the memories I possess, the memories that exist from this life from before that time, are not really my own. I mean, they happened, *but not to me*." Sayoose stared at him, enthralled. "Whatever happened to the continuum, the event, catastrophe," he shook his head, his hair flying about in the breeze, "I'm not even sure what to call it at this point, and I don't really think it matters, but it seems to have taken place thirty-five years ago."

They continued walking in silence as Sayoose considered what she had heard, watching the twisting path as the colorful spires of the Place of Meeting came into view. She was not sure what she would do with what she had learned, but she knew one thing for certain: The Place of Meeting would be far more important to her now than it had ever been in the past.

She had never been overly involved in the spiritual practices of her people in the past, but that was easy to understand given the memories she had been recovering. Religion had never made much sense to Sayoose, and she tended to look at the teachings of Kairtu as nothing more than a collection of fairy tales that had no particular relevance to her life. Fortunately for her, most Waylacorians were not insistent that someone become involved in one of the religions practiced by the people. If you were not genuinely interested in participating, you were left to your own devices. As much as it was practiced and adhered to throughout the continent, practitioners of Kairturism were also generous to those who chose to not believe, so long as they continued to live harmoniously within the community while allowing the congregation to practice their beliefs in peace.

One of the main precepts of Kairturism that Sayoose had always found attractive was that it strived to coexist peacefully with others, even those who chose to not believe in the teachings taught within the Temple. It was, subsequently, a faith that did not proselytize, nor did it ever attempt to force its beliefs on others. When unbelieving family members attended the Place of Meeting they were welcomed with open arms, but if others chose to abstain from attending they knew that they were always welcomed to attend, but they were never pressured to do so or made to feel ostracized for staying away from the services.

Sayoose had never felt a desire to participate in the activities at the Place of Meeting, but she knew that would certainly be changing now that she had met this new Holy Man who understood who she was. She knew she would have to be there as often as her time permitted. Once she was finished with her work in the fields, she thought to herself, she would transform herself into a bird and fly to the Place of Meeting in order to spend time with Shisularan. She looked up at the spires of the building, as though she was seeing them for the first time in her life, and realized that she had not been there for several years.

She had attended the Passing ceremony for Irsfakaar, but that had not taken place within the Place of Meeting. His body had been laid on a pyre to usher his spirit back to the Wellspring, the purported source of energy joining all shapeshifters together. In the absence of a Holy Man in the village the Elder of Tankanal had performed the ceremony. Tankanal's Elder happened to be a small, bent-over man, nearly blind with age named Lartuuk, but the ceremony only entailed wrapping the body of the dead Holy Man in special cloths and anointing it with special oils, then lighting the pyre, which his sons had arranged earlier in the day.

As they arrived at the Place of Meeting it was as though Shisularan had been reading her thoughts, "I presume we will have many opportunities to speak," he said, taking her small hand in his. "After the weekly services conclude it would be easy for us to speak for some time," he looked at her, searching her face for a moment, as though considering something. "Of course," he continued, tentatively, "nobody will think it odd if you make it known that you have a desire to become a Sister of the Temple, which would give us much more time to speak … in private," he smiled again, still holding her hand, and Sayoose was finding that his warm smile was more than a little intoxicating.

Without hesitation she returned the smile, her eyes lighting up, "You know, it has been a secret dream of mine, unspoken of to anyone else, of course, for … well, at least thirty-five years," she began to laugh, and was pleased to see that the Holy Man was joining her in the obvious fabrication.

"Excellent," he said, releasing her hand to reach into his robe. He produced a small piece of parchment, "I anticipated this before leaving Kintakar," he could see the look of confusion on her face. "Give this to your parents and there shouldn't be any questions," he said. "It is an invitation for you to join me here, in order to become a Sister of the Temple; it includes a stipend to make up for your absence, since you will be unavailable to work on their farm," he smiled again. He took her hand again, relishing the touch of her soft skin, "Fear not, my Sovereign, your family shall be well taken care of; I cannot see how they would be able to deny such an offer."

Sayoose was overwhelmed, blushing at his seeming prescience. "I do not … I do not understand," she stammered, "you have only just arrived … how …" she stared at the piece of parchment he had handed her in wonderment.

Shisularan only laughed, "My Sovereign, when the request for a new Holy Man came to the Temple of Kairtu from the Elder of the village of Tankanal I knew my opportunity to finally meet you had arrived. I've had memories of you as the Sovereign for years, but as a Holy Man I had no good reason to make contact with you, until that request finally arrived. Once it did, I jumped at the opportunity to request the assignment, and it was given to me." He leaned toward her and whispered, "In truth, Tankanal is not considered the most glamorous place in Waylacor for a Holy Man to be sent," he chuckled, "the High Sister of the Temple of Kairtu at Kintakar was relieved that I was so eager to come here and asked no questions. What she did not know is that this is why I became a Holy Man in the first place ... to find others in our situation, and you specifically. I knew that your family had been from the village of Tankanal, so I suspected that if you were here, this would be where I would find you. I was also able to find some others, while waiting for this assignment."

She nodded in understanding, "How many others?" her curiosity was burning, like the candles that lit their small home in the dark of night.

He frowned, "To this point, I have found four others. Unfortunately, none of them worked directly within a part of the Alliance that would be able to assist us in repairing the time stream, if it is even possible to such a thing given our present circumstances."

She nodded again, as though she had expected as much.

"But, that is not what we are here to discuss," he brightened again. "When you move to the Place of Meeting you shall be trained as a Sister of the Temple ..." he suddenly laughed, "in between the work we must do in order to solve our larger problems."

"Which are?" she asked, knowing full well what they were.

He looked at her, seemingly surprised, "Well, for one, finding a way to return us to the proper continuum."

"Do you have a spaceship capable of travelling through time?" she looked him directly in the eye, making him feel distinctly uncomfortable for the briefest instant, reminding him that he was in the presence of the most powerful woman in the universe. Even if everything they knew had been drastically changed, she had not been changed, she was still the Sovereign.

"Of course not, my Sovereign," he replied softly, "but there is still much we can do in the meantime ..."

"Yes, of course there is, I apologize, Shisularan," she thought for a moment. "We may have quite a while to wait, but ..." she flashed him another smile, making his heart skip a beat, "I suppose we may just have to have faith, am I correct?" They both looked up at the painted ceiling of the Place of Meeting and laughed.

"Indeed, my young Sister. Faith we shall have; and in abundance," they continued to study the colorful ceiling, which depicted events from the *Sacred Scrolls of Kairtu*.

"I only hope it does not take so long that I end up becoming the High Sister of the Temple of Kairtu at Kintakar," they laughed again, but it faded as the seriousness of their situation settled upon them and they realized that they could easily end up living the rest of their lives in this time stream, knowing full well it was not the one they should be living.

"That isn't going to happen, I assure you," he replied, trying to sound confident. "Although …," he said thoughtfully, "considering the current situation, and the fact that you are currently the only Initiate of Kairtu studying here, there is every likelihood that you will become the High Sister of the Temple of Kairtu here in Tankanal," he paused as Sayoose seemed to want to interrupt him with a question.

When she remained silent he continued, "After all, each Temples of Kairtu is supposed to have its own High Sister, and, as I'm sure you know, Tankanal has been without her High Sister for many years now … since before you were born." She remembered that the previous High Sister of the Temple of Kairtu at Tankanal had died, according to her mother, on the day before Sayoose had been born. Her mother had told her about that day and said she recalled it so clearly because she had attended the ceremony to send the spirit of the High Sister to the Wellspring only a few hours before entering into her confinement, at which time she sent her husband to summon the accoucheuse to aid in the delivery of their child. Shortly after the rising of the sun, the next morning, Sayoose had been born, and they had named her in the tradition of the most faithful Kairturists, naming her after the person who had most recently been ushered into the Wellspring. High Sister Sayoose had served as the High Sister of the Temple of Kairtu at Tankanal for over six thousand years and had been beloved by the entire community.

Shisularan nodded, seeing that Sayoose was remembering the woman for whom she had been named, "Unlike the Holy Men," he continued, "who are permitted to serve throughout Waylacor, the teachings of Kairtu demands that the High Sisters of Kairtu must serve within their own community, from the Place of Meeting they attended as Initiates. This has made it more difficult to find a replacement for a High Sister when they pass unexpectedly." Shisularan smiled warmly again, patting Sayoose on her hand, "but that is nothing for you to be concerned with at the moment," he said softly. "You have much to do at the moment, my dear," he blushed at his inadvertent intimacy, hoping he had not offended her, and was pleased to see that she had either not noticed or was not offended.

He pressed on, "It is beginning to get late and I must prepare for tomorrow's service. I trust you shall be here, before the service begins, with whatever possessions you desire to keep with you as you prepare to begin your studies?" She nodded in response. "Good. Now, I'm sure your parents are wondering where you are, and will be pleased to see the invitation you have received from the new Holy Man," he gave her the traditional kiss on both cheeks, and a gentle hug.

"I shall be here, but," she hesitated, "if I may ask a question?"

He nodded, "Of course, my Sovereign, you may ask anything."

"Why have there been no Initiates to fill the role of High Sister since the passing of High Sister Sayoose?" It seemed like something that needed to be asked.

He looked at her and nodded again, "Even in the Temple of Kintakar the reputation of High Sister Sayoose was well known," he began, his voice filled with an awe that was reserved for someone who was highly revered. "It was also well known that the day after her passing ceremony, when her spirit had been sent to the Wellspring, a female child of the same name was born," he smiled at her.

"Surely you do not expect me to believe ..."

He shook his head, "I'm only telling you what the people here probably believe," he responded, smiling again. "Kairtu teaches that a child born close to the passing ceremony of a High Sister or Holy Man may receive their spirit. When you tell your parents of your desire to begin your training I am quite confident that their reaction will include a reminder of what happened before you were born."

She looked at him, her mind reeling at the ramifications of everything he had said and all that had transpired, and then she smiled, "Thank you, Shisularan," she finally said, "for the first time that I can recall, I feel ... hope," there were tears of joy in her eyes as she turned to leave and began walking home, her heart light and filled with song. She was thinking about how her life, and the lives of her parents, would be changed as her training commenced. More than anything, she would finally be liberated from the despicable casa beans, and the stipend would allow her parents to hire at least one field hand to assist on their farm, leaving them with some extra money by the time they had returned from the market.

As she walked home she could not stop herself from smiling while she hummed a tune from a piece of music that she knew had been written by a Terran composer. His name had been Robert Schumann and the melody was from the lyrical third movement of his *First String*

Quartet; it was a melody that was charged with an expressiveness and melancholy that still managed to lift her spirits higher than any bird could soar. She knew that the composer had lived a tragically short life, it was especially short by Waylacorian standards: he had died after only living forty-six years, and yet he had accomplished so much in his short life. It was music that was ideally suited to the day she was experiencing, but it also provided another example of something else that she knew she should not possibly have been able to know, even as the familiar melody escaped from her lungs, crescendoing around her as it filled the afternoon with the glory of its transcendent beauty.

It had turned out to be a wonderful day.

End of excerpt of *Time Changers*.

ABOUT THE AUTHOR

Peter Amsel was born in Toronto and moved to Sudbury as a young child where he began his early musical training. He continued his studies at the University of Ottawa and then in Montreal, at McGill University. His passion for music has never waned and he continues to compose, but Peter has always been drawn to a love for the written word and has constantly turned to writing as an expressive tool, especially when music seemed inadequate for the emotions he was trying to convey.

His music has been heard on three continents, but that has not stopped him from pursuing his love of writing, something he has enjoyed since even before he began his musical career. *Sun Killers* is Peter's debut novel; it is the first volume of the five-volume *Felis Alliance Series*. The second and third volumes are currently being prepared for publication and will be available before the end of 2016.

Peter lives in Ottawa with an aggressively affectionate black cat, with a white bib and stomach accent, named *CC*.

For information about Peter's creative endeavors and upcoming projects, including exclusive samples of future publications, please visit:
http://bordofskyproductions.ca
Like us on Facebook at:
https://www.facebook.com/bordofskyproductions/